PROFESSOR DAVID PURDIE was born privately and educated publicly. He spent most of his early years as a child, before attending Ayr Academy and Glasgow University where he graduated in Medicine.

He is presently an Hon. Fellow of The Institute for Advanced Studies in the Humanities, part of the School of Literature, Language & Culture of the University of Edinburgh. His principal interest is the literature of the Scottish Enlightenment, particularly the work of Sir Walter Scott, Robert Burns and the philosopher David Hume.

David Purdie is Editor-in-Chief of the current 4th edition of *The Burns Encyclopaedia* (2013) which covers the life and work of the poet and song-writer Robert Burns

A past Chairman of the Sir Walter Scott Club of Edinburgh, his edition of Scott's *Ivanhoe* was published by Luath Press in 2012.

He is also a parliamentary speechwriter and editor for several MPs and MSPs, and for a number of other public figures.

He is in considerable demand at home and abroad as a humorous after-dinner speaker, described in this role by the *Daily Telegraph* as 'arguably our best of the moment.' He lives in Edinburgh, leaving it only when absolutely necessary.

Sir Walter Scott's

THE
HEART OF
MIDLOTHIAN

Newly adapted for the modern reader by
David W. Purdie

Luath Press Limited
EDINBURGH
www.luath.co.uk

First published 2014
Reprinted 2014
Reprinted 2016

ISBN: 978-1-908373-80-9

The paper used in this book is recyclable. It is made from
low chlorine pulps produced in a low energy, low emissions manner
from renewable forests.

Printed and bound by
Harper Collins/RR Donnelley, Glasgow

Typeset in 9.5 point Sabon by
3btype.com

chapter one

Who has e'er been at Paris must needs know the Grève,
The fatal retreat of th' unfortunate brave,
Where honour and justice most oddly contribute,
To ease heroes' pains by an halter and gibbet.[1]
Matthew Prior, The Thief & Cordelier: A Ballad

In former times, England had her Tyburn, to which the victims of justice were conducted in solemn procession along what is now Oxford Street. In Edinburgh, the Grassmarket, a large open street or rather an oblong square, surrounded by high houses was used for this purpose. It was not ill-chosen for such a scene, being fit to accommodate the great number of spectators usually assembled. Few of the houses which surround it were, even in early times, inhabited by persons of fashion or those likely to be offended or even affected by such exhibitions. The place itself is not without some features of grandeur, being overhung by the southern side of the huge rock of the Castle and by the battlements and turreted walls of that ancient fortress.

It was thus the custom to use the Grassmarket esplanade for public executions, the fatal day being announced to the public by the appearance of a huge black gallows tree towards the eastern end. This apparition was of great height, with a scaffold surrounding it and a double ladder placed against it for the ascent of both criminal and executioner. As this was always arranged before dawn, it seemed as if the gallows had grown out of the earth in the course of one night, like the production of some foul demon. I well remember the fright with which schoolboys, when I was one of their number, used to regard these ominous signs. On the night after the execution the gallows disappeared again, conveyed in darkness back to the vaults under Parliament House. This mode of execution has now been exchanged for one similar to that in front of Newgate Prison, though with what beneficial effect is uncertain. The mental sufferings of the convict are shortened; he no longer stalks through a considerable part of the city between attendant clergymen, dressed in his grave-clothes and looking like a walking corpse.

On the 7th day of September 1736, preparations for execution were descried in the Grassmarket. At an early hour the area began to be occupied by several groups who gazed on the scaffold and gibbet with an unusually stern show of satisfaction. Such is seldom shown by a populace whose good nature usually forgets the crime of the condemned and dwells only on his misery. However, the very act for which this condemned man had been convicted had awakened the highest resentment of the multitude. The tale is well known; yet it is necessary to recall the circumstances to better understand what follows.

The contraband trade, though it strikes at the root of government by encroaching upon its revenues and injuring the fair trader, is not usually looked upon by either the commonality or their betters as particularly heinous. On the

---

[1]   La Place de Grève ('gravel square') was the site of public executions under the *ancien régime*. Now La Place de l'Hôtel de Ville, it is the square in front of City Hall.

contrary, in those countries where it prevails, the boldest and most intelligent of the peasantry are engaged in such illicit transactions, often with the approval of the farmers and gentry. Smuggling was almost universal in Scotland in the reigns of George I and II because the people, unused to taxes and regarding them as an invasion of their ancient liberties, had no hesitation in evading them.

chapter two

[Fife] *Ane beggaris Mantle, fringit wi' Gowd*[1]
    King James VI & I

The county of Fife is bound by two firths to the south and north, and by the North Sea to the east. Having a number of small seaports, it was long famed for its successful smuggling trade and harboured many seafaring men who had been buccaneers in their youth. Among these, one Andrew Wilson, originally a baker in the village of Pathhead, was particularly obnoxious to the Revenue Officers. He possessed great personal strength, courage and cunning and was perfectly acquainted with the coast. On several occasions he succeeded in eluding the pursuit of the King's Officers, but became such an object of their attention that he was finally ruined by repeated seizures. The man became desperate. He considered that he himself had been plundered and took it into his head that he had a right to make a reprisal.

Having learned that the Collector of the Customs at Kirkcaldy was to be in Pittenweem carrying a considerable sum of money, Wilson resolved to reimburse himself for his losses. Accompanied by a certain Robertson and two other young men in the smuggling trade, he broke into the house where the Collector lodged. Wilson and his two accomplices entered the Collector's apartment while Robertson kept watch at the door with a drawn cutlass. The Collector, believing his life in danger, escaped through his bedroom window while the thieves stole about two hundred pounds of public money. The robbery was particularly audacious, as several persons were passing in the street at the time. Robertson, however, assured them that the noise they had heard was just a dispute betwixt the Collector and the people of the house. The worthy citizens of Pittenweem felt themselves in no way obliged to interfere on behalf of the obnoxious Revenue Officer and, like the Levite in the parable: The Good Samaritan: Luke 10.29–37 passed by on the opposite side. The alarm was at length raised and the military were called in. The robbers were pursued and captured, the booty was recovered and Wilson and Robertson were tried and condemned to death by hanging.

Many citizens thought that justice might have been satisfied with less than the forfeiture of two lives. The Government's opinion, on the other hand, was that the audacity of the raid required that a severe example be made. When it

---

[1] 'Jamie the Saxt' here refers to Fife's impoverished interior, contrasting it with its coastal seaports and golf links, the former being a rich source of 'gowd' to the treasury of His Majesty.

became apparent that the sentence of death would be executed, a friend outside succeeded in smuggling files and other implements into the prison with which a bar was sawed out of a window by Wilson and Robertson. The latter, a young and slim man, proposed that he exit first, enlarging the gap from the outside if necessary to allow his larger friend to follow. Wilson, however, insisted on going first, but found it impossible to get through the bars and jammed fast. Discovery followed and precautions were taken by the jailors to prevent any repetition. Robertson uttered not a word of reproach. Wilson, much moved by the fact that his obstinacy had prevented Robertson's escape, was now bent on saving his friend's life without further concern for his own.

Adjacent to the Tolbooth, or city jail of Edinburgh, is one of three churches into which the cathedral of St Giles is divided. It is called, from its vicinity, the Tolbooth Kirk. It was the custom that criminals under sentence of death were brought, with a sufficient guard, to this church for public worship on the Sabbath before their execution. It was supposed that their hearts would be moved by uniting their thoughts and voices for the last time with their fellow mortals, as all addressed their Creator. The congregation, it was also believed, could not but be impressed and affected to find their devotions mingling with those trembling on the verge of eternity. This practice, however edifying, was later discontinued – a consequence of the incident we are about to divulge.

The clergyman had concluded his sermon, part of which was directed at Wilson and Robertson, who were in the pew set apart for condemned persons, each secured betwixt two soldiers of the City Guard. The minister had reminded them that the next congregation they would join would be that of the Just or of the Unjust, and that their Psalms must be exchanged in two days for eternal Hallelujahs or Lamentations. They were also told to take comfort in their misery. While all who kneeled beside them lay under the same sentence of certain death, they alone had the advantage of knowing the precise moment at which it should be executed.

'Therefore,' urged the minister, his voice trembling with emotion, 'redeem, my unhappy brethren, the time which is yet left; remember that through the Grace of Him to whom space and time are as nothing, Salvation may yet be assured, even in the brief delay which the Law affords you.'

Robertson was observed to weep at these words, but Wilson seemed as one who had not grasped their meaning and whose thoughts were elsewhere. The benediction was pronounced and the congregation was dismissed, many lingering to indulge their curiosity with a final look at the two criminals, now rising with their guards to depart. A murmur of compassion was heard among the spectators when all at once Wilson, a very strong man, seized two of the soldiers, one with each fist, calling to his companion,

'Run Geordie, *run*!'

Wilson threw himself on a third guard and fastened his teeth on the collar of his coat. Robertson stood for a second as if thunderstruck, but at the cry of 'Run, run!' being echoed from many around, he shook off the remaining soldier, threw himself over the pews, scattered the dispersing congregation – none of whom felt inclined to stop a man taking his last chance for life – gained the door of the church and was lost to pursuit.

The generous bravery of Wilson heightened the feelings of compassion among the public, who also rejoiced in Robertson's escape. This general feeling started a rumour that Wilson would be rescued from the place of execution, either by the mob, by his old associates, or by another act of strength and courage on his own part. The Magistrates, alarmed, thought it their duty to guard against any such disturbance and ordered out the greater part of the City Guard.

Its commander was Captain John Porteous.

chapter three

And thou, great god of Aquavitae!
Wha sways the empire of this city
(When fou we're sometimes capernoity),
Be thou prepared
To save us frae that black banditti,
The City Guard!
      Robert Fergusson, *The Daft Days*

Captain John Porteous, a name memorable in the folklore of Edinburgh, as well as in the records of criminal jurisprudence, was the son of an Edinburgh tailor. His father wished him to follow this trade, but the youth had a wild propensity to dissipation which led him to The Scotch Dutch, an infantry corps long in the service of the States of Holland. Here he learned military discipline. Returning to his native city in the course of an idle and wandering life, his services were obtained by the magistrates of Edinburgh in the disturbed year of 1715 for disciplining their City Guard, in which he received a Captain's commission.[1] It was only by his military skill and his alert and resolute character as an officer of the police that he merited the position, for he was a man of profligate habits and a brutal husband. However, his harsh and fierce activity rendered him formidable to rioters and disturbers of the public peace.

The corps in which he held his command was a body of about one hundred and twenty soldiers divided into three Companies and regularly armed, clothed and embodied. They had the charge of preserving public order and were chiefly military veterans who had the benefit of working at their trades when off-duty. Acting as an armed police force, they repressed riots and street robberies. They also attended all public occasions where popular disturbance might be expected.

The Lord Provost of Edinburgh was, *ex-officio*, commander and Colonel of the corps, which might be increased to three hundred men when the times required it. No drum but theirs was allowed to sound on the High Street between

---

[1] The first major Jacobite rising and the inconclusive, ie drawn, Battle of Sheriffmuir, where the rebels, led by the Earl of Mar, faced a Government army under John Campbell, 2nd Duke of Argyll, of whom *vide infra*. The battle was wittily summarised by Anon: 'Some say that *we* wan, and some say that *they* wan, while some say that *nane* wan at a', man; but *we* ran, and *they* ran and *we*... ach we a' ran awa' man!'.

the Luckenbooths and the Netherbow. The escapades of the celebrated poet Robert Fergusson sometimes led him into unpleasant *rencontres* with these conservators of public order. Indeed, he mentions them so often in his works that he may be termed their poet laureate.[1] He thus admonishes his readers, based doubtless on his own experience:

> *Gude folk, as ye come frae the fair,*
> *Bide yont frae this black squad:*
> *There's nae sic savages elsewhere*
> *Allowed to wear cockad.*

The soldiers of the City Guard were for the greater part Highlanders. Neither by birth nor education were they trained to endure the insults of the rabble, the truant schoolboys, or the idlers with whom they came into contact. The tempers of the old fellows were soured by the indignities which the mob heaped on them on many occasions and frequently might have required the soothing strains of the poet:

> *O soldiers! For your ain dear sakes,*
> *For Scotland's love, the Land o' Cakes,*
> *Gie not her bairns sic deadly paiks,* [blows]
> *Nor be sae rude,*
> *Wi' firelock or Lochaber axe,*
> *As spill their bluid!*

On all occasions when a civic holiday encouraged riot and disorder, a skirmish with these veterans was a favourite recreation of the rabble of Edinburgh. Though the City Guard is now extinct there may still be seen, here and there, the spectre of an old grey-headed and bearded Highlander. His war-worn features appear below an old fashioned cocked-hat, bound with white tape instead of silver lace. His coat, waistcoat and breeches are of a muddy red and, though bent with age, he bears in a withered hand an ancient weapon. This is a Lochaber axe; a long pole with an axe at the extremity and a hook at the back of the hatchet.[2]

Such a phantom of former days still creeps round the statue of Charles II in Parliament Square, and one or two others are supposed to glide around the door of their Guardhouse in the Luckenbooths, when their ancient refuge in the High Street was demolished. Their last march to do duty at Hallowfair[3] was most moving. On this joyous occasion, their fifes and drums had been wont to play the lively tune *Jockey to the Fair*, but on his final occasion the veterans moved slowly to the dirge of: *the last time I cam' ower the muir*.[4]

This old Town Guard of Edinburgh with their grim and valiant corporal, John

---

[1] Robert Fergusson (1750–1774): Scottish poet and inspiration to Burns.

[2] This hook was to enable the bearer of the Lochaber axe to scale a gateway by grappling the top of the door and swinging himself up by the staff of his weapon. Scott.

[3] A market held on Hallowmas, or All Saints Day (1 November) at Edinburgh where it was the occasion of a large cattle-market.

[4] A song by Allan Ramsay (1686–1758).

Dhu – the fiercest-looking fellow I ever saw – were in my boyhood the alternate to the terror and derision of the petulant brood of the High School. Kay's caricatures[1] have preserved the features of some of these warriors. In the preceding generation, when there was perpetual alarm over Jacobite activities and plots, pains were taken by the magistrates of Edinburgh to keep the City Guard in an effective state, but latterly their most dangerous service was to skirmish with the rabble on the King's birthday.[2]

To Captain John Porteous, the honour of his Corps was a matter of high interest and personal importance. He was incensed with Wilson over the affront to his soldiers in liberating his companion. He was no less indignant at rumours of a rescue of Wilson from the gallows, and uttered threats which would later be recalled to his disadvantage. Porteous, despite his readiness to come to blows with the rabble, was entrusted by the Magistrates with the command of the soldiers at Wilson's execution. He was ordered to guard the gallows and scaffold with all the disposable force that could be spared for that duty – about eighty men.

The Magistrates took a farther precaution which deeply affected Porteous's pride; they requested the assistance of part of a regular infantry Regiment. The soldiers were not to attend the execution itself, but were to be drawn up on the High Street, the principal street of the City, as a display of force to intimidate the multitude. Captain Porteous deeply resented the introduction of these Welsh Fusiliers into the city, and their parading on a street where no beating drums but his own might be allowed. As he could not vent his ill-humour on the Magistrates, it increased his indignation at Wilson and all who supported him. This combination of jealousy and rage wrought a change in the man's countenance and bearing, visible to all who saw him on the day when Wilson was to hang.

Porteous was about the middle size, strong and well made, with a military air. His complexion was brown, his face somewhat fretted with the scars of the smallpox, his eyes more languid than keen or fierce. On the present occasion, however, it seemed as if he were agitated by some evil demon. His step was irregular, his voice hollow, his countenance pale and his eyes staring. His speech was confused, indeed his whole appearance so disordered that many remarked he seemed to be *fey*, the state of those driven to their impending fate by an irresistible impulse.

One part of his conduct was particularly diabolical. When Wilson was delivered to him by the keeper of the Tolbooth to be conducted to the Grassmarket, Porteous, not satisfied with the usual precautions to prevent escape, ordered him to be manacled. This was justifiable, given his character and bodily strength, as well as from the fear of a rescue attempt. But the handcuffs being too small for the wrists of a man as big-boned as Wilson, were forced closed to the exquisite torture of the criminal. Wilson remonstrated against such barbarous usage, declaring that the pain distracted his thoughts from the meditation proper to his unhappy condition.

'Your pain,' replied Porteous, 'will soon be at an end.'

---

[1] See John Kay, *A Series of Original Portraits, With Biographical Sketches and Illustrative Anecdotes* (Edinburgh: A & C Black, 1877).

[2] Of King George III: 4 June.

'And your cruelty is great,' retorted Wilson, 'You know not how soon *you* may be asking for mercy. God forgive you!'

These words, long afterwards remembered and quoted, were all that passed between Porteous and his prisoner. However, as they became generally known, they greatly increased the popular compassion for Wilson and the indignation against Porteous.

When the grim procession was completed, Wilson and his escort arrived at the scaffold in the Grassmarket. There appeared no sign of any attempt to rescue him. The multitude looked on with deeper interest than at ordinary executions; on the countenances of many was the stern, indignant expression with which the Cameronians had witnessed the execution of their brethren on that very spot.[1] But there was no attempt at violence. Wilson himself seemed disposed to hasten over the space that divided time from eternity. The devotions, proper and usual on such occasions, were no sooner finished than he submitted to his fate. The sentence of the Law was executed.

When he had hung on the gibbet long enough to be totally deprived of life, a tumult arose among the multitude. Stones were thrown at Porteous and his guards. The mob continued to press forward with howls and threats. A young fellow in a sailor's cap sprang onto the scaffold and cut the rope by which Wilson's body was suspended. Others approached either to carry it off for burial, or perhaps to attempt resuscitation.

This appearance of insurrection against his authority sent Captain Porteous into a rage. He forgot that since the sentence had now been executed, it was his duty not to engage in hostilities with the mob, but to withdraw his men. Instead, he sprang from the scaffold and snatched a musket from one of his soldiers. Commanding his men to open fire, he set them an example by firing his weapon and shooting a man dead on the spot. Several soldiers obeyed his command; six or seven persons were killed and a great many more wounded.

The Captain then proceeded to withdraw his men towards their Guardhouse in the High Street, but the mob were not so much intimidated as incensed by what he had done. They pursued the soldiers with curses and volleys of stones. As they pressed on towards them, the rearmost soldiers turned and opened fire, again with fatal results. It is not known for certain whether Porteous ordered this second fusillade, but the odium of that whole fatal day attached to him and to him alone. Arriving at the Guardhouse, he dismissed his men and went to make his report to the Magistrates.

Apparently by this time Captain Porteous had begun to doubt the propriety of his own conduct, and the reception he met with from the Magistrates made him still more anxious to gloss it over. He denied that he had given orders to fire; he denied he himself had fired; he even produced the *fusee*[2] which he carried as

---

[1]   The Cameronian sect of Presbyterians were the strictest among the Scottish Covenanters. Founded by Richard Cameron (1648–1680), they fiercely opposed any alliance of Church and State. Cameron was killed in action at the skirmish of Aird's Moss. The closest present day sect are the Free Presbyterians who, impressively, regard the Free Church of Scotland (the 'Wee Frees') as dangerous libertines.

[2]   A flintlock rifle.

an Officer, for examination. It was found to be still loaded. Of three cartridges which he was seen putting into his pouch that morning, two were still there; a white handkerchief was thrust into the muzzle of the weapon and emerged unsoiled or blackened. To the defences based on these circumstances, however, it was pointed out that Porteous had not used his *own* weapon, but had been seen to take one from a soldier.

Among the many killed and wounded by the firing were several individuals of higher rank, observing the scene from upper windows. The common humanity of the soldiers had made them fire over the heads of the crowd, this proving fatal to several of those persons. The voice of public indignation was loud, and before tempers had time to cool, the trial of Captain Porteous for murder took place before the High Court of Justiciary.

After a long hearing, the jury had the difficult duty of balancing the evidence of witnesses. Many respectable persons testified to the prisoner commanding his soldiers to fire, and himself firing his *fusée*. Others swore that they saw the smoke and the flash and a man drop. On the other hand, testimony came from others who, though well-stationed, neither heard Porteous give orders to fire, nor saw him fire himself. On the contrary, they averred that the first shot had been fired by a soldier close by him. A great part of his defence was also founded on the turbulence of the crowd, which again witnesses represented differently. Some described a formidable riot, others the trifling disturbance usual on such occasions when the executioner and the men commissioned to protect him were routinely exposed to indignities.

Having considered their verdict, the jury found that that John Porteous fired a gun into the people assembled at the execution, and also that he gave orders to his soldiers to fire, resulting in many persons being killed or wounded. They also found that the Captain and his guards had been assaulted and wounded by stones thrown at them by the multitude.

The Lords of Justiciary passed sentence of death against Captain John Porteous. He was ordered to be hanged on a gibbet at the common place of execution on Wednesday, 8 September 1736. Furthermore, according to Scottish Law in cases of willful murder, all his movable property was forfeited to the King.[1]

chapter four

'The Hour's come, but not the Man.'[2]

On the day when Porteous was to suffer execution, the Grassmarket, extensive as it is, was crowded almost to suffocation. Spectators filled the windows

---

[1] The five signatures affixed to the death warrant of Captain Porteous were headed by Andrew Fletcher of Milton, the Lord Justice Clerk. It was dated 20 July 1736.

[2] Walter Scott, *The Minstrelsy of the Scottish Border* (1802–1803). Notes to *The Water-Kelpie* by the Rev. Dr John Jamieson, author of *An Etymological Dictionary of the Scottish Language* (1808).

of all the lofty tenements around it, and lined the steep, curving street called The Bow, by which the procession was to descend from the High Street. The antique appearance of the houses of The Grassmarket, some formerly the property of the Knights Templars and the Knights of St John, and which still exhibit on their fronts and gables the Cross of these Orders, gave additional effect to the scene. The Grassmarket itself resembled a huge dark sea of human heads, in the centre of which arose the fatal tree; tall, black, ominous – and from which dangled the deadly halter.

Amid so numerous an assembly there was scarcely a word spoken, save in whispers. The thirst for vengeance was allayed by its certainty and the populace suppressed all exultation, preparing instead to observe the scene of retaliation in silent, stern triumph. It was as if the very depth of the popular hatred of Porteous scorned to display itself. Indeed, a stranger might have supposed that so vast a multitude were assembled for some purpose arousing deepest sorrow and which had stilled the noise normally arising from such a concourse. If, however, he had gazed upon their faces, he would have been instantly undeceived. The compressed lip and the stern and flashing eye of almost everyone conveyed the expression of men now in full sight of triumphal revenge.

The usual hour for producing the condemned had been past for many minutes, yet the spectators observed no symptom of his appearance.

'Would they *dare* deny public justice?' men began anxiously to ask each other. The first answer was bold and positive:

'No. They *dare* not!' But when the point was further canvassed, other opinions were entertained and various causes of doubt emerged. Porteous had been the favourite Officer of the Magistracy of the city; he had been described by his Counsel as the person upon whom the Magistrates relied in emergencies of unusual difficulty; and it had been argued that his conduct at Wilson's execution was due simply to an excess of zeal in the execution of his lawful duty.

The mob of Edinburgh, when thoroughly excited, had always been one of the fiercest in Europe and of late had risen repeatedly against the authorities, sometimes with temporary success. They were conscious that they were no favourites with their rulers, and that for Captain Porteous' violence to attract capital punishment would render it dangerous for Officers to effectively repress tumults. There is also the natural desire among governments for the maintenance of authority; and hence what had appeared to be an unprovoked massacre might be viewed otherwise in London by the Cabinet at St James's. There it might be supposed that Porteous was exercising a trust delegated to him by the lawful civil authority. He had been assaulted by the populace, and several of his men hurt; and that in repelling force by force, his conduct could be fairly imputed to self-defence in the execution of his duty.

These powerful considerations induced the spectators to suspect the possibility of a reprieve; and to the causes which might influence their rulers in Porteous' favour, the lower element of the rabble added another. It was said that Porteous repressed the slightest excesses of the poor with severity, while overlooking the license and pranks of the young nobles and gentry. This suspicion impressed the populace and was reinforced when word went round that certain citizens of higher rank had petitioned the Crown for mercy to Porteous.

While these arguments were being canvassed around, the expectant silence of the people changed into that deep, agitated murmur sent up by the ocean before the tempest begins to howl. The crowded populace, their motions corresponding to the unsettled state of their minds, fluctuated to and fro. That which the Magistrates had hesitated to communicate to them was at length announced. It spread like lightning among the spectators.

A reprieve from the Secretary of State's office under the hand of his Grace the Duke of Newcastle had arrived, intimating the pleasure of Queen Caroline, Regent of the kingdom in the absence of King George II in Germany, that:

> *The execution of the death sentence pronounced against John Porteous,*
> *late Captain of the City Guard of Edinburgh and prisoner in the Tolbooth*
> *of that city, be respited for six weeks from the time appointed.*

The assembled spectators uttered a roar of indignation and frustrated revenge, foretelling an immediate explosion of popular resentment. Such had actually been expected by the Magistrates, who had taken measures to repress it. But the shout was not repeated, nor did a riot ensue. The populace seemed ashamed of having expressed their disappointment in a vain clamour and the sound changed, not into silence, but into stifled mutterings. These each group maintained among themselves, and they blended into one deep and hoarse murmur floating above the assembly. Yet still, though all expectation of the execution was gone, the mob remained assembled and stationary, gazing on the preparations for death which had now been made in vain.

'This man, Wilson,' they said to each other, 'this brave man was executed for stealing a purse of gold, while he who shed the blood of twenty of his fellow citizens, is deemed a fitting object for the exercise of the Royal prerogative of Mercy. Is this to be borne? Would our fathers have borne it? Are not we too, Burghers of Edinburgh – and *Scotsmen*?'

The Officers of Justice began now to remove the scaffold, hoping that doing so would accelerate the dispersal of the crowd. The measure had the desired effect. The fatal tree was unfixed from the large stone pedestal or socket in which it was secured, and lowered slowly down upon the wain[1] for removal to its hiding place. Thereupon the populace, after giving vent to their feelings with a second shout of rage, began slowly to disperse.

In like manner, the windows were gradually deserted and groups of burgesses formed up as if waiting to return home when the streets should be cleared. In this case, all ranks regarded the cause as common to all. As noted, it was by no means amongst the lowest class, those most likely to riot at Wilson's execution, that the fatal fire of Porteous' soldiers had taken effect. Thus the Burghers, ever tenacious of their rights as the citizens of Edinburgh, were equally exasperated at the respite of Captain Porteous.

It was noticed at the time, and afterwards particularly remembered, that while the crowd was dispersing, several individuals were seen passing from one group of people to another, whispering to those protesting most violently against the

---

[1] A heavy, four-wheeled, horse-drawn agricultural wagon.

reprieve. These were men from the country, generally supposed to be old friends and confederates of Wilson – and of course highly excited against Porteous.

If it was the intention of these men to stir the multitude to any immediate act of mutiny, it seemed for the time to be fruitless. The rabble, as well as the more respectable part of the assembly, dispersed and went home. It was only by observing the moody discontent or catching the conversation they held with each other that the mind of the citizenry could be gauged. One group was slowly ascending the steep incline of the West Bow to return to their homes in the Lawnmarket.

'An unco thing is this, Mrs. Howden,' said Peter Plumdamas to his neighbour, a rouping-wife, or saleswoman, offering his arm to assist her in the ascent, 'to see the grit folk at Lunnon set their face against Law and Gospel and let loose sic a *reprobate* as Porteous upon a peaceable town!'

'And think o' the weary walk they hae gien us,' answered Mrs Howden, 'and sic a comfortable window as I had gotten, too, just within a penny-cast of the scaffold. I could hae heard every word the minister said. I paid twalpennies for my stand, and a' for naething!'[1]

'I judge,' said Plumdamas, 'that this reprieve wadna stand gude in the auld Scots Law when Scotland was a Kingdom.'

'I dinna ken about the law,' answered Mrs Howden; 'but I ken this; when we had a King, and a Chancellor, and a Parliament o' our ain, we could aye peeble them wi' stanes when they werena gude bairns; but naebody can reach the length o' Lunnon.'

'Weary on Lunnon, and a' that ever came out o't!' said Miss Grizel Damahoy, an old seamstress. 'They hae taen away our Parliament and oppressed our trade. Our gentlefolk will hardly allow that a Scots needle can sew ruffles on a sark, or lace on an owerlay.'[2]

'And now,' responded Plumdamas, 'sic a host of idle English excisemen torment us, that an honest man canna fetch sae muckle as an anker[3] o' brandy frae Leith to the Lawnmarket, but he's like to be robbit o' the very gudes he's bought and paid for. I winna justify Andrew Wilson for taking what wasna his; but if he took nae mair than his ain, there's an awfu' difference between that and the fact this man stands for.'

'If ye speak about the Law,' said Mrs Howden, 'here comes Mr Saddletree, that can settle it as weel as ony Judge.'

The party she mentioned was a grave elderly person with a superb periwig, dressed in a decent suit of sad-coloured clothes. He came up as she spoke and courteously gave his arm to Miss Grizel Damahoy. Mr Bartoline Saddletree kept a highly esteemed shop for harness, saddles &c. at the sign of the Golden Nag, at the head of Bess Wynd.[4] His genius, however, as he himself and most of his neigh-

---

[1] Twelve pennies: a shilling of which, until 1971, there were twenty in the Pound (ie 5p).

[2] From Anglo-Saxon *serc*, a shirt or chemise. In Burns's *Tam o' Shanter*, the 'cutty' (short) sark of the dancing witch Nannie discloses an impressive amount of flesh to the eponymous hero. An 'owerlay' was a cravat or neck-cloth.

[3] A keg containing the equivalent of 8.5 imperial gallons.

[4] An alley leading from Edinburgh's Lawnmarket, at the site of the Tolbooth, to near the head of the Cowgate. It was removed in 1809 to make way for the new libraries of the Faculty of Advocates and the Writers to the Signet, Scott.

bours agreed, lay towards matters of the Law. He was in frequent attendance at the pleadings and arguments of lawyers and judges in Parliament Square, where he was more often to be found than at his own business. However, his active wife both pleased the customers and scolded the journeymen. This good lady let her husband go his own way, improving his stock of legal knowledge, while she controlled the domestic and commercial departments.

Bartoline Saddletree had a considerable gift of words, which he mistook for eloquence and conferred liberally upon society. There was a saying that he had a Golden Nag at his door and a Grey Mare, his wife, in his shop. This was lucky for him, since his fortune increased with little trouble on his part and little interruption of his beloved legal studies.

Saddletree laid down, with great precision, the law upon Porteous's case. His conclusion was that if Porteous had fired five minutes sooner, that is, *before* Wilson was cut down, he would have been *versans in licito*; that is, engaged with discretion in a lawful act and only guilty of excessive zeal, which might have mitigated the punishment.

'Discretion!' echoed Mrs Howden, on whom the finesse of this distinction was wasted, 'whan had Jock Porteous either discretion *or* gude manners?'

'Mrs Howden, Miss Damahoy,' implored the orator, 'mind the distinction. Now, with the body of the criminal cut down, and the execution ended, Porteous was no longer *official*; the act which he had come to protect and guard being ended, he was no better than *cuivis ex populo*.'[1]

'*Quivis*, Mr Saddletree, craving your pardon, with the accent on the *first* syllable,' said Reuben Butler, an assistant schoolmaster of a parish near Edinburgh, who came up behind them just as the false Latin was uttered.

'What means this interruption, Mr Butler? But I am glad to see ye, notwithstanding. I speak as did Counsellor Crossmyloof, and he said "*cuivis*".'[2]

'If Crossmyloof used the dative instead of the nominative case, I would have crossed his palm with a leather strap, Mr Saddletree. That was a grammatical solecism.'

'I speak Latin like a lawyer, Mr Butler, and not like a schoolmaster. All I mean to say is that Porteous merits execution because he did not fire when he was in office, but waited till the body was cut down. He himself thus *exonered*[3] the public trust imposed on him.'

'But, Mr Saddletree,' said Plumdamas, 'do ye really think John Porteous's case wad hae been better if he had begun firing *before* ony stanes were flung?'

'Indeed I do, Plumdamas,' replied Bartoline, confidently, 'he being then in point of trust and power, the execution being but *inchoat*, or underway, but not finally ended. But after Wilson was cut down he should hae gotten awa' fast wi' his Guards up the West Bow.'

'I'll tell ye what it is, neighbours,' said Mrs Howden, 'I'll ne'er believe Scotland is still Scotland if we Scots accept the affront they hae gien us this day. My

---

1 Literally 'anyone among the people'.

2 *Cuivis* is in fact correct. Butler's, ie Scott's, Latin grammar is at fault. Tut.

3 Deserted; annulled.

daughter's wean, little Eppie, played truant frae the school and had just cruppen[1] to the gallows' foot to see the hanging, as is natural for a wean. She might hae been shot wi' the rest o' them!'

'Weel,' said Mrs Howden, 'the sum o' the matter is this; were I a man, I wad hae revenge on Jock Porteous, whatever the upshot.'

'I would claw down the Tolbooth door wi' my *nails* to be at him!' said Miss Grizel.

'Ye may be right, ladies,' said Butler, 'but I would not advise you to speak so loud.'

'Speak?' exclaimed both ladies, 'there will be naething else spoken about frae the Weighhouse to the Watergate till this affair is either mended – or ended!'

The females now departed home. Plumdamas joined the other two gentlemen in drinking their *meridian*, their noonday bumper dram of brandy at their usual place of refreshment in the Lawnmarket. Mr Plumdamas then departed for his shop, while Reuben Butler walked down the Lawnmarket with Mr Saddletree, each talking whenever he could thrust a word in; the one on the Laws of Scotland, the other on those of Latin syntax; and neither listening to a word uttered by the other.

chapter five

Elswhair he colde right weel lay down the law,
But in his house was meek as is a daw.

   Attributed by Scott to 'Sir Davie Lindsay'

'Jock Driver the carrier has been here, speiring about his new graith,'[2] said Mrs Saddletree to her husband as he and Reuben Butler crossed his threshold. 'And the laird of Girdingburst has had his running footman here, and then ca'd himsell, a civil young gentleman, to see when the broidered saddle cloth for his sorrel horse[3] will be ready, for he wants it for the Kelso races.'

'Indeed?'

'And his lordship, the Earl of Blazonbury, is clean daft that the harness for his six Flanders mares, wi' the crests, coronets, housings, and mountings are no sent hame according to your promise given.'

'Weel, weel, gudewife,' said Saddletree, 'if he gangs daft, we'll hae him cognosced.[4] It's a' very weel.'

'It's weel that ye think sae, Mr Saddletree,' she answered, nettled at his indifference to her reports; 'mony a man wad hae been black-affronted if sae mony customers had ca'd and naebody to meet them but women-folk; for a' the lads were aff as soon as your back was turned to see Porteous hanged.'

'Mrs Saddletree,' said Bartoline, with an air of consequence, 'dinna deave me wi' your nonsense; I was under the necessity of being elsewhere. *Non omnia*

---

[1]   Crept.

[2]   Enquiring about his new harness.

[3]   Chestnut.

[4]   Examined to determine if a person is insane or mentally incompetent.

possumus... possimis? I ken our Law-Latin offends Mr Butler's ears, but it means that naebody can do twa things at once, not even the Lord President himsell.'

'Very right, Mr Saddletree,' answered his wife with a sarcastic smile, 'and it wad better become ye, since ye say ye hae skill o' the Law, to see if ye can do onything for Effie Deans. The puir, puir thing is lying up in the Tolbooth yonder, cauld, hungry, and comfortless. She's *our* servant lass, Mr Butler, an innocent lass to my thinking and usefu' in the shop. She was aye civil, and a bonnier lass wasna in Auld Reekie. And when folk were hasty and unreasonable, she could serve them better than me, who's a bit short in the temper. I miss Effie daily.'

'I think,' said Butler, after some hesitation, 'I have seen this girl in the shop; a modest, fair-haired lass?'

'Ay, ay, that's puir Effie,' said her mistress. 'How she was abandoned, or whether she was innocent o' the sinful deed, God in Heaven knows.'

Butler had suddenly become agitated and fidgeted up and down the shop. 'Was not this girl,' he said, 'the daughter of David Deans that had the fields at St Leonard's? And has she not a sister?'

'She has; Jeanie Deans, ten years aulder than hersell. She was here a wee while ago, asking about her sister. And what could I say, except that she should come back and speak to Mr Saddletree? Not that I thought Mr Saddletree could do her muckle good or ill, but it wad serve to keep the puir thing's heart up.'

'Ye're mistaken though, gudewife,' said Saddletree. 'I could hae gien her great satisfaction; I could hae proved to her that her sister was indicted upon the Statute of 1690, Chapter One: *for the mair ready prevention of Child-murder; for concealing Pregnancy and giving no account of the Child borne.*'

'I trust to God,' said Butler, 'that she can clear herself.'

'And sae do I, Mr Butler,' replied Mrs Saddletree. 'I am sure I wad hae helped her as if she were my ain daughter; but I had been ill a' the summer, and scarce out of my room for twelve weeks. And as for Mr Saddletree, he might be in a lying-in hospital, and ne'er find out what the women cam there for. Sae I saw naething o' her, or I wad hae had the truth out o' her. But we think her sister maun be able to say something in Court to clear her.'

'The haill Parliament House,' said Saddletree, 'was speaking o' naething else, till this Porteous business put it out o' mind. It's a presumptive infanticide and there's been nane like it since the case of Luckie Smith the howdie[1] that was hanged in the year 1679.'

'Whatever's the *matter* wi' you, Mr Butler?' said Mrs Saddletree, 'ye're gone as white as a sheet!'

'I... walked here from Dumfries yesterday,' said Butler, forcing himself to speak, 'and this is a warm day...'

'Sit down and rest,' she said, 'Ye'll kill yoursell, man, at that rate. And are we to wish you joy o' getting the Dumfries scule, Mr Butler, after teaching at it a' the summer?'

'No, Mrs Saddletree, I am not to have it.'

'And so ye're back to Liberton scule as the assistant, to wait for dead man's shoon? Frail as Mr Whackbairn is, he may live as lang as you.'

---

[1] Midwife.

'Very likely,' replied Butler, with a sigh. 'I do not know if I should wish it otherwise.'

'Nae doubt it's vexing,' continued the good lady, 'to be in a dependent station; you that deserves muckle better. I wonder how ye *bear* these crosses.'

'*Quos diligit castigat,*[1] answered Butler; 'even the pagan Seneca could see an advantage in affliction.'

He stopped and sighed.

'I ken what ye mean,' said Mrs Saddletree, looking toward her husband; 'there's whiles we lose patience in spite of baith book and Bible. But ye'll stay and take some kale wi' us?'

Mr Saddletree laid aside Balfour's *Practiques*[2] to join in his wife's hospitable suggestion. But the teacher declined all entreaties and took his leave.

'I wonder,' said Mrs Saddletree, looking after him as he walked up the street; 'what makes Mr Butler sae distressed about Effie's misfortune? There was nae acquaintance atween them that ever I heard of; but they were neighbours when her father David Deans was on the Laird o' Dumbiedikes' land. Mr Butler wad ken Davie or some o' her folk... Get up, Mr Saddletree! Ye have sat yoursell on the very brecham[3] that wants stitching – and here's Willie, the new prentice. Ye little Deil that ye are! What takes you raking through the gutters to see folk hangit? Gang in and tell Peggy to gie ye broth, for ye'll be as gleg as a gled.[4] Ye mind he's fatherless, Mr Saddletree?'

'True, gudewife,' said Saddletree, 'we are in *loco parentis* and I hae thoughts of applying to the Court for a commission as factor *loco tutoris,*[5] seeing there is nae tutor nominate and the tutor-at-law declines to act.'

'He was in rags when his mother died,' said Mrs Saddletree, 'and that blue polonie that Effie made for him out of my auld mantle was the first decent thing the bairn ever had on. Poor Effie! Can ye tell me now really, wi' a' your law, will her life be in danger when they canna prove that there ever was a bairn at all?'

'Whoa,' said Saddletree, delighted at finding his wife interested in a legal topic. 'Whoa, there are two sorts of *murdrum* or *murdragium*, or what is popularly called murder. I mean there are many sorts; for there's your *murthrum per vigilias et insidias,*[6] and your *murthrum* under trust. However, the case of Effie, or Euphemia, Deans is one of those cases of murder *presumptive*, that is, a murder of the law's inferring, being derived from certain *indicia* or grounds of suspicion.'

'So,' said the good woman, 'unless poor Effie has revealed her pregnancy to others, she'll be hanged, whether the bairn was stillborn, or alive at this moment?'

'Assuredly,' said Saddletree, 'it being a statute to prevent the crime of bringing

---

1 Butler quotes from the Latin Old Testament; Hebrews 12.6: *quem enim diligit Dominus castigat*, 'the Lord punishes those He loves'. The notion also appears in Lucius Seneca's *Ad Lucilium Epistulae Morales, Moral Letters to Lucilius*; 66.11–13

2 A Dictionary of Scots Law published in 1774 and ascribed to Sir James Balfour of Pittendreich, President of the Court of Session 1567–1568.

3 The collar of a draught horse.

4 As sharp-eyed as a *Milvus milvus* – the Red Kite.

5 A person responsible for a minor's education.

6 Latin: 'By keeping watch and ambush' ie premeditated murder.

forth children in secret. The crime is rather a favourite of the Law, *this* species of murder being one of its ain creation.'

'Then, if the Law *makes* murders,' retorted Mrs Saddletree, 'the law should be hanged for them; or if they wad hang a *lawyer* instead, the country wad find nae fault!'

chapter six

But up then raise all Edinburgh,
they all rose up by thousands three.
   Johnnie Armstrang's Goodnight

Reuben Butler, on his departure from the sign of the Golden Nag, went in quest of a lawyer friend to make inquiries concerning Effie Deans. Everyone, however, was for the moment stark-staring mad on the subject of Porteous and engaged in attacking or defending the Government's reprieve. Butler wandered about until dusk, resolving to visit Deans in the Tolbooth when his doing so might be least observed. He passed through the narrow, partly-covered passage leading to the north-west end of the Parliament Square. He now stood before the Gothic entrance of the ancient prison, which reared up in the middle of Edinburgh's High Street, forming the termination to a huge pile of buildings called the Luckenbooths.[1]

These, for some inconceivable reason, our ancestors had jammed into the middle of the principal street of the City, leaving only a narrow street on the north side for passage. To the south, the side into which the prison opens, was a narrow crooked lane winding betwixt the high, sombre walls of the Tolbooth on the one side and the buttresses of the old St Giles Cathedral upon the other. To give some gaiety to this sombre passage, known as the Krames, were a number of little booths, or shops. Here were hosiers, glovers, hatters, milliners, indeed all who dealt in haberdashery.

Butler found the outer turnkey, a tall, thin old man with long silver hair in the act of locking the outer door of the jail. He asked admittance to Effie Deans, confined upon accusation of child-murder. The turnkey, civilly touching his hat out of respect to Butler's black coat and clerical appearance, replied that it was impossible at present.

'You shut up earlier than usual on account of Captain Porteous's affair?' asked Butler.

The turnkey gave two grave nods and, withdrawing a ponderous key of about two feet in length,[2] he proceeded to shut a strong plate of steel which folded down above the keyhole, and was secured by a steel spring and catch. Butler stood still instinctively while the door was made fast. Then, looking at his watch, walked briskly up the street, muttering to himself:

---

1   Literally 'locked booths', the small shops which lined the ground floor.
2   An item later acquired by Scott and conserved at his Borders home of Abbotsford.

Porta adversa, ingens, solidoque adamante columnae;
Vis ut nulla virum, non ipsi exscindere ferro
Coelicolae valeant.[1]

Having wasted half an hour more in a fruitless attempt to find his legal friend, he left the city for his residence in the small village of Liberton, two miles south of Edinburgh. The metropolis was at this time surrounded by a high wall with battlements and flanking projections at intervals. Access was through gates called in Scots *ports*, which were shut at night. A small fee to the Waiters, or keepers, would procure egress and ingress at any time through a wicket in the large gate. As the hour of shutting the gates was close, he made for the nearest, the West Port, which leads out of the Grassmarket. He reached it in time to pass through the city walls and entered the suburb of Portsburgh, chiefly inhabited by the lower order of citizens and mechanics. Here he was unexpectedly interrupted.

He had not gone far from the gate before he heard the sound of a drum and, to his great surprise, met an advancing crowd occupying the whole front of the street, with a considerable mass behind. They were moving with speed towards the gate he had just passed through, having in front of them a drum beating to arms. While he considered how to escape, they came full on and stopped him.

'Are you a clergyman?' he was asked. Butler replied that he was in holy orders, but was not a placed minister.

'It's Mr Butler from Liberton,' said a voice from behind, 'he'll do the duty as weel as ony man.'

'You must turn back with us, sir,' said the first speaker, in a civil but peremptory tone.

'For what purpose, gentlemen?' said Butler. 'I live some distance from town.'

'You shall be sent safely home; no man shall touch a hair of your head; but you must, and shall, come with us.'

'But to what *purpose?*' said Butler.

'You shall know that in good time. I warn you, look neither to the right nor the left and take no notice of any man's face.'

He was compelled to turn round and march in front of the rioters, two men supporting and partly holding him. During this parley the insurgents had made themselves masters of the West Port by rushing upon the Waiters and taking the keys. They bolted and barred the folding doors and closed the wicket. Seemingly prepared for every emergency, they then called for torches. By the light of these, they secured the wicket with long nails brought for that purpose.

While this was going on, Butler watched the individuals who led this singular mob. The torch-light showed those who seemed most active to be dressed in sailors' jackets, trousers, and sea-caps; others were in large, loose-bodied great-coats and slouch hats. There were also several in women's dress but whose deep voices, masculine deportment and mode of walking gave another interpretation.

---

[1] 'Wide is the fronting gate, and, raised on high / With adamantine columns threats the sky / Vain is the force of man – and Heaven's as vain / To crush the pillars which the pile sustains'. Virgil, *Aeneid*, Book VI; translated by John Dryden.

They moved by a well-concerted plan of arrangement and had signals and nick-names by which they distinguished each other. Butler heard the name 'Wildfire', to which one Amazon seemed to reply.

The rioters left a small party to observe the West Port and told the Waiters, if they valued their lives, to remain in their lodge and make no attempt to repossess the gate. They then moved rapidly along the Cowgate, the mob of the city everywhere rising at the sound of their drum and joining them.

Arriving at the Cowgate Port, they secured it with as little opposition as the former gate, made it fast, and left a small party to guard it. The mob, at first only about one hundred strong, now amounted to several thousand and was constantly increasing. They divided to ascend the various narrow lanes which lead up from the Cowgate to the High Street, beating to arms as they went and calling on all true Scotsmen to join them. They now filled the principal street of the city.

The Netherbow Port might be called the Temple Bar of Edinburgh. Placed across the High Street at its eastern termination, this gate divided Edinburgh from the suburb of the Canongate, just as Temple Bar separates London from Westminster. It was of the utmost importance to the rioters to possess the Netherbow because quartered outside in the Canongate was a regiment of infantry. Commanded by Colonel Moyle, it might have occupied the city by advancing through this gate and thus defeat their purpose. The Netherbow Port was secured with as little trouble as the other gates, a strong party being left to watch it.

The next object of the insurgents was to disarm the City Guard and procure arms for themselves; for scarce any weapons but staves and bludgeons had been yet seen among them. The Guardhouse was then a long, low, ugly building like a long black snail crawling up the middle of the High Street. The insurrection was so unexpected that there were no more than the ordinary Sergeant's Guard of the city corps on duty and even these were without powder and ball. There was a sentinel on guard, the one town-guard soldier to do his duty on that eventful evening. He levelled his musket and ordered the foremost of the rioters to stand off. The young Amazon, whom Butler had observed to be particularly active, sprang upon the soldier, seized his musket, wrenched it from him and threw him down on the causeway. One or two soldiers who turned out to support their sentinel were also seized and disarmed. The mob then occupied the Guardhouse, disarming and then dismissing the rest of the men on duty. It was later noted that although these very city-soldiers had effected the slaughter which the riot was designed to revenge, no harm was offered to them. It was as if the vengeance of the people disdained any head other than that which they regarded as the source of their injuries.

On taking the Guardhouse, the first act of the multitude was to destroy the drums, by which an Alarm might have been conveyed to the garrison in the Castle. For the same reason they now silenced their own drum, beaten by a son of the drummer of Portsburgh, whom they had forced into service. Their next business was to distribute to the boldest of the rioters the guards' guns, bayonets, partisans, halberds, and Lochaber axes. Until this point the rioters had kept silence on the ultimate object of their rising. All knew it, but none expressed it. Now, however, they raised a tremendous shout of, 'Porteous. *Porteous*! To the Tolbooth!'

They now proceeded with the same foresight as hitherto. A strong party, drawn up in front of the Luckenbooths and facing down the street, prevented all access from the eastward and the Canongate beyond. The west end of the defile formed by the Luckenbooths was secured in the same manner. The Tolbooth was now completely surrounded. Those tasked with breaking it open were now secured against interruption.

The alarmed Magistrates, meanwhile, had assembled in a tavern with the purpose of raising forces to subdue the rioters. The Deacons of the Craft Trades were appealed to, but they declared there was little chance of their authority being respected by their Craftsmen if the object was to save Porteous. Mr Lindsay, MP for Edinburgh, volunteered for the perilous task of carrying a message from the Lord Provost to Colonel Moyle requesting him to force the Netherbow Port, enter the city and put down the tumult. But Lindsay declined to take any written order which might cost him his life, if found on him by an enraged mob. The outcome of the Provost's now verbal request was that Colonel Moyle had no written instruction from the civil authorities. Furthermore, having seen in the case of Porteous the verdict of a jury on military men acting on their own responsibility, he declined to move.

The Magistrates dispatched messengers by different routes to the Castle to require the Commanding Officer to march down his troops, discharge a few cannon, or even to throw a shell among the mob to clear the streets. But so watchful were the patrols established by the rioters that no emissary reached even the gates of the Castle. They were, however, turned back without injury.

The same vigilance was used to prevent everybody of the upper orders of society from appearing in the street and observing the movements and identities of the rioters. Every person in the garb of a gentleman was stopped by small parties of two or three who requested that he return home. The Sedan chairs of ladies, even of the highest rank with footmen and blazing *flambeaux*, were intercepted. Those who stopped a Sedan usually made the excuse that there was much disturbance on the streets and that it was necessary for the lady's safety that she turn back. They even offered themselves as an escort, lest some of those who had casually joined the riot might indulge in the violence common on such occasions. It seemed as if the conspirators were like those who assassinated Cardinal Beaton.[1] These held that their action was a judgment of Heaven, to be executed with order and gravity.

Meanwhile, a select body of the rioters thundered on the door of the Tolbooth jail and demanded admission. No one answered, for the outer Keeper had made his escape with the keys and was nowhere to be found. The door was then assailed with sledgehammers, crowbars, and the coulters of ploughs. With these they prized, heaved and battered for some time with little effect. The door, besides being of double oak planks, was also clenched both end-long and athwart with broad-headed nails. It was thus so hung and secured as to yield to no means of

---

[1]   Cardinal David Beaton (1494–1546) was murdered by Norman Leslie, Master of Rothes, William Kirkcaldy of Grange *et al* in the castle of St Andrews.

forcing.[1] The rioters, however, were determined to gain entry; gang after gang relieved each other at the exercise and gang after gang retired exhausted without progress. Butler had been led close to this scene of action; so near, indeed, that he was deafened by the unceasing clang of heavy forehammers against the prison's iron-bound portal. He began to entertain hopes that the insurgents might give up in despair, or that some rescue might arrive to disperse them; and there was indeed a moment at which the latter seemed probable.

The Magistrates, having assembled their officers and some citizens willing to hazard themselves for the public peace, now sallied forth from the tavern where they had convened and approached. Their Officers went before them with torches and a Herald to read the Riot Act, if necessary. They easily drove off the outposts of the rioters, but then had to approach the line of guard which the mob of conspirators had drawn across the street in the front of the Luckenbooths. Here they were received with a volley of stones and then, on their closer approach, with the looted pikes, bayonets and Lochaber axes. One Officer, a strong resolute fellow, went forward, seized a rioter and took a musket from him. However, he was unsupported, and was thrown down on his back and disarmed. The Magistrates, after vain attempts to make themselves heard and obeyed, and possessing no means of enforcing their authority, had no option but to beat a hasty retreat as a shower of missiles whistled around their ears.

The resistance of the Tolbooth gate was baffling the purpose of the mob more than the interference of the Magistrates. The heavy sledgehammers continued to din against it with a noise which echoed from the lofty buildings around the spot and alerted the garrison up in the Castle. It was rumoured among the rioters that the troops would march down to disperse them unless they could execute their purpose quickly; or even that, without quitting the fortress, the garrison might effect the same result by discharging a bomb into the street.

Urged on by such fears, they eagerly relieved each other in the assault on the Tolbooth door; yet such was its strength that it still defied their efforts. At length, a voice was heard to cry,

'Try it with fire!'

The rioters called for combustibles and soon had some empty tar-barrels. A huge, red, glaring bonfire speedily arose close to the door of the prison, sending up a tall column of smoke and flame past its turrets and strongly grated windows. The fire also illuminated the ferocious gestures of the rioters surrounding the place, as well as the pale and anxious groups of those watching the scene from nearby windows. The mob fed the fire with whatever would burn. The flames roared and a terrible shout soon announced that the door had kindled and was being consumed. The fire was allowed to die down, but before being extinguished the leaders rushed over its still smouldering remains. Showers of sparks rose in the air as man after man bounded over the glowing embers.

It was now obvious to Butler that the rioters would be soon in possession of their victim.

---

[1]   It was, however, acquired by Scott for Abbotsford when the jail was demolished.

chapter seven

Shylock: *The evil you teach us, we will execute;*
and it shall go hard, but we will
better the instruction.

The Merchant of Venice, III.1

Captain John Porteous had been delivered that day from the prospect of a public execution, his relief even greater as he had wondered if the Government would risk unpopularity by interfering with his legal conviction. He thought, in the words of Scripture on a similar occasion, that surely 'the bitterness of death was past.'[1] Some of his friends, however, had observed the behaviour of the crowd hearing of the reprieve. They advised Porteous to petition the authorities that he be conveyed under guard to the Castle where he might be secure until his ultimate fate was determined. Porteous, however, was contemptuous of the rabble of the city. Unable to imagine them attempting to storm a strong and defensible prison, he rejected the advice. He spent the afternoon of the day entertaining friends who visited him through the indulgence of the Captain of the Tolbooth. Contrary to the rules of the jail, several of these were permitted to remain to supper with him.

It was thus in an hour of unalloyed mirth, when he was high in confidence, hot with wine and 'full of bread and with all his sins full blown',[2] that the first distant shouts of the rioters mingled with the song of merriment. The first explanation of these clamourings was a hurried call from the jailor to the guests, ordering them to depart since a determined mob had taken the city gates and the Guardhouse. Porteous might have eluded their fury had he thought of slipping on a disguise and leaving the prison along with his guests. It is even probable that the jailor might have connived at his escape or even, in the hurry of this contingency, might not have observed it. But both Porteous and his friends lacked the presence of mind for a plan of escape. The latter fled and the former, in a state of stupefaction, awaited the rioters in his cell. The cessation of the hammering and clanging on the outer gate gave him momentary relief. But his hope that the military had marched into the city from the Castle and dispersed the rioters was soon dashed. The glaring of the flames now illuminating every corner of his cell plainly showed that the mob had forced an entrance.

The sudden glare of light suggested to Porteous the possibility of concealment or escape. To rush to the chimney and ascend it at the risk of suffocation were the only means which occurred to him, but his progress was quickly stopped by the iron grating placed across such vents. The bars which impeded his progress, however, served to support him in the position he had reached and he seized them with the tenacious grasp of one clinging to his last hope. The lurid light which had filled the cell lowered and died away; shouts were now heard within the walls

---

[1] I. Samuel 15.32.

[2] *Hamlet,* III. 3. 80–1. Here Hamlet emphasises that his father, murdered by Claudius, died unshriven, ie unconfessed and unabsolved. His sins remaining 'full-blown', his soul could not enter Paradise. Neither, apparently, could that of Porteous.

and on the narrow winding stair which gave access to the upper apartments of the prison. The huzza of the rioters was being answered by shouts as wild and desperate as their own from imprisoned felons. These now expected to be liberated in the general confusion and welcomed the mob as deliverers. The cell of Porteous was pointed out. The obstacle of the lock and bolts was soon overcome, and from his hiding place the man heard his enemies enter. His place of concealment was obvious. Porteous was dragged down and out with a violence which seemed to indicate an intention to put him to death on the spot. More than one weapon was pointed at him when one of the rioters, the same 'Wildfire' whose female disguise had been noticed by Butler, shouted in a tone of authority.

'Are ye mad?' he cried. 'Execute justice as if it were a crime? We will have him die where a murderer *should* die, on the gibbet. Let him die where he spilled the blood of the innocents!'

A shout of agreement followed this and the cry, 'To the gallows! To the Grassmarket with him!' echoed on all hands.

'Let none hurt him,' continued the speaker; 'let him make his peace with God – if he can. We will not kill *both* his soul and body.'

'What time did he give better folk for preparing?' cried several voices, 'Give him the measure he gave *them*!'

However, the spokesman prevailed. The prisoner was assigned a guard and permitted to give his money and property to whomsoever he pleased. A debtor in the jail received this last deposit from the trembling hand of Porteous, who was also permitted to make brief arrangements for his approaching fate. Felons and others who wished to leave the jail were now set at liberty. With wild cries they either joined the mob or disappeared among the narrow lanes.

Two persons, a man of about fifty and a girl about eighteen, were all who remained within the walls, together with a few debtors who saw no advantage in escape. The persons we have mentioned remained in the strong room of the prison, now deserted by all others. One of the departing inmates called out to the man to also make his escape.

'Rin for it, Ratcliffe – the road's clear!'

'It may be, Willie,' answered Ratcliffe composedly, 'but I've a fancy to leave the trade and set up as an honest man.'

'Stay there and be hanged then!' cried the other and ran off down the prison stair.

Meanwhile, the leader in female attire was at the ear of the young woman.

'Effie, *flee*!' was all he had time to whisper. She turned on him a look of fear mingled with affection and upbraiding, all contending with stupefied surprise. He again urged,

'Effie! For the sake of all that's dear to us, *flee*!' Again she gazed on him and made no answer. A loud noise was now heard and the name 'Madge Wildfire' was repeatedly called from the bottom of the staircase.

'I am coming, I am *coming*,' said the person and then reiterated hastily, 'For God's sake, for your own sake, for *my* sake, run – or they'll take your life!' He left.

The girl gazed after him for a moment and then muttered faintly.

'Better tine life, since tint is gude fame.'[1] She sunk her head upon her hand, oblivious to the tumult around her.

That tumult was now transferred from the inside to the outside of the Tolbooth. The mob had brought their victim out and were about to conduct him to the place of common execution. The leader they called Madge Wildfire had been summoned by the impatient shouts of his confederates.

'I will insure you five hundred pounds,' hissed Porteous, grasping Wildfire's hand. 'Five *hundred* pounds to save my life!'

The other answered in the same undertone, returning his grasp with one equally strong. 'Five *hundred weight* of coined gold should not save you. Remember *Wilson*!' Wildfire added, 'Make your peace with Heaven. Where is that clergyman?'

Reuben Butler had been detained in terror and anxiety a few yards from the Tolbooth doors to await the outcome of the search for Porteous. He was now brought forward and commanded to walk by the prisoner's side and to prepare him for death. His answer was a loud appeal to the rioters to consider what they did.

'You are neither judges nor jury!' cried he. 'By the laws of God or man you cannot have power to take away the life of a human creature, however deserving of death. It is murder even for a Magistrate to execute an offender outwith the place and time prescribed by the Judge! You have no warrant for interference! In the name of Him who is all mercy, show mercy to this man. Do not dip your hands in his blood. Do not commit the very crime you wish to avenge!'

'Cut the sermon short – you are not in your pulpit!' answered one.

'Any more of your clavers,' warned another, 'and we may hang *you* beside him.'

'Peace and hush!' said Wildfire. 'Do this good man no harm – he only discharges his conscience.'

He then addressed Butler. 'Now, sir, we have patiently heard you. We wish you to understand that blood must have blood. We have sworn that Porteous shall die the death he deserves. Speak no more to *us*. Prepare *him* for death – as well as brief time permits.'

They had allowed Porteous to put on his nightgown and slippers, as he had thrown off his coat and shoes in his attempted escape up the chimney. In this garb he was now mounted on the hands of two of the rioters, clasped together in the form called in Scotland 'The King's Cushion'. Butler was close to his side. Porteous at first uttered some supplications for mercy, but finding that there was no chance, his military background and his tough natural disposition combined to bolster his spirits.

'Are you prepared?' said Butler in a faltering voice. 'Turn to Him, in whose eyes time and space have no existence. To Him, a few minutes are as a lifetime and a lifetime as a minute.'

'I know what you say,' answered Porteous sullenly. 'I am a soldier. If they will murder me, let my sins as well as my blood lie at *their* door.'

'Who was it,' came the voice of Wildfire, 'who said at this very spot, when Wilson could not pray because of the agony of his handcuffs, that his pains would

---

[1] 'Better lose life, since lost is good repute'. From Old Norse *tyna*, 'to lose'.

soon be over? If you cannot profit from this good man's words, blame not those more merciful to you than you were to Wilson!'

The procession now moved forward at a slow but determined pace. It was enlightened by many blazing links and torches, there being no secrecy to the occasion. The leaders kept close to the prisoner, his pallid yet stubborn features were distinct in the torchlight as he was carried considerably above the concourse around him. Those who bore swords, muskets and battleaxes marched on each side, forming a regular guard to the procession. As they went along, the windows filled with awakened inhabitants. Some of these muttered encouragement, but in general so appalled were they that they looked on in total astonishment. No one, by act or word, offered the slightest interruption.

The rioters continued to act with the same deliberate air of confidence and security which marked all their proceedings. When Porteous lost one of his slippers, they stopped and replaced it.

As they descended the Bow towards the Grassmarket, it was suggested that a rope be readied. The booth of a man who dealt in cordage was forced open, a coil of rope was selected, and next morning the dealer found that a Guinea had been left on his counter in exchange. Thus the perpetrators showed again that they intended no infraction of law, excepting as concerned Porteous himself.

They at length reached the place of common execution, the scene of his crime and now the destined spot of his death. Several of the conspirators tried to extract the stone filling the socket in which the lower end of the gibbet was normally sunk. However, since it was too secure to be forced, others sought the means of constructing a temporary gallows.

Butler used the delay to turn the people back from their design.

'For God's *sake*,' he cried, 'remember it is the image of your Creator you are about to deface in the person of this man! Wretched he is and wicked he may be, but he has a share in every promise of Scripture. You cannot destroy him, impenitent as he is, without blotting his name from the Book of Life. Do not destroy soul *and* body. Give him time for preparation!'

'What time had *they*,' came a stern voice, 'murdered on this very spot? The laws of both God and man call for death.'

'But my friends,' insisted Butler, disregarding his own safety, 'what hath constituted you to be his judges?'

'We are *not* his judges,' came the reply, 'he has *been* judged and condemned by lawful authority. Heaven has stirred us to execute that judgment when a corrupt Government would have protected this murderer.'

'I am none such!' cried Porteous, 'I acted in self-defence and in the *lawful* exercise of my duty!'

'Away with him; *away* with him!' was the general cry. 'Why waste time making a gallows? That dyester's pole is good enough.'

Porteous was forced to his fate and hanged with remorseless speed. Butler, separated from him by the press, escaped the last horrors of his struggles. He fled unnoticed, not caring in what direction, a loud shout proclaiming that the deed was done. Now at the opening into the Cowgate, Butler cast back a terrified glance and by the red, dusky light of the torches, discerned a figure wavering and struggling as it hung suspended above the heads of the multitude. He observed men striking at it with Lochaber axes; the sight doubled his horror and added wings to his flight.

The street down which the fugitive ran opens to one of the eastern ports or gates of the city. Butler did not stop till he reached it, but found it still shut. He waited nearly an hour, walking up and down in perturbation. At length he called out, rousing the attention of the terrified keepers of the gate who now found themselves free to resume their duties. Butler requested them to open the gate. They hesitated. He told them his name and occupation.

'He is a preacher,' said one; 'I have heard him preach in Haddo's-hole.'[1]

'A fine preaching has he been at *this* night,' said another 'but maybe least said is soonest mended.'

Opening the wicket in the main gate, the keepers allowed Butler to depart and thus carry his horror beyond the walls of Edinburgh. His first intention was to take the road homeward to Liberton. However, other fears and cares connected with that remarkable day induced him to linger near Edinburgh until daybreak. Groups of insurgents passed him as he whiled away the remaining hours of darkness, and these, from the stifled tones of their discourse, their unwonted hour of travelling and their hasty pace, he reckoned to be part of the insurrection.

The sudden and total dispersal of the rioters, their purpose accomplished, was not the least remarkable feature of this affair. In general, whatever the original motive for a mob to form, the attainment of its object usually leads on to further excesses. But not so in the present case; they seemed completely satiated with their vengeance. When life had left their victim, they dispersed. At daybreak there remained nothing of the events of the night, excepting the suspended corpse of Porteous. The weapons taken from the city Guardhouse were found scattered about the streets.

The magistrates of Edinburgh resumed their power, not without trembling at the fragility of its tenure. To march troops into the city and commence an inquiry into the preceding night were the first display of their returning energy. But these events had been conducted on so secure and so secret a plan that there was little to throw light upon the authors or principal actors.

An express was dispatched to London with the tidings, where they excited great indignation and surprise in the Council of Regency. Queen Caroline, as Regent – The King was in Germany – considered that the conspiracy had exposed her own authority to contempt. Retribution was spoken of, to be visited not only on the conspirators but also upon the Magistrates, and indeed upon the City which was its scene. Popular tradition records that at the height of her displeasure, Her Majesty told John, Duke of Argyle, that sooner than submit to such an insult, she would make Scotland a hunting field.

'In that case, Madam,' answered that high-spirited nobleman, with a deep bow, 'I will take leave of your Majesty and go to my own country to get my hounds ready.'

The true import of that reply was realised; and as most of the Scottish nobility

---

[1]   The western part of St Giles Cathedral. Named for the royalist Sir John Gordon, Bt of Haddo (1610–1644), imprisoned there before being beheaded for treason.

and gentry shared the same national spirit, the royal displeasure was checked in mid-volley. Milder courses would be recommended and adopted.

chapter eight

Arthur's Seat shall be my bed,
The sheets shall ne'er be pressed by me,
St Anton's well shall be my drink,
Sin' my true-love's forsaken me.
          Anon: *O' Waly Waly up the Bank*

At Edinburgh, the rising or setting sun may be best seen from the path winding around the foot of the high belt of semicircular rocks, called Salisbury Crags. These mark the verge of the steep slope leading down into the glen on the southeastern side of the capital. From here, the prospect is of a close-built, high-piled city, stretching itself out in the shape of a dragon. To the north is the Firth of Forth, a noble arm of the sea with its rocks, isles, distant shores and a boundary of mountains. To the west, a fair and fertile country flanked by the picturesque ridges of the Pentland Hills. As the path gently circles the base of the Crags, the prospects change at every step, blending them in such a way as to gratify both the eye and the imagination. When scenery so beautiful is lighted up by the tints of morning or evening and displays shadowy depth exchanged with brilliance, the effect approaches enchantment.

It was from this romantic path that Butler saw the dawn break on the morning after the murder of Porteous. He might have taken a shorter road to his destination, that which he chose being circuitous. But to compose himself and also to while away the time until a proper hour for visiting family, he lingered until the morning was advanced. With arms folded and watching the sunrise, he meditated on what he had witnessed and upon the news learned at Saddletree's; for his own fate was connected with that of Effie Deans, the imprisoned handmaiden of Mrs Saddletree.

Reuben Butler was of English ancestry, though born in Scotland. His grandfather Stephen had been a trooper in General Monk's army and one of the dismounted dragoons which formed the 'forlorn hope'[1] at the 1651 storming of Dundee. Stephen Butler was known as Scripture Stephen or Bible Butler from his talents in expounding the Testaments. A staunch Independent,[2] he believed the promise that the Saints should inherit the Earth. As hard knocks had been his share hitherto, he did not lose the opportunity which the storm and then plunder of a commercial city afforded.

---

1   From the Dutch *verloren hoep*, literally 'lost hope'. The foremost Company in an assault on a heavily defended position, where the risk of casualties was high.

2   During the English civil war (1641–1645) the Puritan MPs of the Long Parliament split into two factions: the Independents and the Presbyterians. The former advocated complete separation of Church and State, each congregation to be independent of all other civil and ecclesiastical organisations. The latter favoured a Presbyterian state religion.

The troop to which he belonged was quartered in the village of Dalkeith and formed the bodyguard of Monk who resided in the neighbouring castle. On the eve of the Restoration of Charles II in 1660, the General commenced his march out of Scotland. With him he took only soldiers devoted to himself. Scripture Stephen was not among them, having been 'weighed in the balance, and found wanting'.[1] This was because he opposed the ending of the reign of the Military Sainthood and would not join any party supporting Charles Stuart, son of 'the last man', as Charles I was irreverently termed. As time did not permit the cashiering of such dissidents, Stephen Butler was simply advised to give up his horse and accoutrements to one of Middleton's troopers possessed of a more accommodating military conscience. With this advice came arrears of pay. With indifference he watched his old corps depart south for Coldstream, to establish the tottering government of England on a firmer basis.

The *zone* of the ex-trooper, to use Horace's phrase,[2] was weighty enough to purchase a cottage and two or three fields still known as Beersheba[3] within a mile of Dalkeith. There Stephen established himself with a youthful bride from the village, his financial settlement reconciling her to the gruff manners, serious temper and weather-beaten features of the former soldier. Stephen did not long survive the falling on 'evil days and evil tongues', complained of by Milton in the same predicament.[4] At his death, his consort remained an early widow with Benjamin, a son whose later grim features and sententious mode of expression would have vindicated the honour of the widow of Beersheba, had any one challenged his descent from Bible Butler.

Butler's principles did not descend to his family or extend themselves among his neighbours. The air of Scotland was alien to Independency, however favourable it might be to fanaticism under other colours. Nevertheless, they were not forgotten, and a neighbouring Laird found it convenient to rake up all manner of accusations against the deceased Stephen, among which were his religious principles. Widow Butler was repeatedly fined for 'nonconformity' until Beersheba was wrenched out of her hands and became the property of the Laird. His purpose achieved, he showed some remorse, permitting her to occupy her husband's cottage and cultivate a croft of adjacent land. Benjamin grew up to man's estate, married and brought a wife and a son, Reuben, to share the poverty of Beersheba.

The Laird of Dumbiedikes had hitherto been moderate in his exactions, perhaps because he was ashamed to tax her son too highly, being the only means of support remaining to the widow Butler. Benjamin was a man of few words and few ideas, but was strongly attached to Beersheba. He neither remonstrated with the Laird nor endeavoured to escape, but toiled night and day to accomplish the terms of his taskmaster. He eventually fell into a fever and died, followed by his

---

[1] Daniel 5. 25-7. The interpretation by Daniel of 'Tekel' in *Mene Mene Tekel Upharsin*, the famous writing on the wall interrupting Belshazzar's feast.

[2] Livy's actually. In his account of the Second Macedonian war (200–197BC) he reports that Roman soldiers carried silver in their *zonae*, belts, for making purchases.

[3] The refuge of the prophet Elijah after Jezebel, the ferociously painted wife of King Ahab, ordered his death (I Kings, 19.3). Now the capital of the Negev in Israel.

[4] 'On evil days though fallen, and evil tongues...' John Milton, *Paradise Lost*, 7.

wife. Thus Reuben Butler was left an orphan about the year 1704, his guardian being his grandmother, the widow of Monk's old trooper.

The same prospect hung over the head of another tenant of the hard-hearted Laird of Dumbiedikes. This was a tough, true-blue Presbyterian called David Deans who, though obnoxious to the Laird on account of his principles in Church and State, contrived to maintain his ground upon the estate. This he did by regular payment of mail-duties, kain, arriage, dry multure, lock, gowpen, and knaveship, all those various exactions summed up in the emphatic word *rent*.

But the years 1700 and 1701, long remembered in Scotland for famine and general distress, subdued the stout heart of Deans. Citations by the Ground Officer, decreets of the Baron Court, sequestrations, poindings of outside and inside plenishing[1] flew about his ears, as the Tory bullets had whistled among the Covenanters at Bothwell Brig or Aird's Moss.[2] Struggle as he might, 'Douce David Deans' was routed horse and foot and lay at the mercy of his landlord just at the time that Benjamin Butler died. The expulsion of both families was anticipated. However, on the very day of ejection, the parish minister and an Edinburgh doctor received a hasty summons to attend the Laird of Dumbiedikes. Both men were surprised, since his contempt for both professions had been his theme over an extra bottle, that is to say, at least once per day. The physicians, the one for the soul and the other for the body, alighted in the court of the old manor-house at almost the same time. Gazing at each other in surprise, they expressed in the same breath the conviction that Dumbiedikes must needs be very ill indeed. Ere the servant could usher them to his apartment, the party was augmented by a man of law. This personage was the first to be summoned into the Laird's presence where, after some time, the curers of soul and body were invited to join him.

Dumbiedikes by this time had been transported into the best bedroom, used only upon occasions of death and marriage and hence called the Dead Room. In this apartment, besides the laird himself and Mr Novit the lawyer, was Jock. The son and heir of the patient was a tall, gawky, silly-looking boy of fourteen. Present also was the buxom figure of the housekeeper, a woman betwixt forty and fifty who had managed matters for Dumbiedikes since his lady's death. It was to these attendants that the laird addressed himself. Temporal and spiritual matters, the care of his health and his affairs were now strangely jumbled in a head which had never been of the clearest.

'These are sair times wi' me, gentlemen! Amaist as bad as at the aughty-nine, when I was rabbled by the collegers.[3] They mistook me muckle; ca'd me a Papist, but there was never a papist bit about me, minister. Jock, ye'll tak warning; we maun a' pay our debts and there stands Mr Novit that will tell ye I was never gude at paying debts in my life. Mr Novit, ye'll no forget to draw the annual rent that's due. If I pay debt to other folk, I think they suld pay it to me. Jock, when

---

[1] Seizures of good from home and field.

[2] Covenanter defeats by Government forces in the 'Bishops Wars' of the 17th century.

[3] Immediately prior to the 'Glorious Revolution' of 1688, the students of Edinburgh College, violently and riotously anti-Catholic, were suspected of burning Prestonfield House, home of the Lord Provost Sir James Dick.

ye hae naething else to do, ye may be aye sticking in a tree; it will be growing, Jock, when ye're sleeping. My father tauld me sae forty years sin', but I ne'er fand time to mind him. Jock, ne'er drink brandy in the morning, it files the stamach; gin ye take a morning's draught, let it be *aqua mirabilis*[1] – Jenny there makes it weel. Doctor, my breath is growing as scant as a broken-winded piper's, after four-and-twenty hours at a penny wedding. Jenny, pit the pillow aneath my head – but it's a' useless! Minister, could ye be rattling out some bit short prayer? It wad do me gude maybe, and keep some queer thoughts out o' my head, Say *something*, man.'

'I cannot use prayer like a rat-rhyme,' answered the minister, 'and if you would have your soul redeemed, Laird, you must show me your state of mind.'

'Should ye no *ken* that without me telling ye?' shouted the patient. 'What have I been paying stipend and teind,[2] parsonage and vicarage for, ever sin' the aughty-nine, and I canna get a prayer the only time in my life I *ever* asked for ane? Gang awa wi' your whiggery if that's a' ye can do. Auld Curate Kilstoup wad hae read half the Prayer Book to me by this time. Awa wi' ye! Doctor, can ye do onything better for me?'

The doctor assured him that no medical art could prolong his life many hours.

'Then damn Mass John[3] and you *baith*!' cried the furious patient. 'Did ye come here for naething but to tell me that ye *canna* help me at the pinch? Out wi' them, Jenny – out o' the house! Jock, my curse and the curse of Cromwell on ye if ye gie them either a fee or bountith, or sae muckle as a black pair o' cheverons!'[4]

Clergyman and doctor made a speedy retreat out of the apartment, while Dumbiedikes fell into one of those transports of violently profane language which had procured his nickname of Damn-me-dikes.

'Bring me the brandy bottle Jenny ye *bitch*!' he cried in a voice in which passion contended with pain. 'I can die as I lived, without fashing ony o' them. But there's ae thing,' he said, lowering his voice, 'there's ae fearful thing hings about my heart that brandy winna wash away. The Deanses at Woodend! I sequestrated them in the famine years and now they are to flit. They'll starve! And that Beersheba, and auld trooper Butler's wife and her son, *they'll* starve! Look out, Jock; what kind o' night is't?'

'Snaw coming on, father,' answered Jock.

'They'll perish!' said the expiring sinner. 'They'll perish wi' cauld – but I'll be het eneugh in Hell, if a' the tales be true.'

This last observation was made under breath, and in a tone which made the attorney shudder. He recommended, as an opiate for the conscience of the Laird, reparation of the injuries done to these distressed families. But Mammon struggled on with Remorse to retain a bosom long possessed.

'I canna do't,' he answered, with a voice of despair. 'It would *kill* me to do't!'

---

[1] Latin: Wondrous water. A distilled cordial of alcoholic spirits, sage, betony, balm, and other aromatic ingredients.

[2] Payments to the clergy: the stipend is a Minister's salary. A teind is the tithe, ie a tenth of the produce of the land.

[3] Colloquial Scots for a minister. There is no connection with the Catholic Mass.

[4] Kid gloves.

'But ye maun die whether or no, Laird,' said Mr Novit; 'and maybe ye wad die easier. I'll scroll the disposition in nae time.'

'Dinna speak o't!' replied Dumbiedikes, 'or I'll fling the stoup at your heid. But Jock, lad, be kind to these puir creatures, the Deanses and the Butlers. Dinna let the warld get a grip o' ye, Jock, keep the gear thegither! Let the creatures stay at a moderate rent and hae bite and soup; it will maybe go the better wi' your father in the place he's gaun, lad.'

After delivering himself of these instructions, the Laird felt his mind so much at ease that he drank three successive bumpers of brandy. He then expired, or 'soughed awa', as Jenny expressed it, during an attempt to sing *Deil Stick the Minister*.

His death brought a revolution in favour of the distressed families. John Dumbie, now of Dumbiedikes in his own right, lacked the grasping spirit and active mind of his father. His father's dying recommendations were attended to. The tenants were not turned out into the snow.

The cottage of Deans, called Woodend, was not distant from the Butlers at Beersheba. Formerly there had been but little intercourse between the families, for Deans, being a sturdy Scotsman, had prejudices against both the Southron and the spawn of the Southron. Moreover, as a stanch Presbyterian, he held in dread and horror all Independents and whomsoever he supposed allied to them.

However, despite these national and religious prejudices, the situation of Deans and the widow Butler created some intimacy between the families. They had shared a common danger and a mutual deliverance; they now needed each other's assistance.

On this nearer acquaintance, Deans abated some of his prejudices. He found old Mrs Butler, though not thoroughly grounded in the Real Testimony, was not an Independent and neither was she an Englishwoman. It was therefore to be hoped that although the widow of a Cromwellian dragoon, her grandson Reuben might be not be a schismatic. This was a quality for which Deans had as wholesome a terror as against Papists and Malignants.

Douce Davie had his weak side and perceived that widow Butler looked up to him with reverence and listened to his advice. She even joined in an occasional fling at the doctrines of her deceased husband. This she did in return for the valuable counsels from the Presbyterian in the management of her little farm. These usually concluded with:

'They may do otherwise in England, Mrs Butler, for aught I ken,' or 'it may be different in foreign parts,' or 'they wha think differently on the great foundation of our covenanted Reformation, overturning the government and discipline of the Kirk, and breaking down the carved work of our Zion, might be for sowing the craft wi' aits! But I say peace.'

The intercourse betwixt the families at Beersheba and Woodend thus became intimate at an early period betwixt Reuben Butler and Jeanie Deans. The latter was the only child of Douce Davie by his first wife, Christian Menzies in Hochmagirdle, 'that singular Christian woman,' as he was wont to express himself, 'her name savoury to all that kenned her.'

chapter nine

Reuben and Rachel, though as fond as doves,
Were yet discreet and cautious in their loves,
Nor would attend to Cupid's wild commands,
Till cool reflection bade them join their hands;
When both were poor, they thought it argued ill
Of hasty love to make them poorer still.

George Crabbe, *The Parish Register – Marriages*

Both widow Butler and widower Deans struggled with poverty and the hard, sterile soil of 'those parts and portions'[1] of the lands of Dumbiedikes which it was their lot to occupy. It then became gradually apparent that Deans was to gain the battle and the widow to lose it. Davie was a man and not much past the prime of life, while Mrs Butler declined into the vale of years. This ought to have been balanced by Reuben growing up to assist his grandmother, while Jeanie Deans could be supposed to add to her father's burden. But Douce Davie had so schooled and trained the young minion, as he called her, that from the time she could walk she was employed daily in tasks suitable to her age. This, coupled to her father's lectures, gave her mind a firm and reflecting cast. A strong temperament, free from all nervous affection, reinforced this fortitude of character.

Reuben, on the other hand, was weak in constitution and though not timid, was anxious and apprehensive. He was also somewhat lame from an accident in early youth. As the only child of a doting grandmother, her solicitous attention soon led him to overrate his own importance, a frequent consequence among over-indulged children.

Still, however, the two children clung to each other's society. Together they herded the sheep and cows their elders turned out on the unenclosed common of Dumbiedikes. There the two might be seen sheltering from the weather beneath a whin bush, their faces close together under the same plaid. They went together to school and together they worked at their lessons. Reuben proved as much superior to Jeanie Deans in intellect as inferior to her in constitution and in disregard of fatigue and danger. He was decidedly the best scholar in the parish school and the declared favourite of the master.

Reuben, naturally reserved, became more attached to Jeanie Deans as the schoolmaster assured him of fair prospects in future life and awakened his ambition. However, every advance that Reuben made in learning rendered him less capable of attending to his grandmother's farm. For example, while studying the *pons asinorum*[2] in Euclid, he allowed every *cuddie* on the common to trespass upon a large field of peas belonging to the Laird. Only the exertions of Jeanie Deans with

---

[1] Thomas Beveridge: *A Practical Treatise of the Forms of Process of the Court of Session* (1826).

[2] Latin: The Asses' Bridge. Proposition v in Euclid's *Elements of Geometry*. It states that the angles opposite the sides of an isosceles triangle are themselves equal. This early proposition, easy even for asses, was seen as the 'pons' or bridge by which scholars, if not asisine, might progress to the harder ones to come.

her little dog Dustiefoot prevented great loss of the crop and consequent punishment. Similar accidents marked his progress in his classical studies. He read Virgil's *Georgics* till he did not know bere[1] from barley, and nearly destroyed the crofts of Beersheba in attempting to cultivate them according to the practice of Columella[2] and Cato the Censor.

These blunders occasioned grief to his grandmother and modified the good opinion which her neighbour Deans had entertained of Reuben.

'I see naething ye can make of that silly callant,' said he to the old lady, 'unless ye train him to the Ministry. It's evident he will never do a usefu' day's wark, unless as an ambassador from our Master. I will make it my business to procure a license when he is fit for it, trusting he will be a shaft cleanly polished, to be used in the body of the Kirk; and that he shall not turn again like the sow, to wallow in the mire of heretical extremes and defections, but shall have the wings of a dove, though he hath lain among the pots.'

The poor widow absorbed the affront to her late husband's principles implied in this caution. She took Butler to the High School of Edinburgh and encouraged him in the pursuit of mathematics and divinity, thus parting Jeanie from the companion of her labour and pastimes. It was with more than childish emotion that both regarded the separation, but they were young and hope was high. They separated in hopes to meet again at a more auspicious hour.

While Reuben Butler was studying divinity at the University of St Andrews, his body suffering from the privations necessary in seeking food for his mind, his grandmother became daily less able to cope with her little farm. She was at length obliged to throw it up to the new Laird of Dumbiedikes. That great personage did not cheat her in making the bargain, permitting her to remain in her house as long as it should be 'tenantable'. However, he protested against paying a farthing for repairs, his benevolence being of the passive rather than the active kind.

Meanwhile, through his native shrewdness, Davie Deans gained a footing in the world. He had the possession of some wealth, the prospect of more and a disposition to preserve and increase his store. From his high knowledge of agriculture he became a favourite with the Laird, who was wont to end his daily saunter by calling in at the cottage of Woodend.

A man of slow ideas and confused speech, Dumbiedikes used to sit or stand for half an hour, an old laced hat of his father's on his head, an empty pipe in his mouth, his eyes following Jeanie Deans, or 'the lassie' as he called her. Her father, after exhausting the subject of bestial, ploughs and harrows, often took the opportunity of heading full-sail into more theological subjects. To these sallies the dignitary listened with patience, but without making any reply or indeed, as most people thought, without understanding a single word. Deans denied this stoutly as an insult both to his talents for expounding hidden truths and to the Laird's capacity of understanding them. Said he,

---

[1] A landrace, ie local variant of barley, adapted to northern climes and acidic soils common in Scotland. Burns wrote of 'the bearded bere'.

[2] Lucius Columella's classic treatise on farming, *De re rustica*, (c.AD 60) is in twelve books. He writes in the tradition of Marcus Porcius Cato's *De agri cultura*, on the cultivation of fields, describing the agrarian basis of the early Roman state.

'Dumbiedikes was nane of these flashy gentlefolk wi' lace on their coats and swords at their tails, that preferred riding on horseback to hell, than going bare-footed to heaven. He wasna like his father; nae profane company-keeper; nae swearer; nae drinker; nae frequenter of playhouse, music house, or dancing house. He was nae Sabbath-breaker or denier of liberty to the flock. He clave to the warld and the warld's gear, a wee ower muckle,[1] but then there was some breathing of a gale upon his spirit.'

All this honest Davie said – and all this he believed. It is not to be supposed that the constant direction of the Laird's eyes towards Jeanie went unnoticed by her father. However, this made a much greater impression upon Rebecca Deans, the second wife whom he had taken to his bosom ten years after the death of his first.

Some people had been surprised at this. In general, Deans was no friend to marriages, seeming to regard them as a necessary evil, clipping the wings with which we ought to soar upwards, and tethering the Soul to its mansion of clay. In contrast, Rebecca had no horror of matrimony and did not fail to promote a match betwixt Dumbiedikes and her stepdaughter Jeanie. Her husband would frown whenever this topic was touched upon, but usually ended by taking his bonnet and walking out of the house, lest a gleam of satisfaction diffuse itself over his austere features.

Jeanie Deans was deserving of this mute attention of the Laird of Dumbiedikes. She had grey eyes, fair hair, and a round good-humoured face much tanned with the sun. Her peculiar charm was an air of inexpressible serenity, a result of good conscience and a contented temper. There was thus nothing adverse in her form or manners. Yet, whether from sheepish bashfulness or imperfect knowledge of his own mind, the Laird of Dumbiedikes, with his old laced hat and empty tobacco pipe, came and enjoyed the beatific vision of Jeanie Deans day after day, year after year, without the proposal which would have realised the aim of the stepmother.

This good lady began to grow impatient with the slow pace of the Laird's wooing, especially after she herself presented Douce Davie with another daughter, named Euphemia, or Effie for short. Rebecca argued that as Lady Dumbiedikes would have little need for a dowry, the principal part of her husband's substance would naturally descend to her daughter. Other step-dames have tried less laudable means for clearing the way to the succession of their own children, but Rebecca, to do her justice, only sought Effie's advantage through the promotion of her elder sister. She tried every female art to bring the Laird to a proposal but only saw her efforts, like those of an unskillful angler, merely scaring the trout. Upon one occasion in particular, when she joked with the Laird on the propriety of a mistress arriving at Dumbiedikes, he was so startled that neither laced hat nor tobacco-pipe was seen at Woodend for a fortnight. Rebecca was thus compelled to leave the Laird to his snail's pace, now convinced of the grave digger's aphorism that a dull ass will not mend his pace for beating.[2]

Reuben, in the meantime, pursued his studies at the University, supplementing his finances by teaching the younger lads and thus maintaining himself at the great seat of learning. As is usual among the poorer students of divinity at Scottish

---

[1] Rather overmuch.

[2] *Hamlet* v.i.

universities, he contrived not only to maintain himself but even to send considerable assistance to his sole remaining parent. He obtained his License as a preacher of the gospel with some compliments from the Presbytery bestowing it, but this did not lead to his appointment to a Kirk. Returning from St Andrews, he had to make his aged grandmother's cottage at Beersheba his residence for some months, his only income being from tutoring among the neighbouring families. His first visit was naturally to Woodend. Here he was received by Jeanie with warm cordiality, by Rebecca with hospitality and by old Deans in a mode peculiar to himself.

Highly as Douce Davie honoured the clergy, his approval was not bestowed upon each individual of the cloth. Jealous, perhaps, at seeing his young acquaintance erected into the dignity of teacher and preacher, he immediately assailed him upon various points of religious controversy. This was to discover whether he might have fallen into some of the snares, defections and desertions of the time.

Butler, a man of Presbyterian principles, wished to avoid paining his old friend by debating points of little importance and hoped to emerge like fine gold from the furnace of Davie's interrogations. However, the effect on the mind of that strict investigator was not as favourable as might have been anticipated. Old Judith Butler had hobbled that evening as far as Woodend in order to enjoy the congratulations of her neighbours upon Reuben's return and upon his attainments. She was thus mortified to find that her old friend Deans did not share her warmth.

'Aweel, Mr Deans, I thought ye wad hae been glad to see Reuben amang us again.'

'I *am* glad, Mrs Butler.'

'Since he has lost his grandfather and his father – praised be Him that giveth and taketh – nane in the world has been sae like a father to him as yerself.'

'God is the only father of the fatherless,' said Deans, touching his bonnet and looking upwards. 'Give honour where it is due, gudewife, and not to an unworthy instrument.'

'Aweel, if that's your way o' turning it, nae doubt ye ken best; but I hae ken'd ye, Davie, send a forpit o' meal to Beersheba when there wasna a bow left in the meal-ark at Woodend.'

'Gudewife,' said Davie, interrupting her, 'these are but idle tales to tell me; fit for naething but to puff up the inward man wi' his vain acts. I stude beside the blessed Peden,[1] when I heard him describe the death of our martyrs as only draps of blude and scarts[2] of ink!'

'Weel, neibor Deans, ye ken best; but I maun say that I am sure you are glad to see my bairn again. The lameness is gane now unless he has to walk ower mony miles at a stretch; and he has colour in his cheeks. And he has as decent a black coat as the minister; and...'

'I am very heartily glad he is weel and thriving,' said Deans to cut short the subject. However a woman bent upon a point is not easily pushed aside.

'And,' continued Mrs. Butler, 'he can wag his head in a pulpit now, Deans. Think but of that. A' body maun sit still and listen to him as if he were the Pope of Rome!'

---

1 Alexander Peden (1626–1686): a famous Covenanting minister and preacher.

2 Literally the scratchings of an inked pen.

'The *what*? – The who? – *Woman*!' said Deans, with a sternness far beyond his usual gravity, as these offensive words struck his ear.

'Eh, guide us!' said the poor woman; 'I had forgot what an ill temper ye aye had at the Pope, as did my puir gudeman, Stephen Butler. Mony an afternoon he wad sit and take up his testimony against the Pope and against baptizing of bairns.'

'Woman!' cried Deans. 'Either speak about what ye ken something o', or be silent. Independency is a foul heresy, and Anabaptism a damnable and deceiving error, whilk suld be rooted out of the land wi' the fire o' the spiritual and the sword o' the civil Magistrate.'

'I'll no say that ye mayna be right,' answered the submissive Judith. 'I am sure ye are right about the sowing and the mowing, the shearing and the leading, and what for suld ye no be right about Kirk wark, too? But concerning Reuben...'

'Reuben Butler, gudewife,' said David, with solemnity, 'is a lad I wish heartily weel to, even as if he were mine ain son. But I fear his gifts will get the heels of his grace. He has that muckle human wit and learning, he embroiders the marriage-garment with lace and passments and fits his doctrine into that fine airy dress. But,' added he, seeing the old woman's growing uneasiness, 'affliction may gie him a jag, and let the wind out o' him, like a cow that's eaten wet clover. The lad may do weel and be a burning and a shining light;[1] and I trust it will be yours to see, and his to feel it.'

Widow Butler was obliged to retire, unable to make anything more of her neighbour's discourse, which filled her with apprehension on her grandson's account. And it must be admitted, in justice to Deans, that Butler tended to make a greater display of his learning than the occasion called for. The old man, accustomed to dictate upon theological subjects, had felt humbled and mortified when learned authorities were drawn up and arrayed against him. In fact, Butler had not escaped a tinge of pedantry and was apt to make unnecessary parades of his knowledge.

Jeanie Deans, however, admired this display of learning. The circumstances of their families threw the young people constantly together; their old intimacy was renewed, though now on a footing better adapted to their age. It was now understood betwixt them that their marriage should be deferred no longer than until Butler should obtain steady means of support. This, however, was not speedily accomplished; plan after plan was formed and failed. Jeanie lost the first flush of juvenile freshness while Reuben's brow assumed the gravity of manhood, the desired settlement of a Kirk remote as ever. Fortunately for the lovers, a sense of duty on both sides induced them to bear the waiting with fortitude.

Time rolled on. The widow of Stephen Butler, so long the prop of the family of Beersheba, was gathered to her fathers. Rebecca, spouse of our Davie Deans, also died, her matrimonial and domestic economy unfulfilled. On the morning after her death, Reuben Butler, arriving to offer consolation to his old friend, witnessed a remarkable struggle betwixt the forces of natural affection and those religious stoicism.

On his arrival at the cottage, Jeanie, eyes full of tears, pointed to the little orchard.

---

[1]   David the New Testament: John 5.35. Christ is speaking of John the Baptist.

'My father has been there since his misfortune.'

Alarmed, Butler entered the orchard, and advanced slowly towards his old friend, who was seated in a small arbour and appeared sunk in affliction. He lifted his eyes sternly as Butler approached, as if offended at the interruption. But as the young man hesitated, he rose and came forward to meet him.

'Young man,' said Deans, 'take it not to heart, though the righteous and the merciful perish. It may well be said that they are taken away from the evils to come. Woe to me, were I to shed a tear for my wife of my bosom, when I should weep rivers for my afflicted Church, cursed as it is with carnal seekers and with the dead of heart.'

'I am happy,' said Butler, 'that you can forget your private affliction in your regard for public duty.'

'Forget, Reuben?' said Deans, putting his handkerchief to his eyes, 'She's not to be forgotten on this side of time; but He that gives the wound can send the ointment. I declare there have been times during this night when my meditations hae been so rapt, that I knew not of my heavy loss. It has been with me as with the worthy John Semple, called Carsphairn John,[1] who bore a like trial. And like him I have been this night on the banks of Ulai,[2] plucking an apple here and there!'

Despite the fortitude of Deans, he suffered his loss deeply. Woodend became distasteful to him. As he had obtained both income and experience by his management of that farm he decided to employ them as a dairy farmer, or cowfeeder, as such are called in Scotland. The situation he chose was Saint Leonard's Crags, lying betwixt Edinburgh and the hill called Arthur's Seat and adjoining the extensive sheep pasture named the King's Park from its former dedication to royal game. Here he rented a small house about half a mile distant from the nearest point of the city. An extensive pasture-ground, rented from the Keeper of the Royal Park, enabled Deans to feed his milk-cows, the industry of himself and Jeanie being being exerted in the marketing of their produce.

She had now less frequent opportunities of seeing Reuben, who had accepted the position of assistant in a school some four miles from the city. Here he distinguished himself, becoming acquainted with respectable burgesses whose children would commence their education there. His prospects were thus gradually brightening and on each, admittedly rare, visit to Saint Leonard's, he dropped a hint of this into Jeanie's ear. There was, however, another person whose visits were regular.

When Davie Deans intimated to the Laird of Dumbiedikes his intention to quit Woodend the Laird stared, but said nothing. He made his usual visits at the usual hour without remark, until the day before the move when, observing the great east-country *awmrie*[3] dragged out of its nook and standing with its shoulder to the company, the Laird again stared mightily, and said only,

'Alas!'

---

1   The Rev. John Semple (*c*.1610–1677). Covenanting minister of Carsphairn in Kirkcudbrightshire and a notable eccentric.

2   'Ulai' was the Hebrew name for a river near the ancient Persian city of Susa in modern Iran. It is mentioned twice in the Bible: Daniel 8.2 'I was at Susa in the province of Elam... and I was by the river of Ulai.' See also Daniel 8.16.

3   Cabinet.

Even after the day of departure, the Laird of Dumbiedikes presented himself at his usual hour before the closed door of the cottage at Woodend and seemed as much astonished at finding it shut. On this occasion he was heard to ejaculate, 'Gude *guide* us!'

This was a very unusual mark of emotion. From that moment forward, Dumbiedikes became an altered man. His movements, hitherto predictable, became totally disconcerted. There was not a cottage which he did not enter, no maiden on whom he did not stare. But although there were better farmhouses on his estate than Woodend and certainly prettier girls than Jeanie Deans, somehow the Laird's time was not now so pleasantly filled. No seat accommodated him as well as that at Woodend, the like of Jeanie Deans to gaze upon. After rotating around his little orbit and then remaining stationary for a week, it seems to have occurred to him that he need not circulate on a pivot like the hands of the watch. He realised that he could extend his circle. He bought a pony from a Highland drover and with its assistance and its company he stepped to Saint Leonard's Crags.

Jeanie Deans, so accustomed to the Laird's staring that she was scarcely aware of his presence, always feared lest he start to articulate the admiration which shone from his eyes. Should this happen, farewell, she thought, to all chance of a union with Butler. Her father, however independent in his religious principles, was not without that respect for the Laird of the land, imprinted on the Scottish tenantry. He did not dislike Reuben Butler, but the latter's fund of secular learning was often the object of jealous sarcasm on Deans's part. In short, a match with Dumbiedikes would have been irresistible.

The Laird's daily visits to Woodend having being disagreeable to Jeanie, it consoled her upon leaving her place of birth that she had seen the last of Dumbiedikes, his laced hat and tobacco-pipe. She no more expected him to follow her to Saint Leonard's Crags than that any of her cabbages, left rooted at Woodend, would have undertaken the journey. It was therefore with more surprise than pleasure that on the sixth day after their removal to Saint Leonard's she beheld Dumbiedikes arrive, laced hat, tobacco-pipe, and all, and, with the self-same greeting of,

'How's a' wi' ye, Jeanie? Where's the gudeman?' He was no sooner seated that he added, most unusually, 'Jeanie, I say, Jeanie, woman.' He extended his hand towards her shoulder, fingers spread out as if to clutch it, but in so awkward a manner that when she whisked herself beyond its reach, the paw remained suspended in the air, palm open like that of an heraldic griffin.

'Jeanie,' continued Dumbiedikes in this moment of inspiration, 'I say, Jeanie, it's a braw day out by, and the roads are no that ill for boot-hose.'[1]

Her frown acting as a sedative, the Laird relapsed from that day on into his former taciturn habits. He visited the cowfeeder's cottage three or four times every week when the weather permitted, with apparently no other purpose than to gaze at Jeanie Deans, while Douce Davie held forth upon the controversies of the day.

---

[1]   Boot-hose were linen stockings or boot-liners worn to protect fine-knitted stockings from wear.

chapter ten

Her air, her manners, all who saw admired,
Courteous, though coy, and gentle, though retired;
The joy of youth and health her eyes displayed;
And ease of heart her every look conveyed.

  George Crabbe, *Phoebe Dawson*

The visits of the Laird thus sank again into their usual course, from which nothing was to be expected. Could a lover have won a fair lady as a snake fascinates a bird, by gazing with great greenish eyes, now aided by spectacles, Dumbiedikes would have performed the feat. But fascination seems to be among the *artes perditae*,[1] and this most pertinacious of starers produced nothing beyond a yawn. Indeed, the opinion of many was that the Laird would have been better to redirect his glances at she whose charms outshone even Jeanie's in the cottage at St Leonard's.

Effie Deans had grown into a great beauty. Her Grecian head and profuse brown ringlets, confined by a blue snood of silk, shaded a laughing Hebe[2] countenance, the picture of health and contentment. Her russet short-gown set off a slim figure with a graceful and alluring sweep of outline.

These growing charms, however, had no power to divert neither the steadfast mind nor the fixed gaze of the constant Laird. The neighbouring lads at their evening rendezvous for putting the stone or playing at the long bowls watched Effie Deans and contended to attract her attention. Even rigid Presbyterians, who held indulgence of the senses to be a snare, if not a crime, were surprised into a moment's delight at the sight a creature so exquisite. Yet there were points in Effie's character which gave rise to anxiety not only in David Deans with his rigid ideas, but also in her more indulgent sister. Effie possessed a self-conceit and obstinacy and an irritability of temper best illustrated by a cottage evening scene.

The father was foddering the cattle in his byre and the summer evening was beginning to close in. Jeanie Deans began to be anxious that her sister would not reach home before her father returned. Then it would be his custom to have 'family exercise' – a scriptural reading and prayers – when Effie's absence would give him serious displeasure. For several preceding evenings, Effie had disappeared about the same time, her absences at first so brief as scarce to be noticed, had been gradually extending. Jeanie stood at the door, shading her eyes from the setting sun and looking along the various tracks for her sister. There was a wall and a stile separating the royal domain, or King's Park from the public road; there she saw two figures suddenly appear, as if they had walked close in by the side of the wall to screen themselves. One of them, a man, drew back hastily; the other crossed the stile and advanced. It was Effie. She met her sister with affected liveliness of manner, carolling:

---

1   Lost arts.

2   Greek goddess of Youth and the daughter of Zeus and Hera. She was kept extremely busy as cup-bearer to the Gods on Mount Olympus.

The elfin Knight sate on the brae,
The broom grows bonny, the broom sae fair;
And by there came lilting a Lady so gay,
And we daurna gang down to the broom nae mair.

'Whisht, Effie,' said her sister; 'father's coming frae the byre. Whare hae ye been sae late?'

'It's no late!'

'It's chappit eight and the sun's ahint the Corstorphine hills.Whare can ye hae been sae late?'

'Naewhere.'

'And wha was wi' you at the stile?'

'Naebody. Ask me nae questions and I'll tell ye nae lees. I never ask what brings the Laird of Dumbiedikes glowering here like a cat day after day.'

'Ye ken very weel he comes to see our father,' said Jeanie.

'And Reuben Butler the dominie? Does he come to see our father?' said Effie, delighted to divert the attack. She pursued her triumph over her prudent elder sister, looking at her with a sly air and chanting a scrap of an old song:

Through the Kirkyard
I met wi' the Laird,
The silly puir body he said me nae harm;
But just ere 'twas dark,
I met wi' the Clerk...

Here she stopped and looked full at her sister. Observing tears in her eyes, she flung her arms round her neck and kissed them away. Jeanie, though hurt, returned the sisterly kiss in token of reconciliation, but could not suppress a gentle reproof.

'Effie, if ye will learn fule sangs, make a kinder use of them.'

'And so I might, Jeanie,' continued the girl, clinging to her sister's neck, 'and I wish I had never learned them – and I wish we had never come here!'

'Never mind that, Effie, but dinna vex our father!'

'I will not. I willna gang near ane o' the dances.'

'Dance?' echoed Jeanie Deans in astonishment. 'O Effie, what could take ye to a dance?'

As the word 'dance' was uttered, it reached the ear of old David Deans, who had turned the corner of the house unseen by his daughters. The word *prelate*, or even *pope* could not have produced so appalling an effect upon David's ear. Of all activities, that of dancing he deemed most destructive of serious thought and the readiest inlet to licentiousness. Dancing or attending theatres were flagrant proofs of defection from righteousness and hence causes of divine wrath. The utterance of the very *word* 'dance' by his own daughters and at his own *door* drove him beyond patience.

'Dance?' he exclaimed. 'Dance! *Dance*, said ye? To speak sic a word at *my* door! It's a dissolute, profane pastime, practised by the Israelites at their base worship of the Golden Calf at Bethel and by that lass wha danced aff the head of John the Baptist. That Chapter I will read this night for your farther instruction, since ye need it! Better for her to hae been born a cripple, and carried frae door to door, begging like auld Bessie Bowie than to be a King's daughter, fiddling and capering the way she did. I hae often wondered why onybody that ever bent a knee rightly in a Kirk should *dare* to caper to a bagpiper's windage and a fiddler's squealing. And I bless God that worthy Peter Walker, the packman at Bristo-Port,[1] so directed my path in my young days, that fear of the headsman's axe or the hangman's rope, or the battlefield's bullet or the prison's boot or thumkins[2] and, wherever, cauld, hunger, wetness and weariness stopped the wantonness of my feet! If I hear ye lassies sae muckle as *name* dancing, then as sure as my father's spirit is with the Just, ye shall be no more concern of mine! Gang in, then. Gang in, then, hinnies,' he added, in a softer tone, for the tears of both daughters, especially those of Effie, began to flow, 'Gang in, dears, and we'll seek Grace to preserve us frae all manner of profane folly, whilk causeth sin and promoteth the kingdom of darkness, warring with the Kingdom of Light!'

This scolding by Deans, however well meant, was unhappily timed and deterred Effie from her intended confidence in her sister.

'If I told her,' said Effie to herself, 'that I had danced wi' him four times on the green and at Maggie Macqueens's maybe she'll hing it ower my head and tell my father. But I'm resolved I'll no gang back. I'll lay in a leaf of my Bible,[3] as if I had made an aith no tae gang back.'

And she kept her vow for a week, during which she was unusually cross and fretful, alarming the prudent and affectionate Jeanie. She saw that a sudden, severe curb upon her sister's freedom might be productive of more harm than good. Among higher classes, a young woman, however giddy, is still under the dominion of etiquette and subject to the surveillance of mammas and chaperons. The country girl, however, snatching gaiety during the brief intervals of labour, is under no such guardianship. Thus her amusements become the more hazardous. Jeanie was viewing all this with much distress of mind when a circumstance occurred to relieve her anxiety.

Mrs Saddletree was a distant relation of David Deans and, as she was a woman both orderly in her life and of good repute, an acquaintance was kept up between the families. Now, this careful dame chanced to need a better sort of servant, or rather shop-woman.

'Mr Saddletree,' said she to Davie, 'was never in the shop when he could get his nose into the Parliament House, and it was an awkward thing for a woman to be standing alone among bundles o' leather selling saddles and bridles. I hae looked upon my cousin Effie Deans as the very sort of lass who could assist in the business.'

---

1 Patrick Walker (1666–?). Another Cameronian, that strictest sect of Covenanters. It is thought probable that Walker was the model of David Dean for Scott, whose *Old Mortality* did much to shape the heroic public image of the Covenanters as champions of the freedom of religious conscience.

2 Instruments of torture often used against captured Covenanters. The boot and the thumkins, or thumbscrew, applied agonising compression to the feet and hand respectively.

3 The custom of folding a leaf in the Bible when a solemn resolution is formed, is still held to be an appeal to Heaven for his or her sincerity, Scott.

In this proposal there was much that pleased old David. There was bed, board, and bounty. Effie would be under the eye of Mrs Saddletree, who had an upright walk. She also attended the Tolbooth Kirk, in which there was still to be heard the comforting doctrines of one of those few ministers of the Kirk of Scotland who had not bent the knee unto Baal. Nor had he become accessory to the course of national defections: those unions, tolerations, patronages and prelatical Erastian oaths imposed on the Kirk since the Glorious Revolution of 1688 and particularly in the reign of 'That Late Woman', his term of censure for Queen Anne, last of the Stuarts.

Secure in the soundness of the theological doctrine which his daughter was to hear, the good man was undisturbed by those snares of a different kind; those to which a young, beautiful and wilful girl might be exposed in a populous and corrupting city. He only regretted that she should live under the same roof as Bartoline Saddletree, whom David never suspected of being the ass he was, but considered him endowed with all the legal knowledge to which he made claim. Lawyers, especially those who now sat as Ruling Elders in the General Assembly of the Kirk of Scotland, had been prominent in promoting Patronage, the Abjuration Oath[1] and other heinous measures which, in the opinion of Deans, were a breaking down of the carved work of the sanctuary and a vile intrusion upon the liberties of the Kirk.

David gave Effie many a lecture upon the dangers of listening to the doctrines of a legal formalist such as Saddletree; so much so, that he had little time to cover the dangers of chambering, wild company-keeping and promiscuous dancing,[2] to which most would have thought Effie far more exposed than to theoretical error of religious faith.

Jeanie parted from her sister with mixed feelings of regret, apprehension and hope. She was less confident concerning Effie's prudence than her father, having a sharp estimate of the temptations to which she would be exposed. On the other hand, Mrs Saddletree was a shrewd woman, entitled to exercise over Effie the strict authority of a mistress and likely to do with kindness. Her removal to Saddletree's would also serve to break off idle acquaintances formed in the neighbouring suburb. At parting, Effie sobbed, kissed her sister and promised to recollect all the good counsel.

During the first weeks, Effie was all that her kinswoman expected. But with the passage of time in Edinburgh there came a relaxation of her early zeal in the service of Mrs Saddletree, who became displeased both by Effie's lingering over errands on shop business and by her impatience when rebuked. However, she accepted that the first was natural to a girl to whom everything in Edinburgh was

---

[1] An oath of abjuration not to take arms against the king, and rejecting the Covenants. The oath was offered to suspected Covenanters. If refused, they could be be shot on the spot by an Officer holding a commission from the Privy Council and two witnesses. It was much used in the 'Killing Time' to execute Covenanters in the fields, hills and on their own doorsteps. Their wives and children were then evicted.

[2] Some milder Cameronians made a distinction between the two sexes dancing separately and allowed it as a healthy and not unlawful exercise; but when men and women mingled it was then called *promiscuous dancing*, and considered as a scandalous enormity, Scott.

new – the latter a spoiled child, being subjected to the yoke of discipline. Attention and submission could not be learned at once; Holyrood was not built in a day.

It seemed as if the considerate old lady had presaged truly. Ere many months had passed, Effie became wedded to her duties, though she no longer discharged them with the laughing cheek which had at first attracted every customer. Her mistress sometimes observed her in tears. As time wore on, her cheek grew paler and her step progressively heavier. The cause of these changes did not escape the matronly eye of Mrs Saddletree, but she was ill and confined to bed for the latter part of Effie's service. During his wife's inconvenient illness, Bartoline Saddletree was obliged to take a personal charge of the business inconsistent with his study of the Law. He now lost all patience with the girl, just as neighbours and fellow-servants were remarking with curiosity the changing shape, loose dress and pale cheeks of the once beautiful girl. But to no one would she confide the truth, answering taunts with sarcasm and serious enquiries with sullen denials.

Mrs Saddletree recovered. Effie Deans, unwilling to face an investigation by her mistress, asked permission from Bartoline to go home for a week or two. Lynx-eyed in legal discussion, Bartoline was blind to common life. He allowed Effie to depart without inquiry.

Significantly, it was afterwards established that a full week had elapsed betwixt leaving her master's house and her arrival at St Leonard's Crags. She made her appearance before her sister more as a spectre than the gay and beautiful girl who had left seventeen months before. The long illness of her mistress had, for the last few months, given her an excuse for confining herself to the dusky precincts of the Lawnmarket while Jeanie, fully occupied with her father's household, was rarely in the city. Thus the young women had scarcely seen each other months, nor had a single scandalous rumour reached St Leonard's. Jeanie, alarmed at her sister's appearance, overwhelmed her with inquiries to which Effie returned rambling answers before falling into a hysterical fit.

Certain now that her sister had been delivered of a child, Jeanie had now the alternative of either telling her father, or of concealing it from him. To all questions concerning the name of the father and the fate of the infant, Effie remained as mute as the grave – to which she seemed to be hastening. Indeed, the least reference to either drove her to distraction. Her despairing sister was about to have Mrs Saddletree shed what light she could upon the matter, but was saved that trouble by a new stroke of fate; one which seemed to carry the family's misfortune to the uttermost.

David Deans had been alarmed at the state of health in which his daughter had returned, but Jeanie had managed to divert him from any specific inquiry. It was therefore like a clap of thunder to the old man when, just as noon had brought the usual visit of the Laird of Dumbiedikes, other sterner and most unexpected guests arrived at the cottage of St Leonard's.

These were Officers of Justice, with a Warrant of Justiciary to apprehend Euphemia Deans, accused of the crime of child-murder. The old man, who had in his youth resisted both military weaponry and civil tyranny backed with tortures and gibbets, fainted upon his own hearth. The Officers, happy to escape from the scene, roused the object of their warrant from her bed and placed her in a coach. The remedies which Jeanie applied to bring back her father's senses had scarce begun to operate when there came the noise of wheels in motion. Distracted, she ran from the house but was stopped by female neighbours, attracted by the extraordinary presence of a coach. The affliction of these simple folk, by whom the Deans family was held in high regard, filled the house with lamentation. Even Dumbiedikes was moved from his wonted apathy. Groping for his purse, he said,

'Jeanie, woman, dinna greet; it's a sad wark but siller will help it!' He drew out his purse as he spoke.

The old man now seemed to recover this senses. 'Where,' he said, with a voice that made the roof ring, 'where is she that has disgraced the blood of an honest man? Where is she like the Evil One among the children of God? Where is she, Jeanie? Bring her before me!'

All hastened around him with their sources of consolation: the Laird with his purse, Jeanie with burnt feathers and strong waters and the women with their exhortations.

'But to be the father of a castaway; a profligate; a Zipporah[1] and a *murderess*! O how will the wicked exult! The Prelatists, the Latitudinarians, and them whose hands are hard as horn wi' handing the slaughter-weapons. They will now say that we are such as themselves. Sair I am grieved, neighbours, for the castaway child of mine old age; but sairer for the scandal to all honest souls!'

'Davie! Winna siller help?' said the Laird, still proffering a green purse full of guineas.

'I tell ye, Dumbiedikes,' said Deans, 'even if dollars, or a plack, or the nineteenth part of a boddle wad save her open guilt frae open punishment, that purchase David Deans wad never make! Na, na; an eye for an eye; a tooth for a tooth and a life for a life. It's the law of man and it's the law of God. Leave me, leave me. I maun wrestle wi' this in privacy and on my knees.'

Jeanie, now in some degree restored to the power of thought, joined in the same request. The neighbours departed, leaving father and daughter in the depth of distress.

Thus was it with the afflicted family – until the morning after the death of Porteous...

chapter eleven

HELENA: *Is all the counsel that we two have shared,*
The sisters' vows, the hours that we have spent
When we have chid the hasty-footed time
For parting us—Oh!—and is all forgot?
      A Midsummer Night's Dream, III. 2

---

[1]   The Midianite daughter of Jethro and later the estranged wife of Moses.

Butler remained a long while on Salisbury Crags on the morning which succeeded the lynching of Porteous. For this delay he had his own motives. He wished to collect his thoughts, strangely agitated both by the news of Effie Deans's situation and by the scene he had witnessed. Also, his situation with respect to Jeanie and her father required a fitting time to call upon them. Eight in the morning being then the hour of breakfast, he resolved that it should arrive before his appearance.

Never did hours pass so heavily. Butler shifted his place and widened his walking circle to while away the time. He heard the bell of St Giles Cathedral toll each hour, instantly attested by those of the other steeples. Hearing seven struck, he approached to within a mile of St Leonard's. He descended from his lofty station to the bottom of the deep, grassy valley dividing Salisbury Crags from those smaller rocks named for Saint Leonard. This sequestered dell, as well as other places in the King's Park, was at this time the resort of those who had affairs of honour to settle. Duels were then common among Scotland's haughty gentry. Addicted to intemperance, they both gave provocation and fiercely resented it when given. The sword, then part of every gentleman's dress, was the weapon used for the settlement of such differences. Thus when Butler observed a young man, skulking among the scattered rocks apparently to avoid observation, he assumed that it was for a duel that he sought this lonely spot. Despite his own distress of mind, his sense of duty as a clergyman meant that he could not ignore this person. A tiny interference, he reasoned, may avert a great calamity. My own griefs shall be lighter if they do not divert me from duty.

He quitted the path and advanced. The man, seeing Butler follow him, adjusted his hat fiercely, turned and came forward.

Butler studied his features as they advanced slowly towards each other. The stranger seemed about twenty-five years old. His dress did not indicate his rank with certainty, but from his air and manner he seemed to be dressed below than above his rank. His carriage was bold and his manner unconstrained. His stature was of the middle size and his features uncommonly handsome.

Butler and the stranger met and surveyed each other. The latter, lightly touching his hat, was about to pass by him when Butler, returning the salutation, observed, 'A fine morning, sir. You are on the hill early.'

'I have business here.'

'I do not doubt it, sir,' said Butler. 'Forgive my hoping that it is of a lawful kind?'

'Sir, I never forgive impertinence, nor have you the right to hope about anything that does not concern you.'

'I am a soldier, sir,' said Butler, 'charged to arrest evil-doers in the name of my Master.'

'A soldier! *Arrest* me? Did you reckon with your life before you took the commission?'

'You mistake me, sir, neither my warfare nor my warrant are of *this* world. I am a preacher of the Gospel. In my Master's name I commend good will towards men.'

'A minister!' said the stranger scornfully, 'I know that gentlemen of your cloth in Scotland claim the right of meddling in private affairs. But I have been abroad and know better than to be priest-ridden.'

'Sir, I condemn any clergyman who interferes in men's private affairs out of idle curiosity. But I am of a pure motive. Better to incur your contempt for speaking, than the censure of my conscience for silence.'

'In the name of the Devil!' said the other impatiently. 'Say what you have to say.'

'You,' said Butler, 'are about to violate one of your country's wisest laws. Worse, you are about to violate a law which God himself has implanted in our nature.'

'And what is this Law?' said the stranger in a hollow, disturbed tone.

'Thou shalt do no murder.'

The young man was visibly started. Butler perceived he had made an impression and followed it up. Laying a kindly hand upon the stranger's shoulder he said,

'Think of the alternatives; to kill or be killed. Think what it is to rush uncalled into the presence of the Deity, your heart hot with evil passion, your hand hot from the steel you sent into the breast of a fellow creature. Imagine yourself with the guilt of Cain in your heart – and his stamp upon your brow.'

The stranger gradually withdrew himself. Pulling his hat over his brow, he said, 'Your meaning, sir, I dare say, is excellent, but you are throwing your advice away. I am not here with any violent intention. I am here to save life, not to take it. If you would *do* good rather than *talk* about it, I will give you an opportunity. You see that lone house yonder? Go there. Inquire for one Jeanie Deans. Let her know that I remained here from daybreak expecting to see her, but can abide no longer. Tell her she *must* meet me tonight.'

'Who or what are you,' replied Butler, astonished, 'to charge me with such an errand?'

'I am the Devil!' Butler stepped instinctively back. The stranger went on, 'Call me Apollyon, or whatever name you choose. You shall not find one more odious than my *own*.'

This was spoken with such bitterness of self-upbraiding as to be demoniacal. Butler, though a man brave by principle, was overawed. The stranger now came up boldly, saying in a determined tone,

'And what is *your* name?'

'Reuben Butler.'

The stranger pulled back in agitation. 'Butler!' he repeated. 'Schoolmaster at Liberton?'

'The same.'

The stranger immediately covered his face with his hand. He turned away but stopped after a few paces. He then called out, 'Go your way, and do mine errand. Do not look after me; I will not vanish in a flash of fire. Go, and look not behind you. Tell Jeanie Deans, that when the moon rises I shall meet her at Nicol Muschat's Cairn beneath Saint Anthony's Chapel.'

Amazed that any living man could send so extraordinary a request to his betrothed, Butler strode towards the cottage. By nature neither jealous nor superstitious, Butler was incensed that a profligate gallant might command his future bride to meet at such an hour. Yet the tone in which the stranger had spoken was not that of a seducer. Bold and imperative, it held less of love than threat. Indeed, the place of rendezvous took its very name from a wretch who had there committed a frightful murder.[1]

---

[1] In October 1720, Nichol Muschat took his wife under cloud of night to the King's Park, adjacent to what is called the Duke's Walk near Holyrood Palace and there took her life by cutting her throat. He pleaded guilty to the indictment, for which he suffered death, Scott.

With limbs exhausted with fatigue and a mind harassed with anxiety, Butler ascended from the valley to St Leonard's Crags and Deans's cottage.

chapter twelve

Then she stretched out her lily hand,
And for to do her best;
'Hae back thy faith and troth, Willie,
God gie thy soul good rest!
  Anon, *Sweet William's Ghost*

'Come in,' came the low, sweet voice he loved when Butler tapped at the cottage door. He lifted the latch, and found himself under a roof of affliction. Jeanie sent only one glance towards her lover, meeting him in circumstances so humbling to her honest pride. 'To come of honest Folk' is as highly prized among ordinary Scots as 'to be of good Family' is valued among their gentry. The worth and respectability of one member of a farming family is not only a matter of honest pride, but a guarantee for the good conduct of the whole. Conversely, a stain such as now covered a child of Deans extended its disgrace to all. Jeanie felt herself lowered both in her own eyes and in those of her fiancé. It was in vain that she repressed this feeling. Nature prevailed. The tears she shed for her sister's distress and danger mingled with bitter grief for her own position.

As Butler entered, the old man was seated by the fire, his well-worn pocket Bible in his hands. This was the companion of the wanderings and dangers of his youth, bequeathed to him from the scaffold in 1686 by a fellow Covenanter about to seal their principles with his blood.

The sun sent its rays through a small window at the old man's back, and, 'shining motty through the reek',[1] to use an expression of Burns's, illumined his grey hair and the sacred page he studied. Amidst their sternness, his features retained an expression of stoical dignity born of contempt for earthly things. He boasted, in no small degree, the attributes which Southey ascribes to the ancient Scandinavians; 'firm to inflict, and stubborn to endure.'[2] The whole formed a picture, of which the lights might have come from Rembrandt, but whose outline would have required the force of a Michelangelo.

Deans lifted an eye as Butler entered and instantly averted it, as from an object giving him surprise and pain. He had taken such moral high ground with this scholar that to meet him in his present humiliation merely aggravated his misfortune. Deans raised the Bible with his left hand, partly screening his face and extending his right as far back as he could, and held it out towards Butler. At the same time he turned his body away as if to prevent the preacher seeing his

---

[1] Adapted from Burns's *The Vision*.
[2] Actually 'Stern to inflict and stubborn to endure.' Robert Southey, *To A. S. Cottle*.

countenance. Butler clasped the extended hand, endeavouring, in vain, to say more than, 'God comfort you – God *comfort* you!'

'He will – he *doth*, friend,' said Deans, regaining firmness as he felt the agitation of his guest; 'he doth now, and he will yet more in his own gude time. I have been over proud of my sufferings in a gude cause, Reuben. How muckle better I thought mysell than them that lay in saft beds when I was in the moss-haggs and moors wi' precious Donald Cameron and worthy Mr Blackadder, called Guess-again.[1] And how proud was I to be made a spectacle to men and angels on their pillory at the Canongate afore I was fifteen years old, for the cause of a National Covenant!'

'To think, Reuben, that I that have borne testimony against the defections o' the times yearly, monthly, *daily*, striving and testifying with uplifted hand and voice against all great national snares, such as those nation-wasting, church-sinking abominations of Union, Toleration and Patronage, imposed by that last woman of the Stuarts; also against the infringements of the Eldership, whereanent, I uttered my paper 'A Cry of an Howl in the Desert,' printed at the Bow-head, and sold by all flying stationers in town and country – and *now...*'

Here he paused. Butler, though not in agreement with Douce Davie's ideas on church government, had too much humanity to interrupt him. Indeed, when he paused under the influence of his bitter recollections, Butler threw in his mite of encouragement.

'You have been well known, my old friend, as a true and tried follower of the Cross; one who, as St Jerome hath it *"per infamiam et bonam famam grassari ad immortalitatem"*,[2] which may be freely rendered "who rusheth on to immortal life, through bad and good report". You have been one of those to whom fearful souls cry during the midnight solitude, "Watchman! What of the night?" And assuredly this heavy burden comes with divine permission and special commission and *use*.'

'I *do* receive it as such,' said Deans, grasping Butler's hand, 'and if I have not been taught to read the Scripture in any other tongue but my native Scots, I have learned to bear even this with submission. But, Reuben Butler, what of the Kirk of whilk I have been thought a polished shaft[3] and a pillar, holding from my youth the position of Ruling Elder? What will the profane think of the Elder that cannot keep his own family from stumbling? They will see that my children are as liable to backsliding as the offspring of Belial!'

'But I will bear my cross with the comfort that whatever appeared like goodness in me or mine, was but like the light that shines frae creeping insects on the hillside on a black night. It only appears bright to the eye because all is dark

---

[1]   Rev. John Blackadder (1615–1685) minister of Troqueer, Galloway. A famous Covenanting 'field preacher.' His tombstone says it all: 'Ordained Minister of Troqueer, 1653. Extruded [evicted] 1662. Outlawed for preaching in the fields, 1674. Died after a cruel confinement on the Bass Rock, 1681–1685, *Faithful unto Death*.

[2]   The quotation does not appear in the works of St Jerome (AD *c*.347–420). However the identical quote, again attributed to Jerome, is found in Robert Burton's *Anatomy of Melancholy* I. 484, from which Scott may have extruded it.

[3]   David quotes from Isaiah 49.2.

around it; but when the morn comes o'er the mountains, it is only a puir crawling kail-worm after a'.'

As he uttered these words the door opened and Mr Bartoline Saddletree entered. His three-pointed hat was set far back on his head, a silk handkerchief beneath it to keep it in that cool position. His gold-headed cane was in his hand, his whole deportment that of a wealthy burgher who might one day enter the Magistracy, if not actually descend upon the Curule chair itself.[1]

Although Rochefoucauld says we find something not altogether unpleasant in the misfortunes of our friends,[2] Saddletree would have been angered had anyone told him that he felt pleasure in the disaster of poor Effie Deans and the disgrace of her family. Yet the gratification of playing the person of importance, investigating, and laying down the Law on the whole affair, offered some consolation for the pain he felt for his wife's kinswoman. He had now got a piece of real judicial business on his hands instead of intruding his opinion where it was neither wished nor wanted. He felt as happy as a boy getting his first new watch which actually goes when wound up.

However, besides the subject of Effie for legal disquisition, Bartoline's brain was also loaded with the affair of Porteous's violent death and all its probable consequences to Edinburgh. He had an *embarras des richesses* arising from too much legal and mental wealth. Walking into Deans's cottage was one who not only has more information than the company, but also feels a right to discharge it without mercy.

'Good morning, Mr Deans and good-morrow to you, Mr Butler. I was not aware that you were acquainted with Mr Deans.'

The worthy burgher now sat down importantly upon a chair, wiped his brow, collected his breath and with a deep and dignified sigh, he said, 'Awful' times these, neighbour Deans, awful' times!'

'Sinful', shameful' times!' he answered in a low, subdued tone.

'I arose last morning,' continued Saddletree, 'wi' my mind on what's to be done in puir Effie's misfortune, when a mob strings up Jock Porteous to a beam – and knocks a' thing out of my head again.'

Distressed as he was with his own domestic calamity, Deans could not help expressing interest in the news. Saddletree immediately entered on details of the insurrection and its consequences, while Butler sought private conversation with Jeanie. She gave him the opportunity by leaving the room as if engaged on her morning labour. Butler followed. Deans, closely engaged with his visitor, missed their departure.

Butler found her silent in the dairy, dejected and ready for tears. She was seated in a corner, listless under the weight of her own thoughts.

'I am glad you have come in,' said she, 'for... for I wished to tell ye that all maun be ended between you and me. It's best for both our sakes.'

---

1   The seat of the Chief Magistrate, ie Lord Provost of Edinburgh.

2   François, Duc de la Rochefoucauld (1613–1680), 'Dans l'adversité de nos meilleurs amis, nous trouvons toujours quelque chose qui ne nous déplaît pas.' *Réflexions ou Maximes Morales* (1665).

'Ended!' said Butler in surprise; 'Why should it be ended? This evil lies neither at your door nor at mine. It's an evil of God's sending, and it must be borne. Jeanie, it cannot break plighted troth while they that gave their word wish to keep it.'

'Reuben,' said Jeanie, looking at him affectionately, 'I ken weel that ye think more of me than you. Ye are a man of spotless name, bred to God's ministry and a' men say that ye will someday rise high in the Kirk. Poverty is a bad friend, Reuben, but ill-fame is worse and that ye shall never have through me.'

'What do you mean? What connects our engagement with your sister's guilt? And that, I trust in God, may yet be disproved. How can it affect us?'

'How can you ask me that? Will this stain ever be forgotten? Will it not stick to us and to our bairns and to their very bairns' bairns? To be the sister of a... O my God! No, Reuben, I'll bring disgrace to nae man's hearth; my ain distresses I can bear. But there is nae occasion for buckling them on other folk's shouthers.'

A lover is naturally suspicious. Jeanie's renouncing of their engagement seemed to Butler to chime with the commission of the stranger he had met that morning. His voice faltered as he asked whether anything *other* than a sister's distress had occasioned this.

'And what else could there be?' she replied simply.

'Ten years!' said Butler. 'It's a long time; sufficient perhaps for a woman to weary...'

'To weary of her auld gown,' said Jeanie, 'and to wish for a new ane if she likes to be brave. But not long enough to weary of a friend. The eye may wish change, but the heart, never.'

'Never?' said Reuben, 'that's a bold promise.' He paused, and looking at her fixedly.

'I am charged,' he said, 'with a message to you, Jeanie.'

'Indeed! From whom?'

'From a stranger,' said Butler, affecting to speak with indifference, 'A young man I met this morning in the Park.'

'Mercy!' she said eagerly, 'and what did he say?'

'That he did not see you at the hour he expected, but that you should meet him alone at Muschat's Cairn at moonrise tonight.'

'Tell him I shall certainly come.'

'May I ask,' said Butler, his suspicion increasing, 'who is this man?'

'Folk maun do things they have little wish to do in this world,' replied Jeanie.

'Granted, but what compels you to this? Who *is* this person?'

'I do not know.'

'You do not *know*!' said Butler impatiently. 'You say you are compelled to meet a young man you do not know at such a time and in a lonely place. Jeanie, what am I to think of this?'

'Reuben, believe that I speak truth. I do not ken this man. I do not even ken that I ever saw him; and yet I must give him the meeting he asks. There is life and death upon it.'

'Will you not tell your father, or take him with you?'

'I cannot.'

'Then will you let *me* go with you? I will wait in the Park till nightfall and join you when you set out.'

'Impossible,' said Jeanie; 'there maunna be mortal creature within hearing.'

'Have you considered what you do? The time – the place – an unknown, suspicious character.'

'My life and my safety are in God's hands, but I'll not spare to risk either of them on the errand I maun do.'

'Then, Jeanie,' said Butler, 'we must indeed break off and bid farewell. When there can be no confidence betwixt a man and his betrothed she has no longer regard for him.'

Jeanie looked at him and sighed. 'I thought,' she said, 'that I could bear this parting, but... I did not ken that we were to part in unkindness. But I am a woman and you are a man; it may be different wi' you. If your mind is easier by thinking badly of me, so be it.'

'You are what you have *always* been,' said Butler, 'wiser, better, and less selfish than I ever can be. But why – *why* will you not let me be your protector, or at least your adviser in this?'

'Because I cannot and I *dare* not. But hark, what's that?' The voices from the cottage had become obstreperously loud.

When Jeanie and Butler left, Saddletree entered upon the business which chiefly interested the family. He first found old Deans so subdued by his daughter's danger and disgrace that he listened without reply, or perhaps without understanding, to Saddletree's learned disquisitions. These were on the nature of the crime imputed to Effie and on the steps which ought to be taken in consequence. His only answer at each pause was, 'I am no doubting that you wish us weel.'

Encouraged by this, Saddletree reverted to his other topic of interest, namely the murder of Porteous, pronouncing severe censure on the parties concerned.

'These are desperate when the people take the power of life and death out of the hands of the rightful Magistrate and into their ain rough grip. I am of the opinion, and so I believe is the Privy Council, that taking the life of a reprieved man is nae better than perduellion.'[1]

'If I hadna muckle on my mind whilk is hard to bear, Mr Saddletree,' said Deans, 'I wad dispute that point wi' you.'

'How could you dispute that *perduellion* is the warst and maist virulent kind of treason, being an open convocation of the king's lieges against his authority, especially in arms and by tuck of drum and muckle worse than *Lèse-Majesté*!'

'I tell ye,' retorted Douce Davie, 'it *will* bear a disputer unlike your cauld, legal and formal doctrines, Saddletree. I haud little by that Parliament House, since the downfall of the hopes of the honest folk that followed the Revolution.'

'But, Deans,' said Saddletree impatiently; 'didna ye get both Liberty and Conscience made fast and legally settled on you and your heirs for ever?'

'Mr Saddletree,' retorted Deans, 'I ken ye are one of those that are wise after the manner of this world, and that forgather wi' the lang gowns o' the smart lawyers of this land. But dark is the dolefu' cast that they hae given Scotland

---

[1] Treason.

when their black hands of defection were clasped in the red hands of our sworn murtherers; when those who had numbered the towers of our Zion, and marked the bulwarks of our Reformation, saw their hopes turn into a snare and their rejoicing into weeping.'

'I canna *understand* this,' answered Saddletree. 'I am an honest Presbyterian of the Kirk of Scotland and stand by her and the General Assembly, and the due administration of justice by the fifteen Lords o' Session *and* the five Lords o' Justiciary!'

'Out upon ye, Saddletree – *and* the General Assembly!' shouted David, seeing an opening for his testimony on the offences and backslidings of the land and forgetting his own domestic calamity. 'Out upon your General Assembly and the back of my *hand* to your Court o' Session! The Assembly is a bunch o' cauldrife professors and ministers that sat snug and warm when the persecuted Remnant were wrestling wi' hunger and cauld and fear of death and danger of fire and sword upon wet brae-sides, peat-haggs, and flow-mosses? And now they now *creep* out of their holes like bluebottles in a blink of sunshine, to take the pulpits of better folk that witnessed and testified and fought and endured pit, prison-house and transportation beyond the seas? A bonny nest there's o' them! And as for your Court o' Session...'

'Say what ye will o' the General Assembly,' said Saddletree, interrupting him, 'but as for the Lords o' Session, they are my neighbours, I would have ye ken, for your *ain* safety, that to raise scandal about them, whilk is termed to *murmur* again them, is a crime *sui generis*. *Sui generis*, Deans! D'ye ken what that amounts to?'

'I ken little o' the language of the Antichrist,' said Deans, 'and I care *less* than little for carnal courts. And as to murmur agin them, it's what a' the folk does that loses their pleas, and nine-tenths o' them that win them. Sae I wad hae ye ken that I detest a' your gleg-tongued Advocates that sell their knowledge for pieces of silver; *and* your worldly-wise Judges, that will gie *three days* of hearing in presence to a debate about the peeling of an *ingan*,[1] and no ane *half-hour* to the Gospel testimony – as legalists and formalists wha countenance, by cunning terms of Law, patronages, and Erastian prelatic oaths! And as for that soul *and* body-killing Court o' Justiciary...'

The suffering cause of True Religion had swept honest David along with it thus far; but with his mention of the Criminal Court, recollection of the predicament of his daughter rushed at once to his mind. He stopped short in the midst of his triumphant declamation, pressed his hands against his forehead and fell silent.

Saddletree was moved, but not sufficiently to miss the opportunity of prosing in David's sudden silence.

'Nae doubt, Mr Deans, it's a sair thing to hae dealings wi' Courts of Law. Now, touching this unhappy affair of Effie, ye'll hae seen the dittay,[2] doubtless?'

He dragged out of his pocket a bundle of papers, and began to turn them over.

'This is no it... this is the testimony of Mungo Marsport of that Ilk, against Captain Lackland for coming on the lands of Marsport with hawks, hounds,

---

[1]   Onion.

[2]   Indictment.

lying-dogs, nets, guns, cross-bows, hagbuts and other engines for the destruction of game sic as red deer, capercailzies, moor fowl, paitricks, herons and siclike. He, the said Capt. Lackland not being ane *qualified* person, in terms of the Statute of 1629 that is, not having ane plough-gate of land. Now, the Defence propones that *non constat*[1] at this present time what *is* a plough-gate of land, whilk uncertainty is sufficient to nullify the charge. But in response to these Defences the Pursuer assert that it signifies naething what, or how muckle, a plough-gate of land may *be*, since the Defender has nae lands *whatsoever*.'

Saddletree read on from the paper in his hand, 'Sae, granting a ploughgate to be less than the nineteenth part of a guse's grass, what the better will the Defender be, seeing he hasna a divot of land in Scotland?'

'*Advocatus* for Lackland duplies that the Pursuer must show *formaliter et specialiter*, as well as generaliter, what is the qualification that defender Lackland does not possess. Let him tell me what a plough-gate of land is and I'll tell him if I have one or no. Surely the pursuer is bound to understand his own libel and his own statute that he founds upon. If *Titius* pursues *Maevius* for recovery of ane *black* horse lent to Maevius, surely he shall succeed in obtaining the judgment; but if Titius pursues Maevius for ane *scarlet* or ane *crimson* horse, he shall be bound to show that there is sic an animal in *rerum natura*.[2] No man can be bound to plead to nonsense – to a charge which cannot be explained or understood.'

'He's wrang there,' said Saddletree, 'the better the pleadings the fewer understand them!' He returned to the paper;

'And so the reference unto this undefined and unintelligible measure of land is, as if a penalty was inflicted by Statute for any man who suld hunt or hawk, or use lying-dogs, and wearing a sky-blue pair of breeches, without having... But I am wearying you, Mr Deans. We'll pass to your ain business – though this cause of Marsport *versus* Lackland has made an unco din in the Outer House of the Court of Session.'

'Weel, now here's the Dittay against puir Effie: "Whereas it is humbly meant and shown to us," etc. – these are words of mere style – "that *whereas*, by the Laws of this and every other well-regulated realm, the murder of anyone, more especially of an infant child, is a crime of ane high nature & severely punishable: And *whereas*, without prejudice to the foresaid generality, it was, by ane Act of the second session of the First Parliament of our most High and Dread Sovereigns William & Mary, especially enacted that ane woman who shall have concealed her condition, and shall *not* be able to show that she hath called for help at the birth; in the case that the child shall be found dead or missing, she shall be deemed & held guilty of the murder thereof; and the said facts of concealment and pregnancy being found proven, or confessed, shall sustain the pains of law accordingly; yet, nevertheless, you, Effie, or Euphemia Deans...'

'Read no farther!' said Deans, raising his head, 'I would rather ye thrust a sword into my heart than read a word farther!'

---

[1]   There is no agreement.

[2]   In Nature.

'I thought,' said Saddletree, 'it wad hae comforted ye to ken the best and the warst o't. But the question is, what's to be dune?'

'Nothing,' answered Deans firmly, 'but to abide the dispensation that the Lord sends us. Oh, would that His will had been to take this grey head to rest before this visitation on my house and name! But His will be done.'

'But Deans,' said Saddletree, 'ye'll retain Advocates for the puir lassie?'

'I would if there was ae man amang them,' answered Deans, 'that held fast his integrity. But I ken them weel. They are a' carnal, crafty and warld-hunting self-seekers, Erastians and Arminians, every ane o' them!'

'Ye mauna take the warld at its word,' said Saddletree; 'the very Deil's no sae ill as he's ca'd; and I ken mair than ae Advocate that has some integrity as weel as their neighbours; that is... after a sort o' fashion' o' their ain.'

'It is indeed but a *fashion* of integrity that ye'll find amang them,' retorted Deans, 'and a *fashion* of wisdom, and *fashion* of carnal learning. Gazing, glancing-glasses they are wi' their earthly learning, their flights and refinements, their eloquence frae heathen Emperors and Popish canons! In that daft trash ye were reading to me, they canna call men by ony Christened name, but maun baptize them anew wi' sic Latin names as the accursed Titus, wha was made the instrument of burning the Holy Temple and other heathens!'[1]

'It's *Tishius*,' interrupted Saddletree, 'and no Titus. But it's a case of necessity; Effie maun hae Counsel. Now, I could speak to Mr Crossmyloof, Advocate, he's weel ken'd for a round-spun Presbyterian, and a ruling elder to boot.'

'He's a rank *Erastian*!' cried Deans.

'Then what say ye to the Laird of Cuffabout – he thumps the dust out of a case well.'

'Him? The fause loon. He was in his bandoliers and wad hae joined the Highlanders in 1715, had they crossed the Firth.'

'Weel, what of Arniston? There's a clever chield for ye.'

'Ay, to bring Popish medals into their very library from that schismatic woman in the north, the Duchess of Gordon.'[2]

'Weel, weel, but somebody ye maun hae... What o' Kittlepunt?'

'He's an Arminian.'[3]

'Woodsetter, then?'

'He's a Cocceian!'[4]

'Young Nimmo?'

'He's naething at a'.'

'Ye're hard to please,' said Saddletree. 'I hae run ower the pick o' them for you. Ye maun choose for yourself; but bethink ye that in the multitude of

---

[1] The army of the future Roman Emperor Titus, son of the reigning Vespasian, destroyed the Second Temple at Jerusalem during the Great Jewish Revolt in AD 70.

[2] James Dundas, younger of Arniston, was tried in the year 1711 on a charge of having presented, from the Duchess of Gordon, a medal of the Pretender for the purpose, it was said, of affronting Queen Anne, Scott.

[3] Arminians, followers of Jacobus Arminius (1560–1609), rejected predestination.

[4] Johannes Cocceius (1603–1669), a Dutch theologian who held that Sabbath observance was not mandatory for Christians as it was a Jewish instituion.

Counsellors there's safety. What say ye to try young Mackenzie? He has a' his uncle's *Practiques* at the tongue's end.'

'Sir, wad ye speak to *me*,' exclaimed the sturdy Presbyterian in wrath, 'about a man that has the blood of the Saints at his fingers' ends? Didna his uncle die wi' the name of *Bluidy Mackenzie*,[1] to be sae kend as lang as there's a Scots tongue to speak the word? If the life of my dear bairn *and* Jeanie's and my ain and a' Mankind's, depended on my asking sic a Satanist to speak a word for me or them, they should a' gae doun the water thegither!'

It was the power and tone of this last sentence that broke up the conversation between Butler and Jeanie, and brought them back into the house. Here they found the old man half frantic between his grief and his zealous ire against Saddle-tree's proposed measures. His cheek was aflame, his hand clenched and his voice raised, while the tear in his eye and an occasional quiver in his voice showed that he could not shake off his misery. Butler urged patience, worried by the effects of agitation on his aged and feeble frame.

'I *am* patient,' returned the old man sternly, 'more patient than any one who is alive to the woeful backslidings of this miserable time.'

'But sir we *must* use human means. When you call in a physician, would you question him on his religious principles?'

'Wad I *no*?' answered David, 'I wad indeed. And if he didna satisfy me not a *goutte*[2] of his physic should gang through my father's son.'

It is a dangerous thing to trust to an illustration. Butler had done so and miscarried; but like a soldier whose musket misfires, he stood his ground and charged with the bayonet.

'This is *far* too rigid an interpretation of your duty, sir. The sun shines and the rain descends on the just and the unjust. They are often placed together in life, rendering intercourse indispensable. Perhaps this is so that the Evil may be converted by the Good. Perhaps also that the righteous might, among other trials, be required to occasionally converse with the profane.'

'Ye're a silly callant, Reuben,' answered Deans, 'Can a man touch pitch and not be defiled? Nae lawyer shall ever speak for me and mine that hasna concurred in the Testimony of the scattered yet lovely Remnant which abode in the clefts of the rocks.'[3]

So saying, and as if fatigued both with the arguments and presence of his guests, the old man arose and, bidding them *adieu* with a motion of his head and hand, went to his sleeping apartment.

'It's thrawing his daughter's life awa,' said Saddletree to Butler, 'to hear him speak so. Where will he ever get a Cameronian advocate? Or wha ever heard of a lawyer's suffering either for ae religion or another? The lassie's life is clean flung awa.'

During the latter part of this argument, Dumbiedikes had arrived at the door,

---

1   Sir George Mackenzie of Rosehaugh (1636–1691) The Lord Advocate responsible for persecuting the Presbyterian Covenanters. After the the Battle of Bothwell Bridge in 1679, Mackenzie imprisoned 1,200 Covenanters in a field next to Greyfriars Kirkyard. Some were executed, and hundreds died of maltreatment and exposure. This gained him the nickname of 'Bloody Mackenzie'.

2   Not a drop.

3   Another reference to the Cameronian sect of the oppressed Covenanters.

dismounted, hung his pony's bridle on the usual hook and sunk down on a settle. With more than his usual animation, he followed first one speaker then another, till he caught Saddletree's last words. He rose from his seat, stumped slowly across the room, and, coming close up to Saddletree's ear, said in a tremulous voice,

'Will siller do naething for them, Mr Saddletree?'

'Umph!' said Saddletree, looking grave. 'Siller will certainly do it in the Parliament House, if ony thing *can* do it; but where's the siller to come frae? Mr Deans will do naething; and though Mrs Saddletree's their far-awa cousin and weel disposed to assist, she wadna like to stand to be bound *singuli in solidum*[1] to such an expensive wark. Were a friend to bear a share o' the burden, something might be dune. I wadna like to see the case fa' through without being pled. It wadna be creditable, for a' that daft Whig body Deans says.'

'I will be answerable,' said Dumbiedikes, 'for a score of punds sterling.' He fell silent, staring in astonishment at finding himself capable of such resolution and generosity.

'God Almighty bless ye, Laird!' said Jeanie.

'And ye may mak' the twenty punds *thretty*,' said Dumbiedikes, looking bashfully away from her and towards Saddletree.

'That will do bravely,' said Saddletree, rubbing his hands, 'and ye sall hae a' my skill and knowledge to mak' that siller gang far. Fine I ken how to mak the birkies tak short fees and be glad o' them. Let them ken that ye hae twa or three cases of importance coming up, and they'll work cheap to get the custom!'

'Can I also be of use?' said Butler. 'Alas, my means are only worth the black coat I wear; but I owe much to this family. Can I do nothing?'

'Ye can help to collect evidence, sir,' said Saddletree; 'if we could find anyone to say she had gien the least *hint* o' her pregnancy, she wad be safe. The Crown canna be craved to prove a *negative*. Therefore the charge maun be argued by the accused proving her defences. And it canna be done otherwise.'

'But the *fact*, sir,' argued Butler, 'the *fact* that this poor girl has borne a child; surely the Crown's lawyers must prove *that*?' said Butler.

'Yes,' said Saddletree, after some grave hesitation, 'but I fancy that job's been done for them; for she has confessed her guilt.'

'Confessed to *murder*?' exclaimed Jeanie.

'No, but she confessed bearing the babe.'

'Then what became of it?' said Jeanie. 'Not a word could I get from her but sighs and tears.'

'She says it was taken awa' from her by the woman in whose house it was born.'

'But who *was* that woman?' said Butler. 'I will go to her directly.'

'Wha kens that but Effie herself?' said Saddletree.

'Then it is to Effie that I go,' said Butler. 'Farewell, Jeanie.' Then, coming close up to her, he said, 'Take no rash steps till you hear from me. Farewell!'

'I wad gang too,' said Dumbiedikes in an anxious and jealous tone, 'but my powny winna gang ony other road than frae Dumbiedikes to this house and back again.'

---

[1]   Singly liable for a whole amount due.

'Ye'll do better for them,' said Saddletree, as they left the house together, 'by sending me the thretty punds.'

'*Thretty* punds?'

'Aye,' said Saddletree, 'ye amended your offer to thretty.'

'Did I? I dinna mind that I did,' answered Dumbiedikes. 'But whatever I said, I'll stand to.' Then, bestriding his steed with some difficulty, he added, 'Saddletree, didna ye think Jeanie's tearfu' een sparkled like lamour beads?'[1]

'I dinna ken about women's een, Laird,' replied Bartoline; 'and I care just as little. I wish I were as free o' their tongues; though few wives are under better command than my own. I allow neither *perduellion* nor *lèse-majesté* against my authority.'

The Laird saw nothing in this to call for a rejoinder and so, with a mute salutation, they parted.

chapter thirteen

GONZALO: *I'll warrant that fellow from drowning,*
were the ship no stronger than a nut-shell
and as leaky as an unstaunched wench

   The Tempest, *I.I*

Butler felt neither fatigue nor lack of refreshment, although from the way he had spent the night he might well have been overcome with either. He forgot both, however, as he hastened to assist Jeanie Deans's sister.

Walking rapidly, he was surprised to hear his name called, the voice half-drowned by the trot of a Highland pony. He looked behind, and saw the Laird of Dumbie-dikes making after him. Butler stopped in irritation as the panting rider came up.

'Whoa there!' ejaculated Dumbiedikes, checking the pace of the pony. 'It's a hard-set willful beast, this.'

Fortunately, he had overtaken Butler where the clergyman's road parted from that leading to Dumbiedikes, for nothing could have induced his pony, Rory Bean, to diverge a yard from the path to his own paddock.

Even when he had recovered from the shortness of breath occasioned by a more rapid trot than Rory or he were accustomed to, it was a while ere he could utter a syllable. After some effort Dumbiedikes said, 'I say, Mr Butler, it's a braw day for the hairst.'[2]

'Indeed,' said Butler impatiently. 'I wish you good morning, sir.'

'Stay,' rejoined the Laird, 'that was no what I meant to say.'

'Then pray be quick,' rejoined Butler; 'I crave your pardon, but I am in haste, and *tempus nemini*...[3] you know the proverb.'

---

[1] Amber beads.

[2] Harvest.

[3] *Tempus neminem manet* – 'time waits for no man'. Butler's Latin is, again, faulty in using the dative, rather than the accusative case of *nemo, neminis*, ' nobody'. Tut.

Dumbiedikes did not know the proverb. He was concentrating his intellect on one grand gesture.

'Mr Butler, d'ye ken if Mr Saddletree's a great lawyer?'

'I have no word for it but his own,' answered Butler, drily.

'I see,' replied Dumbiedikes in a tone indicating that he caught the import. 'In that case, I'll employ my ain man o' legal business, Mr Nichil Novit, to act for Effie.'

Having thus displayed more sagacity than Butler had ever expected from him, he courteously touched his gold-laced cocked hat. A punch on the ribs conveyed to Rory Bean that he should now proceed homewards.

Butler resumed his pace with a touch of the jealousy excited by the Laird's attention to Jeanie. 'But,' said he to himself, 'why should I be vexed? He brings wealth. I can only bring empty wishes. In God's name, let each do what he can!' Redoubling his pace, he soon stood before the door of the Tolbooth; or rather he stood before the entrance where the door had been.

The mysterious stranger's message to Jeanie, his conversation with her on their engagement and the scene with old Deans, had so occupied his mind as to drown the recollection of the events he had witnessed the preceding evening. However, his attention was quickly recalled to it by groups scattered about the street in conversations which hushed when strangers approached. Searches were being conducted by the city police, supported by parties of the military, while the Guardhouse had treble sentinels. There were subdued and intimidated glances among the lower orders of society, conscious that they were suspected of complicity in a riot.

The doorless entrance to the prison was now defended by a double file of Grenadiers. Their cries of 'Halt!', the blackened gateway and the winding staircase of the Tolbooth now open to the public eye, recalled the eventful night. On his requesting to speak with Effie Deans, the same silver-haired turnkey of the preceding evening, made his appearance.

'I think,' he replied to Butler's request for admission, 'ye'll be the same that was here to see her yestreen?' Butler admitted he was that person. 'And I am thinking,' pursued the turnkey, 'that ye speered at me when we locked up and if we locked up earlier on account of Porteous?'

'Very likely,' said Butler; 'now, can I see Effie Deans?'

'I dinna ken. Gang up the turnpike stair, and turn into the room on the left hand.'

The old man followed close behind him, keys in hand, including the huge one which had once serviced the outer gate. No sooner had Butler entered the room to which he was directed, than the warder locked it on the outside. At first Butler thought this was only the man's habitual caution, but then he heard, 'turn out the guard!', and immediately afterwards heard the clash a sentinel being posted at the door of his apartment. He called out:

'My good friend, I have business of consequence with Effie Deans. I beg to see her as soon as possible.' No answer came.

'If it be against your rules to let me see the prisoner,' repeated Butler, in a still louder tone, 'tell me so and let me go about my business. *Fugit irrevocabile tempus!*' he muttered to himself.

'If ye had business to do, ye suld hae dune it before ye cam here,' replied the warder outside; 'there's sma' likelihood o' another mob coming to raid us again. The Law will haud her ain now and *that*, sir, ye'll find to your cost.'

'What do you mean?' retorted Butler. 'You must be mistaking me for some other person. My name is Reuben Butler, preacher of the Gospel.'

'I ken that weel enough.'

'If you know me, I have a right to know what warrant you have for detaining me.'

'Warrant?' said the jailor. 'The Warrant's awa to Liberton wi' twa Sheriff's officers seeking ye. If ye had staid at hame, as honest men do, ye wad hae seen the warrant. But if ye come of your ain accord to be incarcerated, wha can help it?'

'So I cannot see Effie Deans?'

'As for Effie Deans,' answered the old man, 'ye'll hae enough ado to mind your ain business; let her mind hers. As for letting you out, that's for the Magistrates. Fare ye weel. I maun watch Deacon Sawyers putting back the doors that *your* quiet folk broke down yesternight, Mr. Butler.'

An indistinct idea of peril which he could not ward off now floated before Butler's eyes. He reflected on the events of the preceding night, in hopes of finding some means of vindicating, or at least explaining, his conduct. He had appeared among the mob; his detention must be founded on that. Worryingly, he could not recollect being observed by any disinterested witness in his attempts to reason with the rioters or to make them release him. The distress of the Deans family and Jeanie's rendezvous, which he could not now hope to interrupt, also intruded on these reflections.

After an hour in solitary confinement, he received a summons to attend the sitting Magistrate and was conducted from the prison guarded by a strong party of soldiers. He was introduced into the Council Chambers where the Magistrates hold their sittings, a short distance from the prison. One or two of the Senators of the city were present, and were about to examine an individual who was brought forward to the foot of the long green-covered Council table.

'Is that the preacher?' said one of the Magistrates, as the City Officer introduced Butler. The man answered in the affirmative. 'Let him sit there for an instant; we will finish this man's business shortly.'

'Shall we not remove Mr Butler?' queried an assistant.

'Let him remain where he is.'

Butler accordingly sat down on a bench at the bottom of the apartment, attended by one of his keepers.

It was a large room, partially and imperfectly lighted. However, one window threw a strong light at the foot of the table at which prisoners were posted for examination, while the upper end where the examiners sat was in shadow. Butler's eyes fixed on the person whose examination was at present proceeding, with the idea that he might recognise some one of the conspirators of the former night. But though the features of this man were striking, he could not recollect seeing him before.

The complexion of this person was dark and his age somewhat advanced. He wore his own jet black hair, which was mottled with grey and was combed smooth down and cut very short. The man's face expressed roguery more than stormy passions. His quick black eyes and sardonic smile gave him a knowing look. His dress was that of a horse-dealer: a close-buttoned jockey-coat, or wrap-rascal, as it was then termed, with huge metal buttons, coarse blue upper stockings called boot-hose and a slouch hat. He only lacked a whip under the arm and a spur upon the heel to complete the character.

'Your name is James Ratcliffe?' said the Magistrate.

'Aye, wi' your honour's leave.'

'Is that to say you could find another name if I did not like that one?'

'I hae twenty to pick and choose upon, always with your honour's leave,' resumed the respondent.

'But James Ratcliffe is your *present name*? What is your trade?'

'I canna say distinctly, that I have *preceesely* a trade.'

'And what,' repeated the Magistrate, 'are your means of living?'

'Your Honour kens that as weel as I do!'

'No matter, I want to hear you describe it.'

'*Describe* it to your Honour? Far be it from Jemmie Ratcliffe!'

'Come, sir, no trifling. Answer!'

'Weel, sir, I maun make a clean breast, for ye see, I am looking for favour. What is't again that the eighth Command says?'

'Thou shalt not steal. Ratcliffe, you are a notorious thief.'

'Highlands and Lowlands ken that, sir, forby England *and* Holland,' replied Ratcliffe.

'And what did you think the end of your calling would be?'

'The gallows,' replied Ratcliffe composedly.

'You are a daring rascal,' said the Magistrate; 'but how are you daring to hope things may be mended today?'

'Dear, your Honour,' answered Ratcliffe, 'there's muckle difference between me lying in prison under sentence of death, and staying there of ane's ain proper accord. It would have cost me naething to get up and rin awa! What was to hinder me from stepping out when the rabble walked awa wi' Jock Porteous yestreen? Does your Honour think I stayed on purpose to be hanged?'

'I do not know what *you* may have proposed to yourself, but I do know what the Law proposes for you. You will hang on the Wednesday of next week.'

'Na, na, your Honour,' said Ratcliffe firmly, 'craving your honour's pardon, I'll ne'er believe that till I see it.'

'You do not expect the gallows, to which you are condemned for the *fourth* time to my knowledge? May I know what it is you *do* expect in consideration of your not escaping with the rest of the jail-birds?'

'There's a vacancy for the post of under-turnkey,' said the prisoner; 'I wadna think of asking the lockman's[1] place; it wadna suit me for I never could kill a beast, much less a man.'

'That is in your favour,' said the Magistrate, 'but how can you possibly be trusted in a prison, when you have broken out of half the jails in Scotland?'

'Wi' your Honour's leave,' said Ratcliffe, 'I'm thus the better to keep other folk in!'

The remark seemed to strike the Magistrate, but he made no further observation and ordered Ratcliffe removed.

When this daring and sly freebooter was out of hearing, the Magistrate asked the City Clerk what he thought of the fellow's assurance.

---

[1] Hangman, or Lockman. So called from the small quantity, *lock* in Scots, of meal which he was entitled to take out of every sack exposed to market in the city.

'If James Ratcliffe is inclined to turn to good,' replied the Clerk, 'there's no man could be of such use to the Town in the lock-up business. I'll speak to Mr Sharpitlaw about him.'

Butler was now placed at the table for examination. The Magistrate conducted his inquiry civilly, but in a manner indicating strong suspicion. With a frankness which became his calling and character, Butler admitted his involuntary presence at the murder of Porteous. Of the circumstances attending the affair, he gave minute details which were taken down by the Clerk.

With the narrative concluded, the cross-examination commenced. This is a painful task even for the most candid witness, since a story concerning alarming incidents cannot be clearly and distinctly told without some ambiguity. Doubt may be thrown upon it by a string of minute questions.

The Magistrate commenced by observing that Butler had said his object was to return to the village of Liberton, but that he was intercepted the mob at the West Port.

'Is the West Port your *usual* way of leaving town when you go to Liberton?' said the Magistrate.

'No,' answered Butler, 'but I chanced to be nearer that port than any other, and the hour of shutting the gates was about to strike.'

'That was – *unlucky*,' said the Magistrate, drily. 'You say you were under coercion of the lawless multitude, and compelled to accompany them through scenes irreconcilable to the calling of a Minister. Did you not attempt to resist or escape from them?' Butler replied that their numbers prevented resistance, while their vigilance blocked escape. 'That was *again* unlucky,' repeated the Magistrate, in the same dry tone. He then proceeded with politeness, but with the stiffness of continuing suspicion, to question Butler on the behaviour of the mob. What had been the manners and dress of the ringleaders? When he reckoned that the caution of Butler must have been lulled asleep, the Magistrate artfully returned to former parts of his evidence, requiring a recapitulation of the minutest details attending each part of the scene. No contradiction emerged however to encourage the suspicion in which he seemed to hold Butler.

At length the questioning reached Madge Wildfire, at whose name the Magistrate and Town Clerk exchanged significant glances. The former's enquiries could not have been more particular on the features and dress of this personage. Butler could say almost nothing of this person's features, which had been disguised with red paint and soot like an Indian going to battle. Besides, there was the projecting shade of a coif, which muffled the hair of the supposed female. Butler declared that he thought he would not recognise Madge Wildfire if placed before him, but that he believed he would recognise the voice.

The Magistrate asked him again to state by what gate he eventually left the city. 'By the Cowgate Port,' replied Butler.

'Was *that* the nearest road to Liberton?'

'No,' answered Butler, embarrassed, 'but it was the nearest way to extricate myself from the mob.'

Clerk and Magistrate again exchanged glances.

'Is the Cowgate Port a quicker way to Liberton from the Grassmarket than Bristo Port?'

'No,' replied Butler; 'but I had to visit a friend.'

'Indeed?' said the interrogator, 'You were in a hurry to relate what you had witnessed?'

'Indeed I was not. Nor did I speak on the subject the whole time I was at St Leonard's Crags.'

'And which road did you take to St Leonard's Crags?'

'By the foot of Salisbury Crags.'

'*Indeed*? You seem partial to circuitous routes,' again said the Magistrate, 'Who did you see after you left the city?'

One by one he obtained a description of every one of the groups who had passed Butler; their number, demeanour and appearance. At length they came to the mysterious stranger in the King's Park. On this subject Butler would fain have remained silent, but the Magistrate had no sooner heard of the incident, than he seemed intent on minute particulars.

'Look ye, Mr Butler, you are a young man, and bear an excellent character; so much I will myself testify in your favour. *But*, at times a sort of fiery zeal affects some of you clergy. Men otherwise irreproachable have done, or countenanced, acts which have shaken the peace of the country. I will deal plainly with you: I am not at all satisfied with your story of setting out, again and *again* to seek your dwelling by two different roads, both circuitous. Also, to be frank, no one we have questioned on this affair thought you were acting under compulsion. Moreover, the waiters at the Cowgate Port declare that *you* were the first to command them to open the gate. This you did in a tone of authority, as if still presiding over the sentinels of the mob who had contained them the whole night.'

'God forgive them!' said Butler; 'I only asked free passage for myself alone. They must have misunderstood.'

'Mr Butler,' resumed the Magistrate, 'you *must* be frank with me if you wish to lessen the risk to yourself. You met another individual in your passage through King's Park to Saint Leonard's Crags. I must know every word which passed.'

Butler, thus closely pressed, had no reason to conceal this unless because Jeanie Deans was involved. He described the whole episode from beginning to end.

'Do you suppose,' said the Magistrate, 'that the young woman will accept such an invitation?'

'I fear she will.'

'Why do you *fear* it?'

'I am apprehensive for her safety at a meeting at such a time and such a place. And with someone who looked like a *desperado* and whose message was inexplicable.'

'Her safety shall be cared for,' said the Magistrate. 'Mr Butler, I regret that I cannot immediately discharge you from confinement, but I hope you will not be long detained. Clerk; remove Mr Butler and provide him with decent accommodation in all respects.'

chapter fourteen

Dark and eerie was the night,
And lonely was the way,
As Janet, wi' her green mantell,
To Miles' Cross she did gae.
      Old Ballad

Jeanie Deans had seen Butler depart without an opportunity to give him any
farther explanation. This induced anxiety in one whose heart, under her russet
rokelay, would not have disgraced Cato's daughter.[1] On reflection, she checked
her emotions while her father and sister were in such deep affliction. From her
pocket she drew a letter flung that morning into her apartment through an open
window. It said:'*If you would save the life and honour of your sister, give a secret
and solitary meeting to the writer.*'

She alone could 'rescue' him, continued the letter, and only he could rescue
Effie. Any mention of the meeting to her father, or any other person, would
prevent its taking place – and would ensure her sister's death.

The message delivered to her by Butler from the stranger in the Park tallied
with the contents of the letter, but assigned a later hour and a different meeting
place. Apparently the writer had used Butler to transmit this change to Jeanie.
She had been on the point of producing the billet to allay her fiancé's suspicions,
but the clear threats in the letter hung on her heart. Equally, there was no way of
predicting how the matter might strike old David. Asking a female friend to
accompany her to the rendezvous might have been expedient, but there again
was the warning; betrayal of the meeting would endanger Effie's life.

Left alone and separated from all earthly counsel, she prayed with fervour that
God would please to direct course. Jeanie arose from her devotions, her heart fortified.

'I *will* meet this man,' she said to herself. 'I suspect he is the direct cause of
Effie's misfortune, but I will meet him, be it for good or ill.'

Her mind composed, she went to her father. The old man did not, at least
outwardly, permit family distress to interfere with his stoical reserve. He had even
chided his daughter for allowing the distress of the morning to interfere with her
domestic duties.

'Jeanie, if ye neglect your warldly duties in the day of affliction, what
confidence can I have of your salvation?'

Jeanie was not unhappy to hear her father's thoughts expand beyond his
immediate distress. She put the household in order.

The hour of noon came. Father and child sat down to their repast. In asking
a blessing on the meal, the old man added a prayer that the bread eaten in sadness
of heart and the bitter waters of Marah[1] might be as nourishing as those poured

---

[1]   In Plutarch's (*Parallel Lives*) Porcia, the daughter of M.Porcius Cato, is praised for her
prudence and courage. Wife to Caesar's assassin M. Junius Brutus, she appears as Portia, 'a
woman well-reputed, Cato's daughter' in the plot of Shakespeare's *Julius Caesar* which he
based on Plutarch. A rokelay is a short cloak.

from a plentiful basket and store. The hours glided on. The sun set beyond the dusky eminence of the Castle of Edinburgh and the screen of the Pentland Hills. The close of evening summoned David Deans and his daughter to the nightly exercise, or family worship.

As they sat down, a chair happened to stand in the place usually occupied by Effie. David Deans saw his daughter's eyes swim with tears. The Scripture lesson was read, the Psalm was sung, the Prayer made; the old man avoiding in all of these any passage applicable to the family misfortune. This was perhaps as much to spare the feelings of his daughter as to maintain the appearance of stoical endurance. His duty done, he wished Jeanie good-night, kissed her forehead, and said,

'The God of Israel bless you, even with the blessings of his Promise, dear bairn!'[2]

She now made preparation for her night walk. It would be easy to leave the house unobserved, but the whole undertaking had terrors for Jeanie, her life spent in the seclusion of their peaceful household. The very hour at which some damsels commence an evening of pleasure was for Jeanie one of awe and solemnity. Her hands trembled as she snooded her fair hair beneath the riband, the only ornament which unmarried women then wore on their heads. She adjusted her scarlet tartan muffler and lifted the latch.

Out in the open fields, apprehensions crowded upon her. The dim cliffs, the interspersed rocks and greensward through which she had to pass glimmered before her in the clear autumn night. As the flitting moon began to peer on the scene with a solemn light, Jeanie's fears took another turn; one peculiar to her rank and country.

chapter fifteen

HAMLET: *The spirit that I have seen*
may be the devil and the devil hath power
to assume a pleasing shape.
    Hamlet. II.2

Witchcraft and demonology were then believed in by almost all ranks, but more especially among the stricter Presbyterians. They, when at the head of the State, had been sullied by their persecution of those imagined to engage in such equally imaginary activities. In this field, Saint Leonard's Crags and the adjacent Chase were a dreaded and ill-reputed district. Jeanie Deans was too well acquainted with such legends to escape their effect on the imagination. Indeed, stories of the occult had been familiar to her from infancy, being the only relief which her father's conversation afforded from the gloomy history of the strivings, captures and executions of the Martyrs of the Covenant.

---

[1] Exodus 15.23. 'And when they came to Marah, they could not drink of the waters of Marah, for they were bitter.' Marah is in Sinai. The word means 'bitter' in Hebrew.

[2] God's Promise, made originally to Abraham. *See* Genesis 12.1–3.

Brought up with supernatural legends, Jeanie began to feel an ill-defined apprehension, not merely of phantoms which might lie in her way, but of the nature of the man she was to meet. However, determined to do anything to save her sister, she glided on by rock and stone, 'now in glimmer and now in gloom',[1] as her path lay through moonlight or shadow, endeavouring to overpower her fears. She also prayed for the protection of that Being to whom night is as noon-day.[2]

The rendezvous was to be in the valley behind Salisbury Crags, which has for a background the north-western shoulder of the hill of Arthur's Seat. On its slopes remain the ruins of what was once a hermitage, dedicated to St Anthony the Eremite.[3] The site was well named, for the chapel lies among pathless cliffs in a deserted area despite being close to a populous city. Beneath the steep slope on which the ruins lie was the place where Nichol Muschat had closed his cruelties towards his wife, by murdering her in circumstances of particular barbarity.

The execration in which this crime was held extended to the place itself. This was marked by a small *cairn*, or heap of stones thrown there in testimony of the ancient British malediction, 'May you have a cairn for your burial place!'

As Jeanie Deans approached this unhallowed spot, she paused and looked to the moon, now rising in the north-west and shedding a more distinct light. She then slowly and fearfully turned her head towards the cairn. Nothing was visible beside the pile of stones, grey in the moonlight. Had her correspondent broken his appointment? Was he just late – or had some turn of fate prevented him from appearing? Were he an unearthly being, as she secretly feared, planning to blast her with the horror of his presence at the rendezvous?

When she was within yards of the heap of stones, a figure rose suddenly up from behind it, asking in a hollow voice, 'Are you the sister?'

'I am sister to Effie Deans!' exclaimed Jeanie. 'Are *you* the cause of my sister's ruin?'

'Curse me for it if you wish.'

'Better to pray God to forgive you.'

'Do as you will. Only swear to follow my directions and save your sister's life.'

'I will do all that is *lawful* to save her!'

'No reservations! Lawful or unlawful, you will swear to act as I counsel, or *else*!'

Jeanie, alarmed at his vehemence, said, 'I will let you ken the morn.'

'Tomorrow! And where will I be tomorrow?' A pistol appeared in his hand. 'Is that all you have to say?'

Jeanie sank to her knees. 'I can promise nothing,' she said.

He cocked the weapon.

'God forgive you!' she cried, hands against her eyes.

'No,' he said, 'I will not add to the deaths of Effie and our child. Take the pistol, shoot me through the head, but follow the *only* course to save her life!'

'Is she innocent or guilty?'

---

[1] From *Christabel* (1797) by Samuel Taylor Coleridge.

[2] Isaiah 58.10. Then shall thy light rise in obscurity, and thy darkness be as the noonday.

[3] St Anthony, regarded as the Father of Monasticism, was born about AD 251 at Fayum, Egypt and spent much of his adult life as a desert *eremite*, or hermit.

'She is guiltless of everything, except trusting me.'

'My sister's child – does it live?'

'No. It was murdered, though not by her!'

'Cannot the guilty be brought to justice?'

'They are now far away. No one can save Effie but *you*!'

'But *how*?'

'Listen to me. I trust you. Your sister is innocent of infanticide.'

'Thank God!'

'The person who assisted at her confinement murdered the child; it was without the mother's knowledge. She is as guiltless as the babe.'

'You said there was a remedy.'

'There is,' answered the stranger, 'and it is in your own hands. Now, you saw your sister before the birth. She *surely* mentioned her pregnancy to you? Her doing so removes the concealment – and the *fact* of concealment is essential to a charge of infanticide. Nothing would be more natural than for Effie to tell you of her pregnancy. *Think*!'

'Woe's me!' said Jeanie, 'for she *never* spoke to me on this. When I spoke to her about her looks, she just cried.'

'You asked her questions? You *must* remember what her answer was; surely an admission that she had been seduced and that she carried the result?'

'But I cannot remember what Effie never told me!'

'Are you so *dull*?' he exclaimed, grasping her arm. 'I tell you you must *remember* that she told you all this, whether she ever said it or no. You must repeat this tale before the Justices and save your sister from the gallows; from being murdered herself!'

'But I shall be perjured! It is the *concealment* for which Effie is blamed; and you would make me lie about it.'

'I see,' he said. 'You would rather let your innocent sister die a condemned murderess, than use your voice to save her.'

'I wad shed my best blood to save her,' said Jeanie, now weeping in agony, 'but I canna change right into wrang, or make true what is false.'

'You foolish, hard-hearted woman. Are you afraid of what they might do to you? The Law would *rejoice* at the release of Effie. They would not suspect your tale. Even if they *did* suspect it, they would forgive you.'

'It is not Man I fear,' said Jeanie, looking upward; 'It is God's name that is called to witness what I say in Court. *He* will know!'

'And he will know the *motive*. He will know that you are not doing this for money or gain, but to save an innocent life.'

'He has given us a Law,' said Jeanie, 'and a lamp for our path. I may not do evil, even if good comes of it. But *you* – you promised her shelter and protection! Why do *you* not bear witness evidence on her behalf. Ye may do it with a clear conscience.'

'A clear conscience, woman?' said he with sudden fierceness, 'I have not known one for many a year. Me, testify? You will not find *me* in the courts of men. Hush! Listen to that...'

A voice was now heard singing. It was one of those wild airs of the old Scots ballads. The sound ceased; then came nearer. The stranger listened attentively, still holding a terrified Jeanie by the arm. The words were now audible:

When the gled's in the blue cloud,
The laverock lies still;
When the hound's in' the green-wood
The hind keeps the hill.

The singer kept a powerful voice at high pitch, so that it could be heard at a considerable distance. As the song ceased, they heard a stifled sound, like of steps of persons approaching. The song came again, but the tune had changed:

O sleep ye sound, Sir James, she said,
When ye suld rise and ride;
There's twenty men, wi' bow and blade,
Are seeking where ye hide.

'I must go,' said the stranger. 'Either return home or remain till they come up. You have nothing to fear. But do *not* tell anyone you saw me. Remember, your sister's fate is in your hands.'

So saying, he turned from her and with a swift and silent step plunged into the darkness on the side remote from the approaching sound. Jeanie remained by the cairn, uncertain whether to fly homeward or await the two or three figures now advancing towards her.

chapter sixteen

GENTLEMAN: *She speaks things in doubt,*
That carry but half sense: her speech is nothing,
Yet the unshaped use of it doth move
The hearers to collection; they aim at it,
And botch the words up to fit their own thoughts.
> *Hamlet,* IV.5

'I could risk a sma' wager,' said the Clerk to the Magistrate, 'that if this rascal Ratcliffe were assured of his neck's safety, he could do more than ten constables to help us out of this scrape of Porteous's. Weel acquent he is wi' a' the smugglers, thieves and *banditti* around Edinburgh. Indeed, he's called the father of criminals of Scotland, going amang them these twenty years as "Daddie Rat".'

'A bonny scoundrel,' said the Magistrate, 'to expect appointment by the City!'

'Your Honour,' said the Procurator Fiscal, whose duties included that of Superintendant of Police, 'Mr Fairscrieve is right. It is just sic as Ratcliffe that my department needs! If he turns his knowledge to the City service, ye'll no find a better man. Ye'll get nae saints to hunt smuggled goods or thieves. Decent sort of men put to this can do nae gude. They dinna like to be out at odd hours and on a dark cauld nights, and far less do they like a clout ower the heid. Jock

Porteous was worth a dozen o' them; for he never had ony fear or conscience about onything your Honours bade him.'

'He was a gude servant o' the town,' said the Bailie, 'though he was an ower free-living man. But if you really think this rascal Ratcliffe could discover these malefactors, I would assure him life and reward. It's an awesome thing, this misfortune for the city, Fairscrieve. It's *very* ill taen by the Regent, Queen Caroline, God bless her! And naebody put into the *Tolbooth* for it, far less hanged!'

'If ye think sae, sir,' said the procurator-fiscal, 'we could easily clap a few blackguards into the prison on suspicion. It will have an active look. I hae plenty on my List that wad be nane the waur of a week or twa inside. If ye thought it no strictly just, ye could be easier on them the neist time. They'll no be lang in gieing ye an opportunity!'

'I doubt that will hardly do in this case, Mr Sharpitlaw,' returned the Town Clerk; 'they'll run their letters[1] and be out again before ye ken where ye are.'

'I will speak to the Lord Provost about this Ratcliffe business,' said the Magistrate. 'Mr Sharpitlaw, you will go with me and receive instruction. Something may also come from this story of Butler's and his unknown gentleman. No man has any business swaggering about the King's Park and calling himself the Devil to the terror of honest folk. I cannot think that Butler himsell headed the mob, but time was when ministers were as forward in a bruilzie[2] as their neighbours.'

'These times are lang past,' said Sharpitlaw, 'If ye get me authority from the Provost, I'll speak wi' this Daddie Rat mysell; for I'm thinking I'll mak mair out o' him than your Honour.'

Sharpitlaw was accordingly empowered to make any arrangement as might seem advantageous to Edinburgh in the present emergency. Accordingly, he went to the jail to see Ratcliffe in private.

Now, the relative positions of a police officer and a professed thief vary according to circumstances. The most obvious analogy of a hawk and its prey is often the least applicable. Sometimes the guardian has the air of a cat watching a mouse; sometimes, more passive still, he uses the rattlesnake's art of fascination, staring at the victim until terror and confusion end resistance.

The interview between Ratcliffe and Sharpitlaw was different from all these. For five minutes they sat silent, on opposite sides of a table, looking fixedly at each other, with a sharp, knowing cast of countenance. They resembled two dogs preparing for a romp, who crouch, watching each other's movements and waiting to see who shall start the game.

'So, Mr Ratcliffe,' said the Officer, conceiving that it suited his position to speak first, 'you're to give up business, I hear?'

'Yes sir, I shall be on that path nae mair; and save your folk some trouble, Mr Sharpitlaw.'

'You know you are under sentence of death.'

'Aye, but so are we a', as the minister said in the Tolbooth Kirk the day Robertson ran off. But naebody kens when it will be executed.'

---

[1] A Scottish form of procedure, answering, in some respects, to the English Habeas Corpus, Scott.
[2] Riot.

'Aye, Robertson.' said Sharpitlaw in a lower, confidential tone. 'd'ye ken where he is?'

'Mr Sharpitlaw, I'll be frank wi' ye. Robertson is rather a cut abune me. A wild Deevil he was and mony a daft prank he played; but except that Collector's job that Wilson led him into, he never did onything near *our* line o' business.'

'That's singular, considering the company he kept.'

'Upon my honour,' said Ratcliffe, gravely, 'He keepit out o' our affairs – and that's mair than Wilson did. Robertson will appear in time; there's nae fear o' that. Naebody lives the life he does but comes out sooner or later.'

'Who or what is he, Ratcliffe?'

'He's far better born than he cares to let on. He's been a soldier, and an officer, and a play-actor and more... He's a Deevil amang the lasses.'

'Like enough,' said Sharpitlaw. 'Ratcliffe, I'll no stand here niffering[1] wi' ye. Ye ken how favour's to be gotten from my Office; ye must be *usefu'*.'

'Certainly, sir, naething for naething. I ken the rules.'

'Right then; the main thing is the Porteous case. Tell me of it.'

'Lord help ye! I was under sentence the haill time. God, I couldna help laughing when I heard Jock begging for mercy in the lads' hands. I thought, tak ye what's comin'; ye'll ken *now* what hanging's about!'

'Come now, Rat,' said the Procurator. 'Ye canna creep awa' through that hole, lad. Speak to the point if you want favours.'

'But how can I speak when ye ken I was under sentence o'death and in the strong room a' the while?'

'We canna turn ye loose again unless ye *earn* it.'

'Well, then... I saw Geordie Robertson among the boys that broke into the jail!'

'That's to the purpose *indeed* – where do we find him?'

'The Deil kens. He'll no likely gang back to ony o' his auld haunts. He'll be out of the country now. He has gude friends despite the life he's led; and he's verra weel educate.'

'You saw him plainly?'

'As plainly as I see you.'

'How was he dressed?'

'I couldna weel see. He had a woman's mutch on his head; but ye never saw sic a ca'-throw.[1] I couldna see a' thing.'

'But did he speak to no one?'

'They were a' gabbling to each other,' said Ratcliffe, unwilling to carry his evidence farther.

'This will no do, Ratcliffe,' said the Procurator; 'you must *speak*!' He tapped the table emphatically.

'It's verra hard, sir,' said the prisoner, 'and but for the under-turnkey's place...'

'Robertson's head will help,' said Sharpitlaw. 'The town maun be shown *good* cause for your freedom.'

---

[1]   Discussing matters; exchanging views.

[2]   Confusion.

'Weel then,' said Ratcliffe; 'it's a queer way of beginning an honest trade… but I heard and saw him speak to the wench Effie Deans, her that's up for child-murder.'

'*Did* ye now, Rat? And the man that spoke to Butler in the Park, and that's to meet wi' Jeanie Deans at Muschat's Cairn. Lay these two together… as sure as I live, Robertson must be the father of the lassie's wean!'

'There hae been waur guesses than that…' observed Ratcliffe, turning the quid of tobacco in his cheek and squirting out the juice. 'I heard something a while syne about him and a bonny lass about the Pleasance. It was a' Wilson could do to stop him marrying her.'

Here a city Officer entered to tell Sharpitlaw that they had in custody the woman he had ordered brought before him.

'It's little matter now, George,' said he, 'the thing is taking another turn. However, bring her in.'

The Officer returned with a tall, strapping wench of between eighteen and twenty. She was remarkably dressed in a blue riding jacket with tarnished lace, her hair clubbed like that of a man and surmounted by a Highland bonnet with a bunch of feathers. A riding-skirt of scarlet camlet, embroidered with tarnished flowers completed the picture. Her features were coarse, yet by dint of her bright black eyes, aquiline nose and a commanding profile, she appeared handsome. She flourished the switch she held in her hand, dropped a curtsey, recovered herself according to Touchstone's directions to Audrey,[1] and opened the conversation without awaiting any question.

'God gie your Honour gude e'en, bonny Mr Sharpitlaw! And gude e'en to ye too, Ratton. Man, they tauld me ye were hanged! Did ye get out o' John Dalgleish's hands like half-hangit Maggie Dickson?'[2]

'Whisht, ye daft jaud,' said Ratcliffe. 'Hearken to what's said to ye.'

'Wi' a' my heart, Ratton. It's great preferment for poor Madge to be brought up the street to speak wi' Provosts, Bailies and Town-clerks and prokitors, at this time o' day – and the haill town looking at me too; this is honour!'

'Ay, Madge,' said Sharpitlaw, 'and ye're dressed up in your braws, I see. These are not your everyday claiths.'

Butler was now brought in.

'A *minister* – in the Tolbooth! Wha will ca' it a graceless place now?'

'Did you ever see this woman before?' said Sharpitlaw to Butler.

'Not to my knowledge, sir.'

'I thought as much,' said the Procurator Fiscal, looking towards Ratcliffe, who answered his glance with a nod of acquiescence.

'But this is Madge Wildfire,' said the Fiscal to Butler.

'Ay, that I am,' said Madge, 'and that I have been ever since I was something better, but I canna mind when that was!' She then chanted:

---

[1] Shakespeare's *As You Like It*, Act v.

[2] Margaret Dickson, hanged in 1724 in Edinburgh for infanticide, revived while being taken to Musselburgh for burial and lived for many years thereafter.

I glance like the Wildfire through country and town;
I'm seen on the causeway, I'm seen on the down;
The lightning that flashes so bright and so free,
Is scarcely so blithe or so bonny as me!

'Haud your *tongue*, ye skirling limmer!' said the Officer, scandalised at her freedom before Sharpitlaw.

'Let her alone, George,' said Sharpitlaw, 'I hae some questions to ask her. But first Mr Butler, take another look of her.'

'Do sae, minister – *do* sae,' cried Madge; 'I am as weel worth looking at as ony. And I can say the single Carritch,[1] and the double Carritch, and Justification, and Effectual Calling.[2] I can say the Assembly of Divines at Westminster, that is, I could say them ance... but, ane forgets.' Madge heaved a sigh.

'Weel, sir,' said Sharpitlaw to Butler, 'what think ye now?'

'As before,' said Butler. 'I never saw this demented creature in my life.'

'Then she is *not* the person whom you said the rioters last night described as Madge Wildfire?'

'Certainly not! They may be near the same height, but I see little other resemblance.'

'Their dress is not alike?' said Sharpitlaw.

'Not in the least.'

'Madge, my bonny woman,' said Sharpitlaw, in a coaxing manner, 'what did ye do wi' your everyday claiths yesterday?'

'I dinna mind.'

'Where were ye yesterday at e'en, Madge?'

'I dinna mind onything about yesterday. Ae day is eneugh for onybody.'

'Madge, wad ye mind something about it, if I was to gie ye this half-crown?' said Sharpitlaw.

'I think,' interjected Ratcliffe, 'I could gar her tell us something.'

'Try her, then,' said Sharpitlaw.

'Madge,' said Ratcliffe, 'hae ye ony friends?'

'Aye! There's Rob the Ranter,' said Madge, with a toss of the head of affronted beauty; '*and* Will Fleming and then there's Geordie Robertson – that's Gentleman Geordie. What think ye o' that?'

Ratcliffe laughed. Winking at the Procurator Fiscal, he went on;

'But, Madge, the lads only like ye when ye wear your braws. They wadna touch you wi' tongs in your auld rags.'

'Liar! Gentle Geordie Robertson put my ilka-day's claise on his ain bonny *self* yestreen. He gaed a' through the town wi' them; and grand he lookit; like ony Queen.'

'I dinna believe a word o't,' said Ratcliffe. 'Thae duds were the colour o' moon-shine in the water, I'm thinking, Madge, the gown wad be sky-blue, or scarlet?'

---

1   *Carritch: The Catechism*, of which there were two: *The Shorter* and *The Larger*. Drawn up in the 1640s, they were a Q&A series describing the Christian faith. Scottish children were 'catechised' endlessly. From Greek: κατηχειν 'to instruct orally'.

2   The Westminster Confession of Faith and the Catechisms.

'It was nae sic thing,' said Madge, letting out, in the eagerness of contradiction, all she would have wished to conceal. 'It was neither scarlet nor sky-blue, but my ain auld brown threshie-coat of a short-gown, and my mother's auld mutch and my red rokelay.[1] He gied me a crown and a kiss for the use o' them, bless his bonny face.'

'And where did he change his clothes again, hinnie?' interrupted Sharpitlaw.

'Ah, ye've spoiled a'thing, Procurator,' snapped Ratcliffe.

And it was so. The question had alerted Madge. 'What was't ye were speiring, sir?'

'I asked you,' said the procurator, 'when and where did Robertson bring back your clothes?'

'What Robertson?'

'The fellow you spoke of. Gentle Geordie you called him.'

'Geordie Gentle?' said Madge, with feigned amazement, 'I dinna ken naebody ca'd Geordie Gentle.'

'Come,' said Sharpitlaw, 'this will not do. You must tell us what you did with these clothes of yours.'

Madge Wildfire made no answer, but regaled the embarrassed investigator with a song:

What did ye wi' the bridal ring—bridal ring—bridal ring?
What did ye wi' your wedding ring, ye little cutty quean, O?
I gied it till a sodger, a sodger, a sodger,
I gied it till a sodger, an auld true love o' mine, O.

The Procurator Fiscal said, 'I'll take some measures with this damned Bess of Bedlam[2] that shall make her find her tongue.'

'Better let her mind settle a little,' said Ratcliffe. 'Ye have already got something.'

'True. A brown short-gown, a mutch and a red rokelay... now, does *that* agree with your Madge Wildfire, Mr Butler?' Butler nodded.

'I am free to say now, sir,' said Ratcliffe, 'since it's come out onyway, that these were what Robertson wore last night in the jail at the head of the riot.'

'That's direct evidence,' said Sharpitlaw. 'If ye stick to that, Ratcliffe, I will report favourably on you to the Provost. Now, I have business for you tonight. I must to home, but I'll be back to you later in the evening. Keep Madge here and try to get her into good tune again.'

So saying, he withdrew.

---

[1]   Head-dress and short cloak.

[2]   The title of an anonymous seventeenth century poem about a madwoman; set to music by Henry Purcell *c.*1682.

chapter seventeen

And some they whistled – and some they sang,
And some did loudly say,
Whenever Lord Barnard's horn it blew,
'Away, Musgrave away!
 Anon, *Little Musgrave and Lady Barnard*

When Sharpitlaw returned to the Heart of Midlothian prison, he resumed his conference with Ratcliffe, of whose assistance he now felt secure.

'You must speak with this wench, Rat – this Effie Deans. Sift her; she will ken Robertson's haunts.'

'I hae spoken to Effie,' said Ratcliffe; 'she's strange to this place and to its ways, Mr Sharpitlaw. She's breaking her heart already about this man. Were she the mean's o' arresting him, it wad break outright. I canna undertake it.'

'Weel, Rat, since ye're that sensitive, I'll speak to the hussy mysell.'

Sharpitlaw entered the dark cell tenanted by Effie Deans. The girl was seated on her little flock-bed in a deep reverie. Some food lay untouched on the table. To Sharpitlaw, her warder said,

'Sometimes she tastes naething from the one end of the day to the t'other, except a drink of water.'

Sharpitlaw took a chair. Ordering the warder to leave, he began in a tone of commiseration.

'How's a' wi' ye, Effie? How d'ye find yoursell, hinny?'

A sigh was the only answer.

'Are the folk civil to ye, Effie? It's my duty to inquire.'

'Very civil, sir.'

'And your victuals,' he continued in the same tone, 'do you get what you like?'

'Very weel, sir, thank ye,' said the prisoner, her tone shorn of the former vivacity of the Lily of St Leonard's.

'He must have been a great villain, Effie, who brought you to this pass,' said Sharpitlaw.

'I blame mysell mair than him. I was bred to ken better; but he, poor fellow...'

'A blackguard a' his life, I dare say,' said Sharpitlaw. 'A stranger in Scotland and a companion of that vagabond. Wilson, Effie?'

'Wad that he had ne'er seen Wilson.'

'Very true. Where was't that Robertson and you were used to meet? Someplace about the Laigh Calton, I'm thinking.'

The dispirited girl had followed Sharpitlaw's observations, artfully adjusted as they were to her own thoughts. Her answers thus became a kind of thinking aloud, a mood into which a prisoner may be led by a skilful inquisitor. But the last observation of the procurator-fiscal was just too direct. It broke the spell.

'What was that I was saying?' said Effie. She started up, shading her dishevelled hair back from a still beautiful face.

'I would help ye if I could,' Sharpitlaw said in a soothing tone, 'and *naething* is sae likely to serve ye, Effie, as finding this rascal Robertson.'

'Dinna misca' him, sir! I hae naething to say against the man – and naething *will* I say.'

'Effie, think what distress he has brought on your family.'

'Heaven help me!' she exclaimed, 'My poor father; Jeanie; that's the hardest to bear! Sir, if you hae ony kindness – for a' the folk here are as hard as stanes – let in my sister Jeanie the next time she comes. When I hear them stop her, it pits me out o' my judgment!'

She looked on him with entreaty.

'You shall see your sister.'

Sharpitlaw rose and left. Rejoining Ratcliffe, he observed:

'You are right, Ratton; there's no making much of that lassie. But ae thing I have cleared; Robertson *is* the father of her bairn. It'll be he that meets Jeanie Deans this night at Muschat's Cairn and there we'll nail him – or my name is not Gideon Sharpitlaw.'

'But in that case, Butler wad hae surely kend the man in King's Park to be the same as headed the mob in Madge Wildfire's claise.'

'Not necessarily. There was the dress, the darkness, the confusion and maybe a touch o' a blackit cork, or a slake o' paint. Ratton, I have seen ye dressed such that your ain master the Devil durstna make oath to ye!'

'True.'

'And besides, the minister *did* say he knew something of the features of the man in the Park, though he couldna mind where or when he'd seen them afore. You and I will go with the party and see him taken.'

'But – surely little use can I be to your honour?'

'Use? You can guide the party; you ken the ground. Besides, I do not intend to lose sight o' *you*, my friend, till I have *him*.'

'Weel, sir, hae it your ain way; but mind he's a desperate man.'

'We shall be armed and we will *settle* him if necessary.'

'But I couldna guide you to Muschat's Cairn at night. I ken the place in daylight, but how to find it by moonshine amang sae mony crags and stanes? They're as alike to each other as the collier to the Deil!'[1]

'Ratcliffe, what's the meaning o' this?' said Sharpitlaw, ominously. 'Have you forgotten your sentence of death?'

'No, sir. If I be necessary, I will gang wi' ye. But there is ane wi' mair skill of the route than me; Madge Wildfire. The daft limmer often sleeps out amang thae hills all night.'

'Weel, Ratcliffe,' replied the Procurator Fiscal, 'if you think she can guide us... but mind, your life depends on your behaviour.'

The rising moon saw the whole party leave the walls of Edinburgh and enter the open ground. Dimly visible were Arthur's Seat, like a couchant lion of immense size, and Salisbury Crags, like a huge girdle of granite. Following the southern side of the Canongate, they reached the Abbey of Holyrood House and from thence into the King's Park. They were at first four in number: an Officer of Justice and Sharpitlaw, well armed with pistols and cutlasses; Ratcliffe, unarmed,

---

[1] ie a working coalminer and the Devil are equally black.

and the female. At the last stile, when they entered the Chase, they were joined by two other Officers. Ratcliffe saw this with concern, having thought it likely that Robertson, a bold and active man, might have escaped from Sharpitlaw and a single Officer without his being involved. But with the present strength, the only mode of saving Robertson, which Ratcliffe was minded to do, was by warning him of their approach. This was why Ratcliffe had suggested Madge; he knew her capacity for noise. Indeed, her clamour already had Sharpitlaw half-determined to send her back with one of the Officers. It also seemed as if the approach to the hills and the moonrise made her even more garrulous. To silence her seemed impossible and threats only made her sulky and intractable.

'Is there none of you,' said Sharpitlaw, impatiently, 'that kens the way to this accursed Nichol Muschat's Cairn, excepting this clavering idiot?'

'Nane o' them kens it except me!' cried Madge. 'I hae sat on the grave frae bat-fleeing time till cock-crow and mony's the fine crack I've had wi' Muschat and Ailie Muschat sleeping below.'

The Officers declared that they had general knowledge of the area, but could not guide the party accurately to it by moonlight.

'What to do, Ratcliffe?' said Sharpitlaw, 'if he sees us before we see him – and that's certain if we go strolling about – we may bid the hunt goodbye.'

'I think we maun try Madge,' said Ratcliffe, 'I'll see if I can keep her in order. Even if he hears her skirling her sangs, he's no to ken there's onybody wi' her.'

'That's true,' said Sharpitlaw. 'Forward!'

Madge, in the lead, stopped short on the top of a little hillock and gazed upward fixedly and silently.

'What the Devil's with her now?' snapped Sharpitlaw to Ratcliffe. 'Get her forward!'

'Patience, sir. She'll no gae faster than she likes herself.'

'Damn her,' said Sharpitlaw. 'I'll see she has time in the Bedlam or the Bridewell – or both!'

Madge, who had looked pensive when she stopped, suddenly burst into a vehement fit of laughter and sang:

> I prithee, dear Moon, now pray show to me
> The form and the features, the speech and degree,
> Of the Man who true lover of mine shall be...

'Are we to stand here all *night*?' said Sharpitlaw. 'Drag her forward!'

'Come Madge, hinny,' said Ratcliffe, 'we'll no be in time unless ye show us the road.'

'That I will, Ratton,' said she, seizing him by the arm, and resuming her route with huge strides. 'And I'll tell ye, blithe will Nichol Muschat be to see ye, for he says there isna sic a villain out o' Hell as ye are.'

She began again:

> When the gled's in the blue cloud,
> The laverock lies still;
> When the hound's in the greenwood,
> The hind keeps the hill.

'Stop that noise, if you have to throttle her!' hissed Sharpitlaw; 'I see somebody yonder. Keep close, boys and creep round the shoulder of the height. George Poinder, stay with Ratcliffe and that yelling bitch. You other two, come with me.'

He crept forward with the stealth of the Indian leading his band to an ambush. Ratcliffe saw them glide off, avoiding the moonlight and keeping in shadow.

'Robertson's done,' said he to himself. 'What needs to be said to Jeanie Deans that he suld risk getting his neck stretched for it? He was once as sharp as MacKeachan's elshin,[1] that ran through sax plies of bendleather and half-an-inch into the King's heel.'

He began to hum a ballad of Wildfire's which bore analogy to Robertson, trusting that it would bring the rest to her mind. Madge no sooner heard this than she sang:

> O sleep ye sound, Sir James, she said,
> When ye suld rise and ride?
> There's twenty men, wi' bow and blade,
> Are seeking where ye hide.

Though Ratcliffe was still some distance from Muschat's Cairn, his cat's eyes picked out Robertson and saw that he had caught the alarm and was off. George Poinder, less keen of sight, was not aware of his flight and nor was Sharpitlaw and his men, whose view was masked by the broken ground behind which they were screening themselves. At length, however, they also perceived that Robertson had fled. They rushed towards the place, Sharpitlaw calling out,

'Chase, lads, *Chase*! Haud the brae – he's on the edge of the hill!' Then to the rear guard he ordered: 'Ratcliffe, detain the Deans woman. George, run and guard the stile at the Duke's Walk. *Ratcliffe*! Come here, but first knock out that mad bitch!'

'*Rin* for it, Madge!' hissed Ratcliffe.

Ratcliffe hastened to the spot where Sharpitlaw waited to deliver Jeanie Deans into to his custody. Madge fled in the opposite direction. Thus the whole party separated in flight or pursuit, excepting Ratcliffe and Jeanie who, held fast by her cloak, remained standing by Muschat's Cairn.

chapter eighteen

ESCALUS: *You have paid the heavens your function,*
and the prisoner the very debt of your calling.
> *Measure for Measure*, III.2

Jeanie Deans had waited in fear and amazement as three or four men advanced rapidly towards her. She was yet more startled to see them suddenly divide and

---

[1] A shoemaker's awl, a long spike. Rob McQuechan, a souter (cobbler), ran his awl into Robert Bruce's heel in a popular tale. According to John Ramsay of Ochtertyre, *Rob McQuechan's Elshin* was the title of the only play planned by Robert Burns.

give chase in different directions to her late companion. Sharpitlaw came straight up to her.

'Your name is Jeanie Deans and you are my prisoner. Which way did he run?'

'I dinna ken, sir.'

'Ye *do* ken. Wha it was ye were speaking wi'?'

'I *dinna* ken, sir.'

'We will try to mend your memory,' said Sharpitlaw. He shouted to Ratcliffe to come and take charge of her while he directed the chase after Robertson. As Ratcliffe approached, Sharpitlaw pushed the young woman towards him and began to scramble up the steep bank with a surprising agility. In a few minutes there was no one within sight and only a distant halloo from one of the pursuers to another. Jeanie was left in the clear moonlight under guard.

When all in the distance was silent, Ratcliffe attempted to put an arm round her shoulder.

'This is a braw night for ye to be on the hill wi' your friend.' Jeanie extricated herself from his grasp and made no reply.

'Lads and lasses,' he continued, 'dinna meet at Muschat's Cairn at midnight to crack nuts!' He again attempted to take hold of her.

'If ye are an officer of justice, sir,' said Jeanie, again eluding his arm, 'ye deserve to have your coat stripped from your back!'

'Very true, hinny,' said he, forcibly getting hold of her, 'but suppose I should strip *your* cloak off first?'

It was fortunate that Jeanie possessed both presence of mind and courage. She saw clearly the danger she was in.

'Dinna speak sae loud,' said she in a low voice; 'he's up yonder.'

'Who? Robertson?' said Ratcliffe.

'Aye. Up yonder;' and she pointed to the ruins of the hermitage and chapel.

'Wait for me here!'

But no sooner had he set off towards the chapel than Jeanie raced off in the opposite direction on the nearest path to St Leonards. At the house, it was the work of a moment to double-bolt the door and to pull a heavy article of furniture against it. Her next anxiety was her father. She went silently to the door of his apartment to see whether he had been disturbed. He was awake, but engaged in his devotions.

It was then that a vague idea first darted across her mind, that something might yet be achieved for her sister's safety, convinced as she now was of Effie's innocence. It came to her mind, as she later described it, like a sun-blink on a stormy sea; and she felt a composure not experienced for many days. She went to bed knowing that, by some means or other, she would be called upon to work out her sister's deliverance.

Ratcliffe, meanwhile, had started like a greyhound from the slips when Jeanie had pointed to the ruins. Whether he meant to aid Robertson's escape or assist his pursuers remains doubtful, but he had no opportunity of doing either. He had no sooner mounted the steep ascent and passed under the broken arches of the ruins, than a pistol was presented at his head, and a harsh voice commanded him, in the King's name, to surrender himself.

'Mr Sharpitlaw!' cried Ratcliffe. 'Is this you?'

'Is it only *you*?' answered the Fiscal, 'what made you leave the woman?'

'She told me she saw Robertson go into these ruins!'

'It's all over now,' said Sharpitlaw; 'we'll see no more of him this night. Call back the people, Ratcliffe.'

Ratcliffe holloed to the now dispersed Officers, who willingly obeyed the signal. There was none among them desirous of a hand to hand *rencontre*, with Robertson.

'Where are the two women?' said Sharpitlaw.

'Both took to their heels, but we know how to find both.'

Like a defeated general, a sulky Sharpitlaw led his discomfited forces to the metropolis and dismissed them for the night.

The next morning early, he was under the necessity of making his report to Bailie Middleburgh, the Magistrate of the day. This gentleman chanced to be the same by whom Butler had been committed and was generally respected by his fellow citizens. He was something of a humorist, while a fortune acquired by honest industry made him fully independent. He was, in short, an acute, patient and upright man.

Mr Middleburgh had just taken his seat, and was animatedly discussing a game at golf played the day before with one of his colleagues, when a letter was delivered to him, addressed 'For Bailie Middleburgh:

> *Sir,*
>
> *I know you to be a considerate Magistrate. I therefore trust that you will not reject what I now place before you, despite my share in the Porteous affair, an action which I will justify at the proper time and place.*
>
> *The clergyman, Butler, is innocent. He had only an involuntary presence in the affair, from which he endeavoured to dissuade us. But it was not for him that I speak.*
>
> *There is an innocent woman, Effie Deans, in your jail. Her sister, one Jeanie Deans, knows that she was seduced by a villain and thus knows of her innocence. The sister, however, is a Puritan and superstitious after the manner of her sect. I pray your Honour to impress upon her, that her sister's very life depends upon her testimony. However, should she remain silent, do not think that the young woman is guilty; and far less think to permit her execution. Remember the death of Wilson was fearfully avenged and there are those yet alive who can compel you to drink the dregs of your poisoned chalice.*
>
> *I say, remember Porteous, and say that you had good counsel*
>
> *from,*
>
> *One of his Slayers*

The Magistrate read over this extraordinary letter again. At first he was tempted to dismiss it as the work of a madman, but on a re-perusal he thought that, amid its incoherence, he could hear a tone of awakened passion, though expressed in a manner quaint and unusual.

'It *is* a severe Statute,' said the Magistrate to his assistant, 'and I wish the girl could escape the letter of it. A child may have been born; but it may have been abducted while the mother was unconscious, or it may have perished for lack of care that the creature herself was unable to give it. And yet if the woman is found guilty under the Statute, she faces execution. The crime has been too common and examples are necessary.'

'But,' said the City Clerk, 'if she told her sister of the pregnancy, it will evade the Statute.'

'Very true,' replied the Bailie; 'I will walk out to St Leonard's one of these days and examine the girl myself. I also know something of the father; Deans, an old true-blue Cameronian. I will speak with father and daughter myself when this Porteous business is over.'

'Butler is to remain incarcerated?' said the City Clerk.

'For the present, yes. But I hope to bail him soon.'

'Do you believe the testimony in that letter?' asked the Clerk.

'Not much. But there is something striking about it too; it is the letter of a man in great agitation, or with some sense of guilt... But now to the point. Butler's private character is excellent. From some inquiries this morning, I understand that he arrived in Town only the day before yesterday. It is thus impossible for him to be in the rioters' conspiracy.'

'But religious zeal catches fire at a slight spark and as fast as a brimstone match,' observed the secretary. 'I hae kend a minister wad just as quiet as a rocket on a stick, till ye mentioned the word 'Patronage,' or siclike, and then *whiz*! he was off and up in the air beyond manners, sense or comprehension.'

'I do not believe,' said Middleburgh, 'that Butler's zeal is so inflammable. But I will make farther investigations. Now, what other business is there before us?'

In the course of their business they were interrupted by an old woman, haggard in look and wretched in appearance, who thrust herself into the Council chamber.

'What do you want, gudewife? And who are you?' asked Bailie Middleburgh.

'Whit do I want!' replied she in a sulky tone. 'I want my bairn! Will your honour gie me back my puir crazy bairn? *His honour* indeed and him the son of a Campvere skipper!'[1]

'Tell us what it is you *want*, woman!' said the Magistrate, 'and do not interrupt the Court.'

'I tell ye,' came the termagant's voice, 'I want my *bairn*! Is na that braid Scots?'

'But who *are* you – and who is your bairn?'

'Wha am I? Wha suld I be but Meg Murdockson and wha suld my bairn be, but Magdalen Murdockson? Your constables and your officers ken us weel enough when they tear the claithes aff our backs, take what siller we hae and haul us to the Correction House in Leith Wynd on bread and water!'

'But what do you *want* here?' snapped the impatient Magistrate. 'Tell your business or go away!'

---

[1] Camp Vere, now Veere, is a seaport on the island of Walcheren in the Dutch province of Zealand. From 1444 to 1799, it was Scotland's 'staple port', ie all exports to the Netherlands were landed at Camp Vere, where the Scottish mercantile community enjoyed the right to be governed by Scots law.

'It's my *bairn*! It's Magdalen Murdockson I'm wantin',' screamed the beldam in her cracked voice. 'Havena I been *telling* ye this – are ye *deaf*?'

'She wants her daughter, sir,' said an Officer. 'Her daughter arrested last night; Madge Wildfire.'

'Madge Hellfire, as *they* ca' her!' echoed the beldam. 'And what business has a blackguard like you to ca' an honest woman's bairn names?'

'An *honest* woman's bairn, Maggie?' answered the Officer, smiling and shaking his head with a calmness certain to provoke the furious old shrew.

'I was honest *ance*,' she retorted, 'and that's mair than *ye* can say, ye born and bred *thief*! Ye could never tell ither folks' gear frae your ain since the day ye was cleekit.[1] When ye were five year auld, ye pykit your mother's purse o' twalpennies, just as she was takin' leave o' your faither at the fit o' the *gallows*!'

'She has you there, George,' said the assistant, and there was a general merriment. Appeased by the success of her sally, she turned to the Magistrate saying that if Madge was not so smart as ither folk, few had suffered as she had done. Meg could prove by fifty witnesses that her daughter had never seen Jock Porteous alive or dead since he had given her a thrashing with his cane for hurling a dead cat at the Provost on the King's birthday.

Despite the appearance and violent demeanour of this woman, the Magistrate felt the justice of her argument. He investigated the circumstances which had led to the arrest of Madge Murdockson or Wildfire. Finding that she clearly had not been engaged in the riot, he directed that the police watch her and allowed her to return home with her mother.

While Madge was being fetched from the Tolbooth, the Magistrate enquired if her mother was privy to the exchange of dress betwixt her and Robertson. But on this point he could obtain no light. She persisted that she had never seen Robertson since his escape from St Giles. If her daughter had changed clothes with him, it must have been at Duddingston, a hamlet two miles out of Town where she could prove that Madge passed that eventful night. One of the town-officers, searching for stolen linen in that village, volunteereed that he had seen Madge Murdockson there.

'I *tauld* ye sae,' said the hag; 'see *now* what it is to hae a character, gude or bad! Now, maybe, I could tell ye something about Porteous that you council chamber bodies *never* could find out.' All turned towards her.

'Speak!' said the Magistrate.

She remained silent, seeming to enjoy the anxious suspense. And then she broke forth.

'A' that I ken about him is that he was no soldier, nor a gentleman, but just a thief and a blackguard, like yoursels, dears. Now, what will ye gie me for that news?'

Madge Wildfire was now brought in.

'Ah! See if it isna our auld Deevil's-buckie o' a mither. Oh Sirs, twa o' us in the Guard at ance!'

Old Maggie's eyes had glistened with pleasure when she saw her daughter set at liberty. But Madge's remark had awakened her savage temper.

'What d'ye mean by that, ye street-raking limmer!' she exclaimed, pushing her

---

[1] Born.

daughter ungently to the door. 'I'se tell thee what ye are, ye crazed Hellcat. Ye'll taste naething but bread and water for a fortnight, and serve ye right for the plague ye hae gien me, ye idle *tawpie*!'

Madge, however, escaped from her mother at the door, ran back to the foot of the table, dropped a very low courtesy to the Judge and said, with a giggle,

'My minnie's sair upset, sir, She'll hae had some quarrel wi' her auld husband – that's Satan, ye ken.'

This explanatory note came in a low confidential tone. Her hearers gave an involuntary shudder.

'*Madge*, ye limmer! If I come to fetch ye!'

'Listen to her,' said Madge. 'But I'll dance in the moonlight, when her and Satan are whirring through the air on a broom-shank. Aye, they'll hae a merry sail ower Inchkeith, and ower the bonny waves poppling against the rocks in the gowden glimmer o' the moon! I'm coming, mother; I'm *coming*,' she ended, hearing a scuffle at the door betwixt the beldam and Officers trying to prevent her re-entrance. Madge waved her hand wildly towards the ceiling and sung, at the highest pitch:

> *Up in the air,*
> *On my bonny grey Mare,*
> *And I see, and I see, and I see her yet!*

And, just as the witches in *Macbeth* seemed to fly up from the stage, with a hop, skip and jump she sprang out of the room.

Efforts to discover the murderers of Porteous now occupied all concerned in the administration of justice. It was thus some weeks before Mr Middleburgh found an opportunity of walking to St Leonard's to see if it were possible to obtain the evidence hinted at in the anonymous letter from the 'slayer' respecting Effie Deans.

In the course of the Porteous inquiries, two circumstances of interest arose. Butler, after investigation, was declared innocent of being an accessory to the death of Porteous. However, since he had been present throughout the affair, he was bailed under the obligation not to quit his residence at Liberton so that he could appear as a witness. The other incident was the disappearance of Madge Wildfire and her mother from Edinburgh. When sought for further interrogation, it was discovered that they had eluded the police and left the city as soon as dismissed from the Council Chamber. There was no trace of them.

Meanwhile in London, Queen Caroline's Council of Regency felt their authority seriously slighted by the murder of Porteous. They brought the Edinburgh Magistrates to be interrogated before the House of Lords on the particulars of the Porteous Mob. The Scots *patois*, in which these functionaries made response, was strange to the ears of the English nobles. The Duke of Newcastle, having asked the Provost for the type of shot with which Porteous's men had loaded their muskets, received the response,

'Oh, just sic as we shoot dukes and ither fools with.' This reply was reckoned a serious contempt of the House of Lords and the Provost might have suffered, had not the Duke of Argyle been present. He rose to explain that 'jouks and foules' did not mean Dukes and other mental defectives. Translated into English, the Provost's phrase actually meant 'ducks and other waterfowl'.

However, Parliament went on to dictate measures without regard either to the temper of the Scots people or to the character of their Kirk ministers. An Act was hastily passed. Two hundred pounds was offered for information on any person concerned in the lynching, with the death penalty stipulated for any person harbouring the guilty. But what was most obnoxious in Scotland from *The Lords Temporal & Spiritual*[1] was a clause requiring the Act to be read out by ministers immediately before the Sermon on the first Sabbath of every month. Ministers repeatedly refusing to comply would be barred from any ecclesiastical position in Scotland. This succeeded in uniting, in common cause, the sterner Presbyterians with those who might privately applaud Porteous's death, though disapproving the manner of it. The very pronouncement of the words 'Lords Spiritual' in a Scottish pulpit was, *quodam modo*,[2] an acknowledgment of Episcopalianism, or Prelacy, anathema to such as David Deans. Moreover, Parliament was infringing the *jus divinum*[3] of Presbyterianism, since only the annual General Assembly, representing Christ as Head of the Kirk, could regulate public worship. Many others saw the Act as an attempt to trample on the rights and independence of Scotland.

Also bitterly resented were the steps taken to punish the city of Edinburgh by taking away her Charter and Liberties. A pretext, taken far too hastily, was being used to degrade the ancient Capital of Scotland. In summary, these ill-considered measures occasioned great discontent and disaffection.

Amidst all these dissensions, the trial of Effie Deans, now imprisoned for many weeks, was about to begin. Mr Middleburgh now found time to inquire into the evidence concerning her and chose a fine day for his magisterial walk to her father's house at the Crags of St Leonard's.

The old man was seated on the turf-seat, at the gable end of his cottage, busy mending his cart-harness. He persevered in his task, just raising his head to note the approach of a stranger. Middleburgh waited, expecting Deans to acknowledge his presence but, as he seemed determined to remain silent, he spoke first.

'My name is Middleburgh; James Middleburgh, one of the present Magistrates of the city of Edinburgh.'

'It may be sae.' answered Deans without interrupting his labour.

'You must understand,' the Magistrate continued, 'that my duty is sometimes an unpleasant one.'

'It may be sae.'

'You must be aware that persons in my position are often obliged to make painful inquiries.'

'It may be sae,' again replied Deans, 'But I do ken there was ance a just and God-fearing Magistracy in Edinburgh, that were a terror to evil-doers, and a joy to such as kept the true Path. In the day of Provost Sir William Dick of Braid, there was a faithfu' General Assembly of the Kirk, walking hand in hand with real Scots Barons and the Magistrates; gentlemen, burgesses and commoners of all ranks, seeing with one eye, hearing with one ear, and all upholding the Ark of

---

[1]   Members of the House of Lords. The term is still in use today.

[2]   Latin: Ablative case of *quidam modus*; 'to a certain degree'.

[3]   Divine authority.

the Covenant. Men delivered up their silver to the State's use, as if it had been sclate stanes. My ain father saw sacks of dollars emptied out o' Provost Dick's window into the carts that carried them to the army at Dunse Law.[1] The window itsell still stands in the Luckenbooths; I think it's a claith-merchant's booth the day, five doors abune Gossford's Close.

But now! Now we think mair about the warst wallydraigle[2] in our ain byre, than about the blessing which the Angel of the Covenant gave to the patriarch Jacob at Mahanaim and Peniel.[3] We wad rather gie a pund Scots to buy an unguent to clear our beds o' the English bugs, than gie a penny to rid the land of the swarm of Arminian caterpillars, Socinian pismires[4] and Deistical Miss Katies[5] that have ascended out of the bottomless pit to plague this perverse generation!'

Once embarked on his favourite subject, the stream of Davie Deans' enthusiasm carried him forward despite his mental distress, his well-stocked memory supplying him with all the tropes of rhetoric peculiar to his sect and holy Cause.

Middleburgh contented himself with saying, 'All this may be very true, my friend. Now, you have two daughters I think, Mr Deans?'

The old man winced, but instantly composed himself and resumed the work laid down in his declamation heat. He answered with sullen resolution,

'Ae daughter, sir. Only *ane*.'

'I understand you have only one daughter here at home with you. But the unfortunate girl who is a prisoner is, I think, your younger daughter?'

The Presbyterian sternly raised his eyes. 'In the world and according to the flesh, she is my daughter. But when she became a child of Belial and a company keeper and a trader in iniquity, she ceased to be a bairn of mine.'

'Alas, Mr Deans we are ourselves all sinners. The errors of our offspring ought not to surprise us, being their part of a common corruption inherited through us. We are not entitled to cast them off because they have lost themselves.'

'Sir,' said Deans, irritated at being schooled. 'I ken a' that, but I dinna enter into my private affairs wi' strangers. And now, here's this Porteous' Act that has come up frae London. That is a deeper blow to this poor sinfu' kingdom and suffering Kirk than ony that has been heard of since the foul and fatal Test...'[6]

---

1   In 1638, General Alexander Leslie commanded the Scottish Covenanting Army on Duns Law (hill) to the north of the Berwickshire town. It faced an English army sent by King Charles I to impose Episcopacy on Prebyterian Scotland. No battle ensued, but the events led directly to the 'English' – actually British – Civil War of 1641–1705.

2   A slovenly animal, or person.

3   Jacob had an interesting life. He had a vision of angels at Mahanaim (Genesis 32.2.), while at Peniel on the Jordan (Genesis 32.24) ' there wrestled a Man with him until the breaking of the day...', an encounter which has occasioned much irreverent mirth among the ungodly.

4   Socinians, followers of the Italian theologian Faustus Socinus (1539-1604) rejected the divinity of Christ. They were clearly numerous and well organised since Davie here calls them 'ants'. The term pismire derives from the quasi-urinary odour of formic acid which perfumes an anthuill. Robert Burns was a socinian.

5   Deists believe that God exists but is not 'immanent' ie takes no immediate interest in human affairs. A 'Miss Katie' was eighteenth century rhyming slang for a mosquito.

6   The Test Act, 1681. It required repudiation of the Covenants and acceptance of King Charles II as head of the Church. This was totally unacceptable to Presbyterians for whom Jesus Christ was, and is, Head of the Scottish Kirk.

'But you must surely think of your own household first, or else you are even worse than Infidels.'

'I tell ye, Bailie Middleburgh, I heard the gracious Saunders Peden[1] in the Killing Time, telling his hearers – and gude Christians they were too – that some o' them wad greet mair for a drowned calf than for a' the oppressions of the day. And what wad Peden hae said of me if I had ceased to think of the Gude Cause for Effie; a castaway and a... It kills me to *think* of what she is!'

'But the *life* of your child, Deans. Think of that. If her life could be saved...'.

'Her life! I wadna gie ane o' my grey hairs for her *life*, if her gude *name* be lost. And yet...' said he, 'I wad gie my auld head they grow on for her life and that she might hae time to amend. But I'll never see her mair. Of *that* I am determined!'

His lips continued to move after his voice ceased, as if repeating the same vow internally.

'Sir,' said Mr Middleburgh, 'I speak to you as a man of sense. If you would save your daughter's life, you must use human means.'

'I understand ye. Mr Novit, the lawyer of the Laird of Dumbiedikes, is to do what can be done for her in the circumstances. Mysell, I will not traffic wi' Courts o' Justice as now constituted. I hae a scruple in my mind anent them.'

'Is that to say,' said Middleburgh, 'that you are a Cameronian, and as such do not acknowledge the authority of our Law Courts or present Government?'

'Sir, under your favour,' replied David, too proud of his polemical knowledge to call himself the follower of anyone, 'I canna see why I suld be termed a Cameronian, especially now that Richard Cameron's famous name has been given to a Regiment of soldiers,[2] whereof many now use profane language as fast as Richard could preach! Furthermore, the martyr's name is rendered vain and contemptible by pipes, drums *and* fifes, playing that vain, carnal tune *Cameronian Rant*, which many dance to; a practice unbecoming and promiscuous with the female sex. A brutish fashion it is.'

'Mr Deans,' said Middleburgh, 'I only meant to say that you as a Cameronian, or a MacMillanite, are one of those who think it inconsistent to take oaths under a Government where the Covenant is not ratified.'

'Sir,' replied the controversialist, forgetting his present distress in the discussion, 'I am not a MacMillanite, *or* a Russelite, or a Hamiltonian, or a Harleyite, *or* a Howdenite![3] I will be led by the nose by nane. I take my name as a Christian from no human vessel of clay. I have my own principles and practice, an humble pleader for the Gude Cause.'

'That is to say then, Mr Deans,' said Middleburgh, 'that you are a *Deanite*, with opinions peculiar to yourself.'

'It may please you to say it,' said David Deans; 'but I have maintained my testimony before as great folk as you – *and* in sharper times. I wish every man and woman in this land had kept the true testimony as weel as Johnny Dodds of Farthing's Acre – and ae man mair that shall be... nameless.'

---

[1] Alexander Peden (1626–1686) covenanting minister.

[2] The Cameronian Regiment, 26th of Foot, raised in 1689 to protect the Glorious Revolution of 1688 and 'The Work of Reformation.'

[3] All various species of the great genus *Cameronian*.

'I suppose,' replied the Magistrate, 'that means that Johnny Dodds of Farthing's Acre and David Deans of St Leonard's constitute the only members of the true Kirk of Scotland?'

'God forbid that I suld make sic a vainglorious claim.'

'This is all very fine, but I have no time to spend debating it. The matter in hand is this. I have directed a Citation to be lodged in your daughter Jeanie's hands. If she appears on the day of trial and gives evidence, she may save her sister's life. If, however, from any scruples of *yours* about the legality of the Court, you deter her from this duty, then you, who *gave* life to the girl, will become the means of her losing it.' Middleburgh turned to leave him.

'Bide awee; *bide* awee, Mr Middleburgh,' said Deans, in great perplexity. But the Bailie, sensible that further discussion could only diminish his last and most forcible argument, declined farther controversy and departed.

Deans sunk down upon his seat, stunned with conflicting emotions. A source of great controversy among those sharing his opinions in religious matters was this. How far could the post-Revolution Government of 1688 be recognised by true Presbyterians, since it did not recognise the national testimony of the Solemn League and Covenant? Latterly, those agreeing in this general doctrine assumed the impressive title of *The anti-Popish, anti-Prelatic, anti-Erastian, anti-Sectarian, true Presbyterian Remnant*. They were further divided into many petty sects, several holding it to be a sin to acknowledge existing Laws, Courts and Governments.

These important and delicate points had been the subject of a stormy meeting in the wild, sequestered valley of the Talla Water[1] in Tweeddale, surrounded by high hills and remote from human habitation. The judgment of most at the meeting was that all payment of tribute to the Government was utterly unlawful and a sacrifice to idols. There was, however, fierce controversy on the lawfulness of paying the duties levied at ports and bridges, for maintaining roads and other necessary purposes. Some, to whom imposts on turnpikes and bridges were repugnant, nevertheless felt free in conscience to pay the usual fare at public ferries. This was despite James Russel, one of the slayers of the Archbishop of St Andrews[2] having spoken against this last shade of subjection to constituted authority. This ardent and enlightened person also expressed great doubts over the naming of the days of the week *and* the months of the year, all of which savoured strongly in his nostrils of Paganism. At length they arrived at the conclusion that those who used such names as Monday, Tuesday and January, February and so forth, were indeed the heirs of the idolaters of old.

David Deans had been present on this memorable occasion, although too young to be a speaker among such polemical combatants. His mind, however, had been heated by the clamour and metaphysical ingenuity of the discussion, and it was a controversy to which he often returned. Though he carefully disguised his vacillation from others – and perhaps from himself – he had never arrived at a precise decision on the subject. He was by no means pleased with the quiet manner in

---

[1]   The meeting was at the Linns, ie waterfalls, of the Talla Water, near Tweedsmuir.

[2]   James Sharpe (1613–1679), Primate of Scotland, was ambushed in his coach on Magus Muir near St Andrews and murdered in front of his daughter.

which King William's government glossed over the errors of the times, when, far from restoring the Presbyterian Kirk to its former supremacy, they passed an Act of Oblivion covering even those who had been its persecutors, bestowing titles and employment on many of them.

At the first General Assembly of the Kirk after the 1688 Revolution, an overture was made for the revival of the League and Covenant. With horror, Douce David heard the proposal rejected as inapplicable to modern times. The reign of Queen Anne had increased his conviction that the post-Revolution government was not truly Presbyterian. However, more sensible than the bigots in his sect, he did not confuse the moderation and tolerance of William and Mary and of Anne, with the oppression of Charles II and James II. The Presbyterian religion, though compelled to tolerate the coexistence of Episcopacy and other sects, was still the National Church. Though the glory of the Second Temple was far inferior to that which had flourished from 1639 till the battle of Dunbar in 1650, still it was a structure that retained at least the form and symmetry of the original model.

Then came the Jacobite insurrection of 1715 and David Deans's horror of a potential revival of prelatical Roman Catholicism. This reconciled him to the government of King George, despite his grief that the Monarch might be leaning unto Erastianism. In short, moved by so many different considerations and despite the present Government being still Uncovenanted, he now felt powerfully motivated to authorise Jeanie's giving testimony in a Court of Justice which he knew all true Cameronians would reckon a step of lamentable defection. The voice of nature, however, now exclaimed in his bosom against the dictates of fanaticism.

'I have been constant and unchanging in my beliefs,' said David Deans to himself. 'But my daughter Jeanie may have a light that is hid frae my auld een. If sae, it is on her conscience and not on mine. If she goes before this Court and holds up her hand for poor castaway Effie, surely I will not say she steppeth over her bounds. If not...' He paused in his argument in a pang of mental anguish. Shaking it off, he resumed,

'And if not, God forbid she should go into defection at a bidding of mine! I willna fret the conscience of one bairn – not even to save the life of the other.'

An ancient Roman might have consigned his daughter to death from different motives, but not upon a more heroic principle of duty.

chapter nineteen

To man, in this his trial state,
The privilege is given,
When tost by tides of human fate,
To anchor fast on heaven.

     Dr Isaac Watts (Attrib.)

With a firm step, Deans sought his daughter's room. It had been the bedroom of both sisters. Deans's eyes rested upon Effie's couch with its dark-green coarse curtains. He found Jeanie gazing at a paper containing a citation to appear as a witness for the defence at her sister's trial. Sharpitlaw, determined to do Effie justice and to give her sister no excuse for not giving evidence, had had his Officer serve a *subpoena* of the Scottish Criminal Court during his conference with David.

This precaution saved Deans from the pain of entering upon a formal explanation of the matter with his daughter; he only said, 'I see ye are aware of the matter.'

'Oh father, we are cruelly stood between God's laws and Man's. What shall we do? What *can* we do?'

Jeanie, it must be observed, had no hesitation about appearing in court. She never doubted but she would be placed in the position of either sacrificing her sister by telling the truth, or committing perjury to save her life. So strongly did her thoughts run in this channel that she linked her father's words, 'Ye are aware of the matter,' to this dilemma. She looked up with surprise, whereupon his next words, as she interpreted them, simply horrified her.

'Daughter,' said David, 'it has ever been my view that in things of controversial nature, each Christian's conscience suld be the guide. Therefore examine your ain mind as to what to do in this matter.' Thinking, wrongly, that he was referring to her testimony in Court and not to her attendance at it, she said,

'But, father, how can this be a *controversial* matter? Mind the Ninth Commandment; "Thou shalt not bear false witness against thy neighbour".'

Deans paused. Applying to her words his own preconceived difficulties – whether or not actually to *go* to court – it seemed to him that a woman was scarce entitled to be scrupulous upon this matter where he had told her follow the natural dictates of her conscience.

'Daughter,' he said, 'I did not say that your path was free from stumbling. He who beareth witness unlawfully and against his *conscience* bears also false witness against his neighbour.'

When David had proceeded thus far, his conscience reproved him for perhaps indirectly undermining his daughter's faith. He therefore stopped, and changed his tone.

'Jeanie, my affections cling too heavily in this hour of sorrow to permit me to keep sight of my ain duty, or to direct you to yours. I will speak nae mair anent this matter. Jeanie, if wi' God and gude conscience ye can go to court, speak in favour of your sister. Worthless and castaway as Effie is, she is the daughter of a saint in heaven that was a mother to you in place of your ain. But if ye arena free in conscience to speak for her in the court, let God's will be done.'

At this, he left the room, leaving his daughter in a state of equal distress and perplexity.

It would have been no small addition to the sorrows of David Deans, had he known that his daughter was applying his arguments not as permission to follow her own opinion on the legality of the court itself, but as an encouragement to transgress a divine Commandment.

'Can this *be*?' said Jeanie, as the door closed on her father. 'Can these be *his* words, or has the Devil taken on his voice and features? O God, deliver me!'

She imagined that her father took the ninth Commandment literally, prohibiting false witness *against* our neighbour, but not a falsehood uttered in *favour* of an accused. But her clear discrimination of good and evil rejected such an interpretation.

She remained in a state of uncertainty, afraid to share her thoughts with her father and wrung with distress on her sister's account. The latter was the more acute since the means of saving her were now in her power, yet prohibited by her conscience. Like a vessel in an open roadstead during a storm, she rested on a cable and an anchor; her faith in Providence and a resolution to discharge her duty.

Reuben Butler's affection and strong sense of religion would normally have been her support in these circumstances, but he was still in custody and unable to visit St Leonard's Crags. With her limited scholarship, she found it impossible to express her dilemma in writing and was thus compelled to trust to her sense of right or wrong. It was not the least of Jeanie's distresses that although she believed in her sister's innocence, Effie could not receive that assurance from her own mouth.

* * *

The double-dealing of Ratcliffe in the matter of Robertson had not prevented his being rewarded. Sharpitlaw interceded for him with the Magistrates, citing his remaining in the prison when the doors had been forced open by the mob. He received a full pardon. Soon afterwards, James Ratcliffe, former thief and house-breaker, was appointed turnkey at the Tolbooth and hence responsible for the custody of other delinquents.

Saddletree and others who took interest in the Deans family tried repeatedly and unsuccessfully to arrange an interview between the sisters. The Magistrates however, anxious for the arrest of Robertson, had given strict orders to the contrary, hoping that by keeping them separate they might extract from one or the other information on that fugitive. On this subject Jeanie had nothing to tell them. She informed Mr Middleburgh that she knew nothing whatever of Robertson, except having met him that night to receive advice respecting her sister. This advice, she said, was betwixt God and her conscience. Of his movements or plans past, present, or future, she knew nothing.

Effie was equally silent, though from a different cause. It was in vain that she was offered a commutation of her sentence and even a full Pardon if she would confess what she knew of her lover. She answered only with silent tears. At length, after a delay of many weeks, in hopes she might be induced to speak, the patience of the Magistrates was exhausted and a day was fixed for the trial.

It was now, and no sooner, that Sharpitlaw kept his promise to Effie Deans. He had been dinned into compliance with it by his next-door neighbour Mrs Saddletree, who declared it a heathen cruelty to keep the twa broken-hearted creatures separate. He issued a Mandate, permitting them to see each other at noon on the day preceding the trial.

chapter twenty

CLAUDIO: *Sweet sister, let me live!*
What sin you do to save a brother's life,
Nature dispenses with the deed so far,
That it becomes a virtue.

Measure for Measure, III.1

Jeanie Deans was admitted into the jail by Ratcliffe. As devoid of shame as of honesty, he opened the now trebly secured door and asked her with a leer whether she remembered him? She shuddered.

'No.'

'What! Not remember moonlight and Muschat's Cairn and Robertson and Rat? Your memory needs redding up.'

Jeanie's distress only increased to find her sister under the charge of such a man. In his new occupation he had shown touches of humanity, but this was unknown to Jeanie, now remembering the scene at the Cairn. He told him of her permission from Bailie Middleburgh to see her sister.

'I ken that weel, my bonny dove. And I am specially charged to stay with you, a' the time ye're thegither.'

'Must ye?'

'Aye, hinny. And what the waur will ye and she be of Jim Ratcliffe's hearing what ye say. If ye dinna speak o' escaping the Tolbooth, no word will I tell.'

Ratcliffe now marshalled her the way to the apartment where Effie was confined.

Shame and fear had contended for mastery in Effie that morning while she looked forward to this meeting. But when the door opened she threw herself on her sister's neck, crying, 'Jeanie, dear Jeanie! It's sae lang since I saw ye.'

Jeanie returned the embrace with earnestness. The sisters walked to the side of the pallet bed, sat down side by side holding hands and silently looked each other in the face. Thus they remained for a minute, while the gleam of joy gradually faded, giving way to an intense expression first of melancholy and then of agony. They wept bitterly.

Ratcliffe, his life spent free of conscience and feeling, witnessed this scene with sympathy. The unglazed window of the miserable cell was open and sunbeams fell upon the sisters. Ratcliffe partly closed the shutter, thus throwing a veil over the sorrowful scene.

'Ye are ill, Effie.'

'What wad I no gie to be ten times *waur*, Jeanie!' was the reply. 'What wad I no gie to be *awa*. And our father; but I am his bairn nae langer. Oh that I were wi' my mother in Newbattle kirkyard!'

'Lassie,' came the voice of Ratcliffe, 'dinna be sae doon-hearted; there's mony a tod[1] hunted that's no killed. Advocate Langdale has brought folk safe through

---

[1] Fox.

waur than a' this, and there's no a cleverer lawyer than Nichil Novit. Sic a lawyer and counsel will see fair play. Ye are a bonny lass, too. Busk up. A bonny lass will find favour wi' judge and jury.'

So lost were the sisters in their sorrow that they had become unaware of Ratcliffe's presence.

'Effie,' said Jeanie, 'how *could* you conceal it from me? Did I deserve this? Had ye spoke but ae *word*, we might hae been sorry and shamed, but this awfu' business had never come.'

'And what gude wad that hae dune? Na, na, Jeanie, a' was ower when ance I forgot my promise when I faulded down the leaf of my Bible. See,' she said, producing it. Jeanie took it and found the mark in the book of Job:

He hath stripped me of my glory, and taken the crown from my head. He hath destroyed me on every side, and I am gone.[1]

'Isna that true?' said Effie.

'Oh, if ye had spoken ae *word*,' again sobbed Jeanie, 'if I were free to swear that ye had said but *ae* word of the babe they couldna touch your life.'

'Could they no? Wha tauld ye *that*, Jeanie?'

'One that kend what he was saying,' replied Jeanie, reluctant to mention Robertson.

'Wha was it? *Tell* me!' said Effie, sitting upright. 'Wha would tak interest in me now? Was it – *him*?'

'Why keep the poor lassie in a swither?' said Ratcliffe, 'Robertson told ye that at Muschat's Cairn.'

'*Was* it him?' said Effie eagerly. 'Oh I see it *was*. Poor lad, and me thinking his heart was as hard as a millstane and him in sic danger himself; poor George!'

Jeanie could not help exclaiming,

'O Effie, how can ye speak so of a man like that?'

'We maun forgive our enemies,' said Effie.

'Ye suffer a' this for him – and ye can think of loving him *still*?'

'Love him? If I hadna loved as woman seldom loves, I hadna been here this day. D'ye think a love like mine is lightly forgotten? No. Jeanie, tell me every word he said and whether he was sorry for me or no!'

'Be sure he had muckle to do to save himsell, without speaking on onybody beside.'

'That's no *true*, Jeanie!' said Effie with a spark of lively temper. 'But ye dinna ken, as *I* do, how he put his life in hazard to *save* mine.' And looking at Ratcliffe, she checked herself and was silent.

'I fancy,' said Ratcliffe, 'ye think naebody has een but yourself. I saw your Gentle Geordie seeking to get *other* folk out of this Tolbooth forbye Jock Porteous. But ye were right then, hinny; better to sit and rue, than flit and rue. And ye needna look sae amazed. I ken mair things than *that*, maybe.'

'Oh my God!' said Effie, springing up, 'd'ye ken about my bairn? My wee

---

[1] Job 19.9.

ane... O man, if ye wad earn a blessing, tell me where they hae put my bairn! Wha took him and what they hae dune?'

'How the Deil suld I ken onything of your bairn, huzzy?' said the turnkey, freeing himself from her, 'Ye maun ask that of auld Meg Murdockson!' His answer destroyed the wild hope which had suddenly gleamed. The prisoner let go her hold of his coat and fell, her face to the pavement of the cell.

When she was composed enough, Effie again begged her sister to tell her of the meeting with Robertson. Jeanie now felt it impossible to refuse.

'Effie,' she said, 'ye should ken better than ask what canna but hurt you. But come weal or woe, I canna refuse what ye ask wi' the tear in your ee.'

Again Effie embraced her, kissed her cheek and forehead, murmuring, 'O, if ye kend how lang it is since I heard his name? If ye but kend how good it is to ken onything o' him, ye wadna wonder that I wish to hear it!'

Jeanie sighed, and narrated all that had passed betwixt Robertson and her, making it as brief as possible. Effie devoured every word, listening in breathless anxiety, holding her sister's hand, eyes fixed on her face. Whispered interjections of 'poor George' betwixt sighs were her only interruptions.

'And this was his advice?'

'Just so,' replied her sister.

'And he wanted you to say something that wad save my life?'

'He wanted,' answered Jeanie, 'that I should be man-sworn.'

'And you tauld him that ye wadna come between me and *death*?'

'I told him,' replied Jeanie, trembling at this ominous turn, 'that I daredna swear to an *untruth*.'

'And what d'ye ca' an untruth? Ye are muckle to blame, lass, if ye think a mother would murder her ain bairn. Murder? I wad hae laid down *my* life just to see a blink o' its ee!'

'I believe,' said Jeanie, 'that ye are as innocent of sic a deed as the babe itsell.'

'I'm glad ye do me that justice,' said Effie. 'Folk like you think the rest of the warld are as bad as the warst temptations could make *them*.'

'I didna deserve that, Effie,' said her sister, smarting at the injustice of the reproach, yet compassionate for the state of mind behind it.

'Maybe no, sister,' said Effie. 'But ye are angry because I love Robertson. How can I help loving one that loves me mair than body and soul? He put his life in hazard breaking into this prison to free me. Had *he* been in your place...' she paused and fell silent.

'I wish it stood wi' me to save ye, even at risk of *my* life!' said Jeanie.

'Aye, lass,' said her sister, 'that's lightly said. But no easily credited frae ane that winna say a certain word for me.'

'But Effie, that word is a wilfu' sin!'

'Weel, Jeanie, we'll speak nae mair on the matter. Save your breath for your catechism. Me, I'll soon hae nae breath to waste.'

'It's damn hard,' interposed Ratcliffe, 'that when three words of yours would let the girl cheat Moll Blood,[1] that you make such scruple about them.'

---

[1] The gallows.

'Never speak mair o't,' said the prisoner. 'Gude-day, sister; ye're keeping Mr Ratcliffe waiting. Ye'll come back and see me, before...'

'Are we to part *this* way?' said Jeanie. 'Effie, tell what ye wad hae me do, and I could find in my heart amaist to say that I *wad* do't.'

'No, Jeanie. God knows that I wadna ask ony creature to do a wrang thing to save my life. I might have fled this Tolbooth on that awfu' night. I might hae gone wi' the man who wad hae taken me through all the warld and fended for me. But as I said, let life gang when gude fame is gane before it. But this prison has broken my spirit. And wherever I look I see that Meg Murdockson telling me I had seen the last of my babe!'

'Mr Novit,' said Ratcliffe, 'wants to see the prisoner, and Mr Langtale too.'

Reluctantly, therefore, and after tears and embraces, Jeanie left the cell and heard its jarring bolts. She offered Ratcliffe money to do what he could for her sister's accommodation. To her surprise, Ratcliffe declined the fee.

'Keep your siller. Your sister sall hae all I can gie. But I hope you'll testify on oath for her. But keep your ain counsel, there's nae harm in that. I'll see she takes a sleep after dinner, for she'll no sleep the night. I ken these matters. I hae never seen ane that sleepit the night afore trial, while mony sleepit as sound as a tap the night before their hanging. And it's nae wonder; the warst may be borne when it's kend. Better a finger aff than aye wagging...'

chapter twenty-one

Yet though thou mayst be dragg'd in scorn
To yonder ignominious tree
Thou shalt not want one faithful friend
To share the cruel fates' decree.
William Shenstone, *Jemmy Dawson*

After his morning devotions, David Deans entered the room where breakfast was prepared. He was afraid to look at Jeanie, still uncertain whether she would go to the Court of Justiciary and give, with good conscience, evidence to acquit her sister. He looked at her dress to see whether she was planning to go out that morning. Her apparel was neat and plain, but conveyed no such intimation.

At length, the sound of St Giles's heavy bell tolled the hour prior to the trial's commencement. Jeanie arose and composedly put on her plaid, a preparation for a distant walk. There was a strange contrast between the firmness of her demeanour and the vacillation of her father. No one would have imagined that the former was a gentle country maiden, her father proud, strong and supported by stern religious opinions. The difference was that Jeanie's mind had already decided her conduct, with all its necessary consequences. In contrast, her father was in torment over what Jeanie might say, or rather swear to, and the effect of her testimony on the trial.

He watched his daughter with a faltering, indecisive look. She returned him a look of anguish as she was about to leave the house.

'Father,' said Jeanie, 'ye had better not come with me.'

'In the strength of my God,' answered Deans, 'I will go forth.'

'Let us go.' Taking his daughter's arm, he began the walk, so hastily that it was hard to keep up with him.

'Your bonnet, father?' said Jeanie, observing that he had come out uncovered. He blushed, turned back and put on his large blue Scottish bonnet. With a slower and more composed step, he replaced his daughter's arm in his and resumed the way to Edinburgh.

The Courts of Justice in Parliament Square occupied the former buildings of the Scottish Estates, or Parliament, and had a grave and judicial aspect. The adjacent small quadrangle, or Close, originally the enclosure adjacent to a cathedral, already showed signs of the scene to be enacted. The City Guard were at their posts, the butts of their muskets repelling the crowd which surged forward to catch a glance at the accused as she passed from the adjacent prison to the Court. They laughed, quarreled and pushed each other about as if assembled for some holiday sport.

When Deans and his daughter arrived in the Close and endeavoured to make their way to the door of the courthouse, they became engulfed in the mob and the subject of their insolence. As Deans repelled with some force the pushing he received on all sides, his figure and antiquated dress caught the attention of the rabble. A tattered caidie, or errand porter, whom David Deans had jostled in his attempt to extricate himself from the vicinity of these scorners, exclaimed in a strong Highland accent,

'Deil pluck out yer Cameronian een! What gies you title to push gentlemans about?'

'Make room for a Ruling Elder,' sneered another; 'he comes to see a precious sister glorify God in the Grassmarket!'

'*Shame* on ye, sirs,' came a loud voice. 'It's her father and sister.'

All fell back to make way. In the space conceded by the mob, Deans stood holding his daughter by the hand. The man who had last spoken was none other than Dumbiedikes, his mouth, like that of the prophet's ass, opened by the emergency.[1] He now joined them and, back to his usual taciturnity, escorted them into the Courthouse. No opposition was offered to their entrance by the guards or doorkeepers.

Admitted within the precincts of the Courthouse, they found the usual number of busy office-bearers and the idle loiterers who attend these scenes. Burghers stared; young lawyers sauntered and laughed, as in the pit of the theatre; others sat apart on a bench and reasoned *inter apices juris*[2] on the doctrines of constructive crime and the true import of the Statute. The Bench had been prepared for the arrival of the Judges and jurors were in attendance. The Crown-Counsel advocates looked over their briefs and notes of evidence. They looked grave and whispered with each other. They occupied one side of a large table placed beneath the Bench; on the other sat the Defence advocates. In this, Scots law was more

---

[1] Balaam's talkative ass. 'And Balaam's anger was kindled, and he smote his ass. And his ass said, what have I done unto thee to be thus smitten?' Numbers 22.28.

[2] Among the subtleties of the Law.

liberal than that of England in not only permitting but enjoining Counsel to appear for all accused persons on trial. Mr Nichil Novit, bustling and important, was actively instructing the Counsel for the panel.[1] Entering the Courtroom, Deans asked the Laird, in a tremulous whisper, 'Where will she sit?'

Dumbiedikes pointed to a vacant space at the bar, fronting the Judges and offered to conduct Deans towards it.

'No!' he said; 'I cannot sit by her. I will keep out of her sight. Better for us baith.'

Bartoline Saddletree, whose repeated interference with Counsel had procured him rebuffs and a request that he mind his own business, now bustled up to Deans to exhibit his importance by securing him, through the Macers,[2] a seat hidden from the general view by a projecting corner of the bench.

'It's gude to have a friend at court,' he continued to his helpless auditor. 'Few folk but mysell could hae got ye a seat like this. The Lords will proceed *instanter* to trial. But, for the Lord's sake, what's this? Jeanie, ye're a cited witness. Macer! This lass is a witness and maun be enclosed and no be at large. Mr Novit, suldna Jeanie Deans be enclosed?'

Novit nodded and offered to conduct Jeanie to the apartment, where in Scottish courts, witnesses are held in readiness to be called to give evidence. They are thus separated from all who might influence their testimony by passing information on the progress of the trial.

'Is this necessary?' said Jeanie, reluctant to quit her father.

'A matter of *absolute* necessity,' said Saddletree. 'Wha ever heard of witnesses no being enclosed?'

'It is so,' said the younger Counsel retained for her sister. Jeanie reluctantly followed the Macer from the court.

'This, Mr Deans,' said Saddletree, 'is ca'd *sequestering* a witness. But whisht! Here's the Court.'

As he spoke, the five Lords of Justiciary in their long robes of scarlet faced with white and preceded by their mace-bearer, entered and took their places upon the bench.

The court rose to receive them. The bustle occasioned by their entrance had scarcely settled when a great noise of persons struggling to enter the Courtroom and the galleries, announced that the prisoner was about to be placed at the bar. In rushed the multitude, struggling and sometimes stumbling over each other. The few soldiers forming the centre of this human tide needed all their efforts to clear a passage for the prisoner. Through the authority of the Court and the exertions of its Officers, the tumult was at length suppressed.

Euphemia Deans was then brought forward and placed betwixt two sentinels with drawn bayonets, as the Prisoner at the Bar.

[1] Thus is the prisoner termed in Scottish law phraseology, Scott.
[2] Scottish Court Officers.

chapter twenty-two

DUKE VINCENTIO: *We have strict statutes, and most biting laws,*
The needful bits and curbs for headstrong steeds,
Which, for these fourteen years, we have let sleep,
Like to an o'ergrown lion in a cave,
That goes not out to prey...
                Measure for Measure, 1.3

'Euphemia Deans,' said the presiding Judge, in a tone of both dignity and pity, 'stand up. Listen to the criminal indictment now to be preferred against you.'

Disorientated by the confusion through which her guards had forced a passage, Effie cast a bewildered look at the multitude of faces which seemed to tapestry the walls from ceiling to floor. However, she instinctively obeyed the command, which rang in her ears like the trump of judgment day.

'Put back your hair, Effie,' said one of the Macers. Her long fair hair, which unmarried women did not cover and which Effie dared not now confine with a maiden's riband, hung over her face. She threw back her locks, showing the court an agonised countenance, yet one so lovely as to draw a universal murmur of compassion. This sound of human feeling removed the stupor of fear, but awakened her sense of shame and exposure. Her gaze, which had at first glanced wildly around, was now down; her cheek, at first pale, now overspread with a blush, deepening to crimson.

All were moved by these changes, except one. Deans, motionless in his seat and concealed by the corner of the Bench from seeing or being seen, kept his eyes fixed on the ground, unable to witness the shame of his house.

'*Ichabod!*' said he to himself. '*Ichabod!*'[1]

The indictment setting out in technical form the crime of which the panel stood accused, was now read and the prisoner was asked if she was Guilty, or Not Guilty.

'Not guilty of my poor bairn's death,' said Euphemia Deans.

The presiding Judge next directed Counsel to plead to the relevancy; that is, to state the arguments in Law and the factual evidence both against and in favour of the accused. After this pleading, it was Court procedure to pronounce a preliminary judgment, before sending the case to the cognisance of the jury.

Counsel for the Crown briefly stated the frequency of the crime of infanticide which had given rise to the Statute under which Euphemia Deans stood indicted. He mentioned the various instances which had reluctantly induced the King's Advocate to determine whether, by strictly enforcing the Act of Parliament, infanticides might be prevented.

'I expect,' he said, 'to be able to establish by witnesses, as well as by the declaration of the accused herself, that she was in the state described by the Statute.'

According to his information, she had not communicated her pregnancy to any party, nor did she claim in her own Declaration that she had done so. This

---

[1] Hebrew אִי כָבוֹד meaning 'Glory is departed from my House. I. Samuel 14.2–3.

very secrecy was the first requisite in support of the Indictment. Her Declaration also admitted that she had borne a male child in circumstances which gave reason to believe that it had died by her hands, or at least with her knowledge or consent. It was not, he said, necessary for him to bring positive proof that the accused was *accessory* to the murder nor even to prove that the child was murdered. It was sufficient to support the Indictment that it could *not be found*. According to the Statute, she who both concealed her pregnancy and omitted to call for the assistance necessary at the birth was held to have planned the death of her offspring. Finally, if she could neither prove that the infant had died a natural death, nor could produce it alive, then under the Statute she must be held to have murdered it – and must suffer death accordingly.

Counsel for the accused, Mr Fairbrother, a man of considerable fame in his profession, did not directly combat the arguments of the King's Advocate. He began by regretting that his Senior at the Bar had been suddenly recalled to the county of which he was Sheriff, and that he, Fairbrother, had had but short warning to act for the accused. He had had little time for enquiries and was afraid that a specimen of his incapacity was his being compelled to admit the accuracy of the Indictment under the Statute.

'However,' he said, 'I trust to make out circumstances which would satisfactorily refute the charge of infanticide. My client's story is a short, but most melancholy one. She was raised in the strictest tenets of religion and virtue, the daughter of a worthy and conscientious father who, in former times, had established a character of courage and religion by becoming a sufferer for conscience's sake.'

David Deans gave a convulsive start at hearing himself thus mentioned. He then reburied his face in his hands, which were both resting against the corner of the elevated bench on which the Judges sat. The advocate continued,

'Whatever may be our opinion concerning the tenets of the Deans family, it is impossible to deny them praise for sound and even rigid morals and for the training of their children in the fear of God. Yet it was the daughter of such a person whom the jury would shortly be called upon, in the *absence of evidence*, and upon mere *presumptions*, to convict of a crime more properly belonging to a heathen than to a Christian and civilised country. It is true that the nurture and instruction which the girl had received had not preserved her from guilt and error. She had fallen sacrifice to her affection for a young man of prepossessing manners, but who was a dangerous character. She was seduced under promise of marriage; a promise which the fellow might indeed have kept, had he not been called upon by the Law to answer to a criminal charge.

This crime, violent and desperate, was itself the preface to another event marked by riot, blood and guilt, the final termination of which has not yet arrived. I believe that no one would hear without surprise the name of the father of the missing infant, the very infant said by the learned Advocate to have been murdered. The father was none other than the notorious George Robertson, accomplice of Wilson and escapee from the Tolbooth Church. Now, no one knows better than my learned friend the King's Advocate that Robertson was the principal actor in the Porteous conspiracy...'

'I am sorry to interrupt, Counsel,' said, the presiding Judge; 'but I must remind the learned gentleman that he is travelling out of the case before us.' Counsel bowed and resumed.

'I judge it necessary,' he said, 'to mention the name and situation of Robertson, because that accounted for the silence upon which his Majesty's Counsel laid so much weight, as evidence that Euphemia Deans planned the death of the yet unborn babe. She had not indeed revealed that she had been seduced from the path of honour. And why not? Because she expected daily to be restored to character by marriage to her lover. Was it natural, was it reasonable, was it fair, to expect that she should in the interim, become *felo de se*[1] of her own character when she had every reason to expect that, by a temporary concealment, it might be veiled for ever? Was it not, on the contrary, *pardonable*, that in such an emergency, a young woman in her situation should not confide in every prying gossip? Was it strange, was it criminal, that she should have repelled their inquisitiveness with denials? The sense and feeling of all who hear me will answer in the negative.

My Lords, I trust I shall remove this case from under the Statute and obtain for this unfortunate young woman an honourable discharge from your Lordships' Bar, by showing that she did *indeed* mention her calamitous circumstances. This she did after Robertson's conviction. He then lay in prison awaiting the fate which his comrade Wilson afterwards suffered, and from which he himself so remarkably escaped. It was *then*, with all hopes of wedlock gone, since a union with Robertson would be seen as an addition to her disgrace; *then* it was, as I trust to show, that the prisoner communicated her unhappy situation to her sister. This is a woman several years older than herself, the daughter of her father by a former marriage.'

'And what if, indeed, you are able to instruct on that point, Mr Fairbrother?' said the presiding Judge.

'If I am able so to do, my Lord,' resumed Fairbrother, 'I trust not only to serve my client, but to relieve your Lordships from what I know you feel to be a most painful duty of your high office. I trust also to give all who now hear me the pleasure of seeing dismissed from hence in safety and in honour, the young and ingenuous creature now at the Bar of your Lordships' Court.'

This address affected many in the audience and was followed by a murmur of applause. Deans, hearing his daughter's beauty and innocent appearance appealed to, was about to turn his eyes towards her, but bent them again on the ground with stubborn resolution.

'Will not my learned friend on the other side of the Bar,' continued the advocate, after a short pause, 'share in this approach? I know that while he discharges his duty in bringing an accused person here, no one rejoices more in their being freely and honourably sent hence?

My learned brother shakes his head.

He lays his hand on the accused's Declaration. I understand him perfectly; he would argue that the facts now stated to your Lordships are inconsistent with the confession of Euphemia Deans herself. I need not remind your Lordships that her present defence is not to be confined within the narrow bounds of her confession; it is not by any account which she may *formerly* have given of herself, but by

---

[1]   Latin: 'Felon of, (ie *to*) oneself.' In this case: assassin of her own reputation.

what is *now* to be proved for or against her, that she must ultimately stand or fall. I need not account for her omitting from her Declaration her confession to her sister. She might not have been aware of its importance; she might have been afraid of implicating her sister; she might even have forgotten it entirely in the distress of her arrest on a capital charge.

Any of these reasons are sufficient to account for her having suppressed the fact. I incline personally to her erroneous fear of criminating her sister, because I observe she has had a similar consideration towards her lover, having never *once* mentioned Robertson's name from the beginning to the end of her Declaration. My Lords, I am aware that the King's Advocate will demand of me how Effie Deans's confession to her sister before her delivery is reconcilable with the mystery of the birth and with the disappearance and even perhaps the murder of the infant – for I will not deny a possibility which I cannot disprove.

My Lords, the explanation of this is to be found in the placability, or may I say the pliability, of the female sex. The *dulcis Amaryllidis irae*,[1] as your Lordships well know, are easily appeased. A woman so atrociously offended by the man she has loved, will retain a fund of forgiveness upon which his penitence, real or affected, may draw, knowing that his bill will be met. We can prove, by a letter to be produced in evidence, that Robertson, from his prison cell, contrived to exercise authority over the mind of this girl. When her delivery approached, the accused complied with that letter. Instead of resorting to the protection of her own family, she was induced to entrust herself to the charge of some agent of Robertson. This agent took her to one of those secret places which, to the shame of our police, still exist in the suburbs of this city. There, with the assistance of a female person, she was delivered of a male child.

What purpose Robertson had in all this, it is hard to tell or even to guess. He may have meant to marry the girl, for her father is a man of substance. But the conduct of the woman with whom he had placed Euphemia Deans is yet *more* difficult to account. The young mother contracted childbed fever[2] during, and on recovering her senses, she found that she was childless. Her infant had been carried away, perhaps for the worst purposes, by the wretch that waited on her. It may have been murdered, for all I can tell.'

He was interrupted by a shriek from the prisoner. She composed herself with difficulty, her Counsel availing himself of the interruption to close his pleading with effect.

'My Lords,' said he, 'in that piteous cry, you heard the eloquence of maternal affection, far surpassing the force of my poor words; Rachel weeping for her children![1] Nature herself bears testimony in favour of the tenderness of the prisoner's parental feelings. I will not dishonour her plea by adding a word more.'

---

[1] *Triste lupus stabulis, maturis frugibus imbres / arboribus venti, nobis Amaryllidis irae.* 'Baneful is the wolf to the sheepfold, the rains to ripened crops / the tempest to trees – and the furies of Amaryllis to me!' Virgil, *Eclogue* III, 80–81.

[2] Also known as puerperal sepsis. A serious and, until the twentieth century, often fatal endometritis (infection of the post-partum uterus) leading to septicaemia.

[3] Matthew 2.18. 'Rachel weeping for her children and would not be comforted, because they were not [alive].'

The Judges, after consultation, recorded their judgment that the Indictment, if proved, was relevant to – and would incur – the penalties of Law; but also that the Defence, that the accused had communicated her situation to her sister, was relevant.

Finally, they referred both Indictment and Defence to the judgment of the jury.

chapter twenty-three

SHYLOCK: *Most learned judge!*
A sentence. Come, prepare.
The Merchant of Venice, IV.I

The jury was empanelled and the case proceeded. The prisoner was again required to plead to the charge, and again she replied, 'Not Guilty.'

The Crown Counsel then called three female witnesses who testified to having noted Effie's pregnancy and taxing her with the fact. Her response had been an angry and petulant denial. But, as frequently happens, it was the statement, or Declaration, by the accused herself which bore hardest upon her case.

In Scotland, an accused person is not compelled to answer to police questioning and may remain silent. But whatever answers he or she chooses to give are formally written down as a Declaration, and may be produced in court. Declarations are not produced as evidence, properly so called, but only as adminicles[1] of testimony, to corroborate legal and proper evidence. This fine distinction reconciles the procedure with the central principle that an accused cannot be required to bear witness against himself.

However, it often happens that Declarations become the *de facto* means of condemning the accused, as it were, out of their own mouths. Although prisoners have indeed the privilege of remaining silent, most feel that a refusal to answer pertinent questions is in itself an indication of guilt. It seldom happens, therefore, that the prisoner refuses to give a judicial Declaration in which, either by letting out too much of the truth, or by inventing a fictitious story, he almost always exposes himself to contradictions, which may sway the minds of a jury.

The Declaration of Euphemia Deans was read to the Court and was as follows: 'The Declarant admitted a criminal intrigue with an individual whose name she desired to conceal.

Being interrogated, what her reason was for secrecy on this point?
Declares, that she had no right to blame that person's conduct more than she did her own, and that she was willing to confess her own faults, but not to say anything which might criminate the father.

Asked: if she confessed her pregnancy to anyone, or made any preparation for her confinement?
Declares, she did not.

---

[1]   Latin: *Adminiculum*, support. In Law, something contributing to prove a point without itself constitutng complete proof.

Asked: why she did not take the steps which the imminent childbirth required?

Declares, she was ashamed to tell her friends, and she trusted the un-named absent person would provide for her and the infant.

Asked: did he do so?

Declares, that he did not do so personally; but that it was not his fault; the declarant is convinced he would have laid down his life sooner than the bairn or she had come to harm.

Asked: what prevented him from keeping his promise?

Declares, that it was impossible for him to do so, he being in trouble at the time and declines farther answers to this question.

Asked: where she was from the period she left the residence of her master, Mr Bartoline Saddletree, until her appearance at her father's residence, at St Leonard's on the day before her apprehension?

Declares, she does not remember.

Interrogatory repeated.

Declares, she does not 'mind muckle' about it, for she was very ill.

Interrogatory repeated.

Declares, she will tell the truth, even if it be the undoing of her, so long as she is not asked to incriminate other folk; admits, that she passed that interval in the lodging of a woman, an acquaintance of the un-named person and that she was there delivered of a male child.

Asked: what was the name of that person?

Declares, a refusal to answer.

Asked: where does that person live?

Declares, she has no certainty, for that she was taken to the lodging aforesaid under cloud of night.

Asked: if the lodging was in the City or its suburbs?

Declares, a refusal to answer that question.

Asked: whether she had ever seen the woman before she was sent to her by the person whose name she refuses to reveal?

Declares, not to her knowledge.

Asked: whether this woman was introduced to her by the said person verbally, or by word of mouth?

Declares, she has no freedom to answer this question.

Asked: if the child was liveborn?

Declares, that – God help her and it – it was alive.

Asked: if it died a natural death after birth?

Declares, not to her knowledge.

Asked: where it now is?

Declares, she would give her right hand to ken. She expects never to see more than the bones of it.

Asked: why she supposes it dead?

Declarant wept bitterly and made no answer.

Asked: when the child was taken away from her?

Declares, that she fell into a fever and when she came to her own mind, the woman told her the bairn was dead; and that the declarant said, if it was dead it had had foul play. That, thereupon, the woman and gave her much ill language; and that the declarant was frightened and crawled out of the house when the woman's back was turned and made her way to Saint Leonard's.

Asked: why she did not tell her story to her sister and father, and enforce a search of the house for her child, dead or alive?

Declares, it was her purpose to do so, but she had not time.

Asked: why she now conceals the name of the woman, and the place of her abode?

Declarant remained silent for a time, and then said, that to do so could not repair the harm that was done, but might be the occasion of more.

Asked: whether she, at any time, had any intention of putting away the child by violence?

Declares, never; so might God be merciful to her. And again declares, never when she was in her senses; but what bad thoughts the Devil might have sent when she was out of her mind, she cannot answer. Solemnly declares, that she would have been drawn with wild horses, rather than hurt the bairn.

Declares that the woman said that the declarant had hurt the bairn when in the brain fever; but the declarant believes this was to frighten her and make her be silent. Declares, that when she cried aloud for her bairn and was like to raise the neighbours, the woman threatened her, saying that they stopped the wean's skirling – and would stop hers if she did not keep quiet. At this, the declarant concluded that the bairn's life was gone and her own in danger from this desperate person.

Asked: why she does not now communicate particulars which might enable a Magistrate to ascertain whether the child is living or dead.

Declares, that she kens the bairn is now dead; or, if living, there is one un-named person that will look after it. That for her own living or dying, she is in God's hands, who knows her innocence of harming her bairn; and that she has altered her resolution of speaking out, which she entertained when she left the woman's lodging, on account of a matter which she has since learned. And declares in general that she is wearied and will answer no more questions at this time.

Upon a subsequent examination, Effie Deans adhered to the declaration she had formerly made, with this addition: a letter found in her trunk was shown to her which she admitted was genuine. In consequence of it, she resigned herself to the conduct of the woman at whose lodgings she gave birth.

Dearest Effie, I have gotten the means to send this to you by a woman who will assist you in your approaching streight. She is not what I could wish, but I cannot do better in my present condition. I am obliged to trust her for myself and you too. I hope for the best, though I am now in a sore pinch.

You will be angry with me writing this, but if I can live to be a comfort to you and a father to our babie, you will have plenty of time to scold. Let none know your counsel. My life depends on this dangerous hag; but she has wiles and wit and has cause to be true to me.

Farewell, my Lily. Do not droop on my account. In a week I will be yours – or no more my own.

Effie refused to say from whom she had received this letter, but it clearly had come from Robertson. It appeared to have been written about the time when 'Handie Dandie', a nickname for Andrew Wilson, and he were planning their first abortive attempt to escape.

The evidence of the Crown being concluded, Counsel for the prisoner began the defence. The first witnesses were examined upon her character. All gave her support and none with more feeling than Mrs Saddletree who declared, in tears, that she could not have had a higher opinion of Effie Deans had she been her own daughter.

Mr Fairbrother now announced his most important witness, upon whose evidence his case must in a great measure depend. His client's character had been attested by the preceding witnesses. It was necessary, however, to produce positive testimony of her innocence than what arose out of her general character. This he undertook to do through the person to whom she had revealed her situation; her natural counsellor, guardian – and elder sister.

'Macer, call into court Jean Deans, daughter of David Deans, cow feeder at Saint Leonard's Crags.'

When he uttered these words, the prisoner started up and stretched half-way over the bar, towards the side at which her sister was to enter. Slowly following the Macer, Jeanie advanced to the foot of the table. Effie's expression now altered from one of shame to an imploring earnestness of entreaty. With outstretched hands, eyes on her sister's face and glistening with tears, she exclaimed,

'Oh Jeanie, *save* me!'

Old Deans drew himself back under the cover of the bench so that when Jeanie entered the court and cast a glance towards where she had left him, he was no longer visible. He sat down on the other side of Dumbiedikes, wrung his hand hard, and whispered, 'Ah, Laird, this is the warst of a'.'

Jeanie advanced to the bottom of the table and, unable to resist the impulse of affection, suddenly extended her hand to her sister. Effie grasped it and kissed it. Jeanie, hiding her face with her other hand, was now also weeping. Many spectators shed tears. The presiding Judge told the witness to compose herself and the prisoner to forbear those marks of affection which, however natural, could not be permitted in that presence.

The solemn oath was then administered by the Judge;

The Truth to tell, and no Truth to conceal, as far as she knew, or should be asked, and as the Witness should answer to God at the great Day of Judgment.

Jeanie, educated in deep and devout reverence for the Deity, repeated the words in a reverently low but distinct voice.

The Judge then added:

'Young woman, you come before this Court in circumstances with which it is impossible not to sympathise. Yet it is my duty to remind you, that the truth, *whatever* its consequences may be, is the truth which you owe to your country and to your God, whose name you have just now invoked. Take your own time in answering the questions which that gentleman,' he pointed to the Counsel, 'shall put to you. But remember, anything that you may be tempted to say *beyond* what is the actual truth, for that you must answer both here – *and* in the hereafter.'

The preliminary questions were then put to her:

Whether anyone had instructed her what evidence she had to deliver? Whether anyone had given or promised her any good deed, hire, or reward for her testimony? Whether she had any malice or ill-will at His Majesty's Advocate, being the party against whom she was cited as a witness?

To these questions she answered with a quiet negative. But their tenor gave great offence to her father, who was unaware that they are put to every witness as a matter of form.

'Na, *na*!' he exclaimed, loudly, 'my bairn is no like the Widow of Tekoah. Nane has putten words into her mouth!'[1]

One of the Judges, better acquainted, perhaps, with books of Law than with the Book of Samuel, enquired after this 'Widow of Tekoah' who might have been tampering with the evidence. The presiding Judge, better versed in Scripture, whispered an explanation to his learned brother. The pause occasioned by this gave Jeanie Deans a moment to collect her thoughts for the task ahead.

Fairbrother, whose practice and intelligence were considerable, saw the witness compose herself. He quietly suspected that she came to bear false witness and perjure herself in her sister's favour.

'But that is her own affair,' he said to himself, 'and it is *my* business to see that she has time to regain composure and to deliver her evidence, be it true, or be it false. *Valeat quantum...*'[2]

'You are, I believe, the sister of the prisoner?'

'Yes sir.'

'Not the full sister, however?'

'No sir. We are by different mothers.'

'True; and you are, I think, several years older than your sister?'

'Yes sir.'

After the advocate reckoned that he had familiarised the witness with the situation in which she stood, he asked:

'Now, did you remark your sister's state of health to be altered, during the latter part of the time when she had lived with Mrs Saddletree?'

'Yes.'

---

[1] Joab did so to the Widow of Tekoah. I. Samuel 14.3. Tekoah is twelve miles south of Jerusalem.

[2] The full legal phrase is: *Valeat quantum valere potest*. Lit. It shall have effect as far as it can have effect. Or, let it have what effect it may.

'And she told you the *cause* of it?' said Fairbrother, in an easy and inductive tone.

'I am sorry to interrupt my learned friend,' said the Crown Counsel, rising; 'but I ask your Lordships' judgment, whether this be not a leading question?'

'If this point is to be debated,' said the presiding Judge, 'the witness must be removed.'

Scottish lawyers regard with scrupulous horror any question shaped by an examining Counsel to convey to the witness the least hint of the desired answer. Although founded on an excellent principle, it is generally easy for a sharp barrister to elude an objection that he is leading the witness. Fairbrother did so, saying, 'It is not necessary to waste the time of the Court, my Lord. But since the King's Counsel objects to the form of my question, I will shape it otherwise. Miss Deans, did you ask your sister any question when you observed her looking unwell?'

'I asked her what ailed her.'

'Very well. Take your own time; and what was her answer?'

Jeanie was now silent, and deadly pale. It was not prevarication; it was the natural hesitation to extinguish the last spark of hope that remained for her sister.

'Take courage, young woman,' said Fairbrother. 'I asked what your sister said ailed her – when you enquired?'

'Nothing,' answered Jeanie.

Her faint but distinct voice, heard in every corner of the Courtroom, ended the awful and profound silence between the question and the answer. Fairbrother's countenance fell; but with great presence of mind, he immediately rallied,

'Nothing? True; you mean nothing *at first*. But when you asked her *again*, did she not tell you what ailed her?'

The question came in a tone indicating the extreme importance of her answer, but with less pause than before, she now replied, 'Alack! She never breathed word to me about it.'

A deep groan passed through the Court, echoed by one deeper and more agonised from Deans. The hope to which he had secretly clung now dissolved. The old man fainted. The prisoner struggled with her guards.

'Let me gang to my father! I will gang to him; I will gang to him. I hae *killed* him!' she cried in tones never forgotten by those who heard them.

The Judge gave directions that Deans and Jeanie be conducted into a neighbouring apartment. As her father was borne from the Court, her sister slowly following, Effie pursued them with staring eyes. When they were no longer visible, she seemed to find, despairing and deserted as she was, a courage she had not yet exhibited.

'The bitterness is past now,' she said, and then boldly addressed the Court. 'My Lords, if it is your pleasure to gang on wi' this matter, this weariest day will hae its end at last.'

The Judge requested to know if Counsel for the accused had further evidence to produce. Fairbrother replied, with a distinct air of dejection, that his evidence was concluded.

The King's Counsel now addressed the jury for the Crown. He said that no one could be more concerned than he by the distressing scene they had just witnessed. But great crimes brought distress and ruin upon all connected with the perpetrators.

He briefly reviewed the evidence, showing that all the circumstances of the case concurred with those required by the Act under which the prisoner was tried.

Counsel for the defence, he continued, had failed to prove that Euphemia Deans had communicated her situation to her sister. Respecting her previous good character, he was sorry to observe that it was such females, those of good report, who were most strongly tempted by shame to infanticide: that the child had been murdered, he entertained no doubt. The inconsistent Declaration of the prisoner left no doubt of this in his mind. Neither could he doubt that its mother was party to this guilt. Who else had an interest in a deed so inhuman? Neither Robertson, nor his agent in whose house she was delivered, had the least motive to commit such a crime unless upon her account or with her connivance and for the sake of saving her reputation.

He reminded the jury that it was not required of him in Law to bring precise proof of the murder, or of the prisoner's accession to it. Finally, he put it to the conscience of the jury, that he was entitled to a verdict of Guilty.

In his own closing statement for the defence, Fairbrother was much cramped by his having failed to lead the evidence he had expected from the sister. However, he fought his losing cause with courage and constancy. He attacked the severity of the Statute under which the young woman was tried.

'In all other cases,' he said, 'the first thing required of the criminal prosecutor was to prove unequivocally that the crime libelled had actually been committed, which lawyers called proving the *corpus delicti*.[1] But this Statute, made doubtless with the best intentions, and under the horror for the unnatural crime of infanticide, ran the risk of *itself* occasioning the worst of murders, namely the death of an innocent person. And this was to *atone* for a supposed crime which may never have been committed by anyone. He was so far from acknowledging the probability of the child's violent death that he could not even accept that there was evidence of its having ever lived.

King's Counsel had pointed to the woman's Declaration; but this was concocted in terror and agony. His learned brother well knew it contained no sound evidence against the party who emitted it. It was true that a judicial confession, in presence of the Justices themselves, was the strongest of all proof, insomuch that it is said in Law that '*in confitentem nullae sunt partes judicis.*'[2] But this was true of judicial confession only – that made in presence of the Justices. Of extrajudicial confession, all authorities held with the illustrious Farinaceus and Matthaeus,[3] '*confessio extrajudicialis in se nulla est; et quod nullum est, non potest adminiculari.*'[4] It was totally void of strength and effect and hence incapable of being supported by other presumptive circumstances. In the present case, therefore, letting the extrajudicial confession go, as go it ought, for nothing,

---

[1]   Latin: Literally, the body of crime. The existence of the offence.

[2]   There is no role for the Judge in confessions; ie the judicial role is not to judge a confession, merely to determine the penalty. A concept dating back to the legal *Digest* of Justinian in the fifth century AD.

[3]   Fairbtother cites two celebrated jurists: the Italian Prospero Farinacci (1544–1618) and the Dutch Anthonius Matthaeus (1601–1654). Both published on penal theory.

[4]   Latin: A confession made outside the Court is nothing; and being so, cannot support the case.

I contend that the prosecution has not made out the second quality of the Statute, that a live child had been born – and that at least ought to be established before any presumption of murder. If any of the Jury should be of opinion that this was dealing rather narrowly with the Statute, they ought to consider that it was *highly* penal – and was therefore entitled to no favourable construction.'

He concluded a learned speech with an eloquent peroration on the scene they had just witnessed, during which Saddletree fell fast asleep. It was now the presiding Judge's turn to sum up.

It was for the jury, he said, to consider whether the prosecutor had made out his case. For himself, he sincerely grieved to say, that no shadow of doubt remained upon his mind concerning the verdict which the trial had to bring in. He would not follow the prisoner's Counsel through the attack he had brought against the Statute of King William and Queen Mary. He and the jury were sworn to judge according to the laws *as they stood*, they were not required to criticise, evade, or even to justify them.

The accused's situation could not be doubted; that she had borne a child, and that the child had disappeared were certain facts. The learned Counsel had failed to show that she had communicated her situation. All the requisites of the case required by the Statute were therefore before the jury.

In the present case, no person who had heard the witnesses describe the appearance of the young woman before she left Saddletree's house, and contrasted it with that of her state and condition at her return to her father's, could have any doubt that a birth had taken place, as set forth in her own Declaration. This, therefore, was not a solitary piece of testimony, but one supported by the strongest circumstantial proof.

The Judge went on to say that he had felt, no less than they, the scene of family misery enacted before them. If they, the jury, before God and with good conscience and mindful of the sanctity of their Oath and the Law, should find the accused not guilty, he should rejoice as much as anyone in Court. Never had he found his duty more distressing than in discharging it this day, and glad he would be to be relieved of the yet more painful task of condemnation which would, otherwise, remain for him.

Having heard the Judge's closing address, the jury bowed and, preceded by a Macer of Court, retired to consider their verdict.

chapter twenty-four

Law, take thy victim; may she find the mercy
In yon mild Heaven, which this hard world denies her!
    Walter Scott (Attrib.)

It was an hour ere the jurors returned. As they slowly traversed the crowd, they appeared as men about to discharge a painful responsibility. The audience was hushed into a profound and awful silence.

'Have you agreed on your Chancellor, gentlemen?' enquired the Judge.

The foreman, called in Scotland the Chancellor of the jury, stepped forward. With a bow he delivered to the Court a sealed paper containing the verdict. The jury remained standing while the Judge broke the seals. Having perused the paper, he handed it gravely down to the clerk of Court, who proceeded to engross in the record the yet unknown verdict. A procedure followed, trifling in itself, but which adds a solemnity to the awe of the occasions when it is used. A lighted candle was placed on the table and the paper containing the verdict was enclosed in a further sheet. Sealed with the Judge's own signet, it would be transmitted to the Crown Office to be preserved among other records of its kind. As all this was transacted in profound silence, the production and then the extinguishing of the candle seemed to reflect the human spark doomed to be quenched. The effect on the spectators is similar in effect to that in England when a Judge dons the fatal black cap. The preliminary forms completed, the Judge required Euphemia Deans to stand and hear the verdict:

We the Jury, having made choice of John Kirk, Esq., to be our Chancellor and Thomas Moore, merchant, to be our Clerk, did, by a plurality of voices, find the said Euphemia Deans guilty as charged.

However, in consideration of her youth, and the circumstances of her case, we do earnestly entreat that the Judge recommend her to the mercy of the Crown.

'Gentlemen,' said the Judge, 'you have done your duty – and a painful one it must have been to men of humanity. I will undoubtedly transmit your recommendation to the Throne. But it is also my duty to tell all who now hear me, but especially to inform you, Euphemia Deans, in order that your mind may be settled accordingly, that I have not the least hope of a Royal Pardon being granted in this case. The increasing crime of infanticide is ascribed to the lenity in which the Laws have been exercised. There is, therefore, no hope whatever of obtaining a remission.'

The jury bowed again and, released from their painful office, dispersed among the mass of bystanders. The Court then asked Mr. Fairbrother whether he had reason to arrest, or delay, the judgment now to follow. The Counsel had spent some time in perusing and reperusing the verdict and weighing every phrase in the minutest scale of legal criticism. But the Clerk of the jury had understood his business well. No flaw was to be found and Fairbrother sadly intimated that he had nothing to say in arrest of judgment. The presiding Judge then addressed the prisoner:

'Euphemia Deans, attend to the sentence of the Court now to be pronounced against you.'

She rose again from her seat with a composure far greater than could have been augured from her demeanour during some parts of the trial. *'The first blows bring a stunning apathy, which renders us indifferent to those that follow.'* Thus said Mandrin[1] when he was undergoing the punishment of the wheel; he spoke for all upon whom successive inflictions have descended with reiterated violence.

---

[1] Louis Mandrin (1725–1756) The famous 'Robin Hood of France' and inveterate foe of the tax farmers of the *ancien régime*. At Valence in Drôme he was 'broken on the wheel', ie he was tied to a wheel and had all four limbs smashed with iron clubs before being strangled in front of 6,000 spectators, many of them sympathetic.

'Young woman,' said the Judge, 'it is my painful duty to tell you, that your life is forfeit. It is forfeit under a Law which, although severe, yet is wise. Its purpose is to render those of your unhappy situation aware what risks they run by concealing their lapse from virtue and making no preparation to save the life of the infant they are to bring into the world. You concealed your situation from your mistress, your sister and other worthy persons. You thus seemed to have been contemplating the death of the helpless creature for whose life you neglected to provide.

How the child was disposed of; whether killed by another, or by yourself; whether the extraordinary story you have told is partly false, or altogether so, is between God and your conscience. I will not aggravate your distress by pressing on that topic, but I do most solemnly adjure you to employ your time remaining to make your peace with God. For that purpose, such clergymen as you may name shall have access to you. Notwithstanding the humane recommendation of the Jury, I cannot afford to you the slightest hope that your life will be prolonged beyond the period assigned for the execution of your sentence. Forsaking, therefore, any thoughts of this world, let your mind be prepared by repentance for death, judgment – and eternity. Doomster, read the Sentence.'[1]

The Doomster then appeared; a tall haggard figure, arrayed in a garment of black and grey, passmented with silver lace. All drew back with an instinctive horror and made way for him to approach the foot of the table. As this Office was held by the public executioner, men shouldered each other backward to avoid even the touch of his garment, some being seen to brush their clothes as if thus contaminated. A sound went through the Court, produced the hard intake of breath by men expecting, or witnessing, what is frightful and affecting. The hardened executioner seemed to sense the general detestation, which made him impatient of being in public, just as birds of evil omen are anxious to escape from daylight and from pure air.

Repeating after the Clerk of the Court, he gabbled the words of the sentence, which condemned Euphemia Deans to be conducted back to the Tolbooth of Edinburgh and detained there until the appointed day of execution; and upon that day, betwixt the hours of two and four o'clock after noon, to be conveyed to the common place of lawful execution, and there hanged by the neck upon a gibbet.

'And this,' came the Doomster's harsh voice, 'I pronounce for *Doom*.'

With that last emphatic word he vanished, leaving among the crowd the horror excited by his presence and errand.

The condemned criminal, for thus she must now be termed, had remained standing motionless at the bar while sentence was pronounced. She was observed to shut her eyes when the Doomster appeared but was the first to break silence when the spectre had disappeared.

'God forgive ye, my Lords,' she said. 'As for myself, I canna blame ye, for ye acted by your lights; and if I havena killed my poor infant, ye may witness that I hae been the means of killing my grey-headed father. I deserve the warst frae Man and God. But God is mair mercifu' to us than we are to each other.'

---

[1]   In Scotland, the title of the official who recited the Sentence after it had been pronounced by the Court and recorded by the Clerk. The Doomster, or Dempster, then legalised it with the words of form, *And this I pronounce for Doom*, Scott. The practice was abolished in 1773 when the Doomster ignored the prisoner and launched a tirade of abuse at the Judges. Ed.

With these words the trial concluded. The crowd surged out of the Court in the same excited mode in which they had entered. Walking homeward, groups of men discussed the principle of the Statute, the nature of the evidence and the arguments of Counsel and the actions of the Judge. The female spectators, more compassionate, were loud against that part of the Judge's closing speech which seemed to cut off the hope of pardon.

'Why, indeed,' said Mrs Howden, 'must he tell us that the poor lassie had to die, when John Kirk, as civil a gentleman as there is in the town, took the pains to plead for her himsell.'

'Neighbour,' said Miss Damahoy, drawing up her maidenly form to its prim dignity, 'this business of having bastard bairns should be putten a stop to. There isna a hussy this side of 30 that you can bring within your doors without writer-lads, prentice-lads and what not coming traiking in after them for their destruction and discrediting an honest house. I hae nae patience wi' them.'

'Neighbour,' said Mrs Howden, 'we suld live and let live. We hae been young oursells and we shouldna think the warst when lads and lasses forgather.'

'Young oursells – and think the warst!' said the spinster. 'I am no sae auld as that, Mrs Howden; and as for that what ye ca' the *warst*, I thank my stars that I dinna ken about the matter!'

'Ye are thankfu' for sma' mercies, then,' said Mrs Howden tartly; 'and as for you being young, ye were present at the last sittin' o' the Scots Parliament, and since that was in the gracious year seven,[1] sae ye can be nae chicken!'

Plumdamas, escorting the two dames, saw the hazard of entering into such a delicate chronology. A lover of peace and good neighbourliness, he brought the conversation smartly back to its original subject.

'The Judge didna tell us about the application for a pardon,' said he 'there is aye a wimple in a lawyer's clew,[2] but it's a wee bit secret.'

'And what is't Plumdamas?' said Mrs Howden and Miss Damahoy together, their acidity neutralised by the powerful alkali in the word 'secret.'

'Here's Mr Saddletree can tell ye that better than me,' said Plumdamas as Bartoline came up, his wife disconsolate on his arm. When the question was put him, he looked scornful.

'They speak about stopping child-murder,' said he contemptuously. 'Do ye think our auld enemies of England care a boddle whether we kill ane anither? Na, na, it's no *that* hindering them frae pardoning the lassie. Here's the pinch. The King and Queen are sae ill-pleased about the Porteous business that no Scot will they pardon again, even if the haill town o' Edinburgh should be a' hanged on a single rope.'

'Send them back tae their German kaleyard then,' said Mrs Howden, 'if that's how they guide us!'

'They say for certain,' said Miss Damahoy, 'that King George flang his periwig intae the fire when he heard o' the Porteous mob.'

'He has done that,' replied Saddletree, 'for lesser things.'

---

[1] 1707, the year in which the Scots Parliament was adjourned – until 1999.
[2] There is always a twist in the ball of thread of a Lawyer.

'Aweel,' said Miss Damahoy, 'he should keep down his anger. Mind you, it's a' the better for his wigmaker!'

'The queen tore her biggonets[1] in a rage,' said Plumdamas. 'As for the King, they say he kickit Sir Robert Walpole[2] for no keeping down the mob of Edinburgh.'

'It's the truth,' said Saddletree; 'and he was all for kickin' the Duke of Argyle too.'

'Kickin' the Duke of *Argyle*!' exclaimed all in astonishment.

'Ay, but *MacCailean Mór's*[3] blood wadna stand for that; there was risk of Andro Ferrara coming in thirdsman.'[4]

'The Duke is a real Scotsman. A true friend to the country,' said several.

'Aye, in troth he is – to King and country baith,' continued Bartoline, 'come in bye to our house now, for it's safest speaking of sic things *inter parietes*.'[5]

Entered his shop, Saddletree thrust his apprentice boy out of it, unlocked his desk and, with an air of grave importance, took out a crumpled piece of printed paper.

'This is new corn. It's no anybody could show you the like o' this. It's the Duke's speech about the Porteous mob. Ye shall hear what Iain Ruaidh Cean[6] says for himsell. My correspondent bought it in the Palace-yard, just under the king's nose!'

Saddletree now read an extract from the speech:

'*I am no minister. I never was a minister, and I never will be one...*'

'I didna ken his Grace was ever destined for the Ministry,' interrupted Mrs Howden.

'He disna mean a minister of the *gospel*, Mrs Howden, but a minister of *State*,' said Saddletree condescendingly and then proceeded:

The time was when I might have been a Minister, but I was too sensible of my own incapacity to engage in any State affair. I thank God that I always placed too great a value on those few abilities Nature gave me, to employ them in drudgery. I have, ever since I set out in the world (and I believe few have set out more early), served my Prince with my tongue; I have also served him with my sword in the profession of arms. I have held employments which I have lost, and were I to be deprived t-morrow of those which remain and which I have endeavoured honestly to deserve, I would still serve him to the last acre of my inheritance – and to the last drop of my blood...

Mrs Saddletree broke in upon the orator:

---

1   Ripped up her caps.

2   The Prime Minister.

3   The title of the Dukes of Argyll *qua* Chief of Clan Campbell. It means 'Son of the great Colin' and refers to the clan's Patriarch, *Cailean Mór Caimbeul*, in English 'Sir Colin Campbell' (of Lochow) who died *c.*1296.

4   Andrea Ferrara was an Italian sword manufacturer whose products were popular in Scotland. A thirdsman was an arbiter in adispute. Hence the implication is that rebellion on the cards.

5   Literally: 'within the walls,' ie indoors rather than in the street.

6   Gaelic for 'Redheaded John', a personal name used in the Highlands for John, 2nd Duke of Argyll, who had bright red hair.

'Mr Saddletree, what *is* the meaning of a' this? Here ye are clavering on about the Duke of Argyle; well I wish the Duke of Argyle would pay his *accounts*! He owes a thousand punds Scots from when he was last at Roystoun. And there's distressed folk upstairs, that's Jeanie Deans and her father. And ye've put the prentice that was sewing the curpel out o' the shop, to play wi' blackguards in the close! Sit still, neighbours, I'll no disturb *you*; but what between Courts o' Law and Courts o' State, and upper and under Parliaments and Parliament Houses, here *and* in London, my husband's gane clean gyte!'[1]

At this, the guests rapidly made their farewells and departed. Saddletree whispered to Plundamas that he would meet him at MacCroskie's shop in the Luckenbooths in the hour of cause; back into his pocket went the Ducal speech.

Mrs Saddletree, now freed of visitors, reclaimed her apprentice from the wynd to the exercise of the awl. She then went upstairs to see her cousin David and his elder daughter, who had found in her house the nearest place of friendly refuge.

chapter twenty-five

ISABELLA: *Alas! what poor ability's in me*
To do him good
LUCIO: *Assay the power you have.*
> *Measure for Measure,* 1.4

When Mrs Saddletree entered the apartment in which her guests had shrouded their misery, she found the window darkened and the old man laid in bed. The curtains were drawn and beside him Jeanie sat motionless. Mrs Saddletree was a woman of more kindness than delicacy. She opened the half-shut window and drew the curtain. Taking her kinsman by the hand, she exhorted him to bear his sorrow like the good Christian he was. But when she quitted his hand, it fell powerless by his side, nor did he reply.

'Is all over?' asked Jeanie, ashen pale. 'Is there nae hope for her?'

'Nane, or next to nane,' said Mrs Saddletree; 'I heard the Judge say it. It was a burning shame to see them sat up yonder in their red gowns to take the life o' a senseless lassie. The only wise thing I heard was by that decent John Kirk of Kirknowe. He asked them to get the King's mercy. But he might just hae keepit his breath.'

'But *can* the King gie her mercy?' asked Jeanie earnestly. 'Folk tell me he canna gie mercy in cases like hers.'

'He can when he likes! There was him that stabbed the Laird of Ballencleuch and yon Englishman that killed Lady Colgrain's gudeman and the Master of St Clair, that shot the twa Shaws[2] and mony mair. To be sure *they* were of gentle

---

1   Lost his reason. A phrase famously used by Lord Auchinleck about son James Boswell when he heard of his association with Dr Samuel Johnson.

2   In 1828, the Author presented Roxburgh Club with a curious volume, 'Proceedings in the Court-Martial held upon John, Master of Sinclair, for the murder of Ensign Schaw and Captain Schaw, 17 October 1708', Scott.

blood and had their kin to speak for them. And of course there was Jock Porteous just the other day. There's mercy to be had, if folk could only get at it.'

'Porteous?' said Jeanie. 'Very true. Now, fare ye weel, Mrs Saddletree; and may ye never lack a friend in time of distress.'

'Had ye no better stay wi' your father, Jeanie?'

'I will be wanted at the Tolbooth. I maun leave him now, or I will never be able to leave him. I am na feared for his life; I ken how strong-hearted he is.'

'Weel, hinny, if ye think it's for the best, better he rests here than gang back to St Leonard's.'

'God bless you! Dinna let him go till ye hear frae me.'

'But ye'll be back belyve?'[1] said Mrs Saddletree. 'They winna let ye stay yonder, hinny.'

'I maun gang to St Leonard's. There's muckle to be dune, and little time to do it; and I have friends to speak to. God bless ye. Take care of my father.'

She had reached the door of the apartment, when she suddenly turned back and knelt at the bedside.

'Father, gie me your blessing. Say only, "God bless ye and prosper ye".'

The old man murmured a prayer.

'He has blessed my journey,' said his daughter, rising. 'I shall prosper.'

And so saying, she left the room.

Mrs Saddletree looked after her, and shook her head.

'I wish she werena travelling, poor thing; but there's something odd about a' thae Deanses. But she'll be gaun to look after the kye at St Leonard's. Grizzie! Come up here and see the auld man wants naething.'

The maidservant entered. Her mistress stared at her.

'Ye silly *tawpie*! What garr'd ye busk up your cockermony that way? This day has gien an awfa' warning about cockups and fallal duds.[2] See what they a' come to!'

Effie Deans was now locked up and deprived of the several liberties she had enjoyed before sentence was pronounced. When she had remained about an hour in a state of horror, she heard the jarring of the bolts of her cell. Ratcliffe showed himself.

'It's your sister to speak to ye, Effie.'

'I will see naebody.'

'She says she *must* see ye, though,' said Ratcliffe.

Jeanie, rushing into the cell, threw her arms round the neck of her sister. Effie writhed to extricate herself from her embrace.

'Why come here tae greet ower me?' cried Effie, 'You have killed me! One *word* from ye would have saved me. Me that wad give body and soul to save *you* frae hurt!'

'You shall not die,' said Jeanie, with firmness; 'say and think what you like o' me. Only promise me that ye willna harm yourself. You shall not die this shamefu' death.'

'A *shamefu*' death I will not die, Jeanie lass. Gae hame to our father.'

'Oh, this is what I feared!'

'Hinny,' said Ratcliffe; 'it's little ye ken o' thae things. Each ane thinks that

---

[1] Later.

[2] Coiffed hair and fancy clothes.

they wad rather die than bide out the sax weeks tae the gallows; but they bide the sax weeks out for a' that. I ken this weel; thrice hae I fronted the Doomster and here I stand.'

'My sister,' said Jeanie, 'shall come out of this place into the face of the sun. I will go to London and beg her Pardon from the King or the Queen. They pardoned Porteous; they may pardon her. If a sister asks a sister's life on her bended knees, they will pardon her; and they will win a thousand hearts by it.'

Effie listened in astonishment, but so earnest was her sister's assurance that she almost caught a gleam of hope. It instantly faded.

'Jeanie, the King and Queen are in London, a thousand miles from this. I'll be lang gane before ye get there.'

'It is no sae far,' said Jeanie. 'Fareweel. Unless I die on the road, I will see the King's face.'

'Sir,' she said to Ratcliffe, 'be kind to her. She ne'er ken'd what it was to need a stranger's kindness till now. Effie, dinna speak; I maunna greet now.'

She tore herself from her sister's arms and left the cell. Ratcliffe followed her and beckoned her into a small room.

'Listen,' said he, 'I think there's a chance of you carrying the day. But you must *not* go to the King till you have made some friend; try the Duke o'Argyle, *MacCailean Mór.* I ken that the great London folks there dinna muckle like him; but they *fear* him, and that will serve your purpose. D'ye ken ony man wha might gie ye a letter to him?'

'Argyle?' said Jeanie, recollecting herself suddenly, 'what kin is he to the Argyle that was hanged in my father's time; in the persecution?'[1]

'His son or grandson,' said Ratcliffe, 'but what o' that?'

'Thank God!' said Jeanie, devoutly clasping her hands.

'Now, hark ye, hinny. Ye may meet rough customers on the Border or the midlands afore ye get to Lunnon. Nane o' them will touch a frien' o' Daddie Ratton. There's nane ruffler or padder,[2] but he knows my gybe!'[3]

This was unintelligible to Jeanie Deans, now impatient to escape from him. He hastily scrawled a line or two on a dirty piece of paper.

'If this does nae gude, it can do nae ill. Show this paper if you have fasherie wi' ony o' St Nicholas's clerks.'[4]

'Who?'

'I mean if ye fall among thieves, my precious, and that is frae Scripture. They will ken a scart o' my guse feather. And now, awa wi' ye! Stick to Argyle, for if onybody can dae the job, it be him.'

Casting a look at the grated windows and blackened walls of the Tolbooth and another at the lodging of Mrs Saddletree, Jeanie turned her back on that quarter – and then on Edinburgh.

[1] Archibald Campbell, 9th Earl of Argyll (1629–1685) Executed at Edinburgh on The Maiden, a primitive guillotine. Grandfather of the 2nd Duke of Argyll.

[2] Footpad or pedler.

[3] Pass.

[4] St Nicholas was popularly thought to be the patron saint of robbers; hence to 'nick' something meant to steal it.

At St Leonard's Crags she sent for May Hettly, a faithful old servant of her father's, explaining that family circumstances required her to undertake a journey. As this would require weeks away from home, she gave instructions on the management of the house and farm.

'My father will return soon,' she said, 'and all must be in order for him. He has had enough to distress him.'

It was deep in the night when all these matters were settled. May Hettly's cottage being at some distance, she asked Jeanie if she wished her to stay overnight.

'Ye hae had an awfu' day,' she said, 'and sorrow and fear are bad companions in the watches of the night, as I hae heard you father say.'

'Ill companions indeed,' said Jeanie; 'but I maun learn to abide them. Better to begin in this house than in the field.'

She sent May Hettly home.

Jeanie Deans's preparations were brief. Her tartan screen served all the purposes of a riding-habit and of an umbrella; a small bundle contained necessary changes of linen. Barefooted she had come into the world and barefoot would be her pilgrimage. Her clean shoes and snow-white thread stockings were reserved for occasions of ceremony.

From an oaken cabinet, in which her father kept old books and his accounts, she extracted one or two documents which might be of some use in her mission. But the most important difficulty had not occurred to her until that very evening. The lack of money.

David Deans was in comfortable financial circumstances. But his wealth, like that of the patriarchs of old, consisted of his flock and herd and in monies lent out at interest to neighbours or relatives. To such debtors it would be vain to apply. Jeanie also had a conviction that her father, however upright, was too little in touch with the times to judge the actions now needed. Jeanie, no less upright but more flexible, knew that to ask his consent to her pilgrimage would be in vain; accordingly, she would tell him only after her departure. Pecuniary assistance from Deans was thus out of the question. Reuben Butler, of whose assistance she might have been assured, was even poorer than herself.

To surmount this difficulty, she now formed a singular resolution.

chapter twenty-six

'Tis the voice of the sluggard, I've heard him complain,
'You have waked me too soon, I must slumber again;'
As the door on its hinges, so he on his bed,
Turns his side and his shoulders, and his heavy head.

    Dr Isaac Watts; *The Sluggard*

The mansion house of Dumbiedikes lay three miles to the southward of St Leonard's. It once had some celebrity due to the 'auld laird,' whose humour and pranks were often recounted in the ale-houses for miles around it. He wore a sword, kept a good horse and a brace of greyhounds; brawled, swore and laid bets at cock-fights and horse-matches. He also followed Somerville of Drum's hawks and Lord Ross's hounds. But the line had lost its splendour in the present proprietor, who cared for no rustic amusements and was as retired, as his father had been extravagant and daring.

Dumbiedikes was what is called in Scotland a single house; that is, having rooms occupying its whole depth from back to front, each of these apartments being illuminated by six cross lights whose diminutive panes and heavy frames permitted scarcely any light to enter. The edifice had a steep roof flagged with coarse grey stones instead of slates. It also had a half-circular turret, battlemented on the top, which served to encase a narrow turnpike stair, by which ascent was gained from storey to storey. At the bottom of the turret was a door studded with large-headed nails. There was no lobby at the bottom of the tower and scarce a dismounting-place ootside the door.

One or two low and dilapidated outhouses, connected by a courtyard wall, equally ruinous, surrounded the mansion. The court had been paved, but the flags being partly displaced, a gallant crop of docks and thistles had sprung up between them. The small garden which opened by a postern-gate through the wall was little more orderly. Over the low-arched gateway which led into the yard, there was a carved stone exhibiting an attempt at armorial bearings. Above the inner entrance there had hung for many years a mouldering hatchment[1] which announced that the late Laurence Dumbie of Dumbiedikes lay with his fathers in Newbattle kirkyard.

The approach to this palace of pleasure was by a road formed by rude fragments of stone gathered from the fields and was surrounded by ploughed but unenclosed land. Upon a baulk or ploughed ridge of land interposed among the corn, the Laird's trusty palfrey was tethered by the head, picking at a meal of grass. The whole place argued neglect; the consequence, however, of idleness and indifference rather than poverty.

Jeanie Deans stood in the inner courtyard of Dumbiedikes House at an early hour of a fine spring morning. She looked with curiosity at the mansion of which, with a little encouragement, she might have been the mistress. She thought the house, though inferior to Holyrood House or Dalkeith Palace, was still a stately structure in its way and the land a handsome estate, if better tended. But Jeanie Deans was a plain, honest girl. While noting the size of her old admirer's property, she harboured no thought of doing what many would not have hesitated to do to on less temptation.

Her present business being with the Laird, she looked around for a domestic to announce her. All was silence. She ventured to open the door of the old Laird's dog kennel which was now, as two tubs testified, a washing-house. She tried another, a shed where the hawks had been once kept, as appeared from a rotting perch and a lure and jesses mouldering on the wall. A third door led to a well-stocked coal shed; a good fire being one point of domesticity in which Dumbie-

---

[1] From early French *achèvement*, a plaque displaying the armorial bearings and achievements of the deceased. It was placed over the house doors at the level of the second floor for up to a year, when it was removed to the parish kirk.

dikes was active. In all other matters of domestic economy he was completely passive and at the mercy of his housekeeper. This was the same buxom dame whom his father had bequeathed to his charge and who, rumour asserted, had feathered her nest pretty well at his expense.

Jeanie went on opening doors until she came to a stable. That Highland Pegasus, Rory Bean, to whom the single entire stall belonged, was her old acquaintance. She had seen him grazing on the baulk and here was his ancient demi-pique saddle hanging on the walls. Beyond the 'treviss'[1] which formed one side of the stall stood a cow which turned her head and lowed at Jeanie. Understanding this appeal, she shook down some fodder to the neglected animal. While she was doing this, a slipshod wench peeped into the stable. Perceiving a stranger discharging the task she had just quitted her bed to perform, she cried,

'The Brownie, the *Brownie*!' and fled, yelling as if she had seen the Devil.[2]

Her terror was due to the old house of Dumbiedikes being reputedly haunted by a brownie, one of those familiar spirits who were believed to help the ordinary labourer and 'whirl the long mop, and ply the airy flail'.[3]

Supernatural assistance could have been well utilised in this family, whose domestics were averse to personal activity. Jeanie had followed the yelling damsel into the courtyard. There she was confronted by Janet Balchristie.

This person was said by scandal to have been the favourite sultana of the last Laird and was now housekeeper of the present. Formerly good-looking and betwixt forty and fifty at the death of her Sultan, she was now a red-faced dame of seventy. Fond of her place and jealous of her authority, Mrs Balchristie was uneasy about the laird's almost daily visits to St Leonard's Crags. She regarded Jeanie Deans with malevolence. She had also an aversion to any tolerably young and good-looking female approaching the house of Dumbiedikes and the proprietor thereof.

'Wha the Deil are ye?' said the fiery dame to Jeanie, whom she did not recognise, 'scouping about a decent house at sic an hour in the morning?'

'I am wanting to speak with the Laird.'

'Hae ye nae name? D'ye think his honour has naething else to do than to speak wi' ilka idle tramper and him in his bed yet?'

'Mrs Balchristie, d'ye no mind me, Jeanie Deans?'

'Jeanie Deans!' said the astonished termagant; then, taking two strides nearer, she peered into her face with a scornful and malignant stare. 'Jeanie *Deans* indeed! Jeanie *Deevil*, they had better hae ca'ed ye! A bonny spot o' wark your sister and you hae done, murdering a puir wean. Your sister's to be hanged for't, as weel she deserves! And the likes o' *you* coming to an honest man's house, wanting into a bachelor gentleman's bedroom at *this* time in the morning! Get awa', gae *awa*'!

---

[1] A screen.

[2] Brownies are, or were, the Scots equivalent of the Scandinavian *tomte* and the German *Heinzelmännchen*, supernatural domestic sprites who perform household chores, usually at night, in return for small items of food.

[3] Adapted from 'Trail'st the long Mop or whirl'st the mimic Flail', a line on Brownies from *Verses* (1788) by the William Erskine. In these he enjoined the Rev. John Home, author of the famous play *Douglas – a Tragedy*, to celebrate Scots traditions.

If it wasna that your father Deans was our tenant, I would call the men and hae ye dookit in the burn[3] for your impudence!'

Jeanie had already turned her back, and was walking towards the door of the courtyard. However, Mrs Balchristie had raised her stentorian voice to its utmost pitch; and thus lost the engagement.

The Laird had been awakened by his housekeeper's verbal assaults, sounds not uncommon in themselves, but remarkable for their early hour. He had turned over in bed in hopes the squall would blow past when he distinctly heard the word 'Deans'. Aware of Balchristie's malevolence toward the family, he wondered if some message from St Leonard's was the cause of this untimely ire. He slipped into an old brocaded night-gown, clapped on his head his father's gold-laced hat in which, contrary to report, he did not sleep, and opened his bedroom window. To his astonishment, he saw the figure of Jeanie Deans retreating from his gate while his housekeeper sent after her a final volley of oaths. His choler rose.

'Listen tae me,' he roared from the window, 'ye auld limb of *Satan*! Wha the Deil gies ye leave to treat an honest woman that way?'

'But,' Janet stammered, 'I couldna think of disturbing your Honour sae early, when this woman could weel call again. To be sure, I might have mistaken between the twa sisters, for ane o' them wasna creditable.'

'Haud your *peace*, ye auld jade,' shouted Dumbiedikes. 'Jeanie, woman, gang into the parlour. No, wait! It winna be redd up yet! I'll come down to let ye in.'

'Never mind me, lass,' said the chastened housekeeper with a forced laugh. 'A' the warld kens my bark's waur than my bite. If ye had an appointment wi' the Laird, ye should hae tauld me.'

'I had no appointment wi' the Laird,' said Jeanie. 'I want just to speak twa words to him – and I wad rather do it standing right here, Mrs Balchristie.'

The Laird appeared.

'Gang in and get breakfast ready,' he barked at his housekeeper. 'Jeanie, woman, come in and rest ye.'

'No, Laird, I canna gang in. I have a lang day's darg[2] before me. I maun be twenty mile away by the night.'

'God deliver us! *Twenty* mile – and on your *feet*?' cried Dumbiedikes.

'I canna come in, Laird,' replied Jeanie; 'the twa words I have to say to ye I can say here; also, that Mrs Balchristie...'

'The Deil flee *awa* wi' Balchristie!' cried Dumbiedikes, 'and he'll hae a heavy lading o' her! I tell ye, Jeanie Deans, I am a man of few words, but I am laird at hame and afield.'

'Laird,' said Jeanie, entering upon her business, 'I am gaun on a lang journey, outby of my father's knowledge.'

'*Outby* his knowledge, Jeanie? It's no right!' said Dumbiedikes.

'I am for Lunnon, where I will get means to speak to the Queen about my sister's life.'

'Lunnon? The *Queen*?' said Dumbiedikes, amazed. 'The lassie's demented!'

---

[1] Ducked in the stream.

[2] Task.

'I am not. I am indeed to Lunnon, if I must beg my way. And that I maun do, unless ye wad lend me a small sum to pay my expense. A little will do it. Ye ken weel that my father's a man of substance and wad not see you come to a loss by me.'

Dumbiedikes, now understanding the nature of the visit, could scarce believe his ears. He made no answer and stood with his eyes rivetted on the ground.

'I see ye are no for assisting me, Laird. Sae, sae fare ye weel. Gang and see my father as aften as ye can – he will be lonely eneugh now.'

'Where are ye gaun, lass?' said Dumbiedikes, gently. Taking her hand, he led her into the house.

They entered an old-fashioned parlour. The laird dropped her hand, shut the door behind them and fastened it with a bolt. Jeanie, surprised at this manoeuvre, remained near the door. Dumdiedikes now pressed a spring-lock fixed into an oak panel in the wainscot. It slipped aside, revealing an iron strong-box in a recess of the wall. This he opened, pulling out two or three drawers filled with leather bags full of gold and silver coin.

'This is my bank, Jeanie lass,' he said. Then, suddenly changing his tone, he said, 'Jeanie, I will make ye Lady Dumbiedikes afore the sun sets. Ye may then ride to Lunnon in your ain *coach* if ye like.'

'Laird,' said Jeanie, 'that can never be. My sister's situation; the discredit...'

'That's *my* business,' said Dumbiedikes; 'But if your heart's ower fu' at present, tak what will serve ye, and be wed when ye come back.'

'Laird,' said Jeanie gently, seeing the need to be explicit, 'I love another man. I canna marry ye.'

'Another man, Jeanie? How is't possible? It's *no* possible, woman. Ye hae ken'd me sae lang!'

'Laird,' said Jeanie, with persevering simplicity, 'I hae ken'd him *langer*.'

'Langer! It's no possible! It canna be; ye were born on this land. O Jeanie woman, ye haena seen the half o' the gear.' He drew out another drawer. 'A' gowd, Jeanie, and there's bonds for siller lent. And the rental book, Jeanie, clear three hunder sterling and no debt! And then my mother's wardrobe, and my grand-mother's; silk gowns, pearline-lace as fine as spiders' webs; and rings, earrings. They are a' in my chamber. Oh, Jeanie, gang up the stair and look at them!'

Jeanie held fast.

'It canna be. Laird, I am *promised*. I canna break my word.'

'Your *word* to him,' said the Laird, 'but wha is he, Jeanie?'

'Reuben Butler.'

'Reuben *Butler*!' echoed Dumbiedikes, pacing the apartment, 'Butler, the *dominie* at Liberton. The son of my *cottar*! He hasna the price o' the auld black coat he wears. But it disna matter...' As he spoke he shut, successively and with vehemence, the drawers of his treasury. 'A fair offer, Jeanie, is nae cause of feud. And as for wasting my substance on other folks...'

The last nettled Jeanie's pride.

'I was *begging* naething,' she said. 'Gude morning to ye, sir. Ye hae been kind to my father and it isna in my heart to think of ye other than kindly.' And so saying, she left the room.

She traversed the courtyard with a quick step, glowing with the shame which an honest mind feels at having asked a favour and being refused. Out of the Laird's property and back upon the public road, her pace slackened. Her indignation also cooled as the consequences of her disappointment began to loom. Must she then actually beg her way to London? Such seemed the alternative. Should she turn back and solicit her father for money? By doing so she would lose precious time besides receiving his prohibition of the journey. She saw no compromise between these alternatives and, walking slowly on, she meditated whether it were not better to return home.

Suddenly, she heard the clatter of horse's hoofs and a well-known voice calling her name. She looked round and saw trotting towards her a pony whose bare back and halter were at odds with the nightgown, slippers, and cocked-hat of the cavalier. It was Dumbiedikes. In the energy of his pursuit he had overcome even the Highland obstinacy of Rory Bean, even compelling that self-willed steed to a canter. This, however, Rory did with the greatest reluctance, accompanying every pace with a sideways motion indicating his determination to turn around, a manoeuvre resisted by the Laird's heels and cudgel.

Coming up with Jeanie, his first words were, 'Jeanie, they say ye shouldna take a woman at her first word!'

'Aye, but ye maun take me at mine, Laird,' said Jeanie, looking at the ground and walking on.

'Then,' said Dumbiedikes, 'ye suldna aye take a man at his first word. Ye maunna gang sillerless, come o't what ye like.'

He put a purse into her hand.

'I wad gie you Rory too, but he's as wilfu' as yoursell!'

'Laird,' said Jeanie, 'though my father will repay every penny of this, I wadna borrow frae a man that wants something mair than the paying back.'

'There's twenty-five guineas there,' said Dumbiedikes with a sigh, 'and whether your father pays or disna pay, I make ye free without another word. Gang where ye like; *do* what ye like; mairry a' the Butlers in the *country* if ye like – and gude morning to you, Jeanie Deans.'

'Laird, God bless you,' said Jeanie, her heart softened by such generosity. 'And the Lord's peace to you, suld we never meet again!'

Dumbiedikes turned and waved his hand. Rory Bean, now more than willing, hurried off homeward so fast that Dumbiedikes, lacking bridle, saddle and stirrups, was too occupied keeping his seat to permit the backward look of a forlorn lover. The sight of him careering off in nightgown, slippers and a laced hat on a bareback Highland pony confirmed Jeanie's original sentiment.

'He's a gude and a kind creature,' said she.

chapter twenty-seven

What strange and wayward thoughts will slide
Into a lover's head;
'O mercy!' to myself I cried,
'If Lucy should be dead!'

Wordsworth & Coleridge, *Lyrical Ballads*

Pursuing her solitary journey from the house of Dumbiedikes, Jeanie gained a little rise from which she saw to the eastward a brook, its meanders shaded with straggling willows and alders. Beyond it she could see the haunts of her early life, the cottages of Woodend and Beersheba. There was the common on which she had herded, and the rivulet where she and Butler had pulled rushes to plait crowns for Effie. The recollection was bitter.

'But fine I ken'd,' said Jeanie, when she later gave an account of her pilgrimage, 'that greeting would do little good. It was mair beseeming to thank the Lord for showing me a man that mony ca'd a Nabal[1] and a churl, but wha was as generous to me as a fountain to a stream. And I minded the sin of Israel at Meribah[2] when the people complained, although Moses had brought water from the dry rock that they might drink and live. Sae, I wad not trust mysell with another look at Woodend and the blue reek[3] that came from it.'

She pursued her journey. It led her towards Liberton with its old-fashioned church among a tuft of trees on a ridge south of Edinburgh. Close by the village was a clumsy square tower, the residence of the Laird of Liberton. The village did not lie precisely in Jeanie's road towards England, but it was the home of Butler. She had resolved to ask him to write to her father about her expedition and hopes; moreover, she simply wished to see him before her perilous pilgrimage.

Another thought pressed on her mind as she approached the village. She had looked anxiously for Butler in the courthouse, but in vain. She knew that he was under a degree of legal restraint but had hoped that he would have secured release for the day. She wondered if he might be ill – and her fears were justified.

Butler, his constitution not strong, did not recover quickly from the mental distress of the Porteous affair. Official suspicion aggravated matters, to which was added the Magistrates' prohibition of any communication with Deans or his family. It had appeared likely to them that Butler might procure a meeting between the family and Robertson, and this they were anxious to prevent or intercept. The measure pressed cruelly hard on Butler, who realised he must now be seen as a deserter by the person dearest to him.

A succession of feverish attacks had also rendered him incapable of the teaching duties on which his bread depended. However, the Principal of the parish

---

[1] I. Samuel 25:3. Now the name of the man was Nabal and of his wife Abigail; she was a woman of good understanding and beautiful but the man was surly and evil in his doings. (King James Version).

[2] Exodus 17.7.

[3] Blue smoke.

school was sincerely attached to Butler for greatly raising its credit. This ancient pedagogue retained a taste for the classics and would relax, after the school day was over, by conning over a few pages of Horace or Juvenal with his assistant. Seeing Butler's debility with compassion, he taught the school himself, insisting that Reuben rest and recuperate.

Such was Butler's situation, scarcely able to drag himself over to the school and fearful over the fate of those dearest to him. Then came the trial and condemnation of Effie Deans to put the copestone upon his misery. He heard a particular account of these events, from a fellow in the village who had been present. Sleep was impossible for most of that night, while in the morning he was awakened from a feverish slumber by a visit from Bartoline Saddletree. He had two children boarded at the Liberton school and liked Butler's company. If anything could have added gall to bitterness, it was Saddletree's prosing account of the trial of Effie Deans and the probability of her being executed. The words fell on Butler's ear like the clang of the death bell.

While this was going on, the cottage which her fiancé rented was being indicated to Jeanie by a lass with a milk pail on her head. She paused at the door on hearing the pompous tones of Saddletree coming from the inner apartment.

'It will be sae, Butler. She maun gang down the Bow wi' the lad in the pioted coat.[1] I am sorry for the lassie, but the Law maun hae its course; *Vivat Rex, Currat Lex*, as the poet Horace has it, in whilk of his Odes I know not.'[2]

Butler groaned. Saddletree, however, poured forth his legal knowledge without mercy. He concluded by saying to Butler, 'Was it na a pity my father didna send me to the University at Utrecht? Wad I no hae been a *clarissimus ictus*, eh?'

'I really do not understand you, Saddletree,' said Butler faintly.

'No understand me, man? *Ictus* is Latin for a lawyer, is it not?'

'Not that I heard of.'

'The Deil ye didna! Man, I got the word this very morning out of a legal memorial. See, there it is, *ictus clarissimus et perti – peritissimus*. It's a' Latin, for it is in Italic type.'

'*Ictus* is the abbreviation for *juris-consultus*, Latin for lawyer.'

'Dinna tell me that, man. There's nae abbreviates except in adjudications; and this is a' about a servitude of water-drap – that is to say, *tillicidian*,[3] but maybe ye'll say *that's* no Latin neither?'

'Very likely. I am unwell and unable to argue with you.'

'Few folk are, Mr Butler. Now, as ye're no weel, I'll sit wi' you to divert ye and explain t'ye the nature of a tillicidian.

'The petitioner, Mrs Crombie, a decent woman, lives in a ground floor tenement or laigh house. All of us wha live at ground level are burdened wi' the

---

1   The magpie coat of the executioner, his livery being black and silver.

2   'May the King live, may the Law take its course.' A line from Act IV.1 of *The History of Sir John Oldcastle* (1600) attributed to Shakespeare in the *Third Folio*, but probably a collaboration. The Surname of Falstaff was originally Oldcastle. It is *not* Horace.

3   He meant *stillicidium*; a dripping of water from the eaves, from Latin: *stilla*, a drop and *cadere*, to fall. The term was originally given by Vitruvius in *de architectura* to the dripping eaves of the roof of an Etruscan temple.

tillicide, that is, that we are obligated to receive the natural waterfall from the superior tenement, whether it be the rain from Heaven falling on our neighbour's house, and from thence by the gutters down to our laigh tenement. Now, the other night a Highland servant lass hurls God *kens* what out of the superior tenement, right on to Mrs Crombie! The lass had shouted *Gardyloo!* out of the *wrang* window,[1] out of respect for twa Highlandmen speaking the Gaelic below the *right* ane...'

This account might have gone on, had not Saddletree been interrupted by voices at the door. Butler's landlady, returning with her pitcher from the well, found Jeanie at her door, impatient at the harangue of Saddletree yet unwilling to enter until he was done or, preferably, gone.

'Was ye wanting the gudeman or me, lass?'

'I wanted to speak with Mr Butler.'

'Gang in by then,' answered the goodwife. She opened the door of a room, announcing, 'Mr Butler, here's a lass to speak t'ye.'

'Good God!' he said, starting from his chair.

'Reuben,' said Jeanie. 'But oh, ye look so ill!'

'No: I am well... quite well,' said Butler. 'Jeanie, can I do anything for you or your father?'

'Jeanie, lass,' said Saddletree, 'what brings you out to Liberton sae early in the morning, and your father lying ill in the Luckenbooths?'

'I want to speak with Mr. Butler about some business of my father and Effie.'

'Is it law business?' said Saddletree; 'because if it is, ye had better take *my* opinion on the subject.'

'It is *not*,' said Jeanie, who had no intention of letting Saddletree into the secret of her journey. She looked at Butler and wrung her hands with impatience.

'Mr Saddletree,' said Butler, 'you will want to hear your sons called up to their lessons.'

'Indeed, Mr Butler. I promised to ask a half day holiday for the schule. The bairns might then gang and see a hanging, which canna but have a good effect on their young minds. Butler, keep Jeanie here till I come back.' He departed.

'Reuben,' said Jeanie urgently, 'I am gaun on a lang journey. I am for London to ask Effie's life of the King and Queen Caroline.'

'Jeanie. Surely not!' said Butler in total surprise.

'And what for no, Reuben? It's but speaking to a mortal man and woman. Their hearts are flesh and blood and Effie's story wad melt them if were they stane.'

'But Jeanie, the difficulty of getting an audience!'

'I have thought of that, Reuben, and it shall not break my spirit. I will have something within me that will keep my heart from failing.'

'Jeanie! Kings do not sit at their gates nowadays to dispense justice as in patriarchal times. King George does everything by means of his ministers.'

---

[1] 'Gardyloo!' Edinburgh's version of the French *'Gare de l'eau!'* (Beware the water!). This was the dreaded cry sent down to pedestrians from housemaids about to empty out brimming receptacles of the day's liquid (and solid) human waste.

'And nae doubt he has a great number o' them. But I'll be decently dressed and I'll offer a trifle o' siller at the gates, as if I came to see the palace. And if they cavil at that, I'll tell them I'm come on a business of life and death. Then they will surely bring me in to speech with the King and Queen Caroline?' Butler shook his head.

'Jeanie, this is a wild dream. You could only see them through some great Lord's intercession.'

'Maybe I can get that,' said Jeanie, 'with a little help from you.'

'From *me*?'

'Aye. Havena I heard you say that your grandfather did some service lang syne[1] to a forbear of this *MacCailean Mór*, Argyle's Duke, when he was Lord of Lorn?'

'He did *indeed*,' said Butler, '*and* I can prove it. I could write to the Duke. Report speaks of him as a good man and a brave. I will beg him to intercede for your sister. There is but a poor chance of success, but we must try all means.'

'Indeed we must try, but *writing* winna do it. A letter canna beseech as the human voice can. A letter's like the music on a spinet; naething but a black score, compared to the same tune sung. It's word of mouth maun do it, Reuben.'

'Right,' said Butler. 'But Jeanie, you must not take on this perilous journey alone. You must give me a husband's right to protect you.'

'Reuben, I fear it cannot be. A pardon will not gie back my sister her good name or make me a fitting bride for a minister.'

'But Jeanie I do not believe Effie guilty. And blame, even if justly laid on her, does not fall on *you*.'

'Reuben, ye ken weel; it is a blot that spreads to kith and kin. Good repute has gane frae us a'.'

'Jeanie, think of your word. Your engagement to me. Would you undertake such a journey without a protector, and who should that be but your husband?'

'Reuben, this is no time to be given in marriage. If it's to be, it maun be in a better season. Ye speak of protecting me, but who will protect *you*? Your limbs tremble with standing just ten minutes; how could you undertake a journey to Lunnon?'

'But I am strong... I am well.'

'Let me depart,' said Jeanie. 'It's a grief to see you like this, but keep up your heart for my sake. If I am not to be your wife, I'll never be wife to a living man. Gie me the letter for this *MacCailean Mór* and bid me God speed.'

Butler did so and put into her hands the paper she desired. Together with the muster-roll in which it was folded up, it was his sole relic of his grandfather, the stern Bible Butler.

'Now Reuben, write to my father. God help me, I have neither head nor hand for lang letters. I trust him entirely to you; and I trust you will be able to see him soon. And remember the auld man's ways for Jeanie's sake! Dinna speak in Latin to him, but start him speaking himself, for he'll hae mair comfort that way. And finally Reuben, the poor lass in yon dungeon! Gie her what comfort ye can, as soon as they let ye see her. God bless ye, Reuben!'

---

[1] Long ago. As in Burns's *Auld Lang Syne*.

And with an affectionate smile, she was gone.

Butler picked up the Bible, the last book which Jeanie had been touching. To his surprise, a paper containing two or three gold coins dropped from the book. With a black lead pencil, she had marked Psalm 37:

A little that a righteous man hath, is better than the riches of the wicked.

Deeply impressed, he pressed the gold to his lips. To emulate her devout firmness was now his ambition, and his first task was to write to David Deans. He described his daughter's journey southward, his letter using every phrase which might reconcile the old man to her extraordinary expedition.

chapter twenty-eight

My native Land – Good Night!
Lord Byron, *Childe Harold's Pilgrimage*, Canto I. IV

Her heart strong and her frame patient of fatigue, Jeanie Deans travelled at a daily rate of twenty miles and sometimes more. She thus traversed the southern part of Scotland, crossed the Border and advanced as far as Durham.

Hitherto she had been either among her own country-folk, or those to whom her bare feet and tartan shawl were objects too familiar to attract attention. However, as she advanced, she began to note sarcasm and taunts. Although she thought it inhospitable to sneer at the attire of a passing stranger, she had the sense to alter those parts of her dress attracting observation. Her shawl was deposited carefully in her bundle and she conformed to the English habit of wearing shoes and stockings for the whole day. With these changes she had little, as she said, to mark her out, except her accent. This drew so many jests couched in a far stronger patois than her own, that she soon found it was in her interest to talk as seldom as possible. Thus she answered civil salutations of passers-by with a civil courtesy. She found the common people of England by no means deficient in hospitality. She readily obtained food and overnight accommodations at very moderate rates, which sometimes mine host declined with a blunt:

'Thee hast a long way afore thee, lass; and I'se ne'er take penny out o' a single woman's purse.' It often happened that mine hostess, struck with 'the tidy, nice Scotch body', procured her an escort, or a seat in a wagon for some part of the way, or gave advice on resting-places.

At York, the pilgrim stopped for the best part of a day, partly to recruit her strength and partly because she had the good luck to obtain lodging at an inn kept by a countrywoman. There she wrote to her father and to Reuben Butler:

Dearest Father,

I make my present pilgrimage more burdensome as it is without your knowledge, which God knows was far contrary to my heart. Nevertheless, I must help my poor sister otherwise I was not, for wealth or for world's gear have done this without your knowledge.

Dear father, speak a word or write to comfort Effie. If she has sinned, she has also sorrowed and suffered, and ye ken that we maun forgie others, as we pray to be forgien.

Dear father, forgive my saying this muckle, for it becomes not a young head to instruct grey age; but fain wad I hear that ye had forgien Effie her trespass.

The folk here are civil, and hae shown me much kindness; they hae some Kirks without organs like ours, and are called meeting-houses, where the minister preaches withouten a gown! Most of the country are Episcopal and I saw twa men that were Ministers following hounds, as bauld as Roslin or Dryden, that young Laird of Loup-the-dyke, or ony wild gallant in Lothian. A sorrowfu' sight!

Dear father,
remember in your prayers your affectionate
daughter to command,
Jean Deans

A postscript said:

When I reach Lunnon, I intend to gang to our cousin Mrs Glass at the sign o' the Thistle, wha sends up your snuff. As she must be well kend in Lunnon, I doubt not to find her.

Mr Reuben Butler, York.

Hoping this will find you better, it comes to say that I have reached this great City safe. I am not wearied with the walking, but the better for it. And I have seen many things which I trust to tell you one day, also the muckle Kirk of this place; and all around the city are mills, whilk havena muckle wheels nor mill-dams, but gang by the wind.

I keep the straight road, and just beck if onybody speaks to me ceevilly, and answer naebody with the tongue but women.

Reuben, I wish I kend onything that wad mak ye weel, for they hae mair medicines in this town of York than wad cure a' Scotland. Keep a good heart, for we are in the hands of He that kens better what is gude for us than we ken oursells. To ken, as I do, that a purpose is right makes the heart strong and is the way to get through the warst of days.

I sall tell ye by writing how I get on wi' the Duke of Argyle when I win to Lunnon. Direct a line, to tell me how ye are, to Mrs Margaret Glass, tobacconiste, at the Sign of the Thistle, Lunnon.

That it be God's pleasure that we may meet again in joy, even on this hither side of Jordan, is the wish of her that is your servant to command,

Jeanie Deans

She sealed her letters carefully and put them into the Post Office with her own hand, enquiring when they were likely to reach Edinburgh. This duty performed, she accepted her Scottish landlady's invitation to remain till the next morning.

Mrs Bickerton, landlady of the Seven Stars in the Castle-gate, York, was a Merse woman.[1] She displayed kindness to her guest and showed such anxiety over her farther progress that Jeanie, though by nature cautious, told her the whole story. Mrs Bickerton raised her hands and eyes in wonder and pity at the recital. She asked about the strength of Jeanie's purse, now reduced to about fifteen pounds by her deposit to Butler at Liberton and by the expense of her journey.

'This would do very well,' she said, 'providing, Jeanie, ye carry it a' to London safe from highwaymen, for ye are going into a more roguish country than the North. Take my advice and hide the gold in thy stays; but keep a piece or two and some silver ready, just in case, for there's bad lads haunting the roads a day's walk from hence... And, lass, dinna gang through Lunnon, asking wha kens Mrs Glass at the sign o' the Thistle! Gang to this honest man.' She put a name and address into Jeanie's hand. 'He kens maist of the Scots in the city. He will find your friend for thee.'

Jeanie took the letter with thanks. Alarmed by the mention of highway robbers, she recalled what Ratcliffe had said to her and gave his paper to Mrs Bickerton. The Lady of the Seven Stars whistled on a silver call, which hung by her side. A serving maid entered the room.

'Tell Dick Ostler to come here.'

Dick Ostler accordingly made his appearance; a shambling creature with a hatchet-face, a game-arm and a limp.

'Ostler,' said Mrs Bickerton, 'thou knowest most people and most things o' the road.'

'Aye, God help me, mistress.'

'Then what is in this paper, man?' she said, handing him the protection which Ratcliffe had given Jeanie. Dick looked at the paper, scratched his head powerfully, and said,

'Ay – maybe I ken summat, mistress.'

'Speak!'

'Why, then,' said Dick, giving the head-band of his breeches a hoist with one hand, 'I dare say this lad's pass will be weel kend on the road.'

'And what sort of a lad was he?' said Mrs Bickerton, winking to Jeanie.

'Jim the Rat? Why he was Cock o' the North within this twelmonth; he and that Wilson, Handle Dandie as they called him. But he's been out o' this country a while, as I reckon; but ony gentleman, as keeps the road[2] this side o' Stamford, will respect Jim's pass.'

The landlady filled Ostler a bumper. He ducked his head and shoulders, bolted the alcohol and left.

'So, Jeanie,' said Mrs Bickerton, 'if thou meetest with ugly customers on the road, show them this bit paper, for it will serve thee.'

Mrs Bickerton, saying that payment was out of the question, furnished Jeanie with credentials to her correspondent in London and to several Inns upon the road. She also reminded her to conceal her money. Finally, she and made her

---

[1]   The Merse is the fertile plain of Berwickshire south of the Lammermuir hills.

[2]   ie any 'road-agent' or highwayman.

promise to revisit the Seven Stars on her way home to Scotland and relate all that had passed.

Jeanie promised so to do.

chapter twenty-nine

And Need and Misery, Vice and Danger, bind,
In sad alliance, each degraded mind.
　　　　　George Crabbe, *The Borough – the Poor*

As our traveller set out early on the ensuing morning Dick Ostler holloed out after her.

'The top of the morning to you, Moggie. Have a care o' Gunderby Hill, young one. Robin Hood's dead and gone, but there be robbers and takers yet in the Vale of Belvoir!'

Jeanie looked at him to request a farther explanation, but Dick had turned back to the steed he was currying and sang as he employed comb and brush:

Robin Hood was a yeoman good,
His bow was trusty yew;
And if Robin said 'stand' on the King's lea-land,
Why should we not too?

Jeanie set out without farther inquiry. A painful day's journey brought her to the Swan at Ferrybridge, the best inn upon the Great Northern Road. An introduction from Mrs Bickerton procured her a pillion and post-horse returning to Tuxford, her longest day's journey yet. She was fatigued by this unaccustomed mode of travelling and it was considerably later than usual next morning that she resumed her pilgrimage.

At noon, the hundred-armed river Trent and the blackened ruins of Newark Castle, demolished in the great Civil War, lay before her. Jeanie had no antiquarian curiosity and went straight to the Saracen's Head in Newark, the inn recommended at Ferrybridge. There she observed a servant girl looking at her several times with fixed and peculiar interest. Then, to her surprise, the girl inquired: 'Is your name Deans, a Scotchwoman going to London upon justice business?'

Jeanie asked whence came the questions. The girl said, 'Two women passed through this morning, making inquiries after one Jeanie Deans travelling to London. They could scarce be persuaded that she had not yet arrived.'

Surprised and somewhat alarmed, Jeanie questioned the wench about the appearance of the two women, but could only learn that the one was aged and the other young; the latter was the taller, while the former talked most and with authority over her companion. Both spoke with the Scots accent.

This conveyed little information, but with a presentiment of evil, Jeanie decided to take post-horses for the next stage, but the landlord could not accommodate her. After waiting in the fruitless hope that a pair of horses that had gone southward would return in time for her use, she resolved to continue on foot.

'It was all plain road,' she was assured, 'except Gunnerby Hill about three miles from Grantham,' which would be her stage for the night.

'I'm glad to hear there's a hill,' said Jeanie, 'for baith my sight and my very feet are weary o' this level ground.'

'If thee's that fond o' hills,' said mine host, 'I carena if thou carries Gunnerby away with thee! It's a murder to my post-horses. But here's to thy journey, for thou is a bold and a canny lass.'

He took a powerful pull at a tankard of ale.

'I hope there is nae bad company on the road, sir?' said Jeanie.

'But there are na sae many footpads now, since they lost Jim the Rat.'

Jeanie resumed her solitary walk. She was alarmed when twilight overtook her in the open ground, intersected with patches of copse and swamps, which extends to the foot of Gunnerby Hill. Common land along the Great North Road is now enclosed, but was then poorly policed and exposed the traveller to a risk of highway robbery. Aware of this, Jeanie slowed her pace when she heard a horse behind and drew to one side of the road to allow the rider to pass. She saw that the horse carried two women, one riding side-saddle and the other on a pillion behind her.

'A braw good-night to ye, Jeanie Deans,' said the foremost female. 'What think ye o' yon bonny hill yonder, lifting its brow to the moon? D'ye think yon's the gate to the Heaven ye're sae fain of?'

The speaker kept changing her seat in the saddle. The woman behind her snapped,

'Hand your tongue, ye moon-raised bitch! What is your business Heaven or Hell?'

'Mither, it's no Heaven but Hell I fear, considering wha I carry ahint me. Come, naggie. Trot on, for a witch rides thee.' She hummed:

> With my curtch on my Foot, and my Shoe on my hand,
> I glance like the wildfire through Burgh and through Land...

The tramp of the horse and increasing distance drowned the rest of her song, but for some time Jeanie heard the sounds ring across the waste. The pilgrim was stunned with apprehension. To be called by name in such a manner and in a strange country by such a person flitting before her seemed almost supernatural. She had not advanced much farther, however, when there came a new and more immediate terror.

Two men started up as she advanced and met her on the road.

'Stand and deliver!' said one menacingly, a short stout fellow in a smock-frock.

'The woman,' said the other, a tall, thin figure, 'does not understand. Your money my precious, or your life.'

'I have very little,' said Jeanie, offering the portion she had kept apart for just such an emergency.

'This won't do, girl!' said the shorter ruffian; 'do ye think we hazard our lives to be cheated? Every farthing you have got, or we will strip you to the skin!'

His companion said, 'No, no, Tom, this is one of the precious sisters. Take her word without the stripping. Hark ye, lass. Look to Heaven, and say this is the last penny you have about ye; and maybe we'll let you pass.'

'Stop!' cried Jeanie, Ratcliffe's pass suddenly occurring to her; 'perhaps you know this paper.'

'What the Devil's this, Frank?' said the more savage ruffian. 'Look at it.'

'A jark from Jim Ratcliffe,' said the other, 'Let the wench go.'

'No! Rat has turned bloodhound.'

'We may yet need a good turn from him all the same.'

'But we promised to strip the wench and send her begging back to her own beggarly country; and now you are for letting her go!'

'For the love of God!' cried Jeanie. 'Dinna ask me to leave the road!'

'What art tha afraid of?' demanded the brutal one, 'Either you come with us, or I'll beat your brains out where you stand.'

'Thou'rt a rough bear, Tom,' said his companion. 'Touch her and I'll rattle thy guts. Never mind him, girl; he will not lay a finger on you if you come quietly.'

Jeanie saw in him of the milder mood, her only protection. She not only followed him, but held him by the sleeve, lest he should escape from her.

They conducted their prisoner along a track. After half an hour's walking in silence, they approached an old barn at the edge of cultivated ground, but remote from any habitation. There was a light in the windows.

One of the footpads scratched at the door. It was opened by a female. They entered. An old woman, preparing food by the assistance of a charcoal fire, demanded in the name of the Devil, what they brought the wench there for and why they had not stripped her and turned her abroad on the common?

'Come, Mother Blood,' said the tall man, 'we'll oblige you, but no more.'

'She has got a jark from Ratcliffe,' said the short fellow, 'so Frank here won't put her through the mill.'

'No, that I will not, by God!' answered Frank; 'but if old Mother Blood keeps her here for a while, or sends her back to Scotland, I see no harm in that.'

'I'll tell *you* what, Frank Levitt,' said the old woman, picking up a knife, 'call me Mother Blood again and I'll plant this gully in you!'

'Mother Blood,' said Frank, 'that puts me out of humour.'

Without hesitation, the old fury hurled her knife at him. He ducked. It whistled past his ear and stuck deep in the clay wall behind.

'Mother,' he said, seizing her by both wrists, 'I'll teach you who's master!' He forced the hag backwards until she sank on a bunch of straw. Letting go of her hands, he held up a menacing finger towards her. This appeared to work; she did not attempt to rise but stared with impotent rage.

'I promise you, old Devil,' said Frank; 'the wench shall not go on the London road, but I will not have you touch a hair of her head!'

Meanwhile, another female personage was added to the party.

'Now, Frank Levitt,' said the newcomer, entering with a hop, step and jump, 'were ye killing our mother, or were ye slitting the grunter's weasand[1] that Tam brought this morning?'

Jeanie immediately recognised the voice of the woman riding foremost of the pair which passed her before she met the robbers.

---

[1] The pig's throat.

'Out, ye mad Devil!' said Tom, disturbed in a draught of liquor, 'betwixt your Bess of Bedlam pranks, and your dam's frenzies, a man might live quieter with the Devil!' He resumed drinking from the broken jug.

'And what's *this*?' said Madge Wildfire. 'Douce Davie Deans's daughter in a gipsy barn, and the night setting in! This is a sight for sair een. Ah, sirs, the falling off o' the godly! And the other sister in the Tolbooth! Sorry I am for her; it's my mother that wishes her ill, no me; though maybe I hae as muckle cause...'

'Madge,' said Frank Levitt, 'take this lass to your kennel!'

'That I will,' said Madge, taking hold of Jeanie's arm and pulling her along; 'decent Christian young leddies like her and me dinna keep company wi' the like o' you and Tyburn Tam at this time o' night. Gude e'en to ye, sirs, and may ye sleep till the hangman waukens ye!' Madge suddenly dropped to her knees and, in the manner of a child, said to her mother,

'Mammie, hear me say my prayers before I go to bed as ye used to do – and say God bless my bonny face.'

'The Deil flay the *hide* o' ye to sole his brogues!' shouted her mother, aiming a punch at the supplicant.

The blow missed, but the old crone seized a pair of fire tongs and would have beaten out her brains, had not Levitt seized her by the shoulder and flung her down exclaiming, 'Madge of Bedlam, get to your hole!'

Madge took the advice. She retreated as fast as she could, Jeanie along with her, into a recess partitioned off from the rest of the barn and filled with straw. The moonlight shone through an open window upon a pillion, a pack-saddle and one or two wallets,[1] the travelling kit of Madge and her amiable mother.

'Now, did ye e'er see in your life,' said Madge, 'sae dainty a chamber? See how the moon shines down on the fresh strae! There's no a pleasanter cell in Bedlam... Were ye ever in Bedlam?'

'No,' answered Jeanie faintly, appalled by the question. Yet she wished to soothe her companion, since even this madwoman seemed to offer a degree of protection.

'*Never* in Bedlam?' said Madge. 'But ye'll hae been in the cells at Edinburgh?'

'Never!'

'I sometimes think thae daft carles of Magistrates send naebody to Bedlam but me. Whenever I am brought before them, thae aye hae me back to Bedlam. But to tell ye my private mind about it, I think ye are at nae great loss. The Tolbooth keeper's a cross-patch[2] and the daftest in the house. Listen! What are they makin' sic a noise for? None o' them gets in here – it wadna be mensfu'![3] I'll sit wi' my back agin the door. It winna be easy stirring *me*!'

Madge arranged herself for sleep on the straw in a half-sitting posture with her back resting against the door.

'Wha but mysell wad hae thought, Jeanie,' said Madge Wildfire, 'of making a bolt of my ain backbone? But this door's no sae strong as yon o' the Tolbooth.

---

[1]   Knapsacks.
[2]   An evil-tempered person.
[3]   Decorous, discreet.

The hammermen of Edinburgh beat the warld in making ring-bolts, fetter-bolts, bars and locks. And they arena that bad at girdles for carcakes neither.[1] My mother had ance a bonny Cu'ross girdle. I thought to have baked carcakes on it for my puir wean that's dead and gane. But we maun a' dee, ye ken, Jeanie. But touching Bedlam, I'd never recommend it! But ye ken what the sang says?'

Pursuing the wanderings of her mind, she sang:

In the bonny cells of Bedlam
Ere I was ane-and-twenty,
I had hempen bracelets strang,
And merry whips, ding-dang,
And prayer and fasting plenty.

'Weel, Jeanie, I am hoarse the night, and I canna sing mair. Troth, I think I am to sleep.'

She drooped her head on her breast, a posture from which Jeanie was careful not to disturb her. However, after nodding for a minute or so with eyes half-closed, her unquiet spirit again assailed Madge. She raised her head and spoke, but with a lowered tone, gradually overcome by the fatigue of a day's journey on horseback.

'I dinna ken what makes me sae sleepy. I never sleep till my bonny Lady Moon gangs till her bed when she's at the full, yonder in her grand silver coach. I have danced to her alone for very joy. And whiles dead folk came and danced wi' me; the like o' Jock Porteous or those I ken'd when I was living... for ye maun ken I was ance dead mysell...' Then, in a low wild tone she sang:

My banes are buried in yon kirkyard
Sae far ayont the sea,
And it is but my blithesome ghaist
That's speaking now to thee.

'But after a', Jeanie my woman, naebody kens weel wha's living and wha's dead; or wha's gone to Fairyland; there's another question. Whiles I think my puir bairn's dead; I ken very weel it's buried; but that means naething. I have had it on my knee a hundred times since it was buried; and how could that be if it were dead, ye ken?' And here she burst into a fit of crying, sobbing herself into a deep sleep.

Jeanie was left to her own melancholy thoughts.

---

[1] A small cake baked on a girdle; eaten on Shrove Tuesday in parts of Scotland.

chapter thirty

Bind her quickly; or, by this steel,
I'll tell, although I truss for company.
    Fletcher, *The Coxcomb*

The imperfect light which shone through the window enabled Jeanie to see that there was scarcely any chance of making her escape by that route. The aperture was high in the wall and anyway too narrow. She then looked at the clay partition, which divided the hovel in which she now was, from the rest of the barn. It was decayed and full of chinks, one of which she noiselessly enlarged with her fingers. This obtained her a plain view of the old hag and the taller footpad, Levitt, in close conference. She was alarmed at the sight of the hideous old woman with her hardened and inveterate malice. Jeanie was now able to overhear part of their conversation. The man was saying:

'Now, dame, I am loyal to my friend. I have not forgot that you planted a chury[1] which saw me through the bars of the Castle of York – and one good turn deserves another. But now that Madge is asleep, tell me what all this is about. Tell me too what's to be done, for damn me if I touch the girl or let her be touched; she has Jim Rat's *pass*!'

'Frank,' said the old woman, 'thou'rt too good for thy trade; thy tender heart will get thee into trouble. This girl is going to London...' the rest was lost, Jeanie being able only to distinguish the word 'sister.' Levitt answered in a louder tone,

'Fair enough; but what is *your* business with it?'

'Business enough. If the bitch dodges the noose, that silly cull Robertson will marry her.'

'And who cares if he does?' said the man.

'Who cares, ye donnard? *I* care! I will strangle her with my own hands if he prefers her to Madge.'

'*Madge*? You're *blind* if ye think he'd ever marry Madge? Marry Madge Wildfire; that's a good one.'

'Listen, ye born and bred thief. Suppose he never marries Madge, is that a reason he should marry another in her place, with Madge crazed and I a beggar – and all due to *him*? But I know something that *will* hang him!'

'Then *let* them hang him!' said Frank contemptuously. 'There's more more sense in that than wreaking yourself on two girls that have done you nor Madge no ill.'

'No ill? And he to marry this jailbird, if ever she gets loose!'

'But there's no *chance* of his marrying a bird of your brood! I cannot for my soul, see what you have to *do* with all this.'

'Would you go nae length for *revenge*? The sweetest morsel ever cooked in Hell. I have wrought hard for it; I have suffered and sinned for it; and, by heaven I will *have* it!'

---

[1]   Concealed a knife.

Levitt had lighted a pipe as he listened to these vindictive ravings, too hardened to be shocked but unable to understand.

'But, mother,' he said, after a pause, 'surely if revenge is your wish, you should take it on this Robertson fellow himself.'

'I cannot.'

'Why not?'

'Because I nursed him at this withered breast,' answered the old woman, folding her hands on her bosom, as if pressing an infant to it, 'and though he proved an adder to me and mine, yet I cannot take his life. He was the first bairn I ever nursed and no man can ever ken what a woman feels for the first bairn at her bosom!'

'To be sure,' said Levitt, 'but they say you havena been so kind to other bairns that have come in your way. Now, never lay your hand on your whittle,[1] for I am leader here and I will have no rebellion.'

The hag, who had grasped a large knife, now let it fall by her side.

'Bairns! Ye are joking, lad; wha wad touch bairns? Madge, puir thing, had a misfortune wi' ane; and t'other lass, Effie...'

Here her voice sank so much that Jeanie could not catch a word she said, until she raised her tone to say,

'So Madge, I think, threw it in the Nor' Loch.'[2]

Madge, whose slumbers were easily broken, was now heard, 'Mother, that's a great lie. I did nae sic thing!'

'Hush, Hellcat,' said her mother, 'or the sister will be waking too.'

'That may be dangerous,' said Levitt, rising and following Meg Murdockson across the floor.

'Rise,' said the hag through the door to her daughter, 'or I sall drive the knife between the planks and into the Bedlam back of thee!'

She followed up on her threat, pricking her with the knife. Madge moved away with a scream and the door opened.

The old woman had a candle in one hand and her knife in the other. Levitt appeared behind her. Jeanie, equal to the crisis, feigned sleep as the old woman passed the light across her eyes. Levitt also looked at her with fixed attention, but then turned the old woman out and followed her back to the outward apartment. Jeanie then heard the highwayman say,

'Now, old Meg, damned if I yet understand this story of yours, or what good it will do you see the one wench hang and torment the other.'

'Never mind, Levitt,' said the old woman. 'I carena whether *she* live or die; it's her *sister*!'

'Well, we'll say no more about it; I hear Tom coming in. I'll couch – and so better had you.'

When Jeanie awoke the sun was high in the Heavens. Madge Wildfire was still in the hovel which had served them for the night, and bade her good morning, with her usual insane glee.

---

[1] Knife.

[2] The North Loch was the northern defence line of mediaeval walled Edinburgh. Drained in the late eighteenth century, the site is now occupied by Princes St Gardens.

'And dye ken, lass,' said Madge, 'there's queer things chanced since ye hae been in the land of Nod. The constables hae been here, woman, and they met wi' my minnie at the door, and they whirl'd her awa to the Justices. We will awa' out and take a walk. We can easily be back before dark and it will be some frolic and fresh air. Ye needna be feared to walk wi' me.'

Jeanie assured Madge that she would walk with her.

'I am thinking,' said Madge; 'that ye will want out o' thae folk's hands; no that they are a'thegither bad, but they have queer ways. There's whiles I think it has never been weel wi' my mother and me since we kept sic company.'

With the haste of a liberated captive, Jeanie snatched up her bundle, followed Madge into the fresh air and looked around for a human habitation. None was to be seen. She wondered where the highway lay. If she regained it, she reckoned on finding a house where she might tell her story and seek protection. But she had no idea of what direction to take and was still dependent on her crazy companion.

'Shall we not walk upon the highway?' said she coaxingly to Madge. 'It's brawer than walking amang these bushes and whins.'

Madge, walking very fast, stopped and looked at Jeanie.

'Aha, lass, ye'll be for taking to your heels, I am judging.'

Jeanie hesitated. She knew not in which direction to flee. Neither was she sure who was the swiftest, but perfectly sure that if overtaken she could never equal Madge in strength. She therefore gave up thoughts of escape for the present and followed Madge along the path.

'Are ye sure ye ken the way ye're taking us?' said Jeanie, thinking they were going deeper into the woods and farther from the highway.

'Do I ken the road? Wasna I mony a day living right here, and why shouldna I ken the road?'

By this time they had gained the deepest part of the woodland. The trees were dense and at the foot of a beautiful poplar was a hillock of moss. Here Madge, joining her hands above her head and, with a loud scream, flung herself down and lay motionless.

'Let me alane – let me *alane*!' cried Wildfire as her paroxysm of grief began to abate. 'Let me alane. It does me good to weep. I canna shed tears but only ance a year, and I aye come to wet *this* turf with them, that the flowers may grow fair and the grass be green.'

'What is the matter with you?' said Jeanie.

'There's reason enough. Mair than ane puir mind can bear. I'll tell you for I like ye, Jeanie Deans. A'body spoke weel of ye when we lived in the Pleasaunts. I mind the drink o' milk ye gae me yon day when I had been on Arthur's Seat for four-and-twenty hours, looking for the ship that somebody was sailing in.'

At this, Jeanie immediately recalled being frightened one morning by meeting a crazy young woman near her father's house. As she seemed harmless, her initial fear became pity and she gave her food which she devoured with the haste of a starveling. The incident, trifling in itself, now seemed important, having clearly made a permanent impression on Madge's mind.

'Yes,' said Madge, 'I'll tell ye about it, for ye are a decent man's daughter and maybe ye'll teach me to find the straight path. I hae been burning bricks in Egypt and in the weary wilderness of Sinai. But whenever I think on mine errors, I am like to cover my lips for shame.' Here she looked up and smiled. 'Here's a strange thing now. I hae spoke mair gude words to you in ten minutes than to my mother in as mony years. It's no that I dinna think gude words; whiles they are just at my tongue's end, but then comes the Devil, and brushes my lips with his black wing, for black it is, Jeanie. He sweeps away a' my gude thoughts and pits in fule sangs and vanities...'

'Madge,' said Jeanie, 'settle your mind and make your breast clean. You'll find your heart easier. Resist the Devil and he will flee from you. There is nae Devil sae deceitfu' as our ain wandering thoughts.'

'That's true too, lass,' said Madge, starting up; 'I'll gang a place where the Devil daurna follow me; and it's a place you will like too. But I'll keep a fast haud o' your arm, lest Apollyon stride across the path just as he did in the Pilgrim's Progress.'[1]

She got up. Taking Jeanie by the arm, she began to walk at a great pace. Soon, and to her companion's joy, they came to a marked path with which Madge seemed acquainted. Jeanie endeavoured to bring her back to the confessional, but the idea was gone. Having now got John Bunyan's parable into her head to the exclusion of everything else, on she went,

'Did ye never read the *Pilgrim's Progress*? And you shall be the woman, Christiana, and I will be the maiden, Mercy; for ye ken Mercy was of the fairer countenance, and the more alluring than her companion. And if I had my little dog here, it would be Great-heart, their guide ye ken. For he was so bold that he wad bark at ony thing twenty times his size; and that was the death of him, for he bit Corporal MacAlpine's heels ae morning when they were hauling me to the Guardhouse, and MacAlpine killed the faithfu' thing wi' his Lochaber axe!'

'Now, Madge,' said Jeanie, 'dinna speak of it.'

'It's very true. But then I maunna think o' my puir bit doggie dying in the gutter. It suffered cauld and hunger when it was living, and in the grave there is rest for a' things; rest for the doggie and me – and my puir bairn.'

'*Your* bairn?'

'Aye to be sure, *my* bairn. What for shouldna I hae a bairn – and lose a bairn too, like your bonnie sister, yon Lily of St Leonard's? The bairn was a blessing; that is, Jeanie, it wad hae *been* a blessing if it hadna been for my mother; a queer woman. Ye see, there was an auld carle wi' a bit land, and siller besides. And so the auld carle...'

'Yes?' said Jeanie, now interested in getting to the truth of Madge's history, which seemed in some extraordinary way to be entwined with the fate of her sister. 'And so the auld carle...' said Madge, 'I wish ye had seen him stoiting about, aff ae leg on to the other, wi' a dot-and-go-one sort o' motion. Gentle George could take him aff brawly. I used to laugh to see George gang hip-hop like him!'

'And who was Gentle George?' said Jeanie, trying to haul her back to her story.

'Oh, he was Geordie Robertson, ye ken, when he was in Edinburgh. But that's

[1]   Properly, *The Pilgrim's Progres from this World to that which is to come* (1679), John Bunyan's celebrated Christian allegory. Apollyon is a pseudonym for the Devil.

no his right name neither. His name is... but what's *your* business wi' his name?' said she suddenly. 'What have ye to do asking for folk's names? Never ask folk's names, Jeanie, it's no civil. Daddie Ratton says the most uncivil thing is the Bailies asking when ye saw sic a man? And if ye dinna ken their names there can be nae mair speiring about it.'

A magpie hopped across the path.

'See there!' said Madge, 'that was the way my old man-friend used to walk. I wanted to marry him for a' that, Jeanie, but then there came to him the story of my bairn. My mother thought he wad be deaved[1] wi' it's skirling, and so she pat it away below the turf yonder. And I think she buried my wits with it, for I have never been just mysell since. And Jeanie, after my mother had taken a' these pains, did the auld man no turn up his nose and wadna say a word to me! But little I care, for I have led a merry life ever since, and every braw gentleman that looks at me, ye'd think he was gaun to fall off his horse for mere love of me. I have ken'd some o' them put their hand in their pocket and gie me as muckle as sixpence – just for my bonny face!'

Thus Jeanie gained a dark insight into Madge's history. She had been courted by a wealthy suitor, whose addresses her mother had favoured, despite old age and deformity. She had been seduced by some profligate and, to conceal this and promote the match, her mother had destroyed the child of their intrigue. The consequence was the derangement of the mind of Madge Wildfire.

chapter thirty-one

So free from danger, free from fear
They crossed the court – right glad they were.
    Samuel Taylor Coleridge, *Christabel*

Pursuing the path with Madge, Jeanie Deans observed more signs of cultivation appearing. Thatched roofs with blue smoke arising were seen far off in a tuft of trees. The track leading in that direction, Jeanie resolved to ask Madge no further questions which might awaken her suspicions.

Madge thus went on uninterrupted; her wild disjointed chat much more revealing about her history than when responding to questions.

'It's a queer thing,' she said, 'but whiles I can speak about the bairn just as if it had been another body's and no my ain; and whiles I am like to break my heart about it. Had you ever a bairn, Jeanie?'

'No.'

'Aye; but your sister had, though – and I ken what became o't.'

'In mercy's name,' cried Jeanie, '*tell* me!'

Madge stopped, looked at her fixedly, then broke into a great fit of laughter.

'Aha, lass, catch me if you can! I think it's easy to mak you believe onything.

---

[1] Deafened.

How suld I ken onything o' your sister's wean? They say maidens' bairns are weel treated. That wasna true of your sister's – and mine… but these are sad tales to tell.

I maun sing a bit to keep up my heart. It's a sang that Gentle George made on me lang syne, when I went to Lockington to see him act on a stage in fine clothes with the player folk. He might hae dune waur than married me that night, as he promised. Better wed over the mixen[1] as over the moor, as they say in Yorkshire:

> *I'm Madge of the country, I'm Madge of the town,*
> *I'm Madge of the Lad I am blithest to own;*
> *My Lady of Beeve in diamonds may shine,*
> *But hasna a heart half so lightsome as mine!*
>
> *I am Queen of the Wake, I am Lady of May,*
> *I lead the blithe ring round the Maypole today;*
> *The wildfire that flashes so fair and so free,*
> *Was never so bright or so bonny as me!*

'I like that the best o' a' my sangs,' she continued, 'because *he* wrote it. I am often singing it and that's maybe why folk ca' me Madge Wildfire. I aye answer to the name, though it's no my ain?'

'Ye shouldna sing on the Sabbath,' said Jeanie as they approached a little village.

'Is this Sunday?' said Madge. 'My mother leads sic a life, turning night into day, that I lose count o' the days. In England folk sing when they like. And then, ye ken, you are Christiana and I am Mercy.[2] Ye ken how they sang on their way:

> *He that is down need fear no fall,*
> *He that is low no pride,*
> *He that is humble ever shall*
> *Have God to be his guide.*

'Jeanie, there's much truth in that book, the *Pilgrim's Progress*.' Jeanie Deans had never read Bunyan. Although he was a Calvinist, he was a member of a Baptist congregation and hence had no place on David Deans's shelf of divinity. Madge, however, had clearly been well acquainted at some time of her life, with his work.

'I am sure,' she continued, 'I am come out of the city of Destruction, for my mother is Mrs Bat's-eyes, that dwells at Deadman's corner; and Frank Levitt, and Tyburn Tam are Mistrust and Guilt, that struck the poor pilgrim to the ground with a great club and stole his bag of silver. But now we will gang to the Interpreter's house, for I ken a man that will play the Interpreter. We'll knock at his gate and the keeper will admit Christiana, that's you Jeanie, but Mercy will be left at the door, trembling and crying. Then Christiana will intercede for me; and then Mercy, that's me, will faint. And then the Interpreter, that's Mr Staunton himself, will

---

[1]   A homely proverb, signifying better wed a neighbour than one fetched from a distance. Mixen signifies dunghill, Scott.

[2]   In *Pilgrim's Progress* the Interpreter has a house in which he teaches pilgrims to lead the Christian life. He is thought to represent the Holy Spirit.

come out and take poor demented me by the hand, and give me a pomegranate, and a piece of honeycomb, and a bottle of spirits, to stay my fainting; and then the good times will come back again and we'll be the happiest folk ever you saw.'

They were now close by the village. The cottages, instead of being built in two direct lines on each side of a dusty road as in Scotland, stood in detached groups. They were separated by large oaks, elms and fruit trees, many in flourish with their crimson and white blossoms. In the centre of the hamlet stood the parish church from whose Gothic tower came the Sunday chime of bells.

'We will wait here until the folk are a' in the church,' said Madge. Jeanie was conscious of her disorderly appearance after the preceding night and of the grotesque demeanour of her guide. She thus readily agreed to rest under the trees until the commencement of the church service would allow them to enter the hamlet without attracting a crowd. She sat down at the foot of an oak beside a placid fountain dammed up for the use of the villagers. This served as a natural mirror as she began to arrange her toilette in the open air and bring her dress into order.

She soon had reason, however, to regret that she had set about this task. Madge no sooner beheld Jeanie arranging her hair, placing her bonnet in order and rubbing the dust from her shoes and clothes, than with imitative zeal she began to bedizen and trick herself out with remnants of beggarly finery, which she took out of a little bundle. Jeanie groaned inwardly but dared not interfere. Across the man's riding hat she wore, Madge placed a broken and soiled white feather, intersected with one from the fantail of a peacock. To her dress, a kind of riding-habit, she pinned a large furbelow of artificial flowers, all crushed and dirty, which had at first bedecked a lady of quality. A tawdry scarf of yellow silk, trimmed with tinsel and spangles was next flung over one shoulder, and fell across her person like a shoulder belt, or baldrick. She then took off her coarse shoes, replacing them by a pair of dirty satin ones with high heels. She had cut a willow switch in her morning's walk and this she peeled till it was transformed into such a wand as a Treasurer or High Steward bears on public occasions. She told Jeanie that since they now looked as decent as young women should do upon a Sunday morning, she would now take her to the Interpreter's house.

Jeanie sighed heavily at her fate. On the Lord's day and during Kirk time too, she must parade the street of an inhabited village with a grotesque madwoman. However, she could see no means of shaking herself free without a quarrel. Madge, on the other hand, was elated with her dazzling dress and appearance. They entered the hamlet observed only by one old woman who, being nearly blind, was only conscious that someone very fine and glittering was passing. She dropped as deep a curtsy to Madge as she would have done to a Countess. Madge smiled, simpered, and waved Jeanie forward with the air of a noble chaperone undertaking the charge of a country lady on her first journey to the capital.

Jeanie followed patiently, eyes fixed on the ground to avoid the mortification of seeing her companion's absurdities. However she started when she found herself in the churchyard, and saw that Madge was making straight for the door of the church. As Jeanie had no mind to join the congregation in such company, she walked aside from the pathway, saying,

'Madge, I will wait here till the church comes out. You go in by yourself.' She was about to seat herself upon a gravestone when Madge turned round in a passion and seized her by the arm.

'Ye ungratefu' wretch! D'ye think I am gaun to let you sit doun upon my father's grave? Rise and come wi' me into the Interpreter's house here, the house of God, or I'll tear every stitch aff your back!'

With one grab she tore off Jeanie's straw bonnet and threw it up into a yew-tree where it stuck fast. Jeanie's first impulse was to cry out, but she thought it perhaps wiser to follow the madwoman into the congregation. There she might find some means of escape, or at least be safe from violence. But her guide's uncertain brain had caught another train of ideas. Holding Jeanie fast with one hand, she pointed to the inscription on the gravestone and ordered her to read it:

This Monument was erected to the Memory of Donald
Murdockson of the King's 36th Cameronian
Regiment, a sincere Christian, a brave Soldier and
faithful Servant, by his grateful and sorrowing master
Robert Staunton.

'Very weel read, Jeanie; it's just the very words,' said Madge, her ire now faded into melancholy. With a quiet and mournful step, she led her companion towards the door of the church.

Gothic parish churches are frequent in England and are perhaps the most decent and reverential places of worship to be found in the Christian world. Yet, despite the solemnity of its exterior, Jeanie, faithful to the presbyterian Kirk, would never have willingly entered an Episcopalian place of worship. However, in her present situation, she was looking for safety. Not even sounds forbidden in the Kirk; those of the organ and flutes accompanying the psalmody, stopped her following Madge into the chancel.

No sooner had Madge put her foot upon the aisle's pavement, and realised that she had the attention of the congregation, than she resumed her extraordinary deportment. She swam rather than walked up the aisle, pulling Jeanie after her. Jeanie would fain have slipped into the pew nearest to the door, leaving Madge to ascend alone to the altar, but this was impossible. She was thus led captive up the whole length of the church. Madge, eyes half-shut and a prim smile upon her lips, moved at a delicate pace. She seemed to take the stares of the congregation as high compliments, returning them with nods and half-curtseys to individuals she seemed to know. Her absurdity was enhanced in the by the strange contrast which she formed to her companion who, with dishevelled hair, eyes downcast and a face glowing with shame, she pulled in triumph behind her.

Madge now encountered the clergyman, who fixed upon her a steady glance both compassionate and admonitory. Opening an empty pew, she entered, dragging Jeanie after her and kicking her shins by way of a warning. Madge then sank her head upon her hand for the space of a minute. Jeanie did not attempt to do the like, but looked round her with a bewildered stare which her neighbours, judging from the company she kept, naturally ascribed to insanity. Every person in their immediate vicinity drew back. One old man, unable to get beyond Madge's reach, had the prayer-book snatched from his hand as Madge ascertained the lesson of the day.

Jeanie continued to look around, wondering to whom she ought to appeal for protection when the service concluded. Her first idea was the clergyman, a gentleman of dignified appearance and deportment. He read the service with a gravity which brought back to attention those younger members of the congregation disturbed by the entrance of Madge Wildfire. It was to the priest, therefore, that Jeanie resolved to appeal when the service was over.

Meanwhile, she was shocked at his surplice, of which she had heard, but had never seen worn by a preacher of the Word. She was also confused by the repeated changes of posture in different parts of the ritual. Madge, to whom they seemed familiar, pulled her up and pushed her down with a bustling authority, making them both the continuing objects of attention. Sensibly, Jeanie decided to imitate what was done around her. The prophet, she reasoned, permitted Naaman the Syrian to bow even in the house of Rimmon.[1] Surely, she thought, if I worship the God of my fathers in my own language, the Lord will pardon me this.

Withdrawing herself from Madge as far as the pew permitted, she endeavoured to show by her attention to the service that she was composed to devotion. Madge, meanwhile, overcome with fatigue, fell fast asleep in the other corner of the pew.

The serious attention with which Jeanie listened did not escape the clergyman. Madge Wildfire's entrance had rendered him apprehensive of disturbance, but he soon saw that despite the loss of her bonnet and the awkwardness of her situation, her state of mind was very different from that of her companion. With the congregation dismissed, the preacher observed Jeanie looking around, clearly uncertain what to do.

A benevolent Christian pastor, he resolved to assist her.

chapter thirty-two

There governed in that year
A stern, stout churl – an angry overseer.
George Crabbe, *The Borough – Parish Clerk*

While the clergyman, the Rev. Staunton, was laying aside his gown in the vestry, Jeanie was coming to an open rupture with Madge.

'We must return to Mummer's barn,' said Madge. 'We'll be ower late and my mother will be angry.'

'I am not going back with you, Madge,' said Jeanie, taking out a guinea, and offering it to her; 'I maun gang my ain road.'

'And me coming a' this way out o' my road to please ye, ye ungratefu' cutty! And to be brained by my mother when I gang hame, and a' for *your* sake! I will do it *mysel'*!'

---

[1]   II Kings 5.15–17. So Naaman said, '… when I bow down in the temple of Rimmon, may the Lord pardon your servant in this thing'. Rimmon was a Syrian cult image, also known as Baal.

'For God's sake keep her away; she is mad!' cried Jeanie to a man standing beside them.

'Madge!' cried the rustic; 'keep thy hand off her, or I'se lend thee a whister-poop.'[1]

Several parishioners now gathered round the strangers, and the cry arose among the boys that there was a-going to be a fight between mad Madge Murdockson and another Bess of Bedlam. The laced cocked-hat of the Beadle now appeared among the crowd. All made way for him. He addressed himself to Madge.

'What's brought thee back again, thou silly donnot, to plague this parish? Hast tha brought another bastard wi' thee to lay at honest men's doors? Or does tha think to burden us with *this* goose? Away wi' thee to thy thief of a mother; she's in the stocks at Barkston. Away wi' ye out o' the parish or I'se be at ye with the rattan!'

Madge stood sulky.

'My puir mother in the stocks at Barkston![2] This is a' your fault Jeanie Deans; but I'll be upsides wi' you, as sure as my name's Madge Wild... Murdockson. God help me, I forgets my very name!' She turned upon her heel and went off, followed by all the urchins of the village crying, 'Madge, canst tha tell tha name?' and pulling the skirts of her dress to exasperate her into frenzy.

Though Jeanie saw her departure with infinite relief, she wished she could have repaid the service Madge had done her. She asked the Beadle whether here was a boarding house in the village and whether she might speak to the clergyman. Said he,

'I shall take thee to his Reverence first, to gie an account o' thysell and to see that thou'll be no burden upon the parish.'

'I do not wish to burden anyone,' replied Jeanie; 'I have money and only wish to get on with my journey.'

'Come then. Our Rector is a good man.'

'I am very willing to see the minister,' said Jeanie; 'although he read his discourse *and* wore the surplice. He preached the root of the matter.'

The clerical mansion was large and commodious, for the living was an excellent one. The advowson[3] belonged to a wealthy family in the neighbourhood who had usually bred up a son or nephew to the Church – and for this very comfortable living. Thus the rectory of Willingham had always been considered as a direct and immediate appanage of Willingham Hall and its Staunton Baronets.

It was situated about four hundred yards from the village on gently rising ground covered with old oaks and elms planted in rows. These fell into perspective and blended together in handsome irregularity. Approaching the house, a handsome gateway admitted them into a lawn interspersed with large chestnut trees and beeches. The front of the house was irregular. Part of it looked very old and had been the residence of the priest in Romish times. Successive occupants had made considerable additions and improvements, each in the taste of his own

---

[1]   Defined as, 'a backhanded blow' by the antiquarian Capt. Francis Grose in *A Provincial Glossary* (1788). Grose, a friend of Burns, commissioned *Tam o' Shanter*.

[2]   A village three miles north of Grantham, Lincs.

[3]   The right to present a clergyman to a living.

age and with little regard to symmetry. These, however, were so happily mingled that the eye saw nothing but what was interesting and varied. Fruit trees on the southern wall, outer staircases, various entrances and a combination of chimneys of different age, rendered the frontage picturesque.

'Mony men would hae scrupled such expense,' he said, 'seeing as the living mun go as pleases Sir Edmund; but his Reverence has a canny bit land of his own and need not look on two sides of a penny.'

Jeanie could not help comparing the commodious building before her to the Manses in her own country which penurious heritors provided but poor accommodation for the minister.

Behind the Rector's house the ground sloped down to a small river, which complemented the landscape by appearing through the willows and poplars crowning its banks.

'Best trout stream in all Lincolnshire,' said the beadle. Ignoring the principal entrance, he conducted Jeanie to a door in the older part of the building. His knock was answered a servant in grave purple livery.

'How do, Tummas?' said the beadle, 'and how be young Master Staunton?'

'Poorly, Master Stubbs. Are you wanting his Reverence?'

'Aye, Tummas; please to say I ha' brought up the young woman as came to service today with mad Madge Murdockson. She seems a decentish kind o' body; I can tell his Reverence only that she is a Scotchwoman.' Tummas desired Mr Stubbs and his charge to step in. He would inform his master of their presence.

The room into which he showed them was a steward's parlour, hung with county maps and three or four prints of eminent persons including the famous Peregrine, Lord Willoughby.[1] In full armour and looking as when he spoke the words of the legend below the engraving:

Ye musquet and calliver-men,
Do you prove true to me,
I'll be the foremost man in fight,
Said brave Lord Willoughbee...

Tummas returned with instructions that Stubbs and the young woman should be taken up to the library. The beadle conducted Jeanie through passages into a handsome little anteroom, adjoining to the library. Out of this a glass door opened to the lawn.

'Stay here,' said Stubbs, 'till I tell his Reverence you are come.'

He opened a door and entered the library. Without wishing to hear their conversation, Jeanie could not avoid it. Stubbs stood by the door while his Reverence was at the upper end of a large room, rendering their conversation audible in the anteroom.

'So you have brought the younger woman Mr Stubbs. What has become of that other being?'

'I let her go her ways back to her mother who is in trouble in the next parish.'

---

[1] Peregrine Bertie, 13th Baron Willoughby de Eresby (1555–1601). Diplomat and soldier. Latterly, he was Governor of Berwick and Warden of the English East March.

'Wretched, incorrigible woman! What sort of person is the companion?'

'Decent like, your Reverence,' said Stubbs; 'for aught I see, there's no harm in her.'

'Send her in then, but remain below.'

This exchange had engaged Jeanie's attention so deeply, that not until it was over did she observe that the sashed door into the gardens had been opened. A young man of pale and sickly appearance was then carried in by two assistants. He was lifted on to the nearest couch as if to recover from the fatigue of an unusual exertion. As they were doing this, Stubbs came out of the library and summoned Jeanie to enter. She obeyed, somehow sensing that the success of her journey depended upon the impression she would make on Mr Staunton. Jeanie's recent violent detention showed that there were persons determined to stop her journey and she felt the necessity of protection, at least until she should get beyond their reach.

While these things passed through her mind, Jeanie found herself in a handsome library and in the presence of the Rector of Willingham. The well-furnished presses and shelves contained books, an orrery, globes, a telescope and other scientific implements which conveyed to Jeanie both admiration and wonder, not unmixed with some fear.

Mr Staunton spoke gently to her. He told her that her appearance at Church had been in discreditable company and that Madge deliberately sought to disturb the congregation. He wished, nevertheless, to hear her own account. He was, he informed her, a Justice of the Peace as well as a clergyman.

'Your Honour is very civil.'

'So, who are you, young woman, and what do you do in this county and in such company?'

'I am no vagrant, sir. I am a decent Scots lass, travelling through the land on my own business and my own expense. I was unlucky to fall in with wicked people; thieves who and stopped me by violence last night on my journey. That puir light-headed creature let me out in the morning.'

'Thieves? You charge them with robbery?'

'No, sir; they took nothing from me. Nor did they use me ill, other than confining me.'

Staunton inquired into the particulars of her pilgrimage. These she related to him from point to point.

'This is an extraordinary and not a very probable tale, young woman. According to your account, violence has been committed, but without motive. Are you aware that in English law, injured persons are put to the expense of appearing as prosecutors?'

'But my business at London is urgent! All I want is for some gentleman, out of Christian charity, to protect me to a town or city where I may hire horses and a guide. It would be my father's opinion that I am not free to give testimony in any English court of justice, as this land is not under direct Gospel dispensation.'

Mr Staunton stared at this and asked was her father a Quaker?

'God forbid, sir,' said Jeanie, 'He has never dealt in sic black commodities as theirs. That's weel kend o' him.'

'What is his name, pray?' said Staunton.

'David Deans, sir, a dairy farmer at Saint Leonard's Crags, near Edinburgh.'

A deep groan came from the anteroom. It prevented the Rector from replying.

'Good God, that unhappy boy!' he exclaimed. Leaving Jeanie alone, he hastened into the outer apartment. Some noise and bustle was heard, but no one entered the library for the best part of an hour.

chapter thirty-three

Fantastic passions' maddening brawl,
And shame and terror over all!
Deeds to be hid which were not hid,
Which, all confused, I could not know
Whether I suffer'd or I did...

Samuel Taylor Coleridge, *The Pains of Sleep*

Left alone, Jeanie anxiously revolved in her mind what course to pursue. Although impatient to continue her journey, she hesitated to do so while old Murdockson and her accomplices were in the neighbourhood. From the conversation she had partly overheard and also from the ravings of Madge, she gathered that her mother had a deep and revengeful motive for obstructing her journey. Could she hope for assistance from Rector Staunton? His appearance and demeanour encouraged her hopes. His tone and language were encouraging. He had served in the Army and retained the frankness of the profession of arms. He was, besides, a preacher, although he wore a surplice and read the Book of Common Prayer. Despite these errors, Jeanie reckoned him very different from the Episcopalian divines of her father's earlier days. These would get drunk in their canonical dress before hounding out the Dragoons against the wandering Cameronians.

The house seemed to be in some disturbance and Jeanie thought it better simply to remain quiet where she had been left. The first who entered was an elderly housekeeper, Mrs Dalton.

'My young master,' she said, 'had a bad accident, a fall from his horse. It makes him liable to fits. He has been taken very ill just now and his Reverence cannot see you for some time. However, fear not, he will do all for you that is just and proper.'

She offered to show Jeanie a room where she might remain till his Reverence was free and where she might change her dress. This done, the old lady hardly recognised the soiled and disordered traveller in the neat, clean woman who reappeared before her. Encouraged by the alteration in her appearance, Mrs. Dalton invited Jeanie to partake of her dinner.

'Tha canst read this Book, canst tha, young woman?' said the old lady, when their meal was concluded, laying her hand upon a large Bible.

'I can indeed.'

'Take thou the book, then, for my eyes are dazed and read. Tis' the only book thou canst not happen wrong in.'

Jeanie selected instead a Chapter of Isaiah, and read it with devout propriety to an appreciative Mrs Dalton.

'Ah,' she said, 'would that all Scotchwomen were sic as thou; but it is our luck here to get born Devils of thy country, every one worse than t'other.'

There now entered Tammas.

'Master wishes to see the young woman from Scotland.'

'Go up to his Reverence, my dear,' said Mrs Dalton, 'and tell him your story. I will fold down the leaf, and will have tea and a muffin against tha come down.'

'Master's *waiting*,' said Tummas impatiently.

'Well, Mr Jack-Sauce, and what is your business to put in your oar? And how often must you be told to call Mr Staunton his Reverence and not 'mastering' him like he were a petty squire?'

The footman said nothing till they got into the passage, when he muttered,

'There are more than one master in this house and a mistress too, in that Dame Dalton.'

Tummas led the way through intricate passages and ushered Jeanie into an apartment darkened by the closing of most of the window-shutters. There was a bed with the curtains partly drawn.

'Here is the young woman, sir.'

'Very well,' said a voice from the bed, but not that of his Reverence. 'Be ready to answer the bell. Leave the room, Tom.'

'There is some mistake,' said Jeanie, surprised at finding herself in the room of an invalid; 'the servant told me that the minister...'

'Don't trouble yourself,' said the voice, 'there is no mistake. I know more about your affairs than my father, and I can manage them better. We have little time to lose. Open the shutters of that window.'

She did so. He drew aside the curtain of his bed and the light fell on his pale countenance. Turban'd with bandages, and dressed in a night-gown, he lay apparently exhausted on the bed.

'Look at me Jeanie Deans. Do you not remember me?'

'No, sir,' said she, surprised. 'I was never here before.'

'Think!'

A terrible recollection flashed on Jeanie.

'Yes. Be calm. Muschat's Cairn and a moonlit night!'

Jeanie sank down on a chair with clasped hands.

'Yes, here I lie when I ought to be in Edinburgh trying to save a life dearer to me than my own. How fares it with her? The horse carrying me north fell with me, on my only good mission in years! Give me some of that cordial. You tremble. You have good cause.'

Jeanie approached him with the cup.

'Tell me,' he said, 'what you are doing in this country? I will help you for her sake.'

'I trust in God and to find if it pleases Him to end my sister's captivity. That is all I seek, whoever be the instrument!'

'The Devil take you Puritans!' cried George Staunton, 'I beg your pardon. What harm can it do to tell me how your sister stands, and how you hope to assist her?'

There was in the look of this young man an impetuosity which seemed to prey on itself, like a fiery steed churning on the bit. In as few words as possible, she told him of her sister's trial and condemnation and of her own journey as far as Newark. To much of what she said he listened as if he were having confirmed what he already knew. But when she pursued her tale to the forced interruption to her journey, extreme surprise and attention appeared. He questioned Jeanie closely about the two men, and the conversation she had overheard between the taller of them and the old woman.When Jeanie mentioned the old woman's allusion to her foster-son, he said simply, 'It is true; but go on.' Jeanie related her journey with Madge and closed her tale.

Young Staunton lay in profound thought. At length he spoke, and with more composure than hitherto,

'You are a good woman, Jeanie Deans, and I will tell you more of my own story than I have told to anyone. I do it because I desire your confidence in return and that you will act on my advice.'

'I will do whatever is fitting for a Christian sister to do.'

'Listen to me. Old Margaret Murdockson was the widow of a favourite servant of my father. She was my nurse as a babe. She lived in a cottage nearby here and had a daughter who grew up to be a beautiful but giddy girl. Her mother tried to marry her off to an old, wealthy churl in the neighbourhood. The girl saw me frequently and we became lovers; but soon after this I was sent abroad. When I returned, I found that both mother and daughter had fallen into disgrace and had been chased from the county. My share in their shame was discovered; my father used very harsh language and we quarreled. I left his house, swearing never to see it or my father again. I joined with others marauding on the Revenue and similar adventures. Have you looked round this rectory? Is it not a sweet and pleasant retreat?'

Jeanie was alarmed at this sudden change of subject.

'Yes.'

'I wish it had been ten thousand fathoms underground! It and its tithes and all that belongs to it. Had it not been for this cursed rectory, I would have followed my own inclination into the Army.' He paused, then went on with more composure.

'The wandering life brought me to Scotland where I got embroiled. I met Wilson, a remarkable man who influenced me. It was then that I met your sister Effie at gatherings of young people in Edinburgh. You know the result of our affair. I was, and am determined to marry her and had a friend attempt a negotiation with my father. But just when I was expecting his pardon, he learned of my activities in exaggerated colours. He wrote enclosing a sum of money and disowning me for ever... I became desperate and joined Wilson in the robbery of the Customs Officer in Fife. We were arrested and condemned. But your sister's pregnancy made me determined to try to save my life... I forgot to tell you that in Edinburgh I had met Murdockson and her daughter again, who seemed hardly to know her old lover. Meanwhile your sister's delivery approached. Effie said she would die a thousand deaths before you should know of the pregnancy, yet her confinement had to be provided for. I knew this woman Murdockson was Devilish but I thought that money would hold her steady. She got a file for Wilson and a spring-saw for me and she undertook to take charge of Effie for the birth. I gave her the money my father had sent me. She would take Effie into her house and wait till I escaped. My plan was to marry Effie and we would then flee to the West Indies.

We made the attempt to escape but it miscarried with Wilson insisting on going first. He then sacrificed himself to allow my escape from the Tolbooth Church which you must have heard of. The bloodhounds were so close behind that I dared not trust myself to my old haunts, but old Murdockson met me and told me that Effie had been delivered of a boy. I told the old hag that Effie was to lack nothing that money could buy – and fled to Fife and my old mates. We heard that the Edinburgh mob would back any attempt to rescue Wilson, even from the foot of the gibbet. I said that I would lead the attack on the guards and I found no lack of men to come with me.

I have no doubt I could have rescued him, but the Magistrates took the precaution suggested by that wretch Porteous, which denied us. They brought the time of execution *forward* by half an hour! It was all over before our rescue attempt began. I made it to the scaffold and cut the rope with my own hand. Too late! The bold man was dead. All that remained to us was vengeance on Porteous, who had kept his men firing on the people. At length and at the hazard of my life, I went to Murdockson's place to find my Effie and my son. Both were gone. She told me that when Effie heard of the failed rescue, she fell into a brain fever, escaped from the house and had not been seen since. I sent a comrade to Saint Leonard's, but before I heard anything, I had to flee to a more distant hiding place. At length I heard of Porteous's condemnation and of your sister's arrest on a criminal charge. I again ventured to the Pleasance and charged Murdockson with treachery to Effie and our son.'

'What did she say?' said Jeanie.

'Nothing. She said she had made a moonlight flitting with the infant in her arms and that she had seen neither of them since. She said Effie might well have thrown the child into the North Loch or the Quarry Holes for what she knew.'

'But why did you believe that she lied?'

'Because, on this second occasion, I saw Madge. From her I understood that in fact the child had been removed during its mother's fever. All this is uncertain; but the character of old Murdockson makes me fear the worst.'

'That agrees with what I heard from my sister,' said Jeanie.

'I am *certain*,' said Staunton, 'that Effie in her senses would never injure any living creature. But what could I do? Nothing! Then came the rage in Edinburgh over the reprieve of Porteous. This gave me the idea of forcing the jail and freeing Effie. I joined with the mob and ordered a trusted friend to take her out to a place of safety as soon as we left the jail with Porteous. But *nothing* could induce her to leave that prison.'

'Effie was right,' said Jeanie; 'and I love her the better for it.'

'My hope,' went on Staunton, 'was acquittal at her trial through your testimony. You remember how I urged it at the Cairn. I do not blame you for your refusal; it was on principle and not on indifference to Effie's fate. I knew not where to turn. I fled Scotland. I came here, where my appearance brought a pardon from my father; and here, in anguish, I awaited the outcome of the trial.'

'With *nothing* for Effie's relief?' asked Jeanie.

'To the last I hoped that it might end favourably. Two days ago the news arrived. I took my best horse and headed for London to appeal to Walpole for your sister's safety.[1] In return I would surrender to him, the heir to Willingham, *alias* George Robertson, breaker of the Tolbooth and leader of the Porteous mob.'

'But would that save my sister?' said Jeanie in astonishment.

'It would indeed. Prime Ministers love the power of pleasing sovereigns by gratifying their passions; and the Queen's passion is revenge for Porteous. However, I had not rode ten miles when my horse, normally the most sure-footed in the county, fell with me. On a level piece of road too, as if struck by a cannonball. I was brought back here in the condition you see.'

A servant opened the door.

'Sir, his Reverence is coming upstairs to wait upon you.'

'For God's sake hide, Jeanie,' hissed Staunton, 'into that dressing closet!'

'No! I willna hide frae the master of this house.'

'But, consider the...'

But before he could complete the warning, his father entered.

chapter thirty-four

And now, will pardon, comfort, kindness, draw
The youth from vice? will honour, duty, law?
George Crabbe; *The Borough – Players*

Jeanie arose from her seat, and made a quiet curtsey as the elder Staunton entered, his astonishment obvious at finding his son in present company. Said he to Jeanie, 'I seem to have made a mistake respecting you. I ought to have left the task of helping you to this young man, with whom you are clearly acquainted.'

'The servant told me his master wished to speak with me.'

'George,' said Mr Staunton, 'still lost to all self-respect? You might have spared your father's house such a scene.'

'Sir, you do me injustice,' said George. 'By my honour you do!'

'Your *honour*!' said his father, turning away with contempt. To Jeanie he said, 'From you I neither ask nor expect an explanation. As a father I request your departure from this house. Your story was only a pretext to gain admission into it. You will find a Justice of the Peace just two miles away with whom you may lodge your complaint of abduction.'

'This shall not *be*,' said George Staunton, starting up. 'Sir, you are naturally humane. Do not become inhospitable on my account. Turn out that eaves-dropping rascal,' here he pointed to Thomas. 'Get me hartshorn drops[2] and I will explain

---

[1] Sir Robert Walpole (1676–1745), 1st Earl of Orford. Norfolk-born Whig politician. First Lord of the Treasury 1721–1742 and Britain's first 'Prime Minister' 1730–1742.

[2] Hartshorn, also known as 'baker's ammonia', is *ammonium bicarbonate* and was formerly used both as preventative and as a restorative in fainting.

my connection with this woman. She shall not lose her good repute through me; I have done too much mischief to her family already.'

'Leave the room,' said the Rector to the servant. He shut the door behind Thomas.

'Now, sir, what have you to say?'

Young Staunton was about to speak, but it was one of those moments for those like Jeanie Deans who possess courage and unruffled temper.

'Sir,' she said to the elder Staunton, 'ye have the right to ask your son to defend his conduct. But I am just a wayfaring traveller, no way indebted to you, unless it be for a meal which in my country, is willingly gien by rich or poor to those in need. And for that I am willing to make payment, if I didna think it would be an affront in a house like this.'

'All very well, young woman,' said the surprised Rector, unsure whether Jeanie's language came from simplicity or impertinence, 'but come to the point! Why do you stop my son from giving his explanation?'

'He may tell what he likes of his ain affairs,' answered Jeanie; 'but *my* family and *my* friends have the right to prevent stories being told anent them without their express desire. Since they canna be here to speak for themselves, I entreat ye wadna ask Mr George ony questions anent me or my folk. He will be neither a Christian nor a gentleman if he answers against my express desire.'

'This is quite the most extraordinary thing I ever met with,' said the Rector, eyeing her modest countenance. He turned suddenly to his son.

'What have *you* to say?'

'I have been too hasty. I have indeed no right to discuss the affairs of this person's family without her consent.'

The elder Staunton looked from one to the other with surprise.

'I *insist* upon knowing the mystery!'

'I repeat, sir,' replied his son, sullenly, 'that I have no right to speak of this woman's family without her consent.'

'And as *I* hae nae mysteries to explain, sir,' said Jeanie, 'I only pray you as a preacher and a gentleman, to permit me to go safely to the next stage-house on the Lunnon road.'

'I shall take care of your safety,' said young Staunton.

'Perhaps, sir,' said his father, 'you intend a disgraceful marriage? *Beware!*'

'Ye needna fear sic a thing,' said Jeanie, 'I wadna wed your son; not for all the land between the twa ends of the rainbow!'

'There is something *very* strange in this,' said the Rector. 'Young woman, pray follow me into the next room.'

'Hear me first,' said George. 'Jeanie Deans, I trust to your prudence. Tell my father as much or as little of these matters as you wish. He shall know neither more nor less from me.'

His father darted an indignant glance which softened into sorrow as he saw him sink back on the couch, exhausted by the scene. He left the apartment, Jeanie following. Entering the small parlour, he shut the door.

'Young woman,' said he, 'there is something in your appearance that marks both sense and innocence. Should it be otherwise, I can only say that you are the most accomplished hypocrite. I ask no secret you are unwilling to reveal, least of all any concerning my son. He has given me too much unhappiness.'

'I understand, sir,' replied Jeanie; 'and as ye speak o' him in sic a way, I must tell ye that that this is only the second time of my speaking wi' him in my life. And what I heard frae him on both occasions, I *never* wish to hear again.'

'Then it is really your intention to proceed to London?'

'Certainly, sir; for I may say that the avenger of blood is behind me.[1] Would that I were assured against mischief on the way.'

'I have made inquiries,' said the clergyman, 'about the characters you described. They have left their rendezvous but may be hiding in the neighbourhood. As you have good reason to fear them, I will put you under the charge of a steady person as far as Stamford and see you into the stage-coach which goes from thence to London.'

'A coach is surely not for the likes of me, sir?' said Jeanie. Staunton explained that she would find the coach cheaper and safer than travelling on horseback. She expressed her gratitude with such feeling that he asked if she had enough money for the journey. She had. This finally removed any doubt in Staunton's mind, respecting her character and purpose. He asked her destination.

'I go to a very decent merchant and a cousin, a Mrs Glass. She sells snuff and tobacco, at the Sign o' the Thistle in the City.'

Jeanie anticipated that such a respectable connection would impress Mr Staunton. She was thus surprised when he answered, 'My poor girl, is this woman your *only* acquaintance in London? Have you really no better knowledge of where she is to be found?'

'I am gaun to see the Duke of Argyle, forbye Mrs Glass,' said Jeanie; 'does your honour think it would be best to go there first? Mayhap his Grace's folk will direct me.'

'*Really*? Are you acquainted with the Duke of Argyle?'

'No, sir.'

'Well!' said he. 'As I must not inquire into the cause of your journey, I cannot advise you how to manage it. But the landlady of the London Inn where the coach stops is a decent person. I use her house myself sometimes. I will give you a recommendation to her.' Jeanie thanked him.

'And now,' said he, 'I presume you wish to set out.'

'I wad not have presumed to use the Lord's Day for travelling. But as I am on a journey of mercy I trust my doing so is lawful.'

'You may, if you wish, remain with Mrs Dalton for the evening. However, have no farther correspondence with my son. He is no proper counsellor.'

'Your honour speaks truly in that,' said Jeanie; 'it was not my will to speak wi' him just now. I dinna wish the gentleman onything but gude, but I never wish to see him again.'

'If you wish,' added the Rector, 'you may attend family worship in the hall this evening. You seem to be a serious young woman.'

'I have been bred in the faith of the suffering Remnant[2] of the Presbyterian

---

[1] Joshua 20.5, 7, 9.

[2] The Cameronian sect of the Covenanters to which Deans belonged.

doctrine in Scotland. I doubt if I can lawfully attend upon your form of worship, testified against by many of our Kirk including my worthy father.'

'Well, my girl,' said the Rector, with a good-humoured smile, 'far be it from me to strain your conscience. Yet you ought to recollect that divine Grace streams to other kingdoms as well as Scotland and is essential to our spiritual wants. Its many springs, are various in character but equally efficacious throughout the Christendom.'

'Ah, but,' said Jeanie, 'though the waters may be alike, yet the *blessing* from them may not be equal. It would have been in vain for Naaman the Syrian leper to have bathed in Pharpar and Abana, those rivers of Damascus, when only the waters of the Jordan were sanctified for the cure.'[1]

'Well,' said the Rector, 'we will not enter the great debate betwixt our national Churches. However, we must try to satisfy you that, besides our errors, we at least preserve Christian charity.'

He sent for Mrs Dalton and consigned Jeanie to her particular charge, assuring her that early next morning a trusty guide and a good horse would be ready for Stamford. He then took a dignified leave of her, wishing her success in the objects of her journey which, he doubted not, were laudable. Jeanie was conducted by the housekeeper to her room.

The evening, however, was not destined to pass without farther interference from young Staunton. A paper was slipped into her hand by the faithful Tummas, intimating his young master's demand to see her and assuring her freedom from interruption.

'Tell your young master,' said Jeanie, 'that I promised his worthy father that I would not see him again.'

'*Tummas!*' said Mrs Dalton severely, 'You should be more creditably employed than carrying messages between your master and girls that chance to be in this house.'

'Mrs Dalton, I was hired to carry messages and not to ask questions. It's not for the likes of me to refuse the young gentleman. If there's no harm meant, there's none done, see?'

'And I gie you fair warning, Tummas Ditton, that if I catch thee at this work again, his Reverence shall clear this house of you.'

Thomas retired defeated and the rest of the evening passed uneventfully.

Jeanie enjoyed the comfort of a good bed and a sound sleep until awakened at six o'clock by Mrs Dalton. Her guide and horse were ready. She rose, said her morning devotions, and was ready to resume her travels. The housekeeper provided breakfast and she then found herself safe seated on a pillion behind a stout and armed Lincolnshire servant of the Rector. They rode in silence along a country road which led by hedge and gateway into the principal highway beyond Grantham. At length her escort said,

'Here be a note for thee,' He handed it over his left shoulder. 'It's from the young master. Every man about Willingham is fain to please him for he'll be Squire one day, let them say as they like.'

[1] II Kings 5.12.

Jeanie broke the seal. She read:

You refuse to see me. You are shocked at my character: but you should give me credit for sincerity – and I am no hypocrite. I desire only to repair your sister's misfortunes, be it at the expense of my honour and my own life.

Now, as you have declined my help, you must take the whole upon yourself. Go to the Duke of Argyle and tell him you know the identity of the leader of the Porteous mob. He will surely hear you on this.

Make your own terms. You know where I am to be found. Be assured I will not flee as that night at the Cairn. I will not stir from this house.

Ask your sister's life, but also make terms for yourself. Ask an office for Butler. You will get anything for delivering to the hangman one whose most earnest desire is to be at rest.

G. S.

Jeanie read it over and then tore it into small pieces. These she dispersed them into in the air a few at a time so that the perilous secret might not fall into any other hand.

Jeanie pondered the question of whether she was entitled to save her sister's life by sacrificing that of another – and one who had done her no injury. In one sense, denouncing Staunton who was the cause of her sister's misfortune might seem an act of just retribution. But Jeanie, educated in a strict morality, had to consider what right had she to barter between the lives of Staunton and of Effie – to sacrifice one for the safety of the other? His guilt was a crime against the public, not against her.

That action was blended with many circumstances which, in the eyes of those in Jeanie's rank of life, mitigated its most atrocious features. The anxiety of the London Government to convict those responsible had led to severe measures against the city of Edinburgh and the Scottish clergy, compelled, against their principles, to announce from their pulpits the reward offered for those involved in the death of Porteous. Jeanie herself felt that denouncing Staunton would actually be a treasonable act against the independence of Scotland. Presbyterians always had a glow of national feeling, and Jeanie trembled at the idea of the name of Deans being twinned with that of Monteath.[1] Yet, the thought of Effie's life, when one spoken word might save it, pressed heavily on the mind of her sister.

'Lord, support and direct me!' said Jeanie. 'He tests me with difficulties beyond my strength.'

While these thoughts passed through Jeanie's mind, her guard began to show some an inclination to talk about the Willingham family.

Jeanie learned that the Rector had been a soldier. During service in the West Indies he had married the heiress of a wealthy planter. Their son George, an only

---

[1] Sir John de Menteith (c.1275–c.1323) still known in Scotland as 'the fause (false) Monteath.' He was the Governor of Dumbarton Castle who in 1306 betrayed Sir William Wallace to the English, by whom he was barbarously executed in London.

child, had passed his early youth under a doting mother and in the society of slaves who gratified his every caprice. His father was a man of worth, but his beautiful wife was wilful and overindulgent to the child. Every restraint imposed on the boy by his father's presence was removed in his absence.

When he was ten years old his mother died and his father returned to England. His mother had placed a considerable part of her fortune under her son's exclusive control and young George was not long in England before he learned of this independence. He also learned how to abuse it, as shown by riotous conduct at his school. His father, having taken holy orders, was inducted by his brother Sir William Staunton Bt into the family living of Willingham. The revenue was a matter of importance to him as he himself derived little from the estate of his late wife.

He took his son to reside with him at the Rectory, but found him uncontrollable. He found the young men of his own rank unable to endure him and he fell into low society. His father tried sending sent him abroad, but he returned wilder than before. The youth was not without good qualities, having a lively wit and a reckless generosity which might pass in society. All these, however, availed him nothing. He became so well acquainted with the turf, the gaming-table, the cockpit and worse, that his mother's fortune was gone before he was 21. He was now in debt and distress. His early history may be concluded in the words of the British Juvenal describing a similar character:

> Headstrong, determined in his own career,
> He thought reproof unjust, and truth severe.
> The soul's disease was to its crisis come,
> He first abused, and then abjured, his home.[1]

'And yet, 'tis pity on Master George too,' continued Jeanie's companion, 'for he has an open hand, and winna let a poor body want if he can help it.'

At Stamford our heroine was deposited in safety by her guide. She obtained a place in the London coach which reached the capital on the afternoon of the second day. The recommendation of the elder Staunton procured Jeanie a civil reception at the Inn where the carriage stopped. Then, with the aid of Mrs Bickerton's correspondent, she found Mrs Glass.

chapter thirty-five

My name is Argyle. You may well think it strange,
To live at the Court and never to change.
  Bannocks o' Barley Meal, Attrib. John, 2nd Duke of Argyll

F ew names deserve more honourable mention in the history of Scotland during this period than that of Field Marshal John Campbell, Duke of Argyle and

---

[1]   George Crabbe, *The Borough*, Letter xii (1810). Crabbe was a close friend of Scott.

Greenwich. His talents as a statesman and a soldier were generally acknowledged.[1] He was not without ambition, but was 'without the illness that attends it' the malady which can excite great men to raise themselves to power while throwing the Kingdom into confusion. Pope has distinguished him as:

> Argyle, the State's whole Thunder born to wield,
> And shake alike the Senate and the Field.

He was equally free from the vices which may afflict Statesmen, such as falsehood and dissimulation; and from those of great Soldiers, such as an inordinate thirst for self-aggrandisement.

His native Scotland stood at this time in a precarious and doubtful situation. She was indeed united to England, but the cement had not yet acquired consistence. The irritant memory of ancient wrongs subsisted and betwixt the fretful jealousy of the Scots and the supercilious disdain of the English, quarrels repeatedly occurred. In the course of these, the Union so important to the safety of both was in danger of being dissolved. Scotland had also the disadvantage of being bitterly divided into factions, which waited only for a signal to break forth into action.

In such circumstances, another man with the talents and rank of Argyle, but with a mind less regulated, might have sought the whirlwind and directed its fury. He chose instead a safer and more honourable course. His voice, whether in Office or Opposition, was raised for both just and lenient measures. During the Jacobite Rising of 1715, his high military services to the House of Hanover were perhaps too great to be either acknowledged or repaid. Thereafter he used his influence to soften the consequences of that insurrection for those of his countrymen whose mistaken loyalty had engaged them in the affair. For this he was rewarded by the esteem and affection of Scotland to an uncommon degree. This popularity with a discontented and warlike people caused jealousy at Court. Here, the very potential to become dangerous may be obnoxious, even though inclination is absent. Besides, Argyle's independent mode of expressing himself in Parliament and of acting in public were ill-calculated to attract royal favour.

He was therefore respected and indeed often employed in state affairs, but was no favourite of George II, his Queen or indeed his ministers. At several periods in his life, the Duke was considered to be in disgrace at Court, although never a declared member of the Opposition in the House of Lords. This rendered him the dearer to Scotland, because it was usually in her cause that he incurred the displeasure of the King. Regarding the Porteous affair, he eloquently opposed the severe measures to be adopted towards the city of Edinburgh. This was gratefully received in that City, the more so since it was understood that the Duke's intervention had given personal offence to Queen Caroline,[2] then acting as Regent during the King's absence in Germany.

---

[1] John Campbell, 2nd Duke of Argyll and 1st Duke of Greenwich KG (1678–1743), known in the Highlands as *Iain Ruairidh nan Cath*, Red John of the Battles.

[2] Caroline of Ansbach (1683–1737). Politically adroit and generally popular, she was Regent four times during her husband's absences in Hanover, where he was Elector. The King refused to marry after her death and had twenty-two years of widowerhood.

His conduct upon this occasion, like that of all the Scottish members of parliament – with one or two unworthy exceptions – was spirited in the highest degree. His reply to Queen Caroline, already given, and some fragments of his speech against the Porteous Bill are still remembered. He famously retorted to the Lord Chancellor that he, Lord Hardwicke, had spoken in the debate more rather as a man of Party, than as a Judge:

'I appeal,' said Argyle, 'to this House and to the Nation. Can I be justly branded as a jobber or a partisan? Have I been a briber of votes? A buyer of boroughs? An agent of corruption for any purpose, or on behalf of any Party?

Consider my life. Examine my actions on the battlefield – and in Cabinet – and see if there lies there any blot to my honour. I have shown myself the friend of my country and a loyal subject of my King. I am ready to do so again, without an instant's regard to the frowns, or the smiles, of a Court; for I have experienced both!

I have given my reasons for opposing this Bill, and have shown it to be contrary to the Treaty of Union, to the liberty of Scotland and indeed to that of England. It is also repugnant to common justice, common sense and to the public interest. The metropolis of Scotland is the former Capital of an independent nation, the residence of a long line of Monarchs by whom that noble city was graced and dignified. Shall such a city, for the fault of an unknown body of rioters, be deprived of its honours and its privileges, of its gates and its Guards? And shall any native Scotsman tamely behold such havoc?

I glory, my Lords, in opposing such injustice. I reckon it my dearest pride and honour to defend my native country, thus laid open to undeserved shame and unjust spoliation.'

Other statesmen and orators, both Scottish and English, used similar arguments and the Bill was gradually stripped of its most oppressive and obnoxious clauses. The matter eventually concluded with a fine of £2,000 upon the city of Edinburgh in favour of Porteous's widow, of which she accepted three-fourths. As was wittily observed at the time, the ferocious Parliamentary debates had simply made the fortune of an old cook-maid; such having been the original occupation of Mrs Porteous. The Court, however, did not forget the rebuff they had received from the Duke of Argyle, who was thereafter to be considered a person in the royal disgrace. The Duke was alone in his study when one of his gentlemen acquainted him that a country-girl from Scotland was desirous of speaking with his Grace.

'A country-girl, and from Scotland? What can have brought the silly fool to London? A lover press-ganged into the Navy I suppose, or some stock sunk in the South Sea funds – and nobody in the world to manage the matter but *MacCailean Mór*... Show her up, Archibald.'

A young woman of modest stature and of countenance pleasing in expression, sunburnt and freckled, was ushered into the splendid library. She wore the tartan plaid of her country adjusted to cover her head, and partly to fall back over her shoulders. A quantity of fair hair surrounded a round, good-humoured face. The solemnity of her mission and her sense of the Duke's rank gave an appearance of awe, but not of fear or bashfulness. Jeanie's dress, in the style of Scottish maidens of her own class, was arranged with scrupulous attention.

She stopped near the entrance of the room, made a curtsey and crossed her hands upon her bosom, without uttering a syllable. The Duke of Argyle advanced towards her. If she admired his graceful manners and his dress-coat decorated with Orders, he was no less struck with her simple modesty in dress and countenance.

'Did you wish to speak with me, bonny lass? Or did you wish to see the Duchess?'

'My business is with you, your Grace.'

'And what is it?'

Jeanie looked uncertainly at the attendant.

'Leave us, Archibald,' said the Duke, 'wait in the anteroom.' The domestic withdrew.

'And now sit down, lass. Take your breath; take your time and tell me what you have to say. By your dress, I guess you are just come down from Scotland. Did you pass through the streets in your tartan plaid?'

'No, sir,' said Jeanie; 'a friend brought me in ane o' their street coaches – a very decent woman,' she added, her courage increasing as she became familiar with the sound of her voice in such a presence. 'Your Grace kens her. Mrs Glass, at the sign o' the Thistle.'

'My worthy snuff-merchant! I always have a chat with Mrs Glass when I purchase my high-dried. Well, to your business.'

'I am muckle obliged. Sir, I am the sister of that Effie Deans, who is ordered for execution at Edinburgh.'

'Ah!' said the Duke, 'I have heard of this. A case of child-murder, under a special Act of Parliament. Duncan Forbes[1] mentioned it the other day.'

'And I am come frae the north, sir, to see what could be done for her in the way of getting a reprieve or pardon – or the like of that.'

'Alas, my poor girl. You have made a long and a sad journey to very little purpose. Your sister is ordered for execution.'

'But I am hearing that there is a Law for reprieving her, if it is the King's pleasure.'

'Certainly there is, but that is purely in the king's breast. The crime has been too common and the Scots crown-lawyers think that an example must be made. Futhermore, the recent disorders in Edinburgh have raised a Government prejudice against the nation at large. What arguments have you to offer against this, except your sisterly affection? What is your influence, if any? Have you any friends at Court?'

'None, excepting God and your Grace.'

'Alas!' said the Duke, 'I could almost say with old Ormond[2] that there is none whose influence is *smaller* with Kings and Ministers. It is a cruel part of the situation of men in my circumstances, that the public ascribe to us influence which we simply do not possess. They expect assistance which we cannot render. But candour and plain dealing is in the power of everyone, and I must not let you imagine that I have great influence to deploy for you. It does not exist. I regret to make your distress heavier, but I have no means of averting your sister's fate.'

---

[1] Duncan Forbes of Culloden, Lord Advocate at the time and later President of the Court of Sesssion. In 1746, the battlefield would be on his estate near Inverness.

[2] James Butler, 1st Duke of Ormonde, Anglo-Irish royalist soldier and poilitician.

'We must a' die, sir,' said Jeanie; 'it is our common doom for our fathers' transgression; but we shouldna *hasten* ilk other out o' the world, as your honour kens better than me.'

'My good young woman,' said the Duke mildly, 'we are all apt to blame the Law which condemns. Now, you seem to have been well educated. You must know that it is both the law of God and Man that the murderer shall surely die.'

'But, sir, Effie – that is my poor sister, sir – canna be *proved* to be a murderer. And if she be not and the Law takes her life, wha is the murderer then?'

'I am no lawyer – and I do admit the Statute is very severe.'

'But you are a law-*maker*, sir, with your leave; and therefore ye have power over the Law.'

'Not in my individual capacity. Though, as one of a large body in Parliament, I have a voice in the legislation. But that cannot serve you. Nor have I any influence with the Sovereign as would enable me to ask any favour from him. What tempted you to address yourself to me?'

'It was yourself, sir.'

'Myself? I am sure you have never seen me before.'

'No, sir. But a' the world kens that the Duke of Argyle is his country's friend and that ye speak for the right. And since there's nane like you in our present Israel, them that think themselves wranged head for refuge under your shadow. If *ye* willna stir to save the blood of an innocent countrywoman, what should we expect frae southerners and strangers? And I had another reason for troubling your honour.'

'And what is that?'

'I hae understood from my father that your honour's house and especially your gudesire[1] and *his* father laid down their lives on the scaffold in the Persecuting Time. And my father was honoured to suffer for his Faith in the cage *and* in the pillory, as is specially mentioned in the books of Peter Walker the packman, that I dare say your honour kens. And, sir, there is a gentleman that takes concern in me, that wished me to gang to your Grace's presence. His gudesire did your ain gudesire some good turn, as ye may see frae these papers.'

With these words, she gave over to the Duke the little parcel received from Butler. He opened it and began to read, immediately exclaiming,

'This is my grandfather's hand sure enough!'

To all who may have friendship for the house of Argyle, these are to certify that Benjamin Butler of Monk's regiment of Dragoons, having been, under God, the means of saving my life from four English troopers about to slay me, I, having presently no other means of recompense in my power, do give him this acknowledgment, hoping that it may be useful to him or his, during these troublesome times.

And I do adjure my friends, tenants, kinsmen, and whoever will do aught for me, either in the Highlands or Lowlands, to protect and assist the said Benjamin Butler and his friends or family on their lawful occasions, giving

---

[1] Grandfather.

them such countenance, and supply as may correspond with the benefit
he hath bestowed on me;
   Witness my hand. Lorne.

'This is a powerful injunction. This Benjamin Butler was your grandfather? You
seem too young to be his daughter.'

'He was nae kin to me, sir. He was grandfather to a sincere weel-wisher of mine.'

'Oh, I understand. He was the grandsire of him to whom you are engaged?'

'*Was* engaged, sir,' said Jeanie, sighing; 'but this unhappy business of my
sister...'

'He has surely not *deserted* you on that account, has he?'

'No, sir; he wad be the last to leave a friend in difficulties, but I maun think
for him as weel as for mysell. He is a clergyman. It would not be seemly for him
to marry the like of me, wi' this disgrace on my kindred.'

'You are a *singular* young woman,' said the Duke. 'You seem to me to think of
everyone before yourself. And have you really come down from Edinburgh, and
on foot, to solicit for your sister's life?'

'It was not a'thegither on foot, sir. I sometimes got a hurl in a wagon and I
had a horse from Ferrybridge and then the coach.'

'Well, never mind all that. Now, what reasons have you for thinking your sister
innocent?'

'Because she has not been *proved* guilty.'

She put into his hand a note of the evidence and a copy of her sister's Declaration.
These were papers which, as promised, Reuben Butler had procured after her
departure and forwarded to Mrs Glass in London to await her arrival.

'Sit down in that chair, my girl, while I look over the papers.'

Jeanie watched with the anxiety each change in his countenance as he went
through the papers with attention, making memoranda as he went along. After
reading them over, he looked up, and seemed about to speak, yet changed his mind
as if afraid of giving too hasty an opinion. He read over again several passages he
had marked as important. At length he rose, after a few minutes' deep reflection.

'Your sister's case must certainly be termed a hard one. It seems contrary to
the spirit of British law to accept that which is not proved; or to punish with
death a crime, which for aught the Prosecutor has shown, may not have been
committed at all.'

'God bless you, sir!' said Jeanie, rising, her eyes glittering through tears.

'But, alas, my poor girl,' he continued, 'what good is my opinion unless I could
impress it upon those in whose hands your sister's life lies? Besides, I am no lawyer.
I must speak with some of our Scottish gentlemen of the gown about this.'

'Sir, will what seems reasonable to you be the same to them?'

'That I do not know. Ilka man buckles his belt his ain gate – you know our
old Scots proverb. But you shall not have come to me altogether in vain. Leave
these papers here. You shall hear from me tomorrow or next day. Take care to
be at home at Mrs Glass's and ready to come to me at a moment's warning.
And... you will please to be dressed just as you are at present.'

'I wad hae putten on a bonnet, sir, but your honour kens it isna our way for
single women.'

'You judged right. I know the full value of the snood. Go now, and don't be out of the way when I send.'

'There is little fear of that, sir, for I have little heart to go about seeing sights amang this wilderness of houses. But if I might say to your Grace that if ye manage to speak to royalty, just think there can be nae such difference between you and them, as between Jeanie Deans from St Leonard's and the Duke of Argyle. So dinna be chappit back or cast down wi' the first rough answer.'

'I am not apt to mind rough answers. Do not hope too much from what I have said. I will do my best, but God keeps the hearts of Kings in his own hand.'

Jeanie curtseyed and, attended by the Duke's gentleman, went out to the hackney coach.

chapter thirty-six

Ascend, while radiant summer opens all its pride,
Thy hill, delightful Shene! Here let us sweep
The boundless landscape.
      James Thomson, *The Seasons – Summer*

Back in the coach, Jeanie underwent a very close catechism from kind, gossipy Mrs Glass on their road to the Strand. There, at the Sign of the Thistle, the good lady flourished in full glory, her shop's motto of *Nemo me Impune*,[1] distinguishing it to all Scottish folk of whatever degree. Said Mrs Glass,

'I hope you showed your breeding in speaking to His Grace of Argyle. What would he think your friends in London, if you had been "My Lording" him – and him a Duke?'

'He didna seem muckle to mind,' said Jeanie. 'He kend that I was landward bred.'

'His Grace kens me weel. I never fill his snuff-box but he says, "How d'ye do, good Mrs Glass? Have ye heard from the North lately?" And I answer, "I hope your Grace's Duchess, and your daughters are well and I trust my snuff gives your Grace satisfaction." At this, the others in the shop begin to look round and if they're Scotsman, aff come the hats. And when he leaves they look after him, and say "There goes the Prince of Scotland, God bless him!" But ye have not told me yet what words he said t'ye.'

Jeanie had no intention of doing so. She had the caution and shrewdness of her country. She answered generally; that the Duke had received her very kindly and had promised to interest himself in her sister's affair and she would hear from him in due course. She did not mention his instruction to be in readiness, nor his hint that she should *not* bring her landlady.

Next day, Jeanie declined all in suggestions to walk abroad and continued to inhale the atmosphere of Mrs Glass's small parlour. The latter flavour it owed to

---

[1]   Properly, *Nemo me impune lacessit.* The motto of all Scottish Regiments. The Latin translates literally as, ' no one assails me with impunity.' But far better rendered as the broad Scots: Wha *daur* meddle wi' me!

a certain cupboard containing canisters of real Havana tobacco, which, whether from respect to the manufacture – or fear of the Eexciseman – Mrs Glass did not care to exhibit in the shop below. It gave the room an aroma that, however fragrant to the connoisseur, was less than agreeable to Jeanie.

'I wonder,' she said to herself, 'how my cousin's silk manty,[1] and her gowd watch, or ony thing in the world, can be worth sneezing all her life in this room, when she might walk on green braes.'

Mrs Glass was equally surprised at her cousin's reluctance to stir abroad, and her indifference to the fine sights of London.

'It would help to pass away the time,' she said, 'to have something to look at.' But Jeanie was not persuadable. The day after her interview with the Duke was spent in that 'hope delayed, which maketh the heart sick.'[2] Hours fled after hours as the day wore away in fruitless expectation.

The next morning a well-dressed gentleman entered Mrs Glass's shop asking her if he might see the young woman from Scotland.

'That is my cousin Jeanie Deans, Mr Archibald,' said Mrs Glass. 'Have you any message for her from his Grace of Argyle? I will carry it to her.'

'I must give her the trouble of stepping down, Mrs Glass.'

'Jeanie, Jeanie *Deans*!' cried Mrs Glass from the bottom of the staircase, 'Come downstairs. Here is the Duke of Argyle's groom of the Chamber desiring to see you.'

This was announced in a voice so loud, as to make all within earshot aware of its importance. Jeanie appeared.

'I must ask the favour of your company a little way,' said Archibald.

'I am quite ready, sir.'

'Is my cousin to go out, Mr Archibald? Then I will hae to go wi' her. James Rasper, look to the shop! Mr Archibald,' she pushed a jar towards him, 'you take his Grace's mixture, I think. Please to fill your box while I get on my things.'

Mr Archibald transferred a modest parcel of snuff from the jar to his own mull, but declined the pleasure of Mrs Glass's company, saying his message was particularly to the young person.

'Indeed?' said Mrs Glass; 'is not that unusual, Mr Archibald? It is not to every-one from a great man's house that I would trust my cousin. Jeanie, you mustna gang through the London streets with a tartan shawl like a Highland cattle drover. Why, you'll have the mob after you! Wait till I bring down my silk cloak.'

'I have a hackney-coach waiting, madam,' said Archibald, 'and I am instructed that she must *not* change her dress.'

Mr Archibald seated himself in the front seat of the coach opposite Jeanie and they drove off in silence. After they had driven nearly for half an hour, without a word on either side, it occurred to Jeanie that the distance and time did not correspond with her former journey to the residence of the Duke. At length she said to her taciturn companion,

'Whilk way are we going?'

---

[1] Scotish version of the English Mantua, a shawl of fine material.

[2] Hope deferred maketh the heart sick, but when the desire be fulfilled it is a tree of life. Proverbs 13.12. (King James Version).

'My Lord Duke will inform you of that himself, madam,' answered Archibald, with the same solemn courtesy which marked his whole demeanour. Almost as he spoke, the hackney-coach drew up. The coachman dismounted and opened the door. Archibald got out, and assisted Jeanie to get down. She found herself in a large turnpike road outside London. On the other side of the road there was drawn up a plain coach drawn by four horses. Its panels were without a coat-of-arms, its servants without livery.

'You are punctual,' said the Duke as Archibald opened the carriage-door. 'You will be my sole companion for the rest of the way. Archibald will remain here with the hackney-coach till your return.'

Jeanie now found herself seated by the Duke's side in a carriage rolling forward rapidly yet smoothly and very different from the lumbering, jolting vehicle she had just left.

'Now, Jeanie,' said the Duke, 'I believe that a great injustice would be done by the execution of this sentence on your sister. This is also the view of several intelligent lawyers of both countries I have spoken with. Nay, pray hear me out before you thank me. I have already told you that my personal conviction is of little consequence unless I can impress it upon others. Now, I have asked an audience of a Lady whose influence with the King is very high. An audience has been granted and I am desirous that you should see her and speak for yourself. You have no occasion to be abashed; tell your story simply, just as you did to me.'

'I am much obliged,' said Jeanie. 'But, sir, I need to ken what to ca' her, is't your Grace – or your Leddyship as we say in Scotland? it I ken leddies are particular about their titles.'

'Call her Madam, and nothing but Madam. Just say what you think is likely to make the best impression. Look at me from time to time – and if I put my hand to my cravat *so* – I am showing you the motion – you must stop. But I shall only do this should you say anything to give displeasure.'

'But your Grace,' said Jeanie, 'if it wasna muckle trouble, wad it no be better to tell me what I *should* say, so that I could get it by heart?'

'No, Jeanie! That would not have the same effect. That would be like *reading* a sermon which we Presbyterians think has far less power than when spoken. Just speak as plainly and boldly to this lady as you did to me the day before yesterday. If you can gain her consent, I'll wad ye a plack,[1] as we say in the north, that you'll get the pardon from the King.'

As he spoke, he took a pamphlet from his pocket, and began to read. Jeanie had the tact to interpret this as a hint that she was to ask no more questions. She remained silent.

The carriage rolled rapidly onwards through fertile meadows, ornamented with splendid old oaks, and giving the occasional sight of a broad and placid river. After passing through a village, the equipage stopped on a commanding eminence, where the English landscape was displayed in its utmost luxuriance. Here the Duke alighted and desired Jeanie to follow him. They paused for a moment on the brow of a hill to gaze on the view below. There were promontories of massive

---

[1] Lay you a wager.

groves of trees, while flocks and cattle herds wandering through the pastures. The Thames, its banks lined with turreted villas and garlanded with forests, flowed slowly by, bearing barks and skiffs, whose white sails and fluttering pennons gave life to the whole.

'A fine scene, Jeanie Deans,' said Argyle. 'Nothing quite like it in Scotland.'

'It's braw rich feeding for the cows, and they have a fine breed o' cattle here,' replied Jeanie; 'but I like just as weel the craigs of St Leonard's – with the sea beyond.'

The Duke smiled and signalled the carriage to remain where it was. Then, taking a footpath, he conducted Jeanie through several complicated mazes to a postern-door set in a high brick wall. It was shut; but as the Duke tapped lightly on it, a person waiting within unlocked the door. They entered, the door being immediately closed and fastened behind them. This was all done quickly, the gatekeeper so rapidly disappearing that Jeanie caught not a glimpse of him.

They found themselves at the end of a deep and narrow alley, carpeted with verdant, close-shaven turf, which felt like velvet underfoot. It was screened from the sun by the branches of lofty elms which united high above the path. In the solemn obscurity of the light they admitted, like the aisle of a Gothic cathedral was the path now taken by Jeanie Deans and the Duke.

chapter thirty-seven

I beseech you –
These tears beseech you, and these chaste hands woo you
That never yet were heaved but to things holy –
Things like yourself – You are a God above us;
Be as a God, then, full of saving mercy!
      John Fletcher & Ben Jonson
      Duke Rollo of Normandy, or *The Bloody Brother*

Encouraged as she was by the courteous manners of her noble companion, it was not without fear that Jeanie felt herself in a remote place with a man of such rank. She had also, however, an eager desire to know where she now was and to whom she was to be presented.

She remarked that the Duke's dress was much plainer than that in which she had formerly seen him. He bore no insignia or honours and was attired as plainly as any gentleman of fashion in the streets of London. This rather conflicted with the opinion which Jeanie had begun to entertain, that perhaps he intended her to plead her cause in the presence of Royalty.

'Surely,' said she to herself, 'he wad hae putten on his braw star and garter, were we coming before the face of majesty.'

There was sense in Jeanie's reasoning, but she was not aware of the relationship then existing betwixt the Government and the Duke of Argyle, who was at this time in open opposition to the administration of Sir Robert Walpole. He was also thought to be out of favour with the royal family, despite rendering them vital services in war. It was, however, a maxim of Queen Caroline to treat her political friends with caution lest they be one day her enemies, and to treat political opponents with the same circumspection. Since Margaret of Anjou,[1] no queen consort had exercised such weight in the political affairs of England. Her husband, whose finest quality was his courage on the field of battle,[2] reigned as King of Great Britian without ever acquiring English habits. While jealously pretending to act according to his own will, he would quietly take and follow the advice of his adroit Queen. He entrusted to her the delicate duties of steadying the waverers, confirming such as were already friendly and regaining those whose goodwill had been lost.

While retaining all the winning address of an elegant and accomplished woman, Queen Caroline was possessed of a masculine soul. She loved the real exercise of power, rather than simply the show of it. Whatever she did herself that was either wise or popular, she always saw to it that the King should have the full credit, conscious that by adding to his respect, she maintained her own.

It was a consistent part of Queen Caroline's policy to keep up private correspondence with those who, in public, seemed to stand ill with the Court. By this means she kept in her hands the threads of many a political intrigue and thus might prevent discontent from becoming hatred, or opposition rising into open rebellion. If her private correspondence with persons out of favour chanced to be discovered, it was represented as apolitical and mere societal intercourse. With such an answer even Sir Robert Walpole had been compelled to accept on discovering that the Queen had given a private audience to Pulteney, afterwards the Earl of Bath, his most inveterate enemy.[3]

Following her policy of occasional intercourse with persons apparently alienated from the Crown, Queen Caroline had taken care not to break entirely with the Duke of Argyle. His high birth, and the regard in which he was held in Scotland, ranked him as one not to be neglected. Furthermore, there was his great service to the House of Brunswick in the 1715 rising when, almost single-handedly, he had halted the banding together of all the Highland chiefs. It was well known that flattering overtures had been made to the Duke from the Jacobite court at St Germains.[4] The temper of Scotland was still seen as a volcano which might slumber for years, yet still be capable of eruption. It was therefore of the highest importance for the Sovereign to retain some hold over the Duke. Queen Caroline preserved the means of doing so by means of a lady with whom, as the wife of George II, she might have been thought to be on less than intimate terms...

The Queen's adroitness had contrived that one of her principal attendants, Lady Suffolk, should be both her husband's mistress and her own confidante. By

---

[1]   The wife of King Henry VI of England; as such she was Queen Consort 1445–1461 and 1470–1471. She also claimed to be Queen Consort of France from 1445–1453.

[2]   King George II was the last British monarch to command troops in battle; at Dettingen in Bavaria (1743) during the War of the Austrian Succession.

[3]   William Pulteney (1684–1764) 1st Earl of Bath. Whig politician.

[4]   King Louis XV set up the Jacobite Court-in-Exile of James Edward Stuart ('The Old Pretender'), son of James II, at the Chateau of St Germain en Laye, near Versailles.

such dexterous management, Caroline secured her influence against the danger which might have threatened it – the thwarting influence of a rival. If she submitted to the mortification of her husband's infidelity, she was at least guarded against its most dangerous effects. She was also at liberty, now and then, to bestow a few civil insults upon her 'good Howard,' but treated her generally with decorum.[1]

Lady Suffolk lay under strong obligations to the Duke of Argyle, and through her the Duke maintained an occasional correspondence with the Queen. This, however, had been much interrupted by the position he had taken in the debate on the Porteous mob. This was an affair which the Queen regarded as a premeditated insult to her own authority as Regent, rather than what it was – an outbreak of popular vengeance. However, communications remained open betwixt them, though disused of late on both sides.

From the narrow alley which they had traversed, the Duke turned into one another, but broader and still longer. For the first time since entering these gardens, Jeanie saw persons approaching.

They were two ladies; one of whom walked a little behind the other, yet not so far as to prevent her from hearing and replying to whatever was addressed to her by the foremost person. As they slowly advanced, Jeanie had time to study their features and appearance. The Duke also slackened his pace, as if to give her time to collect herself. He told her not to be afraid. The lady who seemed the principal person had remarkably good features, though somewhat injured by the smallpox. Her eyes were brilliant, her teeth good and her countenance expressed majesty or courtesy at will. Her form, though rather *embonpoint*,[2] was graceful, and the firmness of her step gave no room to suspect what was actually the case, that she suffered occasionally from the gout. Her dress was rather rich than gay, her manner commanding and noble.

Her companion was of shorter stature, with light brown hair and expressive blue eyes. Her features, without being absolutely regular, were perhaps more pleasing than if they had been critically handsome. A pensive expression predominated when she was silent, but gave way to a pleasing and good-humoured smile.

When they were within twelve yards of these ladies, the Duke made a sign that Jeanie should stand still. Stepping forward with the grace natural to him, he made a low bow, formally returned by the leading personage.

'I trust,' she said, with an affable smile, 'that I see so great a stranger at court as the Duke of Argyle has been of late; and in as good health as his friends could wish.'

'I have been perfectly well,' the Duke replied. 'The necessity of attending to business before the House, and a recent journey into Scotland, has rendered me less assiduous in attending the *levée* and the drawing-room, than I could have desired.'

'When your Grace *can* find time for a duty so frivolous,' replied the Queen, 'you shall be well received. I hope my readiness to comply with the request you

---

[1] Henrietta Howard, Countess of Suffolk (1689–1767) Witty and intelligent, she is thought to have been the model for Chloe in Alexander Pope's *The Rape of the Lock*. Her correspondents included Horace Walpole and Jonathan Swift.

[2] French: *En bon point*, Literally: in good condition, the English meaning being 'plump'.

made to Lady Suffolk yesterday, is proof that at least *one* member of the royal family has not forgotten your Grace's former important services.'

This was said with good humour and in a conciliatory tone.

The Duke replied that he was deeply gratified by the honour which her Majesty was now doing to him. He trusted also that she would soon perceive that it was in a matter essential to his Majesty's interest, that he had had the boldness to give her this trouble.

'You cannot oblige me more, my Lord Duke,' replied the Queen, 'than by giving me the advantage of your experience in the King's service. Your Grace is aware, that I can only be the medium through which any matter is subjected to his Majesty's superior wisdom; but if it is a suit affecting your Grace personally, it shall lose no support by being presented to the King through me.'

'It is not a suit of mine, madam,' replied the Duke, 'although I feel in full force my obligation to your Majesty. It is a business which concerns his Majesty as a lover of justice and of mercy. I am convinced also that it may be useful in concil-iating the unfortunate irritation at present subsisting among his Majesty's subjects in Scotland.'

There were two parts of this speech disagreeable to Caroline. In the first place, it removed the flattering notion she had conceived that Argyle sought her personal intercession in making peace with the administration. She was also displeased that he should talk of the discontent in Scotland as an irritation to be conciliated, rather than actively suppressed. She thus answered hastily,

'His Majesty has loyal subjects in England, my Lord Duke, for which he thanks God and the Law. That he has subjects in Scotland, I think he may thank God and his *sword*.'

The Duke, though a courtier, coloured slightly. Instantly realising her error, the Queen added, without displaying the least change of countenance and as if the words were an original branch of the sentence, '*And* the swords of those real Scotchmen who are friends to the House of Brunswick, *particularly* that of his Grace of Argyle.'

'My sword, madam,' replied the Duke, 'like that of my fathers, has been always at the command of my lawful King and of my native country. But the present is a matter of more private concern, and respects the person of an obscure individual.'

'What is the affair, your Grace?' said the Queen. 'Let us discover what we are talking about, lest we misunderstand each other.'

'The matter, Madam, regards the fate of an unfortunate young woman in Scotland, now lying under sentence of death for a crime of which I think it highly probable that she is innocent. And my humble petition to your Majesty is to obtain your powerful intercession with the King for a royal pardon.'

It was now the Queen's turn to colour, and she did so over cheek and brow. She paused a moment as if unwilling to trust her voice with an initial expression of displeasure. Assuming an air of dignity and an austere control, she at length replied:

'My Lord Duke, I will not ask your motives for addressing to me such an extraordinary request. As a Peer and a Privy Councillor entitled to request an audience, your road to the King's closet was open without giving me the pain of this discussion. *I*, at least, have had enough of Scotch pardons.'

The Duke was prepared for such a burst of indignation and was not shaken by it. He did not attempt a reply with the Queen in the first heat of displeasure, but remained in the same firm yet respectful posture which he had assumed during the interview. The Queen, trained to self-command, perceived the advantage she might lose by yielding to passion. She then added, in her original affable tone,

'You must not judge uncharitably of me. I am moved at the recollection of the gross insult done in Edinburgh to the royal authority at the very time when it was vested in my unworthy person as Regent. Your Grace cannot be surprised that I should both have felt it at the time – and recollected it now.'

'It is certainly not a matter to be forgotten,' answered the Duke. 'My thoughts of it have been long before your Majesty, and I must have expressed myself very ill if I did not convey my detestation of the murder. I might indeed differ from his Majesty's advisers on whether it was either just, or politic, to punish the innocent instead of the guilty. I trust your Majesty will permit me to be silent on a topic in which my opinion has not the good fortune to coincide with those of more able men.'

'We will not prosecute a topic on which we will probably differ,' said the Queen. 'One word, however, I may say privately, for you know our good Lady Suffyle here is a little deaf. The Duke of Argyle, when disposed to renew his acquaintance with his master and mistress, will find few topics on which we should disagree.'

'Let me hope,' the Duke, bowing at so flattering an intimation, 'that I shall not be so unfortunate as to have found one on the present occasion.'

'I must first impose on your Grace the duty of confession,' said the Queen, 'before I grant you absolution. What is your particular interest in this young woman? She does not seem qualified to excite the jealousy of my friend your Duchess. Though she has not the air *d'une grande dame*, I suppose she is some 30th cousin in the terrible chapter of Scottish genealogy?'

'No, Madam, but I wish some of my nearer relations had half her worth and honesty.'

'Her name must be Campbell at least?'

'No, madam; her name is not *quite* so distinguished, if I may be permitted to say so.'

'Ah! But she comes from your Inverary or Argyle-shire?'

'She has never been north of Edinburgh in her life.'

'Then my conjectures are all ended,' said the Queen, 'and your Grace must take the trouble to explain the affair of your *protégée*.'

With the precision and easy brevity acquired by habitually conversing in society, the Duke explained the singular Statute under which Effie Deans had received sentence of death. He detailed the exertions which Jeanie had made in behalf of a sister, for whose sake she was willing to sacrifice all but truth and conscience.

Queen Caroline listened with attention; being fond of debate and argument, she soon found grounds in what the Duke had told her for raising difficulties.

'It appears to me, my Lord,' she replied, 'that this is a severe Law. But still, it is adopted upon good grounds I am bound to suppose. It is the law of the country and the girl has been convicted under it. The presumptions which the law construes as proof positive of guilt, exist in her case. All your Grace has said concerning her possible innocence may be a good argument for annulling the Act of Parliament, but while it stands, they cannot be admitted in favour of an individual convicted under that Statute.'

The Duke saw and avoided the snare. He was conscious that replying to the argument would inevitably lead into a discussion in which the Queen's opinion was likely to harden to the point where she became obliged, out of respect to consistency, to let the criminal suffer.

'If your Majesty,' he said, 'would condescend to hear my countrywoman herself, perhaps she may find an advocate in your own heart; one more able I to combat the doubts suggested by your understanding.'

The Queen seemed to acquiesce. The Duke made a signal for Jeanie to advance from where she had been watching; and from where she had also been observing countenances too long accustomed to suppress emotion, to convey any meaning to her. Queen Caroline smiled at the awestruck manner in which the quiet, demure figure advanced towards her and yet more at the sound of her broad Scots accent.

'Stand up, young woman,' said the Queen kindly, 'and tell me what sort of people your country-folk are, where child-murder is so common as to require the restraint of Law?'

'If your Leddyship pleases,' answered Jeanie, 'there are mony places *besides* Scotland where mothers are unkind to their ain flesh and blood.'

It should be observed that at this time, disputes between King George and Frederick Prince of Wales were then at their highest and that the public laid the blame on the Queen. She coloured smartly and darted a penetrating glance first at Jeanie, then at the Duke. Both sustained it unmoved; Jeanie from total ignorance of the offence given, the Duke from his habitual composure. But in his heart he thought, 'Oh my poor girl. That luckless answer has shot dead your only hope of success.'

Lady Suffolk good-humouredly and skilfully interposed in this awkward crisis.

'You must tell this lady,' she said to Jeanie, 'the particular causes which make this crime common in your country.'

'Some think it's the Kirk Session; it's the cutty stool, if your Leddyship pleases,' said Jeanie, looking down.

'The what?' said Lady Suffolk, to whom the phrase was new.

'The stool of repentance, madam, if it please your Leddyship,' answered Jeanie, 'for loose living and for breaking the Seventh Commandment.'

Here she raised her eyes to the Duke, saw his hand move to his chin and, totally unaware of what she had said, gave double effect to the innuendo by stopping short and looking embarrassed. Lady Suffolk retired like a covering party placed betwixt their comrades and the enemy and coming suddenly under fire. Deuce take the lass, thought Argyle to himself; another shot and a hit with both barrels!

Indeed, the Duke felt confusion as master of ceremonies to this innocent offender. Jeanie's last sally, however, had obliterated the bad impression arising from the first. Her Majesty had not so lost the feelings of a wife in those of a Queen, that she could enjoy a jest at the expense of Lady Suffolk. She turned towards the Duke, a smile marking her pleasure and observed,

'The Scotch are truly a rigidly moral people.' She then asked how Jeanie had travelled down from Scotland.

'Upon my feet mostly, madam.'

'What, all that immense way on *foot*? How far can you walk in a day?'

'Five and twenty miles and a bittock.'

'And a what?'

'And about five miles more,' said the Duke.

'I thought I was a good walker,' said the Queen, 'but this shames me sadly.'

'May your Leddyship never had sae weary a heart, that ye canna be sensible of the weariness of the limbs,' said Jeanie. That was better, thought the Duke; it's the first thing she has said to the purpose.

'And I didna *a'thegither* walk the haill way neither, for I had whiles the cast of a cart; and I had the cast of a horse from Ferrybridge, and divers other easements,' said Jeanie, cutting short her story as she observed the Duke making the sign again.

'Even with these accommodations,' said the Queen, 'you must have had a very fatiguing journey. And, I fear, to little purpose. Even if the King were to pardon your sister, in all probability it would do her little good for I suppose your people of Edinburgh would hang her out of spite.'

She will sink herself now outright, thought the Duke.

He was wrong. The shoals on which Jeanie had inadvertently touched in this delicate conversation were submerged and unknown to her. This rock was above water, and she avoided it.

'I am confident that baith town and country wad rejoice to see his Majesty taking compassion on a poor unfriended creature.'

'His Majesty has not found it so in a *recent* instance,' said the Queen; 'but I suppose my Lord Duke would advise him to be guided by the rabble themselves as to who should be hanged and who spared?'

'No, madam,' said the Duke; 'I would advise his Majesty to be guided by his own feelings and those of his royal consort. Then I am sure punishment would only attach itself to guilt and even then with reluctance.'

'Well, my Lord, all these fine speeches do not convince me of the propriety of showing any mark of favour to your... I suppose I must not say *rebellious*, but at least your very *disaffected* and intractable metropolis. Why, the whole nation conceals the murderers of Porteous; otherwise, how is it possible that with so many engaged in so public an action that not *one* has been recognised? Even this wench, for aught I can tell, may be a depositary of the secret. Young woman, had you any friends engaged in the Porteous mob?'

'No, madam.'

'But I suppose,' continued the Queen, 'if you were possessed of such a secret, it would be a matter of conscience to keep it to yourself?'

'I would pray to be guided what was my duty, madam.'

'Yes, and take that which suited your own inclinations.'

'Madam,' said Jeanie, 'I would hae gaen to the end of the earth to save the life of John Porteous or any other man in his condition. But I would not be the avenger of his blood; that is for the civil Magistrate. He is dead and gane to his place. They that have slain him must answer for their ain acts.

But my sister, Madam, my puir sister Effie still *lives*, though her days and hours are numbered! She still lives and a word of the King's mouth might restore her to a broken-hearted auld man that never in his daily and nightly prayers, forgot to ask God that his Majesty might be *blessed* with a long and a prosperous reign and that his throne, and the throne of his posterity, might be established in righteousness.

Oh Madam, if ever ye kend what it was to sorrow for a sinning and a suffering creature, whose mind is sae tossed that she is fit neither tae live or die, have some compassion on our misery. Save an honest house from dishonour and a girl not eighteen years of age from an early and dreadful death!

Alack; it is not when we sleep soft and wake merrily that we think on other people's sufferings. Our hearts are light within us then, and we are for righting our ain wrangs and fighting our ain battles. But when the hour of trouble comes to the mind or to the body – and seldom may it visit your Leddyship, and when the hour of *death* comes as it does to high and low, lang and late may it be yours!

My Leddy, *then* it isna what we hae dune for oursells, but what we hae dune for *others*, that we think on maist pleasantly. And the thoughts that ye hae intervened to spare the puir thing's life will be sweeter in *that* hour, come when it may, than if a word of your mouth could hang the haill Porteous mob at the tail of ae tow.'[1]

Tears rolled down Jeanie's cheeks, her features glowing and quivering with emotion as, with a pathos both simple and solemn, she pleaded her sister's cause.

'This is eloquence,' said her Majesty to the Duke.

'Young woman,' she continued to Jeanie, '*I* cannot grant a pardon to your sister, but you shall have my intercession with his Majesty. Take this housewife case,' she continued, putting a small embroidered needle case into Jeanie's hands; 'do not open it now, but at your leisure. You will find something in it which will remind you of your interview with Queen Caroline.'

Jeanie would have fulsomely expressed her gratitude, but the Duke, concerned that she might say more than enough, touched his chin once more. The Queen now turned to Argyle,

'Our business is, I think, ended for the present, my Lord Duke. I trust, to your satisfaction. Hereafter I hope to see your Grace more frequently, both at Richmond and St James's. Come, my Lady Suffolk, we must wish his Grace good-morning.'

They exchanged their parting courtesies. As soon as the ladies had turned their backs, the Duke, conducted Jeanie back through the tree-lined avenue.

Her tread was that of one sleepwalking.

chapter thirty-eight

QUEEN: *So soon as I can win the offended king,*
I will be known your advocate.
        Cymbeline; I.I

---

[1]   Rope.

The Duke of Argyle led the way in silence to the small postern by which they had been admitted into Richmond Park, long the favourite residence of Queen Caroline. It was opened by the same half-seen janitor and they found themselves beyond the precincts of the royal demesne. Still not a word was spoken on either side. Jeanie Deans's mind was too agitated to permit the asking of questions. They found the ducal carriage where they had left it began their return to town.

'I think, Jeanie,' said the Duke, 'you should congratulate yourself on the outcome of your interview with her Majesty.'

'And that was the Queen hersel'?' said Jeanie; 'I suspected it when I saw that your honour didna put on your hat; and yet I can hardly believe it, even when I heard her speak it herself.'

'It was certainly Queen Caroline. Have you no curiosity to see what is in the little pocket-book?'

'Do you think the Pardon will be in it, sir?'

'No. Her Majesty told you it was the King, not she, who must grant it.'

'That is true, too,' said Jeanie; 'but I am confused. Does your honour think there is a certainty of Effie's pardon then?' He held in her hand the unopened pocket-book.

'Kings are kittle cattle to shoe behind,[1] as we say in the north,' said the Duke; 'but his wife knows his trim and I have not the least doubt that the matter is quite certain.'

'Oh, God be *praised*!' said Jeanie; 'and may she ne'er lack the heart's ease she has gien me! And God bless your Grace too! Without you I wad ne'er hae won near her.'

The Queen's present was now opened. Inside the case was the usual assortment of silk and needles, with scissors, etc.; but in the pocket was a bank-bill for fifty pounds.

The Duke told Jeanie of the value of the bill as she was unaccustomed to see notes for such sums. She immediately expressed her regret at the mistake which had taken place.

'For the hussy[2] itsell,' she said, 'was a very valuable thing for a keepsake, with the Queen's name written in the inside in her ain hand doubtless – *Caroline* – as plain as could be and a crown drawn aboon it.'

She tendered the bill to the Duke, asking him to return it.

'No, Jeanie, this is no mistake. Her Majesty knows you have been put to great expense and she wishes to make it up to you.'

'I am sure she is ower generous. But it glads me that I can now repay Dumbiedikes his siller without distressing my father.'

'Dumbiedikes? A freeholder of Midlothian, is he not?' said Argyle, whose occasional residence in the county made him acquainted with most of its landed persons. 'His house not far from Dalkeith; wears a black wig and a laced hat?'

'Yes sir.'

'My old friend Dumbie. Is he a cousin of yours?'

---

[1] Metaphorically, Kings' reactions are difficult to predict when operations are performed in their name by others.

[2] A housewife's case.

'No, sir.'

'Then a well-wisher?'

'Yes...' answered Jeanie, blushing and with hesitation.

'Aha! Then if the Laird is interested in you, my friend Butler must be in some danger?'

'Oh no, sir!' Jeanie blushed deeply.

'Well,' said the Duke, 'you are a girl who may be safely trusted with your own matters. I shall inquire no farther into them. But as to the Pardon, I must see it pass through the proper forms; and I have a friend in Office who will do me this favour. Jeanie, I shall send an express messenger up to Scotland who will travel with it safer and more swiftly than you can do. Meanwhile you may write of your success to your friends by post.'

'Does not your Grace no think that I should just take it in my lap and slip hame again?'

'No,' said the Duke. 'The roads are not safe for a travelling single woman. And I have a plan for you besides. One of the Duchess's attendants and one of mine, you know Mr Archibald, are going up to Inverary in a light calash[1] with four horses I have bought. There is room enough in the carriage for you to go with them as far as Glasgow, where Archibald will find means of sending you safely to Edinburgh. And on the way I ask that you teach my woman the mystery of cheese-making, for she is to have charge in the dairy. I dare say you are as tidy about that as about your dress.'

'Does your Honour like cheese?'

'Cakes and cheese are dinner for an Emperor, let alone a Highlandman.'

'Some folk think our cheeses as gude as the real Dunlop; and if your Grace wad but accept a stane or twa, proud it wad make us.'

'The Dunlop,' said the Duke; 'is the very one of which I am so fond. I will take it as a favour were you to send one to Caroline Park. But mind to make it all yourself Jeanie, for I am a good judge.'

This discourse introduced a topic upon which the two travellers, so different in rank and education, each found a good deal to say. The Duke was a distinguished agriculturist and proud of his knowledge in that department. He gave Jeanie his observations on the breeds of cattle in Scotland and their capacity for the dairy, receiving much information from her practical experience in return. He promised her a couple of Devonshire cows in reward for the lesson. In short, his mind was so transported back to his rural activities that he sighed when his carriage stopped opposite to the old hackney-coach with Archibald in attendance. The Duke cautioned Jeanie not to be too communicative to her landlady on what had passed.

'There is,' he said, 'no use of speaking of matters till they are actually settled. Refer the good lady to Archibald if she presses you hard with questions. He knows how to manage her.'

He then took a cordial farewell of Jeanie, telling her to be ready in a week to

---

1   Also called a Barouche. A four-wheeled open carriage with facing passengers and an elevated coachman's seat.

return to Scotland and saw her safely into her hackney-coach. His own carriage then rolled away.

The hackney coach rumbled over the execrable London pavement at a rate very different from that which had conveyed the ducal carriage to Richmond. At length it deposited Jeanie Deans and her attendant at Scotland's national sign of the Thistle. Mrs Glass, full of eager curiosity, rushed out with a cataract of questions:

'Had she seen the Duke, God bless him; the Duchess? Had she seen the King, God bless him too; the Queen; the Prince of Wales? Had she got her sister's pardon? Was it out and out, or only a commutation? What had kept her so long?' Archibald, who had received an instruction from his master, advanced to her rescue.

'Mrs Glass,' said Archibald, 'his Grace desired me particularly to say, that he would take it as a great favour if you would ask the Miss Deans no questions, as he himself wishes to explain to you how her affairs stand. He will also consult you on other matters which she cannot well explain. The Duke will call here at the Thistle tomorrow.'

'His Grace is very considerate.' said Mrs Glass.

'Thank you,' said Archibald. 'I must now return to my Lord directly.' And, making his adieus civilly to both cousins, he left.

'I am glad your affairs have prospered, Jeanie my love,' said Mrs Glass; 'I will ask you no questions because his Grace intends to tell me all. But whether you or he tells it, will make no difference, ye ken. If I ken beforehand what he is going to say, I will be much more ready to give my advice. So you may just say whatever you like, wi' nae questions frae me...'

Jeanie was embarrassed. She wished to gratify her hospitable kinswoman. Prudence, however, suggested that her secret interview with Queen Caroline was not a subject for the gossip of Mrs Glass, whose heart was better than her discretion. She therefore answered in general: the Duke had had the kindness to make enquiries into her sister's affair; he thought he had the means of putting it straight; he would tell all to Mrs Glass himself.

This did not quite satisfy the mistress of the Thistle. Searching in spite of her promise, she urged Jeanie with farther questions.

'Had she been a' the time at Argyle House? Was the Duke with her the whole time? Had she seen the Duchess and specially Lady Caroline Campbell?' Jeanie gave the general reply that she knew so little of the town that she could not tell exactly where she had been. She had not seen the Duchess to her knowledge, but had seen two ladies, one of whom bore the name of Caroline. More she could not tell.

'It would be the Duke's eldest daughter, Lady Caroline, no doubt of that,' said Mrs Glass. 'And so, as the cloth is laid and it is past three o'clock and I have been waiting an hour for you, I have had a snack myself. As we say in Scotland, there is ill talk between a full body and a fasting!'

chapter thirty-nine

Heav'n first taught letters for some wretch's aid,
Some banish'd lover or some captive maid;
Alexander Pope, *Eloisa to Abelard*

By dint of unwonted labour with her pen, Jeanie Deans contrived to write and give to the postman next day no less than three letters. The first was brief. It was addressed to George Staunton, Esq., at Willingham Rectory, Grantham:

> *Sir,*
>
> *I have my sister's pardon from the Queen's Majesty, whereof I do not doubt you will be glad. I have had to say naught of matters whereof you know the purport.*
>
> *I pray for your better welfare in bodie and soul. I also pray you will never again see my sister. And so, wishing you no evil, but that you may be turned from your iniquity, I rest your humble servant,*
>
> *J. D.*

The next letter was to her father. It commenced –

> *Dearest Father,*
>
> *This comes with my duty to inform you that it has pleased God to redeem the captivitie of my poor sister. This comes through the Queen's Majesty, for whom we are ever bound to pray. I spoke with the Queen face to face, for she is not muckle differing from other grand leddies, having a stately presence and een like a blue hunting hawk.*
>
> *All this good was, alway under the Great Giver to whom all are but instruments, wrought for us by the Duke of Argyle, ane true-hearted Scotsman, and not pridefu', like other folk, but skeely in bestial. He has promised me twa Devonshire kye, of which he is enamoured, although I do still haud by the Ayrshire breed. I have promised him a cheese.*
>
> *Father, since it hath pleased God to be merciful to Effie, let her have your pardon, whilk will make her a vessel of Grace.*
>
> *Let the Laird ken that we have the means to repay him in ane wee bit paper as is the fashion here, whilk I am assured is gude for the siller. Through Mr Butler I hae gude friendship with the Duke, through the kindness between their forbears in the Troubled Time.*
>
> *Mrs Glass has been kind like my very mother. She has a braw house and lives wi' twa servant lasses and a man and a callant in the shop. And she is to send you a pound of her snuff. The Duke is to send the pardon by an express messenger, since I canna travel sae fast; and I am to come doun wi' twa of his servants – that is, John Archibald, a decent gentleman that says he has seen you lang syne, when ye were buying beasts in the West and Mrs Dolly Dutton, that is to be the dairymaid at Inverara.*

They bring me on as far as Glasgow, whilk will make it nae pinch to win hame, whilk I desire most of all things. May the Giver of all good things keep ye; whereof devoutly prayeth,

your loving daughter,

Jean Deans

The third letter was to Butler:

Master Butler,

It will be pleasure to you to ken, that all I came for is done, thanks be to God. Your forebear's letter was right welcome to the Duke of Argyle. He wrote your name down with a lead pencil in a leathern book, whereby it seems he will present you to either a Schule or a Kirk; he has enough of baith, as I am assured.

And I have seen the Queen, which gave me a hussy-case out of her own hand. She had not on her crown and skeptre, but they are laid by for her to be worn at need. They are keepit in a Towr, whilk is not like the tour of Libberton, nor event Craigmillar, but mair like to the castell of Edinburgh.

Also the Queen was very bounteous, giving me a paper worth fiftie pounds I am assured, to pay my expenses here and back again.

And mind, this is no meant to haud ye to onything whilk ye wad rather forget, if ye suld get the charge of a Kirk or a Schule. Only I hope it will be a Schule, and not a Kirk. I wish I kend what books ye wanted, Reuben, for they hae haill houses of them here. Many they are obliged to set out in the street, whilk are sald cheap. London is a muckle place and I hae seen sae muckle o' it, that my poor head turns. And as ye ken, I am nae great penwoman, and it is near eleven o'clock o' the night. I am cuming home in good company, and safe; but I had troubles in cuming here whilk makes me blyther of travelling wi' folk I ken.

My cousin, Mrs Glass, has a braw house here, but poisoned wi' snuff.

But what matters these things in comparison of the great deliverance vouchsafed to my father's house, in whilk you, as our dear well-wisher, will rejoice and be glad.

I am, dear Reuben, your sincere

well-wisher in temporal and eternal things,

J. D.

Three days later came the expected coach. Four servants in dark brown and yellow livery clustered behind on the footboard and attended the Duke in laced coat, gold-headed cane, Star and Garter, and very grand.

To Mrs Glass he enquired of Miss Deans but without requesting to see her.

'The Queen,' he told Mrs Glass, 'had taken the case of Miss Euphemia Deans into her gracious consideration and, moved by the character of her elder sister, had interceded for mercy with his Majesty. In consequence of which, a Pardon has been dispatched to Scotland releasing Euphemia Deans on condition of her banishment from Scotland for fourteen years. The King's Advocate had insisted on this, having pointed out to his Majesty's ministers that within the last seven years, twenty-one instances of child-murder had occurred in Scotland.'

'Weary on him!' said Mrs Glass. 'What for needed he to say that of his ain country and to the English? I used to think the Advocate a douce and decent man, but it is an ill bird that fouls its ain nest. And what is the poor lassie to do in a foreign land? Wae's me, it's just sending her to play the same pranks again, this time out of the sight or guidance of her friends.'

'That need not happen,' said the Duke. 'Why, she may come down to London or go over to America and marry well. Is she pretty? Her sister is a comely lass.'

'Oh, far prettier is Effie than Jeanie, though it is long since I saw her mysell.'

'So much the better,' said the Duke. 'And now I hope you will approve of the measures I have taken for restoring your kinswoman to her friends.' These he detailed at length. 'And now, Mrs Glass, tell Jeanie not to forget my Dunlop cheese when she gets to Scotland. Mr Archibald has orders to settle her expenses.'

'Your Grace's pardon, but the Deanses are well off people in their way. The lass has money in her pocket.'

'True,' said the Duke; 'but where *MacCailean Mór* travels, he pays. It is our Highland privilege to take from all what *we* want, and to give to all what *they* want.'

'Your Grace is better at giving than taking.'

'To the contrary,' said the Duke, 'I will fill my snuffbox out of this canister without paying you a *bawbee*!'

He departed.

The banishment grieved her. She was relieved, however, by a letter from her father. It brought his blessing and approval of the steps she had taken.

'If ever a deliverance was dear and precious,' said the letter, 'it is this. The Duke of Argyle is a noble and true-hearted nobleman, who pleads the cause of the poor and of those who have none to help them. His reward shall not be lacking unto him.

I receive this dispensation anent Effie as a call to depart out of Haran,[1] like righteous Abraham of old, and leave my father's kindred and the ashes of them who have gone to sleep before me. I am strengthened in this resolution to change my domicile, hearing that farms are to be had at easy rent in Northumberland.

The Laird has been a true friend and I have paid him back the siller for Effie's misfortune, whereof Mr Nichil Novit returned him no balance, as the Laird and I expected. But 'Law licks up a',' as the common folk say.

As for the Queen, and mercy and the Grace ye found with her, I can only pray for her weel-being and for the establishment of her house for ever upon the throne of these Kingdoms. I doubt not but that you told her Majesty that I was that David Deans who, at the Revolution, noited thegither the heads of those ungracious Graces the prelates that stood on the High Street after being expelled from the Convention – parliament.[2]

---

[1] Harran was a temporary home of the patriarch Abraham. It is in present day Turkey. From there, Abraham departed for Shechem in Canaan. Genesis 11.27–32.

[2] The Convention of Estates of 1689 was dominated by the Presbyterians. It expelled the Epispalian Bishops from the assembly.

I have now seen my misguided daughter. She will be at freedom the morn, provided she shall leave Scotland in four weeks. Her mind is misdirected, however. She casts her eyes backward on Egypt as if the wilderness were harder to endure than the brick furnaces and the savoury flesh-pots. I need not bid you make haste here for you are, excepting my Great Master, my only comfort in these straits. Reuben Butler has been as a son to me in my sorrows.

I charge you to withdraw your feet from the delusion of London, that Vanity Fair where ye sojourn. Go not to their Episcopal worship, whilk is an ill-mumbled Mass, as weel termed by Jamie the Saxt,[1] though he and his unhappy son later strove to bring it ower back into his native Kingdom, whereby their race has been cut off as foam upon the water and shall be as wanderers among the nations: See the prophecies of Hosea, ninth & seventeenth, and the same, tenth & seventh. But as for us and our house, let us say with the same prophet, 'Let us return to the Lord, for he hath torn, and he will heal us – He hath smitten, and he will bind us up.'[2]

As Deans had scarcely ever mentioned Butler before without some gibe either at his carnal gifts and learning, or at his grandfather's heresy, Jeanie saw a good omen from no such qualifying clause being added.

Her three weeks' residence in London becoming tedious to her, it was with satisfaction that she received a summons from Argyle House, requiring her to be ready in two days to join their northward party.

chapter forty

One was a female, who had grievous ill
Wrought in revenge, and she enjoy'd it still;
Sullen she was, and threatening; in her eye
Glared the stern triumph that she dared to die.
George Crabbe, *The Borough*

On the morning appointed, Jeanie took a grateful farewell of Mrs Glass and placed herself, her goods, purchases and presents in a hackney-coach and joined her travelling companions in the housekeeper's apartment at Argyle House. While the carriage was being readied, she was informed that the Duke wished to speak with her. She was ushered into a splendid saloon to find that he wished to present her to his Duchess and daughters.

'I bring you my countrywoman, Duchess.'

The Duchess advanced and, in a few kind and civil words, assured Jeanie of the respect generated by her affectionate and firm character, adding,

'When you get home, you will perhaps hear from me.'

'And from me.' 'From me.' 'And from *me*, Jeanie,' added the young ladies, one after the other.

---

[1] King James VI & I.
[2] Hosea 6.1

Jeanie, overpowered by these compliments, and unaware that the Duke's investigation had covered her behaviour on her sister's trial, could only answer by blushing and saying,

'My thanks!'

'Jeanie,' said the Duke, 'you must have *doch an' dorroch*[1] or you will be unable to travel.'

There was a salver with cake and wine on the table. He took up a glass, drank 'to all true hearts that love Scotland', and offered a glass to his guest. Jeanie declined, saying,

'I have never tasted wine in my life.'

'How comes that, Jeanie?'

'Sir, my father is like Jonadab the son of Rechab who charged his children that they should drink no wine.'[2]

'Then, Jeanie, if you will not drink you must eat!' He gave her a large piece of cake.

'Take it with you, Jeanie,' said he; 'you will be glad of it before you see St Giles. I wish to Heaven I might see it as soon as you! And so, my best service to all my friends about Auld Reekie and a blithe journey to you.'

He shook hands with his *protégée*, and committed her to the charge of Archibald, knowing that his unusual attention to her would ensure the same from his domestics.

Accordingly, in the course of her journey, she found both her companions paying her every civility so that her return, in terms of comfort and safety, formed a distinct contrast to her journey to London. Her heart also was relieved of the weight of grief, shame and fear, which had loaded her before the interview with the Queen at Richmond. But the human mind, when freed from real misery, becomes open and sensitive to lesser calamities. She was now much disturbed that she had heard nothing from Reuben Butler.

'It would have cost him sae little fash,' she said to herself; 'for I hae seen his pen go as fast ower the paper, as ever it did when it was on the grey goose's wing. Maybe he may be ill, but then my father wad hae said something about it. But, I shall wish him weel; and if he has the luck to get a Kirk in our county, I sall gang and hear him to show that I bear nae malice.'

As she imagined the scene, a tear stole over her eye.

Approaching Carlisle, they noticed a considerable crowd upon an eminence at a little distance from the high road. From some people heading towards that busy scene they heard that the cause of the concourse was,

'To see a doomed Scotch witch and thief get only half of her due upo' Haribeebroo' yonder; for she was only to be hanged, when she should hae been boorned alive.'

'How interesting, Mr. Archibald,' said May Dutton, the Argyles' new dame of the dairy. 'I never seed a woman hanged in a' my life, and only four men. It makes a goodly spectacle.'

---

[1] Gaelic: *Deoch an doruis*, literally: drink of the door.

[2] *See* Jeremiah 35.6–19. His name was adopted by The Rechabites, a total abstinence society. The sounds of singing from the pier would alert Para Handy aboard the *Vital Spark* that Dougie the Mate had, once again, 'broken with the Rechabites.'

Archibald, however, was a Scotsman and a man of sense and delicacy. The cause of Jeanie's expedition to London was known to him. He answered drily that it was impossible to stop as he must be early at Carlisle on some business of the Duke's. He bade the postilions press on.

The road at that time passed at about a quarter of a mile's distance from the eminence called Haribee or Harabee-brow which, though of modest height, is nevertheless visible from a great distance owing to the flatness of the Eden valley. Here many an outlaw and border-reiver of both kingdoms wavered in the wind during the wars and hostile truces between the two countries.

The postilions drove on, wheeling as the Penrith road led them round the verge of the rising ground. Yet still the eyes of Mrs Dutton turned towards the scene of action. All could plainly discern the outline of the gallows-tree against the clear sky, the dark shade formed by executioner and condemned upon the tall ladder. One of the objects, launched into the air, gave unequivocal signs of mortal agony though appearing in the distance not larger than a spider dangling at the end of her invisible thread. The remaining form descended and rejoined the crowd. This termination of the tragic scene drew forth a squeal from Mrs Dutton. Jeanie instinctively turned away, the sight of a female undergoing what her beloved sister had so nearly faced being too much for her mind. Faint, she turned to the other side of the carriage with a sensation of sickness and loathing. Archibald, calm and considerate, had the carriage pushed forward till they were beyond sight of the spectacle. Seeing Jeanie's paleness, he stopped the carriage and went in search of a draught of water.

While Archibald was absent, spectators of the execution began to pass the stationary vehicle on their way back to Carlisle. From their half-heard words, Jeanie, her attention involuntarily rivetted on them, discerned that the victim had died 'game' that is, sullen and impenitent, neither fearing God nor man.

'She has gone to hor master, with his name in her mouth,' said another; 'Shame the country should be harried wi' Scotch witches and Scotch bitches. Hang 'em and drown 'em, says I.'

'Silence wi' your fule tongues,' said an old woman, hobbling past, 'this was nae witch, but a bluidy-fingered thief and murderess.'

'But isna the daughter o' yon hangit body as rank a witch as sho?'

'I dunno, but folk are speaking o' swimming her i' the Eden.'

Mr Archibald returned with water as a crowd of boys and girls, and some of the rabble of more mature age, came up from the place of execution, grouping themselves around a tall, fantastically dressed female who was bounding in the midst of them. A horrible recognition hit Jeanie – and it was mutual. With a sudden burst of strength, Madge Wildfire broke away from her circle of tormentors. Clinging fast to the door of the calash, she screamed,

'Jeanie Deans! They hae hangit our mother! O gar them let me cut her down!'

Archibald, embarrassed by the madwoman clinging to the carriage and drawing a crowd around it, was now looking out for a constable to whom he might commit her. Seeing no such person, he tried to loosen her hold on the carriage, so that they might escape by driving on. Madge, however, held on fast, renewing her frantic entreaties to be allowed to cut her mother down. There now came up, however, a group of fierce-looking graziers among whose cattle there had been a fatal distemper, imputed to witchcraft. They tore Madge from the carriage, exclaiming, 'Stop folk on't king's highway? Hast no' done enough wi' thy murders and witcherings?'

'Oh, Jeanie Deans, Jeanie *Deans*!' cried Madge. 'Save my mother! I will take ye to the Interpreter's house – and teach ye a' my bonny sangs – and I will tell ye what came o' the...'

The rest of her entreaties were drowned in the shouts of the rabble.

'Save her, for God's sake!' cried Jeanie to Archibald.

'She is mad, but innocent. She is *mad*, gentlemen!' called Archibald; 'do not maltreat her. Take her before the Mayor.'

'Aye, we'll tak care o'her,' grimly answered one of the fellows; 'gang on thy way, man, an' mind thine own matters.'

It was clear nothing could be done to rescue Madge. Archibald could only bid the postilions hurry on to Carlisle to obtain assistance for the woman. As they drove off, they heard the hoarse roar with which a mob prefaces acts of riot, yet even above that they could discern the screams of the victim. In Carlisle, Archibald, at Jeanie's urgent entreaty, found a Magistrate who went with him and managed to rescue the woman. When they came to the muddy pool in which the mob were ducking her, the Magistrate succeeded in rescuing her. She was unconscious. Revived, she was carried to the workhouse.

Wildfire was not expected to survive the treatment she had received, but Jeanie seemed so agitated that Archibald did not think it prudent to tell her the worst at once. Indeed, she appeared so affected by the incident that although their intention was to go on to Longtown that evening, he judged it advisable to pass the night at Carlisle.

Jeanie wished to see Madge Wildfire. Connecting some of her wild flights with George Staunton's story, she hoped to hear the fate of her sister's infant. She did not cherish great hopes of useful intelligence, but with Madge's mother now silent for ever, it was her only chance. Jeanie hastened to the workhouse hospital with her companions. They found Madge in a large ward of ten beds, of which the patient's was the only one occupied.

Madge was singing when they entered. It was her usual wild snatches of songs and old airs, but a voice with now softened and subdued by bodily exhaustion. There was death in the plaintive tones of her voice which yet had something of a mother's lullaby. Jeanie went to the bedside and, though she addressed Madge by name, there was no sign of recognition. On the contrary, the patient changed her posture, and called out,

'Nurse—*nurse*! Turn my face to the wa', that I may never answer to that name!'

The attendant arranged her as she desired, her face to the wall and her back to the light. As soon as she was quiet in this position, she began to sing again. The strain, however, was different, rather resembling the music of Methodist hymns, though the measure of the song was similar to that of the former:

Doff thy robes of sin and clay;
Christian, rise, and come away.

The strain was solemn and affecting, sustained by a voice naturally fine but one which weakness had softened. Even Archibald, a *pococurante* by profession,[1] was affected. The dairy maid blubbered. Jeanie felt tears rise to her eyes. Even the nurse seemed moved. The patient was evidently growing weaker, as was shown by her difficulty of breathing. Nature was succumbing in the last conflict. But the spirit of melody, which must originally have been so strong, seemed to rise over her pain and weakness. It was remarkable that in her songs there could always something appropriate. She sang softly a fragment of some old ballad:

> *Cauld is my bed, Lord Archibald,*
> *And sad my sleep of sorrow;*
> *But thine sall be as sad and cauld,*
> *My fause true-love, to-morrow!*

Again she changed the tune. It was to one wilder and less regular. Of the words, only a fragment or two could be made out by the listeners:

> *Proud Maisie is in the wood,*
> *Walking so early;*
> *Sweet Robin sits on the bush,*
> *Singing so rarely.*
>
> *Who makes the bridal bed,*
> *Birdie, say truly?*
> *'Tis the grey-headed sexton,*
> *That delves the grave duly.*
>
> *The glow-worm o'er the grave and stone*
> *Shall light thee steady;*
> *The owl from the steeple sings,*
> *'Welcome, proud Lady...*

With the last notes her voice died away and she fell into a slumber, from which the attendant assured them that she would never awake; it proved true.

Madge Murdockson parted with existence without again uttering a sound of any kind.

chapter forty-one

> *Wilt thou go on with me?*
> *The moon is bright, the sea is calm,*
> *And I know well the ocean paths...*
> *Thou wilt go on with me!*
>   Robert Southey, *Thalaba the Destroyer*

---

[1]   Of an incurious, indifferent nature. From Italian: *Poco curante*; little caring.

The agitation caused by these scenes had so tired the normally robust Jeanie that Archibald judged it necessary that the party have a day's repose. It was in vain that Jeanie protested against the delay. Resistance to the Duke's man was in vain and indeed she was eventually glad to go to bed and sleep without interruption.

Archibald was attentive in another particular. He had observed that both the execution of the old woman and the miserable fate of her daughter had had more powerful effects upon Jeanie's mind than those expected from her common humanity. Archibald was ignorant of the connections between his master's protégée and these unfortunate persons, excepting that Jeanie had seen Madge in Scotland. He therefore ascribed the strong impression made upon her to Jeanie's associating them with the recent circumstances of her sister. He became anxious to prevent anything which might further recall these to Jeanie's mind.

That evening, a pedlar brought his wares to Longtown, amongst which was a large broadsheet titled:

Last Speech and Execution of Margaret Murdockson and the barbarous Murder of her Daughter, Magdalene Murdockson, called Madge Wildfire; and of her pious conversation with his Reverence Archdeacon Fleming.

Archibald purchased the entire stock of these tracts and was about to commit the whole to the fire when it was rescued by May Dutton saying that it was a pity to waste so much paper. She promised to put the parcel into her own trunk and keep it out of the sight of Miss Deans.

Next morning they resumed their journey, travelling through Dumfries-shire and part of Lanarkshire, until they arrived at Rutherglen, about four miles from Glasgow. Here an express brought letters to Archibald from the Duke's principal agent in Edinburgh.

He said nothing of their contents that evening, but when they were seated in the carriage the next day, Archibald informed Jeanie that the Duke wished him to take her a stage or two beyond Glasgow. There were, it seemed, riots in the city, rendering it unadvisable for Miss Deans to travel alone and unprotected from Glasgow to Edinburgh. By going forward farther, they would meet one of his Grace's subfactors under whose protection she might journey in safety. Jeanie remonstrated against this arrangement.

'I hae been *lang* frae hame,' she said. 'My father and sister will be anxious to see me and there are other friends that arena weel in health. I will pay for a man and a horse at Glasgow and surely naebody wad meddle wi' sae harmless a creature as me. I am muckle obliged by the offer; but I long for Saint Leonard's.'

Archibald exchanged a meaningful look with Dolly Dutton. Jeanie saw it and cried, 'Mr Archibald – Mrs Dutton, if ye ken of onything that has happened at Saint Leonard's, for God's sake tell me and dinna keep me in suspense!'

'I really know nothing, Miss Deans,' said he.

'And I – I am sure I knows as little,' said Dolly.

Jeanie suspected that something was being concealed from her and it was only the repeated assurances of Archibald that her father, sister and friends were well – as far as he knew – that pacified her alarm. However, her distress was so obvious that Archibald, as a last resort, put into her hand, a slip of paper:

Jeanie Deans,

You will do me a favour by going with Archibald a day's journey beyond Glasgow, and asking them no questions. This will greatly oblige your friend,

Argyle & Greenwich.

This laconic epistle from a nobleman to whom she was obligated, silenced all Jeanie's objections, but only added to her curiosity. Glasgow seemed not now to be an objective of her fellow travellers. They held to the left bank of the Clyde, travelling through beautiful, changing views of that noble stream till it began to assume the character that of a navigable river.

'You are not gaun intill Glasgow?' said Jeanie.

'No,' replied Archibald; 'there are riots and as our Duke is in opposition to the Court, perhaps we might be too well received! Or the mob might take it in their heads to remember that the Captain of Carrick came down upon them with his Highlandmen in the time of Shawfield's mob in 1725, and then we would be too *ill* received.[1] At any rate, it is best for us and for me in particular to leave the good people of the Gorbals to act according to their own inclinations.'

The carriage rolled on with the Clyde expanding itself, becoming tidal and gradually assuming the dignity of an estuary.

'Which way lies Inverary?' said Jeanie, gazing on the dusky Highland hills, which now, piled above each other, and intersected by many a loch, stretched away on the opposite side of the river to the northward. 'Is yon high castle the Duke's?'

'That is the old castle of Dumbarton,' replied Archibald, 'the strongest place in Europe. Sir William Wallace was Governor of it in the great war with the English and his Grace is Governor now. It is always entrusted to the best man in Scotland.'

'And does the Duke live up on yon rock?'

'No, he has a deputy governor who commands in his absence; and he lives in that white house at the bottom of the rock. His Grace does not reside there himself. Now, as to our lodging, we will soon be in a house of the Duke's on the pleasant island of Roseneath. There we take ship for Inverary where we meet the company who will escort Jeanie to Edinburgh.'

'An *island*?' said Jeanie, who had never quitted *terra firma*. 'Then we maun gang in ane of these boats; they look unco sma'.'

'Mr Archibald,' said Mrs Dutton, 'I will not consent to it; I was never engaged to leave the country and I desire you will bid the coachmen drive round the other way to the Duke's house.'

'I am sorry I cannot oblige you, madam. Roseneath happens to be an *island*.'

'If it were *ten* islands,' stormed the now incensed dame, 'that's no reason why I should be drowned in going overseas to it.'

'No reason indeed why you should be drowned, ma'am,' answered the groom of the chambers, 'but an admirably good one why you cannot proceed to it by *land*.'

---

[1]   In 1725, there was an unusually powerful riot in Glasgow, this one over the malt-tax. The insurgents were called 'Shawfield's Mob' from their violence being directed at Provost Daniel Campbell of Shawfield MP. Brought in to restore order were Argyll Highlanders, lampooned as '*Campbell of Carrick and his Highland thieves*'.

They turned off the high road and proceeded towards a hamlet of fishing huts, where there was moored a shallop.[1] The vessel bore a flag with a boar's head, crested with a ducal coronet and by it waited with three seamen and as many Highlanders.

The carriage stopped, and the men began to unyoke their horses, while Archibald superintended the removal of the baggage from the carriage to the little vessel.

'Has the *Caroline* been long arrived?' he said to a seaman.

'She came from Liverpool in five days and she's lying down at Greenock.'

'Let the horses and carriage go to Greenock then,' said Archibald, 'and be embarked there for Inverary. They may lodge in the stables of my cousin Duncan Archibald. Ladies, pray make ready; we must not lose the tide.'

'Miss Deans,' said Mrs Dutton, 'you may do as you please, but I will sit here all night rather than go into that there painted eggshell. Fellow, *fellow*!' she snapped at a Highlander who was lifting a travelling trunk. 'That trunk is *mine*, and that there band-box and that pillion mail and those seven bundles, and the paper-bag. Touch one of them at your peril!'

The Gael kept his eye fixed on the speaker while turning towards Archibald. Receiving no signal, he shouldered the *portmanteau*, ignoring the remonstrances which he would have ignored even if understood. He moved off with Mrs Dutton's wearables and deposited the trunk containing them in the boat.

The baggage stowed, Mr Archibald handed Jeanie out of the carriage and she was then transported through the surf and placed in the boat. He then offered the same to Mrs Dutton, but she was resolute in her refusal to quit the carriage. There she sat in solitary state, threatening all concerned with legal action for wages, damages and expenses. Archibald did not remonstrate, but spoke two or three words to the Highlanders in the Gaelic. They approached the carriage cautiously, then seized the occupant, hoisted her on their shoulders horizontally and rushed down with her to the beach. Through the surf they went and deposited her in the boat in a state of mortification and terror. The men then jumped in themselves; one tall fellow remaining till he had pushed off the boat and then tumbled in among his companions. They took to their oars and began to pull from the shore. The sail was then spread and the vessel drove merrily across the firth.

'You Scotch villain!' cried the infuriated Dutton to Archibald. 'How dare you use a person like me in this way?'

'Madam,' said Archibald composedly, 'it is high time you realised that you are in the Duke's country now. There is not one of these fellows but would throw you out of the boat as readily as into it, were such his Grace's pleasure.'

'Lord have mercy!'

'However, I assure you, you will find the Highlands have their pleasures. You will have a dozen cow-milkers under you at Inverary and you may throw any of *them* into the loch if you have a mind, for the Duke's head people have almost as much power as himself.'

'Miss Deans?' said Dutton to Jeanie, who sat by the side of Archibald at the helm; 'Are you not afeard of these wild men with their naked knees, and of this nutshell of a thing, that pitches like a skimming-dish in a milk pail?'

---

[1] A light sailing boat used mainly for coastal fishing or as a tender for larger vessels.

'No, madam,' answered Jeanie, 'I am not feared; for I hae seen Hielandmen before. And as for the deep waters, there is a Providence by sea as well as by land.'

chapter forty-two

ROSELLIA: *Did Fortune guide,*
Or rather Destiny, our bark, to which
We could appoint no port, to this blest place?
John Fletcher, *The Sea Voyage*, II.I

The islands in the Firth of Clyde were then secluded spots, frequented by no travellers and few visitants of any kind. They are of exquisite, yet varied beauty. Arran, a mountainous island, abounds with the grandest and most romantic scenery. Bute is of a softer and more woodland character. The Cumbraes, in contrast to both, are green, level and bare. They form a natural bar across the mouth of the firth of Clyde, though leaving large intervals of sea. Roseneath, a smaller isle, lies higher up the firth and towards its western shore near the opening of the Gareloch and Loch Long which wind down from the mountains of the Western Highlands to join the Clyde estuary.

The picturesque island of Roseneath had from early times been an occasional residence of the Earls and then Dukes of Argyle, who maintained a fishing lodge there. The touched the landing place, which was partly shrouded by low and wide-spreading oak-trees, intermixed with hazel bushes. Two or three figures were seen awaiting their arrival. To these Jeanie paid little attention, so that it was with an electric shock of surprise that, upon being carried by the rowers out of the boat to the shore, she was received in the arms of her father!

She extricated herself from his affectionate embrace, and held him at arm's length, to satisfy her mind that it was no illusion. But the form was indisputable; douce David Deans himself, in his best Sunday coat, with broad metal buttons, waistcoat and breeches of the same, his strong leggings of thick grey cloth, copper buckles and broad Lowland blue bonnet, thrown back as he lifted his eyes to Heaven in speechless gratitude. His features, usually so stern and stoical were now melted into joy and gratitude.

'Jeanie, my maist dutiful bairn, the Lord of Israel be thy father, for I am hardly worthy of thee! Thou hast redeemed our captivity and brought back honour to our house. Bless thee, my bairn, for He has made thee his instrument.'

'And Effie, father?'

'Ye will hear, ye will hear,' said David hastily.

'And *Effie*?' repeated her sister. 'And the Saddletrees – Dumbiedikes?'

'All weel, praise be to His name!'

'And Reuben Butler? He wasna weel when I gaed awa.'

'He is quite mended.'

'Thank God. But father, *Effie*?'

'You will never see her mair, my bairn,' answered Deans in a solemn tone. 'You are the ane leaf left now on the auld tree!'

'Why? Is she dead?'

'No. She lives in the flesh. Would that she were alive in faith – and free from the bonds of Satan.'

'Lord protect us! Has she left with that villain?'

'Aye,' said Deans. 'She has left the father that prayed for her, and the sister that travailed for her. She has even left the land of her people. She is ower the Border wi' that son of Belial.'

'Wi' that, that *fearfu'* man?' said Jeanie. 'O Effie! After sic a Deliverance!'

'She went from us, my bairn, because she was not *of* us,' replied David. 'She is gone forth into the wilderness of the world. The peace of the warld gang wi' her, and a better peace when she has the grace to turn to it! But be it sae. Let her gang. Let her bite on her ain bridle; the Lord kens his time. But never, Jeanie, *never* let her name be spoken betwixt you and me! She hath passed from us like the brook which vanisheth when summer waxeth warm, as Job saith.[1] Let her be forgotten.'

A melancholy pause followed. Jeanie would fain have asked more about her sister's departure, but the tone of her father prohibited. She was about to mention her interview with Staunton at his father's rectory, but thought that it was likely to aggravate his distress. She would wait until she could enquire about her sister's elopement from Reuben Butler.

But when was she to see him? This was a question she could not forbear asking herself. Meanwhile her father said, pointing to the opposite shore of Dumbartonshire,

'Is that no a pleasant abode? His Grace of Argyle has asked me, as one skilled in flocks and herds, to superintend a store-farm, whilk his Grace had taen into his ain hand for the improvement of stock.'

Jeanie's heart sank. However, she said,

'It seems a goodly and pleasant land. It slopes bonnily to the western sun. The pasture must be fine for the grass is green despite the drouthy weather. But it is far frae hame and I wad be often thinking on the gowans and the yellow king-cups on the Crags of St Leonard's.'

'Dinna speak on't, Jeanie,' said her father. 'I wish never to hear it named mair. The rouping[2] is ower, and the bills are paid. I brought a' the beasts that I thought ye wad like best. There is Gowans and there's your ain brockit cow and the wee hawkit ane, the petted creature.'

Jeanie found new occasions to admire the beneficence of the Duke of Argyle. While establishing an experimental farm on the skirts of his immense Highland estates, he had been at a loss to find a proper person to take charge of it. However, his conversation upon country matters with Jeanie during their return from Richmond, had persuaded him that Deans's long experience and success in farming were perhaps what he needed. He wrote to his man of business in Edinburgh, instructing him to enquire into the character and worth of David Deans and, if satisfactory, to engage him on liberal terms to superintend his new farm in Dumbartonshire.

---

[1] Job 6.17.

[2] A public auction, usually of farming implements and produce.

The proposal was made to David by the Duke's man on the second day after his daughter's pardon had reached Edinburgh. His resolution to leave St Leonard's had been already formed; the honour of an express invitation from the Duke of Argyle was in itself flattering to David who, by accepting, would repay to a degree the great favour he had received at Argyle's hands. The appointment included the right of grazing stock of his own and David's keen eye saw that the situation was convenient for dealing in Highland cattle. There was the risk of her'ship[1] from the neighbouring mountains indeed, but the awesome name of the Duke of Argyle would mean security and a little *blackmail*[2] would assure his safety.

There were two points on which he haggled. The first was the character of the clergyman with whose worship he was to join; and on this delicate point he received satisfaction. The other was the condition of his youngest daughter, obliged as she was to leave Scotland for so many years. The Duke's man of law smiled, and said,

'There is no occasion to interpret that clause too strictly. If the young woman left Scotland for a few months and then came to her father's new residence by sea from England, nobody would know of her arrival. The heritable jurisdiction of his Grace excludes all other Magistrates from his estates. Living on the verge of the Highlands, she might indeed be said to be out of Scotland and beyond the bounds of statute Law.'

Old Deans was not entirely satisfied with this reasoning, but the elopement of Effie, which took place on the third night after her liberation, led him to close with the proposal. The Duke had apprised Archibald of this and directed him to bring Jeanie to Roseneath.

Father and daughter communicated these matters to each other as they walked slowly towards the Lodge which showed itself among the trees half a mile from the little bay where they had landed. As they approached the house, David Deans told his daughter with a grim smile – the closest his visage ever came to mirth – that there was baith a worshipful gentleman and a reverend gentleman therein. The worshipful gentleman was his honour the Laird of Knocktarlitie, bailie of the Rosneath estate for the Duke of Argyle. Said Douce Davie,

'He is a Highland gentleman, tarr'd wi' the same stick as mony of them, namely a choleric temper, and a neglect of the higher things that belong to Salvation, and also a gripping unto the things of this world, without muckle distinction of property. However, he is also ane hospitable gentleman with whom it would be wise to live on a gude understanding.

'As for the reverend person, he is the candidate of the Duke for the kirk of the parish in which the farm lies. He is likely to be acceptable to the Christian souls of the parish. They hunger for spiritual manna, having been fed but upon sour Hieland sowens by the Rev. Duncan MacDonough, the last minister, who began every Sunday – and Saturday – with a mutchkin of *usquebaugh*.[3] But I need say

---

[1] A Scottish word which may be said to be now obsolete, meaning the practice of plundering by armed force, Scott.

[2] Protection money paid to Highland reivers to prevent cattle rustling.

[3] Gaelic: Whisky.

no more of the new lad for I think ye may hae seen him afore. And here he is come to meet us.'

She had indeed seen him before.

It was Reuben Butler.

Ivanhoe

Sir Walter Scott
Newly adapted for the modern reader
by David Purdie
ISBN 978-1-908373-58-8 HBK £19.99
ISBN 978-1-908373-26-7 PBK £9.99

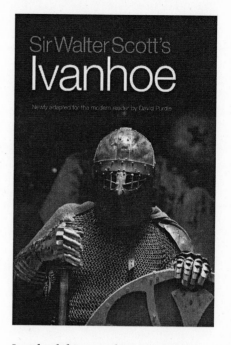

Fight on, brave knights. Man dies, but glory lives!

Ivanhoe has been cut down to size in this modern retelling of Scott's classic novel: the original text has been slashed from an epic 194,000 words to a more manageable 95,000.

Banished from his father's court, Wilfred of Ivanhoe returns from Richard the Lionheart's Crusades to claim love, justice and glory. Tyrannical Norman knights, indolent Saxon nobles and the usurper Prince John stand in his way. A saga of tournaments and melees, chivalry and love, nobility and merry men, Ivanhoe's own quest soon becomes a battle for the English throne itself...

This is exactly what's needed in order to rescue Sir Walter Scott.
ALEXANDER McCALL SMITH

Knights getting shorter... [Ivanhoe] has been brought up to date by Professor David Purdie who is president of the Sir Walter Scott Society and should know the ropes.
THE HERALD

I applaud this new, shorter version of Ivanhoe which makes this wonderful novel, once so popular, accessible to a new generation of readers who will be able to enjoy its classic blend of history and romance.
PROFESSOR GRAHAM TULLOCH, Editor of the Edinburgh Edition of the Waverley novels

Details of these and other books published by Luath Press
can be found at: **www.luath.co.uk**

Luath Press Limited

committed to publishing well written books worth reading

LUATH PRESS takes its name from Robert Burns, whose little collie Luath (*Gael.*, swift or nimble) tripped up Jean Armour at a wedding and gave him the chance to speak to the woman who was to be his wife and the abiding love of his life. Burns called one of 'The Twa Dogs' Luath after Cuchullin's hunting dog in Ossian's *Fingal*. Luath Press was established in 1981 in the heart of Burns country, and now resides a few steps up the road from Burns' first lodgings on Edinburgh's Royal Mile.

Luath offers you distinctive writing with a hint of unexpected pleasures.

Most bookshops in the UK, the US, Canada, Australia, New Zealand and parts of Europe either carry our books in stock or can order them for you. To order direct from us, please send a £sterling cheque, postal order, international money order or your credit card details (number, address of cardholder and expiry date) to us at the address below. Please add post and packing as follows: UK – £1.00 per delivery address; overseas surface mail – £2.50 per delivery address; overseas airmail – £3.50 for the first book to each delivery address, plus £1.00 for each additional book by airmail to the same address. If your order is a gift, we will happily enclose your card or message at no extra charge.

ILLUSTRATION: IAN KELLAS

Luath Press Limited
543/2 Castlehill
The Royal Mile
Edinburgh EH1 2ND
Scotland
Telephone: 0131 225 4326 (24 hours)
Fax: 0131 225 4324
email: sales@luath.co.uk
Website: www.luath.co.uk

Printed by RR Donnelley at Glasgow, UK